Adélaïde de Clermont-Tonnerre

The Last of Our Kind

Translated by Adriana Hunter

HODDER

First published in France by Éditions Grasset

First published in Great Britain in 2018 by Hodder & Stoughton
An Hachette UK company

This paperback edition published in 2019

1

Paperback ISBN 978 1 473 65806 6
eBook ISBN 978 1 473 65805 9

Typeset in Sabon MT Std by
Palimpsest Book Production Ltd, Falkirk, Stirlingshire

Printed and bound in Great Britain by Clays Ltd, Elcograf S.p.A.

Hodder & Stoughton Ltd
Carmelite House
50 Victoria Embankment
London EC4Y 0DZ

www.hodder.co.uk

For Laurent

Manhattan, 1969

The first thing I saw of her was her ankle, delicate, whip-sharp, circled by the strap of a blue sandal. I'd never had fetishes before that May day, and if I'd had to instinctively focus on part of a woman's anatomy, I would have gone for another part of her body, definitely not her feet. I noticed feet only if they were ugly or ungroomed, which didn't happen a lot. I was lucky enough to be loved by beautiful women, and I made it a point of honour to reciprocate their affections. And that's exactly what we were discussing . . .

'You want all of them,' complained Marcus, who was having lunch with me.

My friend and associate, who had trouble seducing just one, elaborated: 'You sit down somewhere, look around, have a drink and bang! Within fifteen minutes there are two fluttering around you.'

'It's exasperating,' Marcus added indignantly. 'I think I'd be more scared to come near you, built like a giant, with your square jaw and washed-out eyes—'

'My eyes are *not* washed out! They're light blue . . .'

'They're washed out. *Mine* are blue, but they don't have anything like the same effect. Girls love telling me their life story, their problems, talking about their parents, their first tooth. I listen for weeks while they confide in me, I'm just about to get what I'm there for, and you come along and in just fifteen minutes you're in bed with them.'

'I never stole anyone from you!' I protested.

'No, it's worse than that! You don't do anything to steal them from me and they *still* fall into your arms . . .'

'If you tell me which ones you like, I won't even look at them.'

'I don't want a girlfriend who'll forget me the minute you walk in the room, where's the value in that?'

Marcus was painting a very exaggerated portrait: I didn't just sit there waiting for women to throw themselves at me, I worked at doing what it took to get them. I'd told him my golden rules over and over, but he thought my direct approach 'simplistic'. He was happier making excuses for his own shyness by citing this so-called magnetism of mine. Though he was richer than me, his principles wouldn't allow him to use this advantage. He hindered himself with a complicated mental strategy when, contrary to popular belief, women are predictable. To sleep with one, you have to:

(A) Find what's beautiful about her – because there's beauty in each and every one of them – and show her that you like it.

(B) Ask for, even beg for, sex.

(C) Always accompany the request with enough humour not to lose face if she says no.

(D) Be straightforward and down-to-earth, and avoid sending her three pages of literary quotations which will make you look like a nutcase.

I'd told Marcus twenty times he needed to make his intentions clearer, but it wasn't in his nature. He had a gift for eliciting confessions, from men and women, without knowing how to use them to his advantage. I had the same aptitude for getting girls into my bed.

*

I'd just turned fourteen when they started taking an interest in me, after my fight at high school with Billy Melvin. He was two years older than me and he terrorised the pupils of Hawthorne

High. One day Billy called me a 'complete zero', in reference to my family name, Zilch. I did not take it well.

His face was screwed up with loathing, like he was staring into the sun. He said he didn't want anyone to be taller than him. I was already getting close, and it infuriated him. I was no better disposed towards him. I hate guys like that who think they're entitled to everything because they've always had everything. The reverence around them and their contempt for the rest of humanity make me sick. I like money, but I respect it only if it's been earned, not inherited by people like Billy. You only had to look at him to know he was stupid. I didn't like his square face and his freckly skin. I didn't like the way he behaved. I didn't like how he walked or talked or looked at people with his pinched nose and his air of superiority. It has to be said, I didn't like much in those days.

When I heard Billy Melvin say yet again, 'You're a complete zero, Zilch, a big fat zero taken in by a couple of losers out of charity,' I flew into one of those rages that sometimes overwhelmed me. Marcus says all the colour drains from my face; I feel as though someone else has taken possession of me and I have no control over anything. I grabbed hold of Billy's arm, swung him around me twice like we learned in shot-put, and sent him hurtling into one of the huge windows that the school was so proud of. Billy was dazed for a few seconds, then he shook himself like a Doberman emerging from a pond and launched himself at me. We fought on the ground. We were rabid. It took a prefect and the captain of the football team grabbing us around the waist to separate us. His nose bleeding and one ear torn, Billy Melvin limped and cursed. The neck of my T-shirt was ripped down to my waist, the knuckles of my left hand were wrecked and I had a cut under my chin that dripped beads of red onto the concrete in the school yard. That wound, incompetently sutured, has left me a W-shaped scar: W for Werner – I'm very pleased with it.

We were both excluded from school for a week. The principal used the opportunity to saddle us with community work. He wanted to curry favour with the mayor of Hawthorne. We had to work in silence for two days, sweeping up and collecting leaves on Lafayette Avenue – where the mayor lived. Then we cleaned, sanded down and repainted his garden fence before moving hundreds of boxes of archives to the town hall so he could make his office space larger.

This exclusion earned me a serious row with Armande, my mother, and unofficial congratulations from Andrew, my father. Ever since I was tiny, his eyes have softened when he looks at me. He'll feel my shoulders or my biceps and marvel, 'Now that's fine craftsmanship! Good, solid stuff.' The fact that I'd given a thrashing to a boy two years older than me appealed to him, even if it did mean trouble for me.

When we returned to school, Marcus – who was already drawn to the law – arranged peace negotiations. They culminated in the signing of a peace treaty he had drafted. This agreement, supplemented with a map of the school, divided the yard along a diagonal line running from the changing-room door to the canteen. The girls' and boys' bathrooms were cross-hatched and declared neutral territory. Marcus was passionate about history and he baptised them 'Switzerland'. It's been a long-standing joke for Marcus and me. To this day, when we need to pee, we 'go to Switzerland'.

This dramatic exploit, and the relative victory of not having been beaten up by Billy, earned me new male friends and my first girlfriend: Lou. She cornered me in the gym one day and rammed her tongue into my mouth. She tasted like cherry-flavoured candy and, after the initial daring of the kiss, her tongue felt kind of limp. I found the experience too wet and didn't appreciate being approached rather than doing the approaching, but Lou was the prettiest girl in Hawthorne. She had long brown hair, an insolent attitude that belied her pleated skirt, she was two years older than me – Billy's age, then – and had breasts that already stretched her sweaters and turned boys' heads at school. Lou was the sort of chance you don't turn down. In the school's Entrepreneur Club where we 'the future elite of the business world' was being nurtured, our teacher always said we had to 'identify opportunities and grab them'. Although overwhelmed by Lou's onslaught, I conducted a conscientious analysis of the situation by opening my mouth and responding to her demands. I concluded that Lou corresponded with the type-two model: 'an opportunity involving moderate risk', one of the situations with the highest potential benefits. Proud to be following in the footsteps of the great businessmen who had built our country, and even though I was slightly taken aback, I very willingly grabbed hold of this girl who was offering herself to me.

I started by touching her breasts, using the same technique as when regulating the hot and cold water in the shower, astonished by how soft they were when I'd imagined them much firmer, then I grasped her backside with both hands and, not knowing how to proceed, shook it vigorously up and down. These experimental manoeuvres produced absolutely no reaction, and I very soon ran out of ideas. So, after a moment's hesitation, I pressed my advantage further and explored between Lou's legs, whereupon she had the good grace to stop me . . . When I stepped out of the gym, I had a knockout girl on my arm.

Outside the school building she wound herself around me like ivy on a tree. The history teacher, an embittered old man who only liked Marcus (the sole pupil who took a passionate interest in the conquests of kings with unpronounceable names in tiny countries in eras so long gone that hominids had barely come down from the trees), came and told us to 'behave ourselves'. I gave him a swaggering reply that betrayed none of the raging doubts and male hormones jostling for position inside me. Lou stood by my rebellion, unleashing an 'Alright, alright! This *is* a democracy, you know!' Then, with her eyes still pinned on the fusty teacher, she licked my ear before taking all of it into her mouth, which caused a painful thrumming sound for the rest of the day. With this performance, which far outstripped the wildest things the teacher had ever attempted with his puritanical wife, the man turned the same claret colour as his knitted tie and walked away without further ado.

Lou was a highly prized catch. She further increased the cachet conferred on me by the fight and peace treaty with Billy. My buddies attributed disproportionate seductive powers to me. I wasn't so convinced myself, but there was no escaping the fact that since I'd been 'going out' with Lou – a strange choice of words because it seemed to me that the main aim wasn't to go out with Lou, but to get into her, something with which she obstinately refused to comply – girls gazed at me with love-struck eyes. They giggled when I walked past, and admitted to Marcus that they loved my blue eyes or my 'oh-so-cute' smile. There was even one, whose name I've forgotten, who noticed I was always hungry and made me a cake every day. Her presents infuriated Lou, but she had no desire to start cooking herself, so she settled for taking her share of the cake. She was watching her figure so she handed this portion out to her friends and watched them eat it with the satisfaction that slim girls derive from exercising their restraint while – before their very eyes – other, chubbier girls are ruled by their greed.

Since then I've never had any trouble with women. I got used to it. They came easy, and although some may have resisted, it didn't last long. The more tenacious ones would play hard to get. Whether or not I snared them quickly, I viewed them as pleasantly diverting, no more – a flippancy that led, over the years, to my bad reputation. I'm respectful but rarely sentimental. I don't get attached very easily. One of my girlfriends, a psychology student – oh, how I loved the way she kept her glasses on when we made love – analysed this character trait. According to her, the fact that I'd been adopted had made me wary. I had a phobia of abandonment, she explained, and it drove me to have more and more partners. Basically I think women are all obsessed with relationships, with building on them and being 'serious'. They want men to fall in love and they call the ones who can't bastards. They think love has the power to wash away the sins of the flesh. Unlike Marcus, which is why he'll never go far in this field, I coped very well without the outdated bleaching agent of emotions. I was a young man at just the right time. In the sixties girls felt it their duty to make the most of their freedom. They went in for a sort of competition in which they could take pride in exercising their sexuality rather than suppressing it. I made the most of it, I'll admit that. Love was just a game, but this charmed period came to an end at Gioccardi's restaurant the day a young woman crushed my carefree ways with her blue sandals.

Marcus and I were having lunch on the street level of the SoHo trattoria, where we ate nearly every day. The owner welcomed my dog Shakespeare like some sort of god, and made him generous bowls of food. That was worth a lot because plenty of people were afraid of Shakespeare. Up on his hind legs, he reached six feet. His tawny bear-like coat was not enough to distract people from his jaws which, if he hadn't been so good-natured, could have polished off a man in a matter of seconds. I was hungrily eyeing my spaghetti al pesto, when the ankle that would change my view of women appeared on the tiled steps. It immediately captivated me. Its owner, who was coming down from the floor above, paused briefly. She was talking to someone. It took me a while to identify her teasing voice in the hubbub of conversation and clink of cutlery. She spun round on her feet with the agility of a dancer. I was awed by her childish toes and their glossy nails. She kept talking, her voice insistent: she wanted to eat downstairs. The upstairs room was almost empty. There was no one there, it was gloomy. A man's voice – I could see his brown loafers – protested that it was quieter upstairs. The girl's left foot came down another step, revealing the beginnings of a calf. It went back up, came down again, and then finally made up its mind. As she was gradually revealed, my eyes drank in the slender line of her tibias, her knees, the first glimpses of thigh with that diagonal indent of muscle that drives me crazy in a woman. Her skin, which was lightly sun-kissed and surreally perfect, then disappeared under a corolla of blue fabric. A belt showed off her waist, where I now longed to rest my hands. Her sleeveless dress meant I could see her arms, which had a rounded, appetising coolness. Higher still, from her collar emerged an elegant neck I could have broken with one hand. She hurried down the last three steps laughing. A light came into the room with her, the light from her hair. Behind her – she was dragging him by his tie – was a man of about forty in sandy-coloured pants and a blazer with a yellow pocket handkerchief. Dragged by the neck, red and extremely put out, he was trying to follow her without falling over. She released him by letting his tie slip between fingers so fine, they were almost transparent.

'Ernie, you're boring!' she exclaimed.

I was watching her so attentively that, alerted by an animal instinct, she met my eye and froze for a fraction of a second. The moment she turned her insolent eyes on me, I knew I liked her more than any woman I'd ever known or just seen and wanted. I felt as if a kind of lava flowed through me, but the young woman seemed unperturbed, or, if she was affected, my dazzling creature had enough poise not to show it. The man with the blazer was irked by the interest I showed in her, and stared at me irritably. My body tensed instantly. I was ready to fight. He had no business being in this restaurant. He didn't deserve this goddess. I wanted him to leave her to me and get the hell out. I gave him a sardonic smile, hoping he would come over and provoke me, but Ernie was a coward. He looked away. My beauty turned gracefully on her heel when the waiter, as awestruck as I was, showed her to their table. He moved aside chairs in her path as she walked forward, her head slightly lowered, with the modest expression peculiar to women who know they're being admired.

'Are you aware that I asked you a question one minute, fifteen seconds ago already?' Marcus asked, looking at his new watch, a birthday present from his father. He had set the timer.

I couldn't tear myself away from her, even though Ernie, with his big lumpen outline, was trying to block her from my view. She sat with her back to the room.

'Don't you think she's sublime?' I asked, half dreaming.

Marcus, who had identified the source of my distraction one minute and forty-five seconds ago, and counting, didn't look up from his watch-face as he replied, 'She is very pretty, and very much with someone, I'm sure you will have noticed . . .'

'Do you think they're together?'

The idea that the radiant girl and the ageing dandy were together – at the time forty felt to me like the beginning of decrepitude – was unbearable.

'I have absolutely no idea, Wern,' Marcus replied. 'But if, for once, we could have lunch and talk without you unhingeing your cervical vertebrae to look at everything in a skirt, it would do my ego a lot of good.'

'Darling, forgive me, I don't pay you enough attention,' I teased, putting my hand on his.

'You make me feel invisible. It's excruciating. Especially as we do have a few small details to sort out before this afternoon's meeting.'

Our fledgling construction company was going through a treacherous phase in its development. We'd reinvested what we'd earned on our first deal and topped it up with the highest possible loan to rebuild two neighbouring buildings in Brooklyn. When we'd secured a demolition licence and permission for the rebuild, and resolved the countless problems inherent in any construction project in New York, some municipal pen-pushers had suspended the work on an obscure point of land registry law. This dirty trick had enraged me. The Brooklyn Borough president didn't give a damn about the law, he just wanted to corner us into lining his pockets a second time. We had a hearing scheduled for four o'clock that afternoon, arguments to fine-tune and a future to save, but I was struggling to concentrate: I was captivated by the object of my desire a few tables away. She sat very upright, her shoulders not touching the back of the chair. Her hands, which fluttered around her, accompanied her words with complex choreographies. My partner studied me with a strange look in his eye. He knew how much I liked women, but he also knew that our business had always taken priority. The stranger tipped her head back and stretched, moving with the languid suppleness of a panther. The curve of her shoulders hollowed. Her river of hair had a life of its own. I wished I could hold it and bury my face in it.

'Is there a problem, Mr Werner?' asked Paolo, the manager.

He stood with a bottle of Marsala in his hand, looking at my untouched plate. I was one of his favourite customers and he derived a Sicilian *mamma* sort of pride from watching me eat there several times a week, swallowing down two pounds of pasta, a whole dish of lasagne, a rib of beef or two pizzas to myself. That day, though, I hadn't touched the spaghetti that was cooling in front of me.

'Is there something wrong with the pasta? Not enough salt? Overcooked?' he quick-fired at me, his eyes probing my plate, trying to establish a diagnosis.

I wasn't listening to him. The woman had just described a swift circle with one hand to gather her mane of hair over one shoulder, partly revealing the nape of her neck. Why did she feel so familiar? How could I get to talk to her? Paolo picked up my plate and wrinkled his nose as he sniffed at it like a hunting dog.

'Giulia!' he railed. 'What have you done to Signor Zilch's pasta?'

Paolo's fury made everyone in the room turn around, including my stranger. I studied her so greedily, so feverishly it must have amused her because she smiled at me before turning her back on me. I had to have her. I wanted to know everything about her, her smell, her voice, her parents, her friends; where she lived, and who with; how her bedroom was decorated, the dresses she wore, the texture of her bedsheets, whether she slept naked, whether she talked in her sleep. I wanted her to tell me about her sorrows and her dreams, her needs and longings.

'I've told her twenty times!' Paolo grouched. 'She'll never make pesto. It's all in the hand . . . you need strength, you have to crush while you turn the mortar,' he explained, furiously miming the rotation technique. 'Giulia tosses it up like a vinaigrette, with her wrist soft instead of keeping her arm straight and strong.'

I wanted to get up, be one step ahead of her. Smash in the face of the cretin with her, take her hand, steal her away, know everything about her.

'Is he sick? Is he not feeling OK?' Paolo asked, having tasted the spaghetti and found nothing amiss – a capitulation which produced a triumphant smile from Giulia who had come out of the kitchen for this emergency.

Marcus tried to take the plate back from Paolo.

'Don't worry, Paolo, the pasta's delicious and Wern is totally fine, he's just in love.'

'In love!' Paolo and Giulia exclaimed in unison.

The thought of me being in love seemed incompatible with

the succession of girls they'd seen at my table over the last few months. They looked at my face to evaluate the progress of this emotional scourge.

'In love,' Marcus confirmed.

'But who with?' protested Paolo, wanting to know the identity of the pernicious creature who was spoiling his best customer's appetite.

'The blonde in the blue and white,' Marcus summarised blandly, tipping his chin towards the stranger.

We spun out our lunch. Paolo tried to get information about the girl by chatting to her for a while, but Ernie batted him away. We ordered our fourth coffees. Shakespeare, who was used to seeing us devour our meal in twenty minutes, grew impatient. I petted his head half-heartedly, and he lay back at my feet with a sigh. I couldn't take my eyes off the girl, and replied only absently to Marcus's questions while he used his silver pen and a leather-bound notebook to jot down the list of arguments intended to convince the Borough president. When I saw Ernie pay his check, my adrenaline levels rose. My beauty was going to vanish into the jungle of Manhattan and I had no idea what to do. They stood up. I followed them in the hope of being noticed or catching her attention again. I was looking for a reason to stop her when, as luck would have it, the strap of her bag caught on the door handle and broke, spilling some of her things on the floor. She knelt down and I rushed to help her. I was quite overcome when the V-shaped pendant on her necklace wedged between her breasts. The corners of the gold jewel dug into her skin. It didn't seem to bother her but the sight of it made my head spin. I gathered up everything I could lay my hands on. There were felt pens, an ink eraser, loose sheets of paper with strange patterns scribbled on them, a hairbrush, a Carmex lip balm, a denim baseball cap and a corkscrew, which really surprised me. This utilitarian object and the general mess in her bag made her seem more human, and even more desirable. Ernie was relegated to the street. The narrowness of the doorway meant he couldn't contribute, and the seams of his too-tight clothes would have given way if he'd attempted to crouch down.

'Thank you, we can manage . . .' he said, trying to get rid of me. 'Please stand up! Listen, I said we don't need any help!'

I passed everything I'd collected to her. She looked up and I was struck by the colour of her eyes. They were a deep violet, shot through with intelligence and sensitivity. She opened her bag wide for me to throw the things in, and I dropped a notebook which opened to reveal sketches of naked men. She closed it with an amused smile, then looked me right in the eye again.

'Thank you, that's very kind.'

Her voice, which was firmer and deeper than her fine features had led me to expect, sent a shiver through me. The way she stared at me did too. She was direct and open, as if she wanted to assess me in a matter of seconds – and succeeded. When she stood back up I got a waft of her perfume, all amber and flowers. I regretted the fact that I hadn't managed to touch her hand, but now Ernie leant in, grabbed her wrist and pulled her outside. Before I had time to come up with some pretext to hold her back, she stepped into the degenerate dandy's chauffeured Rolls. Watching her disappear behind those tinted windows caused me physical pain. It literally knocked the breath out of me to think I'd never see her again. I started running like a madman, with Shakespeare at my heels. At the sight of such a huge dog bowling freely along the sidewalk, passers-by started screaming. Marcus, who had used this interlude to 'go to Switzerland', was now chasing after me.

'Wait!' he cried. 'What the hell's gotten into you?'

I made Shakespeare jump into our yellow Chrysler and pulled away at full throttle with Marcus stepping into the car on the move and calling me an 'unstable social element' and a 'psycho-path in a manic phase'. I was desperately trying to find the Rolls. When Marcus saw the powerless rage screwing up my face, he murmured anxiously:

'Wern, you scare me sometimes.'

Saxony, Germany, 1945

It was a February night, another night of disgrace for humanity. Acres of ruins blazed under acrid, ash-laden rain. For hours on end Dresden had been an endless inferno annihilating bodies, hopes and lives. As far as the eye could see the city was the incarnation of chaos in an era of global despair. The bombing had been so intensive that, right across what had once constituted the centre, not a single building was left standing. The bombs had blown them away like dead leaves. Then came incendiary bombs which had created the all-consuming furnace now feeding off men, women, children and injured troops home from the east who thought they had been spared. The darkness was lit up by a fairground display of crackling sparks. In the deepest part of the night, the sky had taken on the scarlet and gold shades of an autumn sunset. Separate pools of light had gradually flowed together into an incandescent sea, and even at 22,000 feet, the pilots sowing the seeds of death could feel the heat of the blaze in their cockpits.

On the ground, a storm of flames swallowed up anyone close by who no longer had the strength to withstand the powerful draught of oxygen feeding the fire. It seemed it would never stop. As the hours passed, smoke and ash rose high in the sky, throwing a shroud over the Florence of the Elbe. In this daytime gloaming that attacked lungs and eyes, only the baroque silhouette of the Frauenkirche, the Church of Our Lady, still stood tall. A few surviving Red Cross workers had gathered crowds of wounded there. Victor Klemp, the surgeon who had initiated this emergency unit, tried to organise the horror. For a while he had believed that God was punishing his nation for a sin that he had suspected but had refused to acknowledge. Now that death had humbled him in the most hideous fashion a hundred times every hour, he no longer believed God could want this suffering. He no longer believed God was interested in this world; and this church, the only vertical structure rearing up from the sediments of destruction, seemed neither a miracle nor a sign from heaven, but a final, repulsive provocation. Victor Klemp had not slept for seventy-two hours. His tunic and his face and neck were spattered with the blood and entrails of his failures, and his hands shook with exhaustion. He had long since abandoned any delicate operations, and was dazed by his own calculating steeliness: it took him a matter of seconds to reach a prognosis. He fought only for those who had the best chance of survival. The injured and dying came to him in such quantities and he had such a paucity of medical supplies that he was forced, with just a glance, to condemn ten times more than he saved. He no longer had anything to ease the suffering of the dying or of those on whom he operated. No morphine, no alcohol, no humane words. In some cases, he felt he should put them out of their agony. It was the only act of compassion they could still be shown. Victor Klemp had turned to the captain of one of the few army units in the area and formulated his request very clearly:

'Put a bullet in their heads,' he said, terrified to hear himself say such a thing. 'All those I send to you have no hope.'

The officer had looked him squarely in the eye and, not judging him but speaking with a complete, helpless calm that Victor Klemp would never forget, he had replied, 'We don't have enough bullets to show them mercy, doctor.'

Woefully regular tides of endless new cases were brought to him by civilians and soldiers. To him, these unfortunate souls were now simply wounds, fractures, ravaged organisms, future amputees. After the third wave of bombings, one makeshift stretcher caught his attention in this stream of faceless, nameless wounded. It was carried by two boys in uniform and on it lay a woman. Neither the filth and dust on her face nor her pallor could disguise the harmony of her features lit up by eyes of a pure, icy blue. Her hair, dirty as it was, had a light of its own. Emerging from under the blanket that the soldiers had laid over her were one shoulder and one arm which seemed, in just a few inches of bare skin, to concentrate everything that was sweet and gentle in the world. Further down, beneath the thick rough fabric, the swell of her breasts and abdomen indicated that she was pregnant. She couldn't have been twenty-five years old.

'What's wrong with her?' the doctor asked the stretcher-bearers because the young woman seemed so calm.

He watched the horror intensify on their faces.

'She was on the ground on Freiberger Strasse, partly trapped under rubble . . .' the taller of the two tried to explain. 'We pulled her free . . .'

The words withered in the young soldier's mouth and he gestured towards the blanket where cloying dark patches were forming. Becoming impatient, the doctor reverted to his harsh attitude. He snatched up the blanket. Under shreds of clothing, just below the knee, the young woman's legs had been cut clean off. Despite the improvised bandages, she was bleeding to death. The sight was all the more shocking because in between the two stumps swaddled in red and from which hung torn underwear and burned shreds of a flowery dress clinging to the wounds, another opening gaped. She was giving birth. The victim's eyes locked onto Victor Klemp's.

'I have no hope, doctor,' she said in an extraordinarily clear voice. 'But my child does.'

The groans and cries filling the church seemed to stop.

'Help me,' the woman's voice rang out.

It was not a plea. It was an order. Pity would have irrevocably distanced the surgeon from the woman, but the energy that she communicated to him with her voice and eyes made up his mind. He went into action: with the soldiers' help he tightened the tourniquets on her stumps. Without even a moan, the woman passed out. Two injured men were moved out of a side chapel so she could be attended to there. With a sweep of his hand, Klemp cleared the top of a wooden table cluttered with shattered glass and rubble from the vaulted ceiling, with soiled bandages and the vestiges of votive candles. He laid the woman down and she regained consciousness.

'What's your name?' the doctor asked.

'Luisa.'

'Luisa, I promise you shall see your child.'

The baby was engaged in the birth canal but the doctor decided to go beyond his meagre knowledge of obstetrics and attempt a caesarean. He was afraid of losing the baby, and although he knew it would kill the mother, she was in no state to see her labour through to the end anyway. The soldiers, who had seen plenty of bloodshed despite their youth, looked away when he made his incision just above her pubic bone. For fear of touching the baby, he did not cut deeply with the scalpel, choosing to work through the membranes one at a time by tearing them with his fingers. It was carnage. Luisa kept passing out and coming back round. Not one of the three men dared imagine her pain. The brief moments when she was unconscious were a relief to them. Victor Klemp talked to her the whole time, a sequence of words with no true meaning, intended only to encourage himself and keep Luisa alive. His fingers finally reached what he thought was the uterus because, unlike the other tissues, it resisted being torn by hand. He made a second incision. What he was inflicting on this woman whom he had so recently looked in the eye seemed more barbaric to him than all the butchery of the previous hours. Liquid spurted out as he drove his hands into the warm, wet cavity, feeling for the infant. He felt its tiny body and, not entirely sure what he was holding, pulled at it. Victor Klemp had to use his strength to free the baby's head which was held within the mother's pelvis. The baby was blue. The doctor cut the cord as best he could, and, suddenly starved of oxygen, the new-born gave a wail that brought the mother round.

'It's a boy, Luisa, a good strong lad,' Victor Klemp announced.

She just blacked out again. The doctor sat down with the baby on his lap and made a clumsy knot of his umbilical cord. He cleaned the infant with a rag and what little water he could find then took off his tunic, which had once been white, so that he could remove his shirt and wrap the baby in it. Luisa came round when she felt the weight of her son between her breasts.

'Is he alive?'

'Very much so, Luisa.'

She was lying down too flat to see him properly, and was too weak to put her arms around him.

'With all his fingers and toes?' she insisted.

'All of them, it's a boy, he's magnificent,' the three men replied in a muddle of strangled voices.

Discreetly avoiding looking, they put the soaking blanket back over her. One of the soldiers lifted the child above his mother's face. The baby made a cat-like mewling until he was put back onto Luisa's breast. Victor Klemp held the young woman's elbow and put her hand on her baby so that she could touch him. Feeling her hand, the baby moved softly, and the three men saw Luisa's eyes fill with tears.

She met Victor Klemp's eye again.

'He's under your protection now, doctor,' she said and, without giving him time to reply, she added, 'Find Marthe Engerer, my sister-in-law. She's in Dresden.'

Victor Klemp said some soothing words and then there was silence again before Luisa looked at her baby.

'He's called Werner,' she said. 'Werner Zilch. Don't change his name. He's the last of our kind.'

She closed her eyes, stroking the nape of her baby's neck with her index finger, while Victor Klemp crouched beside her, holding her free hand. The young woman's eyes closed again. This moment of calm lasted a minute, perhaps two, then Luisa's finger stopped moving on her little boy, and her other hand slackened between Victor Klemp's cradling palms. He had the powerful sense, although it was absurd for such a rational man, that he could feel the dying woman's soul travel through him. A palpable shifting of waves for a fraction of a second, then she was gone. The doctor laid Luisa's still-supple arm down onto the table by her side. He looked at the child curled up against his mother, reassured by a warmth that would soon dwindle, resting on a heart that had stopped beating. The two soldiers looked to the doctor for confirmation. He turned away. He had seen many atrocities these last few days, but he had never felt so vulnerable. When he looked up, he saw a picture of the Virgin and Child. The Madonna, spared by the bombing, had watched over them through this appalling miracle. An incredulous laugh full of despair shuddered from the doctor's chest. Suddenly noticing the shrieks of the wounded and the groans of the dying, that he had not heard during those interminable minutes, Victor Klemp sat down. There, at the foot of that table on which the dead half-woman lay with her child, he felt his body convulse while the two soldiers beside him wept like the children they were.

Manhattan, 1969

Marcus spotted the Rolls before I did.

'Over there!' he yelled, pointing. I cut in front of two drivers who regaled me with a concerto of hooting.

An ashen-faced Marcus fastened his seat belt, which he never did, while in the back Shakespeare tumbled around the corners, whimpering. I managed to tailgate Ernie's Rolls, which headed north up Madison Avenue for thirty-five blocks.

'This isn't very discreet,' Marcus warned, 'you should leave a car in between you.'

'I don't want to take the risk,' I replied through clenched teeth.

'We don't have the same definition of the word "risk",' he quipped with reference to the perilous manoeuvre I'd just undertaken.

There wasn't much traffic and we sped swiftly northwards. As the minutes passed, Marcus seemed increasingly tense. When we were beyond the Rockefeller Center where the traffic was starting to stagnate, he couldn't take any more.

'We don't have time for this, Werner, we need to be in Brooklyn in under forty-five minutes.'

'We have time,' I proclaimed, like an act of faith, hands clamped on the metal steering wheel, eyes pinned on the Rolls.

The chauffeur in front turned left onto 51st Street, passed Fifth Avenue, then the Avenue of the Americas, and finally stopped. Marcus said nothing, silence being his most severe form of condemnation. For a few minutes nothing happened. I pictured Ernie inside the car, kissing the young woman, caressing her, perhaps undressing her, and the thought drove me crazy. Luckily she stepped out of the car. She covered ten or so yards with supple, assertive strides. The blue skirt of her dress flapped against her thighs. She took some keys from her purse, got into a green Ford and pulled away. I followed her. Marcus looked at his watch anxiously. When she continued to head west of Central Park, taking us further still from Brooklyn, he gave me an ultimatum.

'If you haven't found her apartment within five minutes, we're giving up, Wern. We can't be late, they'll crucify us!'

All my attention was focused on that green car that kept leading us further away. Her driving was just like her, lively and fluid.

'That's enough now, Wern!' Marcus cried. 'I refuse to let you ruin a ten-million-dollar project for a girl you saw for five minutes in a restaurant.'

'She's the love of my life,' I replied.

I realised how definite this declaration sounded, but I'd never been surer of myself than I was then.

'You didn't even talk to her!' Marcus howled, doubly amazed because until then, lust followed by amnesia had been my only feelings in matters of love.

'She's the one, Marcus.'

'I can't believe you're doing this.'

The green car came to a stop, double-parked outside a brick building. My blonde obsession emerged from the Ford with a flat square package under her arm. She went inside. I cut the engine.

'There's no way you're waiting for her! Do you hear me, Wern? If she's the love of your life, then fate will make sure she crosses your path again. Right now, you're starting the car and turning around.'

Never before had Marcus so seriously implied that our friendship could end. I looked up at the building, my hands clammy and my mind at boiling point. I needed to find a solution. Marcus glowered at me and, in less urgent circumstances, I would have brushed him aside with a flourish, but I knew he was right. We'd staked everything on this operation in Brooklyn. If the work didn't start up again very soon, we were ruined. I turned on the ignition and reversed about five yards. Marcus sighed. He encouraged me with a 'Thanks, Wern, we . . .' but his face dropped dramatically when he saw me shift into first and bear down on the Ford. The impact was more violent than I'd expected. I completely caved in the Ford's left wing, along with the front of our car. Shakespeare was projected between the two of us and landed with his front paws on the dashboard, his stomach straddling the gearshift. Marcus was speechless. I leapt out and leant on the hood of the green car to write on the back of a couple of business cards:

Dear sir,

A momentary lapse of concentration on my part caused this regrettable accident. Please forgive me for the damage I've caused your vehicle. Do get in touch with me as soon as you have a moment so that we can proceed with a statement and an amicable settlement of this problem.

Allow me to reiterate my most abject apologies.

Werner Zilch.

I thought the note was legible despite my 'spidery scrawl', as my handwriting had been described all through my schooldays. I left it on the windshield and set off towards Brooklyn, driving like a madman on the run. Marcus didn't utter a single word on the journey. The front bumper held until we arrived outside Brooklyn city hall where it came loose on one side, forcing us to park amid a deafening racket.

'You know how to make an entrance,' my partner pointed out, tight-lipped.

We hadn't had time to drop Shakespeare at the apartment so

we had to leave him on his own in the car, which he loathed. We ran to get to our hearing, ten minutes late. Marcus was, as usual, beautifully turned out but I now looked a complete mess: in the stress of the chase I'd crumpled my jacket and drenched my shirt. My hair, which I hadn't had time to flatten, had reclaimed its independence and was tangled. Marcus gesticulated with his hands, indicating I should run my hands through it to smooth it down, which I did with no noticeable results: my hair sprang back into its tangle as soon as it was released from my combing fingers.

The Borough president received us in a pretentious, stately, wood-panelled room. When he saw me he raised an enquiring eyebrow, but, wearied by his job and several decades of local politics, he'd lost the capacity for astonishment. He indicated two chairs at his meeting table, a long way from his desk decked with gilded bronzes, which was where he stayed, doing nothing.

'My deputy will be joining you shortly,' he said.

His doleful expression looked as if it was filtered through the tilted slats of a window shutter. He stared at me openly and unashamedly. I was irritated by the buzzing of a fly doggedly bashing into the shade on a lamp behind us. It flew past me a couple of times, but the third time, I caught it with one hand and crushed it.

'You just killed my pet fly,' the town councillor protested.

'Excuse me?'

'That was my fly.'

I saw Marcus blanch. He started stammering apologies.

'But surely,' I interrupted him, 'you didn't have a relationship with that particular fly?'

'I'm joking! It *is* funny, isn't it?'

'Enough,' I replied, mentally gauging just how senile he was, and dropping the remains of the fly onto the dark parquet floor.

'How tall are you?' he asked me.

'Six feet four inches.'

'You also have big feet.'

Marcus shot me a mocking look.

'They're in proportion to my height,' I said, stretching out one of my legs to show him my shoe.

That drew another exasperated glance from Marcus, as the shoe wasn't polished, but the councillor was more interested in the size of my foot than what it was wearing, and adjusted himself in his seat. Contrary to our expectations, his questions bore no relation to the technical details of our project.

'You look strong too. I guess hoodlums don't like rubbing you the wrong way,' he said.

'No one likes rubbing me the wrong way when I'm in a bad mood.'

'Where are you from? You have a very Slavic build.'

Marcus looked disconcerted but I fielded the question calmly.

'Yes, apparently I'm originally from Germany.'

'Apparently?' the councillor asked.

'My parents adopted me when I was three.'

'And how old are you now?'

'Twenty-four.'

'So young! So healthy!' he enthused. 'Isn't it a little ambitious, at such a young age, to be launching into a project on this scale, eighty-five apartments in two buildings?'

'Well, you yourself were first elected at twenty-three,' I replied, glad that Marcus and I had prepared for the meeting.

We watched as he puffed himself up and slid his right hand down the full length of his tie, several times. With his other hand, he absent-mindedly fondled the inside of his thigh.

'I was very handsome at the time, you know. I attracted a lot of attention. Older men chased me . . .' he ventured, to sound us out.

Luckily for us, his deputy arrived. It was to this henchman that we'd given the first back-hander a few months earlier, to persuade him to stop his administrative harassment. He was carrying the files relating to our site in a brown plastic letter tray. He was slim and pale with a pointed nose and a slippery expression. As soon as he appeared there was tension in the room.

'You're late, my friend,' the Borough president said.

'You know I had an equally important meeting that just finished,' his deputy countered.

'Well, then why did you summon these delightful young men so early? You kept them waiting.'

The shrew sat at the same table as us, and the president stood up and slowly made his way over to join us. It became clear that they'd decided on well-defined roles. The president played the part of the debonair patriarch while his deputy barked and bit and sniffed out the weaknesses. First, he tried to impress us with his legal jargon, but he wasn't prepared for Marcus's agility in all matters of the law. Next, he drowned us in technical gibberish which I picked apart with the same aptitude. Lastly, they made their request clearer. They wanted an advance and couldn't care less whether their arguments were valid. We were at their mercy and they knew it. I'd have liked to strangle them on the spot, but judging by the way the president was writhing on his leather chair, I knew that the more verbal – and, if possible, physical – abuse I gave him, the more he'd enjoy it. That's the problem with masochists, it's impossible to do them harm without doing them good. This thought helped me recover my composure.

We didn't have any money left, we needed to find a compromise, so I suggested one of the apartments. The old man's greed reared its head again: he wanted a unit on the top floor with a roof terrace. It was one of our most expensive assets, and the negotiations became more heated. As we defended every square inch of our fortress, I wondered what sort of protégé the president was planning to install in his future penthouse. From the information I had, I knew that the woman he'd married to make a career in politics was already luxuriously accommodated in their house in Manhattan, and their two children also had good homes. As for the shrew, he was happy to settle for a studio, not out of modesty, but because his boss felt hierarchy should be respected: if he was having an apartment with a terrace, his deputy could only lay claim to one fifth of its footprint, and at least three floors lower down. I point-blank refused to give them parking spaces, or the private elevator, or to fit out the kitchens which they would have to do themselves.

Judging by the rumbling sounds coming from his stomach, the president was hungry. I played on this by holding back on the finer details and announcing that I'd cancelled all our other appointments and even dinner so that we could settle this problem. Seeing his teatime snack and his dinner receding until late in the evening, the president suddenly looked very tired and gave in. Having just extorted one of the jewels of our project, he had the nerve to say I drove a 'hard bargain', and must have inherited this 'rigidity' from my ancestors.

'Of course, rigidity is important in a young man . . .' he added, which made me want to smash his teeth in.

I'd made the most of my charm during the negotiations but now that he'd screwed us, I'd have happily forced him to swallow his own innuendos and his tie along with them, particularly as he was still stroking it obscenely. Marcus nervously brought the conversation back to legal matters. We couldn't sign a standard agreement, which would have left evidence of their scheming, so the president and his deputy told us how to proceed: the next morning we were to take the contracts of sale for the said apartments to their low-life attorney so they could draw up the deeds to the properties using nominees. We would be given the authorisation to continue work on site early that afternoon.

We all stood up. I said my goodbyes with a murderous look in my eyes. I didn't know how I would do it, but I was determined to reduce these Mafiosi-dressed-as-big-wheels to dust.

My associate looked at me and gestured towards the door, and we turned away without another word.

Marcus, who didn't like silence, said, 'We did OK, in the end.' Ever the fatalist, when I didn't answer, he added, 'We're all somebody's prey and somebody's predator.'

In the parking lot, I used my belt to reattach the Chrysler's bumper. Shakespeare, who was furious at having been shut in alone, had shredded the rear seat and parts of the headrests. In three hours, Marcus's car had been ruined. This man who couldn't bear mess and damage – a consequence of his privileged childhood – rolled his eyes in resignation.

'What with you and Shakespeare, I wonder why we still pay demolition companies.'

I didn't have the heart to scold the dog. I was too familiar with the ravages of abandonment myself.

Dresden, February 1945

Victor Klemp went back to his horrifying choices between those who were barely alive and those even closer to being dead. He left the first of the two soldiers to carry Luisa's lifeless body to join the other corpses. The second found himself entrusted with the new-born baby and a new problem: finding food for him. Accounts of the miraculous birth did the rounds of the survivors inside the church, all of them still fighting for others or against themselves. A wonderful energy gripped these exhausted people. They needed to find a woman who could suckle the child, and soon. The young soldier carried the baby inside his shirt to give him the comfort of skin-to-skin contact. He asked anyone who was conscious whether they'd seen a woman with a baby anywhere. In vain. The tiny boy was quiet at first but after an hour he started to cry. He attached his tiny mouth to the distraught soldier's skin, instinctively rooting for a breast he couldn't find.

The young soldier left the church just as day was breaking. There was fire everywhere, everywhere fire. Right in the middle of February, the heat was appalling. He saw terrible sights: adults eaten away by flames and reduced to the size of children, scraps of arms and legs, whole families burned, buses full of charred passengers. He paled when he saw a group of unrecognisable men in the same uniform as his. Occasionally he saw wild-eyed figures emerging from the ruins. Lots of people were looking for their children and other family members. A mother to feed this baby? No, they hadn't seen one. They hadn't noticed. They couldn't remember. Milk? No, not a drop. He'd have to get out of the city, go and ask for help in nearby villages. The baby was still crying, his pink throat completely dry. An old man offered the soldier a pinch of sugar and he dissolved it in what little water was left in his flask. He rubbed his little finger clean as best he could against his sweater, then dipped it in the sugared water and put it in Werner's mouth. The child sucked avidly on the finger and started crying again as soon as it was withdrawn. The soldier held him close, walking aimlessly in search of another increasingly improbable miracle.

Soon the baby stopped wailing and his silence panicked the soldier even more than his crying. Feeling this frail little body against him, he was filled with despair. He sat on the stump of a column which, only a few days earlier, had graced the front of the law courts. He didn't have the strength to watch the baby die in his arms, so decided to abandon him; it would be too inhuman to witness his death throes. He spotted a flat stone among the ruins and settled the child in that apocalyptic cradle. He walked a few paces away, devastated. The baby whimpered and the soldier turned back, consumed with remorse that such a thought had even occurred to him. He was so hungry himself . . . He picked up the bundle and started walking again, startled by a terrifying sound. He spun around and, instead of the Frauenkirche that he had left an hour earlier, he saw a huge column of brown dust rise into the sky. This last survivor of the chaos, a majestic edifice of stone which had watched over the city for more than two centuries, had just collapsed. In a flash, he saw a sea of faces: the doctor who had brought the baby into the world, his fellow soldier who had helped him free Luisa, the people he had asked for milk, the children and nurses he had met. He stood rooted to the spot, refusing to believe that these people who, only moments earlier had talked to him and smiled at him, were no longer there. He sat down, too overwhelmed to weep or gauge the extraordinary privilege it was to be alive still.

An hour or two later he saw two women and a little girl, all of them grey with dust, come around the corner of what had once been a street full of shops. He ran over to them so desperately that they were frightened. One of them shakily raised a knife, shouting at him to back away. He opened his shirt to show them the baby.

'Do you have any milk?' he begged.

They shook their heads and stepped closer.

'He doesn't look good,' the older woman said laconically.

'His mother's dead. He hasn't eaten since he was born.'

'Is he your son?' asked the other woman.

'No, he's not my son, but I don't want him to die.'

'You need to find a cow,' the little girl announced pragmatically.

'They were all eaten a long time ago, sweetheart,' said the older woman.

'A mummy, then?' the child suggested.

'His is dead,' the soldier said again, wiping his nose on the back of his dusty sleeve.

'I saw one last night.'

'A cow?' the three adults asked in amazement.

'No, a mummy.'

'When? Where?'

'Last night, in the cellar, a lady who had a baby in a basket.'

'What cellar, darling? I don't remember,' the mother asked the girl.

'You know, the lady who lifted me up when you were outside . . . you know, Mummy, so you could get me out through the hole.'

'The lady in the red coat?'

'Yes,' the girl said with some relief.

'But she didn't have a baby!'

'There was a baby in her basket. I saw him when we were running away from the fire. The mummy was running with her basket. There was thunder everywhere.'

The young woman crouched down on a level with the girl.

'Tell us, Allestria. It's very important.'

'The mummy was thrown to the ground. I saw the baby . . . he made a sun shape,' explained the little girl, making a big circular movement with one arm. 'I saw him in the air. I saw him fly. Then he fell on the ground.'

'Oh, my darling,' the mother said, holding her daughter to her.

'I heard the mummy scream, but you told me to run,' she added.

'We were in a cellar near the city hall,' the young woman said, looking up at the soldier. 'The building collapsed. We were almost trapped. I remember this woman now. I don't know if she's still alive. She was wearing a red coat.'

'He fell,' the little girl said again, her eyes wide with terror.

The women agreed to retrace their steps with the soldier. He ran more than walked, stopping when he had to help the women climb over or around obstacles. It took them twenty minutes to get to what was left of the city hall. Every now and then the soldier looked inside his shirt. Werner was motionless, but still breathing. The little girl pointed to the place, and all four of them started asking passers-by about the woman in the red coat. Most of them, stunned by events, walked past without answering. Others just shrugged their shoulders. No one had seen the woman. Eventually an old man gave them fresh hope. He'd come up from the river where, in the night, his wife had saved the young mother who'd been about to throw herself into the water.

'My wife took hold of her and made her sit on the ground. She cradled her most of the night. That's how my Julia is. Always helping other people . . . The young woman wanted to kill herself, but Julia wouldn't let her. There have been enough deaths for all eternity in the last—'

'Where are they?' the soldier interrupted.

'You'll find them on the banks, near the old bridge,' the man said.

He had set off in search of food. Did they have anything they could share? The women shook their heads sadly. The soldier was already heading for the river, and they followed a little way behind him. It took another fifteen minutes to reach their destination. Hundreds of survivors had gathered along the riverbank, thinking they could take refuge in the water if the fire followed them here. The women lost sight of the soldier briefly, then saw him again. He was making his way over to two women: one was very elderly and must have been Julia, the other was younger and was wearing a coat which, under all the dust, was definitely red. He showed them the baby insistently but, quite unexpectedly, the young woman backed away. The soldier followed her, imploring her. When he put a hand on her arm she spun around furiously.

'It's not my Thomas!' she screamed. 'It's not my son!'

The soldier's companions and Julia gathered around the woman to reason with her. No one was saying this was her son. Everyone could understand her pain, but this baby was about to die, she alone could save him. He hadn't suckled since he was born, the night before. Without her help he would die within the hour. In case prudishness was playing a part in the young woman's inexplicable reaction, at Julia's request, the soldier handed over the child and walked a little way away. The women tried to show Werner to the bereaved mother, but she started screaming again, saying she didn't want anything to do with him, even trying to strike him. When an onlooker made a bitter comment she became so hysterical that Julia took her by the shoulders and shook her vigorously.

'You're going to feed this child and that's all there is to it.'

They sat the reluctant mother down and opened her red coat. Under a beige cardigan the young woman's luxurious dress had large round stains over her breasts.

'He'll do *you* good, too,' Julia said forcefully.

The unwilling wet nurse stopped struggling. The little girl sat facing her, a pleading expression in her eyes. The girl's mother unbuttoned the milk-stained dress while Julia held Werner to the woman's breast. They were all tense, ready to defend him ferociously. The baby was so weak he didn't respond when he felt the nipple. The woman in the red coat stared straight ahead, her jaw clamped and her eyes blank. The old woman very gently squeezed her breast so that a few drops of milk fell on the baby's mouth and face. He didn't move straight away, but the smell of milk gradually brought him back to life. When his lips closed over the dark areola, the group of women gave a cry of joy. Reassured by their smiles, the soldier raised his face and clenched fists towards the sky triumphantly. A tear of relief trickled past his ear and down his neck, followed by another which he brushed away with his hand. He sat down a few paces away, watching Werner regain his strength with every mouthful. Several long minutes later, the rebellious mother looked down at the child that the other women were holding to her breast. He turned his unfocused eyes on her, and she softened. Also weeping, but in her case for the child she'd lost, she finally put her arms around this orphan that life had entrusted to her.

Manhattan, 1969

Back at our apartment, which we used as an office, the ever-dependable Donna was waiting for us. She was a single mother and had become our assistant after walking out of the door of the Madison Avenue attorney's office where she had been working. She'd never explained why. The salary we could afford to give her was much lower than she'd had in her previous job, but she'd accepted it without batting an eyelid in exchange for a guaranteed profit-share in the company – if and when there were any profits – and on condition that she could bring her daughter with her when her nanny was delayed. We suspected she'd had an affair with one of her former bosses, but she never talked about her daughter's father. Whenever people asked, she would say, 'There is no father.' Anyone who argued that even a rudimentary understanding of biology suggested that there had to be a father was treated to such a lacerating glare that they lost the urge to pursue the subject. If you didn't push her on her entrenched ideas, Donna was a pearl. We couldn't have dreamed of a more efficient secretary and she'd helped us avoid a lot of beginner's mistakes. She made a point of keeping a certain distance with us, talked about herself as if she were already over the hill, and was impervious to my charms, which piqued me at first. With hindsight, I'm glad of it, because she fielded my girlfriends' calls so adroitly and diplomatically – but not without an element of unvoiced criticism – that I was spared a good many scenes.

After our negotiations in Brooklyn, we'd dropped the car at the garage, and now almost before I had my foot through the door, I asked her whether she'd had a call for me from a young woman. She looked at me enquiringly and replied that, unfortunately, the only people who'd tried to contact us were:

'Mr Ramirez from the demolition company at 2.35, Mr Roover about delivering the metal beams at 3.54, Mr Hoffman calling urgently about a water leak in building B, and your father, Marcus, who had an alarming conversation with one of your suppliers and wanted to know whether he could help . . .'

Marcus loathed his father's intrusions into our affairs. Personally, I was very aware of the support he had given us. Frank Howard's prestigious signature on the plans for our first two projects and the international credibility of his architectural firm had made a lot of things possible. Frank frequently wanted news of the construction sites, and constantly offered to give a helping hand, which his son refused to accept. My friend couldn't understand his father's sudden interest in him when he'd spent most of his childhood abandoned to nannies. He met his advances with fierce independence and reserve in every aspect of his life. Marcus was not the expansive type. He had a way of finding something to talk about with absolutely anyone, in absolutely any situation, but used this capacity to get people to speak only to protect his secrets all the more closely. He took an interest in others to be sure other people didn't take an interest in him.

'You can tell him the work's starting again this afternoon,' he grouched.

Donna's face lit up.

'We were fleeced like complete rookies,' I said, lowering the mood as I felt the resentment rise in my throat again.

'But we're starting up again?'

'We're starting up again. You'd have been sorry to leave us, admit it . . .'

'I'd have been very sad to see Z & H close down,' she said, reverting to her slightly brisk manner. Donna used our official name, even though the company comprised only the three of us, when she wanted to bring a conversation back onto a professional footing, or to lend more weight to our future multinational.

She granted herself barely a moment to celebrate, then picked up the telephone to let our partners know. I concentrated on the logistics of starting construction again but my stomach made such a loud noise that Marcus and Donna burst out laughing. I emptied the refrigerator, alternating a jumble of sweet and savoury, then eventually called Paolo at Gioccardi's. I ordered some antipasti, two bottles of Chianti and four pizzas: one for Marcus, one for Donna and two for me. Paolo was kind enough to bring dinner to the apartment, and we spent the rest of the evening putting our war machine back into action. Marcus drew up the sales contracts for the two apartments that it had cost us to continue construction work. He seemed very satisfied with his work and told me he'd 'hidden a grenade' in the agreement and hoped he'd camouflaged it sufficiently well for our two corrupt officials not to notice it. I was delighted. Meanwhile, I brought all our subcontractors, who were scattered across different projects, up to date. I had to persuade them, charm them or outright threaten them – exploding into the receiver at them as only I knew how – to ensure they'd be ready to start work the next day. When I'd finished mobilising these slackers and killing my vocal cords, I still prowled around the telephone, followed by Shakespeare, who wouldn't let me out of his sight. My jumpiness made Marcus laugh.

'Oh my, does TLOYL have you trained already!'

'TLOYL?' I asked.

'The Love Of Your Life.'

This acronym was soon abbreviated to 'TL' and took its place in the language of memories and indecipherable private references that Marcus and I had built over the course of our friendship.

The long-awaited call didn't come until the following morning.

Marcus and I were preparing to go out and Donna hadn't yet arrived. I threw myself at the telephone. Shakespeare thought I was playing and started bounding around, yelping and almost knocking over a chair, which I straightened with my foot because my hands were busy with the phone.

I recognised her voice immediately.

'Hello, could I speak to Mr Zilch please?'

'You're speaking to him,' I said, subconsciously accentuating the deeper notes of my voice, which made Marcus laugh, particularly as Shakespeare was undermining my credibility.

'I'm the owner of the green Ford . . . You left your contact details on the windshield.'

'Thank you for calling me, and I apologise. Your car's in a terrible state! I was on my way to conclude a big business deal . . .'

Marcus glared at me. He thought these attempts to sell myself were boorish and, as he explained to me later in the harshest tones, 'You don't apologise. You beg the injured person to forgive you.'

'Where can I meet you to give you the statement?' I asked.

She suggested the bar in the Pierre Hotel. Despite my flustered state, I had the presence of mind to ask her name.

'Rebecca,' she murmured so gently, it made me shiver. She didn't give her family name.

'How will I recognise you?' I added, to bolster my story of an accident.

'I'll be wearing a claret-coloured leather jacket,' she said.

She arranged to meet me an hour and a half later. Even before I'd hung up I was reaching feverishly for my keys and wallet, ready to set off.

'Are you planning to go like that?' Marcus asked, grabbing me by the collar. 'I hope you're joking! Your shirt's crumpled, your pants are creased, you're wearing no jacket, no tie . . .'

'I won't wear a tie, they strangle me,' I protested, rubbing my neck nervily.

'. . . Your shoes aren't polished, you didn't shave, I don't know what to say about your hair, and I hope you brushed your teeth, at least.'

I opened my mouth wide and blew a gust of minty breath in his face.

'I would have taken your word for it, but that's fine,' he concluded, 'as for the rest . . .'

Marcus had an innate sense of style and was impeccably brought up. His mother died when he was only eight, at a time when his father, Frank Howard, was building his first large-scale projects. Constantly travelling and obsessed with his revolutionary constructions, which included the notorious Vancouver Institute of Modern Art and the suspension bridge in Rio de Janeiro, Frank left his son in the hands of the best tutors. His ideas about education were far more conservative than his three-dimensional visions, and he wanted Marcus to be transformed into an archduke. The boy learned to dance, kiss a lady's hand and speak French, unlike me who – although my mother was from Normandy – could just about massacre three words. He played piano, excelled at bridge and tennis (the sport that had brought us together some fifteen years earlier), and was well versed in the history of the United States and Europe along with the history of art and architecture. Marcus was a walking anachronism, in other words he was ill-equipped for real life. Ever since *Homo sapiens* emerged from caves, the world has not been gentle with anyone, but in New York, honesty and consideration proved particularly bad handicaps. I'd decided to teach him to defend himself; he had assigned himself the mission of civilising me.

So, when the whole future of my love life was in the balance, I yielded to Marcus's injunctions. Donna, who wasn't used to seeing me smartly dressed, complimented me on my outfit when we met her on the stairs. Even Marcus pronounced me 'present-able' when he dropped me off by taxi at the Pierre and slipped the forms for the statement into my hand. He meanwhile would take the contracts to the corrupt attorney. I was baptising a pair of shoes that I'd bought at Marcus's insistence a few weeks before. Because the soles weren't worn in, I slipped a good three feet across the marbled chequerboard floor of the sumptuous lobby and only just avoided a fall. As I descended the small flight of steps into the lounge, I scanned the softly lit room. The barman stood idle behind his copper counter. To his left were two businessmen in conversation. My heartbeat accelerated when I saw the love of my life already seated at a table behind one of the square columns. She had scooped her hair into a loose chignon which accentuated her graceful looks. She was wearing beige pants and a dark-red leather jacket. Beneath it, the fabric of her blouse was so fine it afforded glimpses of her shape and her skin. She was drawing in a notebook.

'Miss Rebecca?' I asked, making my way over to her and reaching out my hand.

She looked up and studied me for a few seconds.

'I know you,' she breathed in amazement. 'You were at that Italian restaurant yesterday . . .'

'Oh yes, you were at Gioccardi's!'

'Exactly! Gioccardi's!'

She stood up and shook my hand.

'You had a big dog . . .' she said.

'He's called Shakespeare.'

'And you helped me . . .' I saw her stop to think. 'But surely you didn't . . .'

She opened her violet eyes wide. My future was being played out right there. She sat back down and I sat opposite her. We stayed like that for a moment looking at each other, then I saw the beginnings of a smile on her face. Soon she was smiling openly, incredulously.

'Well, Mr Zilch, you don't beat about the bush! You could have just asked for my number.'

'I didn't dare,' I said, treating her to my bashful, through-my-hair gaze which had enjoyed considerable success.

'You'd rather run into my Ford?'

'It was the only idea that came to mind,' I admitted.

'Addressing the note to "Mr", now that was crafty.'

I should have reacted, taken the advantage, but I was paralysed by a shyness I'd never experienced. The ensuing silence completely crushed me.

'Are you going to offer me a drink?' she teased.

I leapt up to find the waiter and bring him over.

'What would you like? Would champagne earn your forgiveness?'

Rebecca smiled. She looked at her watch, revealing her wrist, and seemed to think the time was right.

'A bloody Mary, please.'

Ordering a vodka cocktail at just 11.30 a.m. struck me as neither very appropriate nor very ladylike, but Rebecca, as I would later discover, rarely complied with the diktats imposed by society on the fairer sex. I asked whether she was an artist and she said she was. I wanted to see the drawings in her sketchbook but she laughed out loud.

'I don't think that's a good idea.'

'Why?'

'Because you were shocked enough that I ordered vodka at this time of day, so my drawings . . .'

'Quite the opposite, I'm delighted you're having vodka,' I stammered, disconcerted.

'Still, you'd have been happier if I'd opted for a soft drink.'

I tied myself in knots with hazy assessments of the vitamin content of vodka, moved on to the inspiration artists need to take from artificial stimuli, developed a point about the Russian soul before landing – although I couldn't say how – on the potato farming that went into making this spirit. I was pathetic. Rebecca indulgently took her sketchbook from her bag and handed it to me.

'At your own risk,' she warned.

I leafed through the pages across which sprawled the studies of naked men I'd glimpsed the previous day. An irrepressible feeling of jealousy surged through me.

'Reassure me that these drawings are the fruit of your imagination . . .'

'I have models.'

'Naked models?' I squeaked.

'You see, you're shocked.'

'Not at all, I'm jealous.'

'I could draw you, if you like.'

'Do I inspire you?'

Through half-closed eyes, Rebecca unashamedly looked me up and down, as if appraising a monument or livestock.

'With your dishevelled hair, your angular frame and your slightly too-long arms, there's something a bit Egon Schiele about you . . . Still, your face has character. I like the cheekbones,' she added, running a finger over her own cheeks, 'and the jaw . . . it's as if your face were a triangle inside a square . . . you're interesting.'

'I've no idea who this Mr Chile is,' I retorted, put out to be examined so coolly.

'So, let's move on to the car,' she said.

The love of my life was in nothing like the same turmoil as me. I cursed myself. She had thrown me a lifeline but I hadn't had the presence of mind to take it. Her peers had accustomed me to more adulation but, in normal circumstances, I knew how to run this show. With Rebecca, I felt like a bad tennis player pelted with shots and forced to run all over the court. I was about to bring the conversation back to her studio and her work, hoping she would issue her invitation again, when we were interrupted by a heavy-set guy I immediately recognised. It was the lardy fop who'd been with Rebecca at Gioccardi's. He was dressed just as pretentiously as the previous day, but seemed to have abandoned his manners.

'Can you explain what's going on?' he asked, ploughing towards us.

'Ah, Ernie, there you are!' exclaimed Rebecca with feigned enthusiasm.

He didn't even bother returning her greeting.

'What's *he* doing here?'

'Please, Ernie, this is the man who drove into my car, that's why I asked him to come. You know I'm hopeless with paperwork. Mr Zilch, can I introduce Mr Gordon, my father's lawyer and right-hand man. Ernie, Mr Zilch.'

'Rebecca, don't tell me you don't recognise him!' the lawyer asked, not even looking at me. I may have taken up a good deal of space, but he was behaving as if I was part of the scenery.

'Recognise who?'

'This guy! He's been chasing after you since Gioccardi's.'

'Come on, Ernie, you're mad,' she replied in such bad faith I was impressed. 'Don't you think I'd remember!'

Ernie, who was as red as his pocket handkerchief, turned to me.

'You're pretty sick, sweetheart. If you think you'll get your own way by destroying my client's car, you've lost your mind. Here's my card. If your insurance hasn't contacted my office in the next two hours, I'll subpoena you for harassment and attempted murder. Rebecca, get your things, we're leaving.'

Rebecca seemed to be finding the situation very amusing. She pushed a little further.

'Ernie, I promise you you're imagining things. Mr Zilch is very kind. Sit down and have a drink with us . . .'

'We're going!' he snapped, grabbing her elbow.

'You're assaulting your client. Let her go.'

'Listen, my dear little man,' he said, even though I was head and shoulders taller than he was, 'I've known Rebecca since she was born, in the days when you were still crying in your mother's skirts. You can't teach me how to behave with her.'

'Would you like me to intervene, Rebecca?' I asked, adopting a chivalrous posture not at all customary to me.

'I would ask you to address my client as Miss Lynch,' the lawyer chipped in.

'I wasn't aware of your client's surname, but since you've been kind enough to communicate it to me, I'll be delighted to address Miss Lynch with all the respect she deserves. And, as you seem susceptible to protocol and decorum, may I warn you that if you use "sweetheart", "my dear little man" or any other such term again, I'll land my fist in your face.'

This seemed to make an impression on him but he soon composed himself.

'I can see what you're up to, you filthy dowry-hunter.'

I turned to Rebecca.

'Dowry-hunter,' I said, 'that's not very nice . . . that's even worse than sweetheart or my dear little man, wouldn't you say, Rebecca?'

'I agree, Ernie. You're being very unfair. May I remind you that Mr Zilch has known me only a half-hour and until two minutes ago, he didn't even know my surname.'

Beneath her innocent exterior, my beauty was having enormous fun. Ernie flushed scarlet. He was about to explode with anger. He looked me in the eye at last.

'You know perfectly well who she is. No, Rebecca, we're leaving,' he ordered, taking her arm.

Seeing him touch her again made me furious. I grabbed him abruptly by his tie knot and slammed him against the column behind our table. I heard his head smack against the stone and his breathing accelerate. I could sense the staff panicking behind me. The barman sprang out from behind his counter. A waiter was already picking up the telephone to call security. I shot a questioning look at Rebecca. She looked very satisfied it had come to this, but didn't want to go any further.

'Don't worry, Mr Zilch. He won't do me any harm. You can

let him go,' she said calmly and with a raised hand and a smile that swept away all tension, she stopped those who were preparing to intervene.

Ernie coughed and adjusted his clothes shakily.

'That isn't the last you'll hear of this,' he announced with a scowl that he probably hoped looked fierce.

He didn't dare get too close to Rebecca, but with a tilt of his head instructed her to pick up her bag and follow him. She complied.

'Goodbye, Mr Zilch. It was a pleasure,' she trilled when she was almost at the door.

'Goodbye, Miss Lynch,' I replied while Ernie, who felt he was now out of my reach, shook Rebecca's arm firmly.

'I know you're particularly drawn to every loser on the planet, but I forbid you to speak to that man.'

'Come on, Ernie! You're not my father, just his employee.'

When Rebecca disappeared, I was flooded with regret. I hated myself for reacting so badly during our meeting. I felt I was right back where I'd been the day before and, worse, I'd created new obstacles. Ernie would try to persuade Rebecca I was unstable, dangerous even. I hadn't even had the presence of mind to ask her for her telephone number when she'd called a few hours earlier. I knew her name and what she did. I surmised that her family was influential, but that struck me as very flimsy material to fuel any hope of seeing her again.

When I left the Pierre I didn't have enough money to take the subway. With the setback on the construction site, I didn't have so much as a dollar left in my pocket and I'd handed my last bills over to the hotel barman. He'd made it clear, with all the restraint peculiar to the staff of great hotels, that Ernie was a regular and an obnoxious customer. I'd given him a majestic tip which meant I now had to walk home. As I strode past block after block, I replayed that first meeting a hundred times. The wind was whistling down the avenue, forcing me to walk with my head down, holding my collar with one hand. I turned left down 47th Street to get away from it. Laundries in basements spewed clouds of steam from their windows. I went over and over Rebecca's words, her every gesture and expression, trying to find anything I might have missed. Far from reassuring me, each new assessment only made me hate myself more. I couldn't find any reason for the love of my life to want to call me again.

Germany, February 1945

'Find Marthe Engerer, my sister-in-law. She's in Dresden,' Luisa
had said after bringing Werner into the world and before leaving
it herself.

In this inconceivable lottery of disaster, Marthe Engerer had
miraculously survived. She was a Red Cross nurse and had been
imprisoned in a cellar for hours. A collapsed wall had blocked
the doorway. The bars on the street-level window were so solid
that her efforts to pull them away had achieved nothing. She
had then worked loose the bricks between her cellar and the
next one, only to find dead bodies and a staircase that was also
obstructed. When the second wave of bombing hit, she put her
head between her knees again. She knew bombs came in fours.
She listened to the sinister whistling followed by an explosion,
and counted: 1, 2, 3, 4. When there was one missing, she held
her breath, praying it wouldn't land on her head, then she heard
the detonation and started counting again. There was a long
wait between the second and third waves of bombing. Time
enough for the day to dawn, judging by a tiny ellipse of light
which appeared on one of the stones blocking the narrow
opening; time enough to dare to hope that the worst was over.
It was hellishly hot in the cellar and her reserves of water were
evaporating before her eyes.

Marthe was more worried about her sister-in-law than herself.
The two women were inseparable; they had been childhood
friends and had wed the Zilch brothers on the same day. Marthe
had married the elder brother, Kasper, a choice she had regretted
ever since that wretched Saturday in June 1938. Luisa fell for

the younger brother, Johann, very likely the kindest husband in Silesia, where the four of them were born. Physically the brothers looked confoundingly alike; they could have been twins but there was in fact eleven months between them. Eleven months and a whole infinity. Johann was calm and gentle, absorbed in his scientific research. Kasper was quite a different story . . .

Another bomb shook the walls and spattered more cement on Marthe's head. Fear drove away her reminiscences. Here in this cellar, which at this rate would become her tomb, she had no idea of the scale of the damage. Her sister-in-law was out there in the city alone, and about to give birth. Since Johann's arrest, poor Luisa had become a mere shadow of herself.

The SS had come one morning and hammered on the door to the couple's apartment on the Peenemünde base. Informed by so-called friends that Johann had spoken out against the war effort and had even hinted at sabotage, they had arrested him with no more concrete justification. For the last four years, Johann had been working with von Braun, who invented the V2, the first ballistic missile with a range of almost 300 kilometres. These weapons, on which Hitler was depending to change the course of the war, were the object of paranoid Gestapo surveillance. It seemed no one was spared their suspicion, not even von Braun. When Johann was imprisoned, the great scientist had tried everything in his power to have his friend and employee released.

Panic-stricken, Luisa had come and thrown herself at the feet of General Hans Kammler, who oversaw all missile projects. The general had promised he would do what he could. The young woman, already four months pregnant at the time, had then gone to the headquarters of the secret police and insisted on being given news of her husband. When no one had answered her questions, she had sat herself down in the waiting room and stayed there all day, with no result. She had returned the next day, and the next. She had arrived every morning as the office opened, and left only when it closed. In the end, her perseverance had irritated the SS. Indifferent to her condition, they had threatened her, jostled her and even put her in a cell overnight to 'teach her some respect and save her the journey'. Marthe, who regularly spoke to Luisa on the telephone, had begged her to move somewhere safe.

'Come and join me in Dresden,' she had said. 'You can't stay there. Think of the baby. I'll look after you. It's all quiet here. No fighting, no police, just refugees . . .'

The baby growing inside her had eventually persuaded Luisa to leave. Were it not for the child, she would have let herself die at General Kammler's door or at the Gestapo headquarters. Marthe had taken her in in a state of anxiety bordering on insanity. During the day Luisa had paced like a caged animal; at night she'd called for Johann in her sleep and woken screaming. Marthe had rocked her in her arms for hours, as if soothing a frightened little girl.

When the bombing stopped, Marthe sat on the ground with her back against the wall of that cellar where the heat made her head spin, and worried herself sick. Her beloved Luisa, so beautiful and so fragile . . . Who was looking after her? The thought turned Marthe's heart to liquid, her legs to rags. The heat was making her delirious. Panting and frantic with thirst, she hopped from one thought to another, one image to another, unable to control the stream of concerns. She thought of Kasper again and shuddered, praying he was dead.

The lozenge of light had disappeared from the cellar by the time her fellow Red Cross workers located her. She called out incessantly. Oxygen was growing scarce. She could hear her rescuers puffing as they pulled aside rubble and clumps of brick. It was several hours before she breathed a first trickle of air from outside. An eternity before it was followed by light. She fell, helpless, into her colleagues' arms. They supported her all the way to the kitchen of their offices. There Marthe gulped water greedily, letting it spill over her cheeks and down her neck. When she'd finished the flask she put it down and ate her fill of stale crackers which she softened by dunking them in a cup of coffee so sugary it was like syrup – sugar was one of the few foodstuffs the Red Cross had in good quantities. Then she put on a clean uniform and climbed into the first rescue truck that stopped by to refuel.

Now she was hit by the scale of the tragedy. Smoke billowing from ruins burned her nostrils, windpipe and lungs. There was no escaping the spectacle of horror. Yet Marthe still refused to imagine the worst. She had to look for Luisa, she had to find her. Every time they stopped she questioned people. Her desperate search was delayed by tending to the injured, but this was her only way of staying in the rescue truck and getting closer to the city centre.

'Luisa Zilch . . . Have you seen her? A young woman, twenty-four, blonde, blue eyes you'd never forget, pregnant, nearly full term, or perhaps with a new-born already . . . she was on Freiberger Strasse when the bombing started . . .'

'Freiberger Strasse? Oh, you poor dear . . . There's nothing left of it. Not a single building . . .'

Marthe examined, disinfected, cleaned and bandaged, asking the same questions again and again. Have you seen Luisa Zilch? Have you met anyone coming from the city centre? Are there any survivors? Have you seen Luisa Zilch, a young woman, very beautiful, pregnant or with a baby? Have you seen survivors in the city centre? Every time she was given an almost identical reply. Freiberger Strasse? Good God, no. The city centre, it's hard to say. But miracles do happen. We have to believe in miracles, you know, we have no choice. Some people, moved by the anxiety in her eyes, felt more comfortable lying to her. Yes, they'd heard that there were survivors. You had to keep looking. Then Marthe would fall silent, more troubled than if they'd tried to discourage her. Hour after hour a sense of foreboding grew, snuffing out the hope that still lingered in her heart. Working silently, she cleaned, removed debris with surgical tongs, cut away, sewed up and applied dressings before asking yet more people whether they'd seen a woman of twenty-four, with unforgettable blue eyes, pregnant or with a baby . . .

Meanwhile, on the banks of the Elbe, an extraordinary chain of solidarity was developing around Werner. His innocence became the thread of hope to which these people who'd lost everything decided to cling. The miracle of his birth was relayed among thousands of survivors. They all took it upon themselves to let others know, first new arrivals and later the emergency services who managed to reach them and hand out drinking water, food rations, clothes and blankets. Anke, the reluctant wet nurse, had emerged from her delirium and now protected the baby with mechanical gestures she had made a thousand times for another infant. Sated at last, Werner himself lay asleep against her, huddled inside her red coat. People forced Anke to eat and drink more than she wanted. Every hour she offered her breast to the little creature who'd so quickly learned how to come back to life.

While Marthe bandaged the badly burned back of the umpteenth casualty – a projectile from an incendiary bomb had carved into his flesh – he told her he'd heard talk of a new-born baby on the banks of the Elbe, where people were looking for a Marthe Engerer, the child's aunt. He didn't need to say any more. If people were looking for her because of the child, how could she not deduce that Luisa was gone?

When, two hours later, Anke placed the baby in her arms, Marthe felt a surge of loathing for this ruddy-coloured, wrinkled little being. He was responsible for Luisa's death. Who else was there to blame? Herself, for making her sister-in-law come to Dresden in the hope of protecting her? The British, who had scattered their bombs, sowing death as far as the eye could see? Fate? God? The Devil? Who could find any meaning in this absurdity? She asked what had happened to her sister-in-law – a term that so poorly reflected her feelings for Luisa! There were so many other names she wished she could give her, so many words she wished she could whisper in her ear as she stroked her hair, and kissed her face, and – though only in her dreams – her lips . . .

Marthe gave little Werner back to Anke and asked again what had happened to his mother. The soldier who had saved Werner paled. He explained how the building had collapsed, how they had pulled her free and taken her to the Church of Our Lady, then he described Dr Klemp, the injured, Luisa's strength, the birth, and her death. The soldier told Marthe that Luisa had at least seen her son, she had felt him against her breast and stroked him with her finger. He was very careful to dampen the horror, but the truth devastated Marthe. She wanted to get away but managed to run only a few paces before she collapsed onto her hands and knees in the mud. Her back shuddering, she vomited on the ground. Throughout her chaotic existence, she had asked only two things of God: for him to rid her of Kasper and to save Luisa. He had just denied her the more important of her pleas.

Manhattan, 1969

'Rebecca Lynch? Nathan Lynch's daughter?'

'I guess,' I told Marcus. 'Who's Nathan Lynch?'

'You have the same sixth sense for a good catch as you have for real estate . . .' he mused.

'Tell me instead of talking in riddles.'

The stormy atmosphere that had been hanging over Manhattan had just exploded into a liberating deluge. We had a meeting with the agency who sold our apartments off-plan. Next we were seeing the designer we'd hired to mastermind the advertising campaign. We were running down 14th Street, me inadequately sheltered under a raincoat that I wore over my head, Marcus holding the walnut handle of his umbrella under which I refused to crouch. As we made our way to the car, which had come out of the garage the day before, he gave me a résumé of Rebecca's father's life. The collector, bibliophile and philanthropist Nathan Lynch was the fifth child and only son of Celestia Sellman and John D. Lynch, who were both descended from very old American dynasties. His mother had bequeathed him the most substantial reserves of natural gas in Venezuela as well as a gold and copper mine in north-west Argentina. From his father he'd inherited an even more colossal fortune built up in the twentieth century by his grandfather, Archibald. Nathan had left Harvard *summa cum laude*, before completing his studies at the London School of Economics, where he befriended John F. Kennedy and, according to Marcus, was more or less engaged to one of the future president's sisters. Citing a good ten family names a minute, Marcus demonstrated that Lynch was related to all the great and the good of America and just as many barons and destitute countesses in Europe, whose prestigious but crumbling estates he maintained thanks to a foundation for safeguarding architecture.

I was already lost in the Lynch family tree when Marcus, who knew all the inter-marriages of major American families inside out, rattled off the husbands of Nathan's sisters, all of whom had chosen heirs to more or less declining lineages. Nathan had fallen out with them since meeting Rebecca's mother, Judith Sokolovsky, a prodigiously talented violinist. His shrewish sisters had greeted 'the bohemian' with unusual spitefulness. Nathan had found their sarcasm unbearable and, when they refused to attend his wedding to Judith, he had stopped talking to them.

Things did not improve when, following a corruption scandal that implicated the administrators of their family capital, Nathan took control of the Lynch trust at the age of twenty-nine. He then dropped his activities in the Venezuelan gas fields and separated his money from his sisters', to set up the Lynch Bank and make his own money grow with such genius that he now had one of the greatest fortunes in the United States. The four tattletales, whose husbands were more talented at spending capital than accruing it, had conceived such bitterness towards him that it had killed three of them in the space of twenty years. The last of them, ruined by and then dumped by her husband, had made amends and, out of charity, Nathan had accommodated her in one of his numerous apartments. He had also become the most powerful real-estate owner in Manhattan.

'My father knows him very well,' Marcus added.

He told me that a few years earlier Nathan Lynch had commissioned Frank Howard to build the head office for his foundation in Chicago.

Seeing my face light up with hope, Marcus sighed. Even before I'd started haranguing him and even though he hated asking anything of his father, he agreed.

'Fine,' he said, 'I'll do it. I'll call my father to get information. I should warn you, you haven't chosen an easy option. I'd never seen Rebecca before Gioccardi's, but I know how she operates. A school-friend of mine was crazy about her and she drove him nuts. She's her father's only daughter. A little princess who's been given everything. She hasn't had the spankings she needed, and judging by the beatific look on your face every time she comes into sight, there's nothing to suggest that – despite your strong character – you have it in you to cope with her.'

The thought of spanking Rebecca gave me pause for thought. A variety of scenarios spooled through my mind, submerging me in a sort of sensuous contemplation that strained my trousers in an uncomfortable way. I slipped one hand into my pocket, keeping the other on my raincoat. I adjusted the fabric restraining me to make myself more comfortable, missing a step as I did, like a horse doing a flying change.

Just then we caught sight of the Chrysler. As Marcus stepped down from the sidewalk to take the wheel, I heard him curse – a Marcus-style curse, somewhere between 'drat' and 'holy mackerel', which was in fact a violent demonstration of his displeasure.

'This can't be happening!' he exclaimed.

The car's left wing, which I'd just had repaired, was completely destroyed. My own anger was flaring up when I noticed a soaking-wet white envelope slipped under one of the windshield wipers. I opened it with feverish fingers, sheltering the card from the weather as best I could.

Dear sir,

A momentary lapse of concentration on my part caused this regrettable accident. Please forgive me for the damage I've caused your vehicle. Do get in touch with me as soon as you have a moment so that we can proceed with a statement and an amicable settlement of this problem.

> *Allow me to reiterate my most abject apologies.*
> *Sincerely,*
> *Rebecca Lynch.*

Under her name, the card identified her soberly as 'painter', and gave her address and telephone number. I stood rooted to the spot, holding the note in both hands. Marcus, who hadn't yet grasped what was going on, grew impatient.

'So, did he leave an address? A name?'

Still sheltering it, I showed him the precious card. He read it, heaved a sigh and handed it back to me.

'You've found a way of courting that needs a serious budget for bodywork. Have you ever thought of sending poetry or serenading each other?'

'If she did this, it means she likes me,' I said enthusiastically.

'If she did this and she doesn't like you, I'll take it very badly,' replied Marcus who, skulking under his umbrella, was still battling with the driver's-side door.

'What do you suggest?' he sighed, eventually giving up.

He was obviously referring to our meeting with the real-estate agency, but all I could think about was Rebecca.

'I'll call her,' I said.

I headed back the way we'd come, jumping in all the puddles.

'Not only do we have a meeting in fifteen minutes,' Marcus yelled after me, 'but Rebecca Lynch is a spoilt child. She always gets what she wants. You should make her wait a little.'

He called 'Wern! Wern!' a few times to try to stop me, then he too retraced his steps. He knew he had no chance of bringing me to my senses.

Germany, February 1945

Marthe Engerer sat on a metal trunk by the banks of the Elbe, holding an envelope and two grubby pieces of paper. In the space of a day her life had been turned upside down, and now here were these telegrams to put her world into turmoil all over again. Von Braun, who had tried and failed to contact both her and Luisa, had addressed these two messages to her at the Red Cross centre. The first should have delighted her, but left her in a sort of apathetic state, a staggering indifference in view of the loathing that had consumed her for the last seven years:

= KASPER DEAD IN TRAGIC ACCIDENT =
= ALL THOUGHTS WITH YOU =
= VON BRAUN =

For a long time Marthe had believed that she would celebrate if and when her husband died. She would no longer live in dread of seeing him appear at every street corner to drag her by her hair back to a state of slavery. She would no longer carry the knife she slipped into her garter by day and put under her pillow by night. She would stop having the nightmares that made her leap out of bed, knife in hand, ready to fight for her life when there was no one there. At last freed of Kasper, she'd pictured herself dancing on his grave, sharing out what she inherited to charities and keeping only what belonged to her, what her parents had given her, and of which Kasper had dispossessed her, enough to start a new life far away from Germany, in Canada or the United States. And yet when she read and re-read that telegram, she felt no joy, but a sort of stupefaction. After years battling this enemy, she found it impossible to understand this sudden absence, or to allow herself to believe in it.

She thought back to her wedding day. Kasper hadn't yet revealed his true character: he gave her flowers and gifts, and called her his 'pixie', his 'little Marthe'. He took her for charming excursions in his new Daimler, and advised her on her clothes and how to wear her hair . . . True, he'd asked for her hand a little quickly. Initially she thought this was out of jealousy, to stop his younger brother marrying first. Kasper was aggressive with Johann, and their competitiveness extended into every field of life. Although peaceful by nature, Johann had learned to fight back. Naturally, Marthe took this into consideration but when she admitted her misgivings to Kasper he swept them aside. He cajoled and charmed her. Kasper had a way with words and he could get what he wanted from anyone. At first glance he would spot your weakness, where to put his hook into you.

Marthe had wanted to believe him. And the thought of being in the same family as Luisa had pleased her more than anything else. Their children would be first cousins, they would raise them together and grow old together. Marthe had pictured herself preparing big summer lunches with Luisa: they would spread dazzling white tablecloths and set out baskets of freshly picked strawberries and redcurrants, apricots and peaches, along with biscuits and jams that would end up smeared on their children's faces. She had imagined anniversaries with singing and dancing, long autumn walks through the woods looking for chestnuts and mushrooms, musical evenings in winter and fireside conversations in the Zilch family home which could accommodate so many people . . . In her innocence, she had said yes.

On the day that the four of them were to be married, though, when the future sisters-in-law were preparing for the ceremony together she had seen, in the mirror, that something wasn't right. No, really, it was blindingly obvious: she wasn't radiant as Luisa was. During the wedding lunch each couple had presided over one end of the table. At this point it was still possible that they were heading towards the same future, that they were as lucky as each other. Of course, Kasper was less attentive, not taking her hand as Johann did Luisa's; not filling her glasses with wine and water the moment they were empty; or stroking her cheek; or delving through the fruit bowls to find a pair of cherries so that, like Luisa, she could giggle and wear them as earrings. Marthe had tried to reassure herself: Kasper had every right to be reserved, he was not obliged to be as demonstrative as his brother . . . It was attractive, elegant even, this lordly restraint of his. She had brushed aside her worrying intuitions until the evening. Then came the night. That first night that would be followed by so many others. Kasper's violence had revealed itself so suddenly.

The day after the ceremony, Luisa had basked in a languid happiness that Marthe would never forget. Her eyes and lips swollen, her skin like fruit gorged with juice, her hair left loose over quivering shoulders, she had changed. She seemed pervaded by secret well-being, a fulfilment that tingled in the air around her person. Marthe, on the other hand, had simply been in pain. She felt she had been crushed, broken. Inside her empty body, her very essence had been reduced to a feeble flame guttering in the wind. A flame that wanted only to go out. It was a long time before she confided in Luisa. She'd been ashamed, and frightened too. Kasper had been so good at keeping up the pretence. When Luisa finally grasped how serious the situation was, she tried everything to help Marthe. The two young women loved each other as much as their husbands fought.

Marthe let a good twenty minutes slip by, her eyes blank. A refugee with a badly burned arm came to her for help. She stood up, opened the trunk and took out what she needed to tend to him. When he walked away, Marthe sat back down and re-read von Braun's second telegram. If she had felt broken before, the few words in this message pulverised her:

= *JOHANN HOME IN PEENEMÜNDE* =
= *WEAK BUT ALIVE* =
= *INFORM LUISA FOR HER IMMEDIATE RETURN* =
= *VON BRAUN* =

All the should-have-beens and the might-have-beens weighed heavy on her heart. Give or take just another twenty-four hours, Luisa would have set off for Peenemünde. She would have been reunited with her husband. She would be alive. Marthe bridled helplessly at the cruelty of fate. Ever since she'd been told of Luisa's last words, they'd haunted her: 'He's called Werner. Werner Zilch. Don't change his name. He's the last of our kind.' The baby wasn't the last of the Zilches, Luisa had been wrong: Johann was alive.

Three weeks earlier Luisa had succumbed to a sort of madness, convinced that her husband was dead. She'd lost all hope overnight and had woken one morning screaming, her hands clutching her swollen belly. Marthe had come running to see her sister-in-law sobbing convulsively on her bed, saying the same words over and over: 'He's dead. I dreamed of him. He came to say goodbye to me. They've killed Johann.' The panicked ramblings of a pregnant woman. Marthe had soothed her as best she could, but Luisa wouldn't be persuaded otherwise: they had killed him.

'But who? Who do you mean?' Marthe had asked.

'The people who took him. Who were against him.'

Nothing seemed to temper her conviction or her pain. Marthe would have so loved to stride into the apartment they shared on Freiberger Strasse, and announce, 'Luisa, I have wonderful news.' She would have loved to take Luisa in her arms and see her face light up when Johann telephoned; to see the weeks of waiting wiped off her face, all the tension that had pinched her features and hardened her mouth since the day of Johann's arrest. Just one minute of conversation would have restored Luisa's serenity, the glow of someone who loves and knows herself to be loved.

Luisa had been wrong. Johann was alive, and free. It was true that no one still believed he could be . . . von Braun had fought tooth and claw to save his friend, without success. Using the respect he still commanded and his rank in the SS, although he didn't like to brag about it, the inventor of the V2 had emphatically told anyone who would listen – and even those who wouldn't – that the rockets couldn't be completed without Johann Zilch. Did they want to disappoint Hitler? Were they trying to sabotage the ultimate weapon that the Führer was relying on to change the course of the war? Von Braun demanded Zilch's immediate return. What had poor Johann done? A momentary lapse, a wave of despondency. Who hadn't suffered the same? Granted, he'd said some unfortunate things, von Braun wasn't denying that, but the boy had had too much to drink, was that such a crime? Zilch had confided in people he thought were friends. Yes, he'd expressed doubts about the outcome of the war and the legitimacy of their mission, but it was obvious Johann hadn't meant a word he'd said. He'd just had two consecutive sleepless nights, resolving extraordinarily complex technical problems. Just imagine how tired he was. There was no one more devoted to the Führer than that boy! Von Braun gave his word on that.

The man generally viewed as 'head of missiles' could throw his weight around all he liked, it made no impression on senior Gestapo officers. They reminded the aeronautical pioneer that he himself had made more than one slip of the tongue, and would do well to watch himself and the rest of his team. Over the telephone they took pleasure in hammering home the things Johann had said, as if to make von Braun face the facts as they clearly enunciated every syllable: 'I dreamed of conquering space, exploring the moon and touching the stars. The war has turned our dream into a *murderous weapon*. I'm serving my country, *but don't ask me to take pleasure in it, don't ask me to feel pride. We have blood on our hands.*'

'Blood on our hands!' the SS officers had barked. It was unacceptable! And in front of five witnesses! How could von Braun defend such a traitor? An ungrateful wretch who showed so little respect for the sacrifices made by the Reich! And what of the German blood that had been spilt? Did the degenerate ever think about that? Did he? Von Braun refused to back down. He contested every word, fought his corner and warned of considerable delays, of errors in the missiles' guidance system that only Johann Zilch would be able to correct. He was arrested and interned for two weeks himself. The only result of his efforts had been to put all of them in danger.

Night was closing in. Exhausted, Marthe tried to analyse the situation as calmly as possible. The baby was restless in her arms, squalling intermittently. She lifted him up and down in the air for a few minutes as if exercising with dumbbells. He seemed satisfied with this and settled down. Marthe had made a nappy for him out of gauze and a long strip of cotton. She hadn't managed to find him a hat so she'd eased his head into a large knitted woollen sock, which gave him an impish look. Then she had wrapped him in a tea-towel, the cleanest thing she'd found, and a shawl donated by one of the refugees. The baby had slipped his fingers through it as if through the mesh of a net. Anke was asleep on the bare ground, rolled up in a brown felted wool blanket. Marthe glanced around the thousands of survivors camping along the riverbank, and made a decision: she had to get to the child's father as soon as possible, she must head for Peenemünde and the military base. Before coming to Dresden, Luisa had asked von Braun to be her baby's godfather, and he had accepted. The scientist would do everything in his power to help them. With the other members of the V2 team, he was among the most precious people the Reich had. Their safety was an affair of state and Marthe intended to make the most of that.

She discovered that a lorry taking an injured senior officer back to Berlin was due to leave within the hour. Hiding her contempt for men, as she had learned to over the years, she rinsed her face with water from her flask, coloured her cheeks and lips by rubbing them furiously with her fingers, untied her headscarf, released her brown hair, removed her coat despite the cold, and opened the top three buttons of her uniform. She went and found the lorry driver and the officer, whose arm was held in place with a neck-scarf. Lively and bright-eyed, she simpered and leant forwards expertly. Within ten minutes she'd secured what she wanted: room in the lorry for Anke, the baby and herself. She extended her charm offensive to the man responsible for provisions, who handed her three hunks of bread, some orange squash, two tins of red beans and five dried sausages, which was more than twice the rations for two people. As soon as her benefactors had turned away, her expression reverted to one of plain determination. Her victories served only to bolster her scorn for men. The rare few with any intelligence were dangerous perverts, the rest halfwits who could be manipulated with a smile and a glimpse of bare flesh. She went to wake Anke.

'But why would I want to go to Berlin, let alone Peenemünde!' Anke tried to protest. 'Why head north? I don't know anyone there . . .'

Marthe didn't give her a choice. The baby needed her. And anyway, no good would come to her if she stayed here alone. Marthe gave an apocalyptic appraisal of the evils that would befall the heartbroken Anke if she refused to come with her, and she painted such a dismal picture of the perils lying in wait, not to mention the remorse that would follow her beyond the grave if she put the tiny baby's life in danger, that the wet nurse – reeling from Marthe's authoritative diatribe, traumatised by her own bereavement, the bombings and this other child that had been thrust upon her – abandoned all attempts at resistance. She let herself be persuaded.

Marthe transformed once again into a seductress when the time came to climb into the lorry, only reverting to her gruff self once she, Anke and Werner were settled inside. The three soldiers escorting the officer didn't succeed in softening her up, and the dangers along their way soon meant they were in no mood for conversation. On the outskirts of the city a lone fighter plane was doggedly targeting vehicles fleeing the inferno. Even though their lorry bore the insignia of the Red Cross, which was visible from a great height, it only narrowly escaped a line of machine-gun fire. The passengers were terrified. They hung on tightly to avoid being thrown against each other. The fires had blazed with such heat that much of the asphalt had melted or burned. The lorry's progress was slowed considerably by great craters in the roads, fallen bridges, the burning carcasses of vans, human and animal corpses, and the exodus of thousands of refugees fleeing the Russians who were said to be on their way. Even the grass had turned red.

Little Werner slept, blissfully oblivious, on Marthe's lap. Even if, at that precise moment, she struggled to imagine loving this tiny parcel of flesh, she couldn't help being soothed by his trust, his almost indiscernible breathing, his perfectly closed eyes with their fair lashes, and that greedy mouth which closed over his wet nurse's breast every couple of hours. He would fall asleep again almost before he'd finished feeding. One of the soldiers offered several times to take the baby so that Marthe could rest, but she refused. Although she wouldn't admit it to herself, she liked feeling his small warm body against her.

Once they were far enough from Dresden for the tension to ease, the Nazi officer cornered Marthe. He thought he would be free to enjoy himself in Berlin for a while, and would be delighted to put his hotel room at her disposal.

'Thank you,' she replied briskly, in tetchy mode again, 'but my husband's waiting for me in Peenemünde. I shan't be stopping in Berlin.'

'What does your husband do?' the officer rallied to mask his disappointment.

'He works tirelessly alongside Dr von Braun, to change the course of this war now that you soldiers appear to have lost control of it.'

The name von Braun made quite an impression on the passengers. Despite Marthe's scathing attack, a respectful silence settled over the lorry. Aware that an invisible shield now protected her, Marthe hugged Werner a little more tightly, and closed her eyes.

'Who shall I say is calling?' asked a woman's voice with a slight foreign accent.

'Werner Zilch.'

A long silence followed my name. I thought the line had been cut.

'Hello? Can you hear me?'

'I didn't quite get your name, sir . . .'

'Zilch, Werner,' I said again, clearly enunciating the syllables. The woman on the other end probably didn't have a good grasp of English.

'How do you spell that?'

'Z.I.L.C.H.'

This time she took even longer to reply.

'Rebecca is out,' she eventually said coldly. 'She will contact you.'

She hung up. Furious with my reception from this snob, I called straight back. I let it ring about twenty times, then the receiver was picked up and put back down in its cradle without a word. I suspected Ernie had been undermining me, I was probably *persona non grata*. I paced angrily around the living room of our apartment. Shakespeare got under my feet and I unintentionally stood on one of his paws. He yelped in pain. I yelled at him to sit down, which he did – on the sofa – with a dignified but offended expression which he kept up all day: my dog is very touchy.

I tried calling Rebecca's house again, without success. My anger was suffocating and I had to exercise all my self-control not to go there in person, hammer on the door of the Lynch family home, demand an apology from the idiot who'd answered the phone and insist on speaking to TLOML immediately. However much I hated being resisted and – worse – ignored, I was sufficiently lucid not to give in to this impulse. Donna confirmed that this was the right decision; she herself hated having her hand forced.

'There's nothing worse than finding a man on your doorstep when you haven't invited him,' she told me solemnly.

I followed her womanly advice and turned towards a less intrusive seduction strategy. Rebecca's response had a bit of panache. Inflicting on my car, or in fact Marcus's, what her own had suffered was feisty and amusing. I wanted to make a coup of my own but my dreams of grandeur evaporated in mediocre reality: I was broke and Marcus was no better off than me. Of course our finances would improve. Reassured that building work had resumed, the agency had relaunched its campaign to sell our apartments, but we wouldn't be cashing our buyers' down payments for several weeks. It was exasperating. I was potentially sitting on a goldmine, but I couldn't afford to take Rebecca to a restaurant. In order to pull out all the stops I had to pawn my watch. It was a 1940s Patek, the only thing of any value that I owned. My father, Andrew, had given it to me for my eighteenth birthday, and it felt all the more precious because it had somehow escaped his weakness for extravagant wagers. All through my childhood, his bad luck had deprived my mother, my sister and me of a good many of life's little pleasures and sometimes even of its necessities.

Marcus came with me to a dive in Queens, not far from Ozone Park. The staircase up to the place was so narrow my shoulders didn't fit. The only way I could climb it was sideways. The second-floor premises were painted blue and smelled of socks and sweat. All the hardship in the world seemed to have congregated there. Along one wall was an indescribable accumulation of clutter, and opposite it were three counters where the cashiers worked. Marcus handed over his tie-pin set with pearls and diamonds. I took the Patek from my wrist. As I handed it to the expert, my brow furrowed and my throat tight, I hesitated. It felt like abandoning a family pet. I liked the feel of it, the way its movement beat like a tiny heart. I usually removed it only to wash. And now, without that brown leather strap softened with wear around my wrist, I felt naked. That watch had brought me luck.

'It has to be said, it's never stopped you being late,' Marcus encouraged me, patting my shoulder.

I handed it over, wincing at the careless way the cashier wrapped my treasure in a filthy old piece of felt and stapled a number to it. I stashed a few hundred dollars in my wallet and left that sordid place as quickly as I could.

The sum secured seemed paltry in comparison to the memories attached to my watch and the ambitions I harboured for the evening I was planning. First I had three bouquets of flowers delivered to the Lynches: the first thanked Rebecca for our meeting at the Pierre; the second came with the statement documents; and the third was accompanied by an invitation to dinner the following week. She accepted. I was both wildly happy and horrified, as we sometimes are when a prayer we never thought would be granted is answered. I thought long and hard about a location. She was so spoiled and I had such a high opinion of her that even the most luxurious hotels – which would, anyway, be prohibitively expensive – didn't seem worthy of her. Our apartment was too ordinary. I couldn't see myself taking her for a picnic in Central Park, or slicing a champagne cork from the bottle on a ferry or a little boat on the Hudson River.

After long discussions with Marcus I decided I would do whatever was most likely to surprise her, and therefore charm her. I felt that the way I arrived in the first place was a key element in stage-managing the evening. We laughed a lot about the options as we had our ritual end-of-the-day drinks, in which Donna – ever concerned to keep her distance – declined to partake. Slightly under the influence, we came up with outlandish scenarios: I could turn up on a bicycle, in a rickshaw or in the Chrysler absolutely covered in flowers, hippie-style. Marcus insisted I rode a horse. I was a good horseman since my time at Yale, which I had financed partly with my winnings at rummy (a discipline my father had taught me), and partly by working as a stable lad in the university stables. I mucked out the loose boxes, swept the yard, and picked out the horses' feet. I also learned to play polo there. I trained every day and sometimes even played when, on the morning of a match, the faculty elite needed a substitute because one of the team had overslept. It was also my job to break in novice ponies because the daddy's boys were afraid they'd do themselves an injury on them. Despite the chivalrous vibe that such a means of transport would undeniably have given me in Rebecca's eyes, I thought it too pretentious and too much of a cliché. I opted simply for a chauffeured rental limousine. A black one. White was my first choice but Marcus thought that 'horribly conspicuous'. Organising everything else took several hours of thought fuelled by Chianti, and required crockery, cutlery, glasses, thirty gallons of paint, a caterer, a crane and two days of setting up.

On the evening of our date, I was outside her place at eight o'clock. Marcus had described the Lynch residence as one of the most beautiful homes in Manhattan. That part of 80th Street, east of the park, seemed to constitute a series of compressed French castles, as if their classical lines had been to a weight-loss spa to show off their height all the better. The façades vied with each other in their elegance, but the Lynches' house was truly resplendent, surpassing even its neighbours. According to Marcus, it dated from the late nineteenth century and was 'a jewel of neo-Renaissance architecture'. From what I could see from the limousine, it was five storeys high. The windows, embellished with stone sculptures, wouldn't have put a cathedral to shame. When locked, the heavy wooden door with carved designs looked like it would take ten men with a battering ram to break it down. Several years earlier, Marcus had accompanied his father to dinner with Nathan Lynch. He'd described the majesty of the place: the double marble staircase, the fireplaces made of stone from Burgundy, the vast antique carpets, the works of art, the sculpted ceilings and the dining room that could seat fifty people. Parked outside this palace, I grasped more fully the gulf that lay between me and the love of my life.

I thought back to my modest family home in Hawthorne, New Jersey, and to my adoptive parents, loving people for whom I felt great affection, though we had little in common. My mother advocated a humdrum sort of happiness and modest ambitions, while I wanted to matter, to build something, to be someone. My father sipped the bitter brew of his own regrets. Dreaming big felt shameful to them, risky even: they weren't equipped to cope with disappointment. My mother had gone beyond the imaginable by leaving her native Normandy for the handsome soldier she'd met in the mad days of the French Liberation. Her obsession became protecting her two children from the countless dangers that could bring heartbreak on a family, and her husband from the moral and financial collapse that beckoned him. Behind his handsome ex-GI features and his flair as a real-estate agent, Andrew concealed terrible fragility and weakness. My mother wrapped him in her tenderness and thoughtful attention, as if to maintain the halo of magic and glory that she had attributed to him when she first set eyes on him, back at that dance in Rouen. My mother's passion for him was her calling, her justification, her identity. My father was consumed with doubts and dissatisfaction, but she saw someone exceptional in him. He longed for a better life, she made do with what we had. He was crippled by unrealised dreams, she was moulded by commendable intentions and modest pleasures. He dreamed of luxury, beautiful cars and large hotels; she loved her home, her little garden, her orderly closets and well-stocked kitchen. She protected him from himself, managed their accounts frugally, gave him only pocket money for his rummy, and didn't resent him when, succumbing once more to the foolish hope that chance would arbitrarily change their life, he emptied the kitty and blew months of savings in one evening.

In fact my mother was never angry with him. I admired her patience and thought I knew the reasons behind it. The difficulties they'd faced trying to have children partly explained their asymmetrical relationship. I never knew whether it was my mother or father who was responsible for their problems conceiving, particularly as my sister Lauren was born a year after they adopted me. We often asked them about it, with no success. They formed a united front, refusing to open up. My parents obstinately protected their secret, but the past had destroyed their confidence. Outside her safe and reassuring domestic space, my mother was afraid of everything: water which could drown us, fire which might burn us, the very air which could carry viruses, the walk to school which could be dotted with prowlers, trees we were bound to fall from, and grass where snakes could be hiding. She was even afraid of beautiful summer evenings, battling to keep us inside, closing the windows (which we threw open as soon as her back was turned) because she feared mosquitoes, bats, lightning bugs and the intoxicating effects of heat and moonlight which she believed could make us go mad. The only place my mother was happy was in shops, clean stylish spaces where anything new was displayed in the most appealing, stage-managed way: colourful, delightful and summarised in simple words on boxes adorned with charming images. She had a feverish desire to buy up this safe, idealised and well-meaning world which knew no sickness, violence or old age, as illustrated on packets of breakfast cereal and washing powder, cans of vegetables, boxes of biscuits, revolutionary beauty creams and homely shampoos. She accumulated her provisions in the kitchen and garage with all the satisfaction of a housewife who'd experienced the privations of the French Occupation.

The war, which had made my mother so wary, had also succeeded in robbing my father of any illusions. During the carnage of the landings, the human animal had been revealed to him in all its horror. He saw civilisation as merely a sophisticated route to disaster. It did nothing to change the fundamental violence, small-mindedness, bitterness and cruelty that constituted the essence of our species. Unlike my mother, who so enthusiastically embraced consumer society, my father didn't believe in the American dream. He'd seen with his own eyes the boys who'd been sent over the Atlantic to have holes shot through their skin in Europe, and those who'd stayed home in peace, studying, sipping beer and licking vanilla ice-cream from cornets. They'd been safe, the bastards, tucked away under Uncle Sam's flag and between the thighs of the women whom the soldiers had left behind. My father no longer believed people had equal opportunities in life and that you could climb up the ladder by working hard. In his view, only chance could change his fate. His life would improve only thanks to the arbitrary stroke of a magic wand, the result of pure luck which he tried to provoke by playing cards every Saturday in his rummy club or by staking his occasional commissions on tired old nags.

I was disgusted by his fatalism: 'Why bother getting up in the morning if you can't change anything? Why bother marrying? Why bother buying a house and raising children?' Unlike him, I believed in the infinite power of will, and was determined to forge a world for myself through hard work alone. I didn't know where I came from, who I had to thank for this face carved with a machete, these washed-out eyes, this sandy mane and this outsized frame which meant I had to fold up, chin to knees, on buses and at the movies. I was free of any inheritance, any past, and I felt I was master of my own future. I had a burning desire to prove who I was, to see my name – which too often invited ridicule – inspire respect and, if need be, fear. My parents thought I was a strange creature. My lowliest aspirations were way beyond their wildest dreams. And I obstinately refused to set limits on myself.

There at the foot of the Lynch residence, I didn't allow myself to feel intimidated. I nodded at the chauffeur to go ring the doorbell, and watched while he talked to a thin, ageing woman in a nun-like skirt and a purple silk blouse tied firmly at the neck. A wave of anger washed over me when I realised it might have been this woman who had hung up on me when I tried to call Rebecca. The chauffeur returned to the car.

'She's on her way,' he told me through the window. He stayed beside the car, ready to open the door for my damsel, who kept us waiting fifteen minutes.

I was expecting a primped and preened young lady, but a tomboy emerged from the house. She was wearing a man's jacket over beige slacks; a white shirt with an open neck, and a blue tie that had been knotted and artfully slackened. In this outfit that might have been worn by a Yale student, her lioness's tumult of blonde hair, her cheerful self-assurance and her defiant swagger lent her an air of freedom that was almost wild. A blast of life came into the car with her. She didn't kiss me and I didn't move to kiss her. We greeted each other without touching, exaggerating this obsequious formality to disperse the embarrassment that had overcome us. Her eyes, though, glittered with impatience: she wanted to know where we were going. Determined to prove more enterprising than at our first meeting, I wagered a kiss on the lips that she wouldn't guess where we were having dinner. She accepted the challenge.

The car set off and she started asking questions, demanding clues, asked whether she was getting warm. To no avail. The names she suggested were all places I'd considered. Sensing she would lose the bet, she insisted on having the first and last letters of the street. I supplied them without a shred of concern: the private road in question had only just been named. Rebecca seemed amazed when we arrived downtown, almost anxious when the car turned onto Brooklyn Bridge, openly alarmed when the chauffeur stopped at the foot of a building under construction and took two pairs of boots from the trunk. Remembering her feet, which had made such an impression on me in their blue sandals at Gioccardi's, I'd guessed her size. We put on our boots to avoid dirtying our shoes in the dirt and dust of the site, and went down into what would be the parking lot. Rebecca didn't look very reassured but she put on a brave face. She didn't really know me at all; she'd only met me twice for a few minutes and in rather chaotic circumstances. She must have been cursing her impulsiveness for entrusting herself to a man crazy enough to run after her out of a restaurant, destroy her car and now take her to this sinister place where he could be planning to sink her body into a concrete block. I tried a joke and she gratified me with a smile dazzling in its falseness; I sensed she'd lost the confidence of our first meeting.

There were no rails on the staircases yet so I took my beauty's hand. She shuddered nervously when I touched her. I stayed on the outer edge, which was punctuated by metal spikes that would hold the banisters. She must have been fit because her breathing was still steady after climbing five flights.

'What's on the menu then, Werner? Cement soup followed by brick pâté with mortar sauce?' she teased.

Hearing her say my name felt like a physical caress. I assured her that I admired her figure too much to serve up such an indigestible meal. At last we reached the tenth and highest floor. Flushed and with her hand on her pounding heart, she heaved a sigh of relief.

'A girl has to earn her dinner with you!'

The metal door was closed. I let her catch her breath. She was warm and took off her jacket, the fine fabric of her shirt cleaving to her shape. She took a hair elastic from her pocket, drew back her lips slightly to put it between her teeth, and used both her hands to lift her long curls into a tantalising ponytail. I've always had a weakness for this hairstyle which reveals the nape of a woman's neck. Once the hair elastic was in place she loosened her tie a little further. The sight of this strip of silk snaking between her breasts invited me to imagine other sights. An electric shock shot through my groin. To avoid finding myself in an embarrassing situation, I took out the key and opened the door, sure that my surprise would have an effect.

Rebecca stifled a cry. Up on the roof – its floor covered with pale gravel and its walls with beige render – she discovered a forest. The workmen had used one of the cranes to lift up most of the trees that would be planted around our two buildings in the next few weeks. Lined up along opposite sides of the rooftop, they now formed an alley that framed the spectacular view over Brooklyn Bridge and across to Manhattan. Rays from the sinking sun carved the sky with gold, scarlet and black. Piano music wafted to us. The instrument was hidden behind a wall of vegetation further along the terrace. It was playing Frank Sinatra's 'I've Got You Under My Skin', an amused nod from Marcus who, ever the supportive friend, was supplying the background music for the evening.

I smiled at the teamwork involved in getting the piano up here. We'd been to fetch it from Marcus's father, Frank. Having brought it here in our construction manager's truck, we then hauled it up by crane, while Marcus – terrified that his long-time companion in moments of solitude might lose a leg or end up shattered on the ground – tensely watched its unlikely upward flight. We'd originally pictured using his grand piano, which was still kept at Frank's home, but had been forced to rein in our ambitions. The instrument was so heavy that even four of us could hardly shift it; the upright would be more than adequate. To complete the magic of the location, I'd made hundreds of lanterns using brown paper bags filled with sharp sand, with a candle burning in each one. Scattered among the trees, these improvised candle-holders created an enchanting light. Rebecca looked delighted but flustered. I wanted to claim the kiss I'd duly won in our bet, but she was just starting to relax and I didn't want to rush her.

That was when Shakespeare bounded out of hiding. Marcus definitely was in playful mode because he'd put a huge red bow around the dog's neck. Rebecca jumped back but I reassured her by pulling her close and lifting a commanding index finger to make Shakespeare sit.

'Are you afraid of dogs?' I asked.

'That's not a dog, it's a pony!'

'Don't worry, he's very friendly.'

I'd lowered my hand again so Shakespeare, whose training was not exactly rigorous, took the opportunity to demonstrate his affection by standing on his hind legs and putting his paws on my shoulders, as he usually did. Rebecca backed away again.

'Down, Shakespeare!' I ordered, pushing him off me. 'Sit! There . . . Say hello to Rebecca.'

'On his hind legs he's almost as tall as you are!' she said, impressed.

Shakespeare sat down, thumping his tail on the ground reassuringly.

'You can stroke him,' I said. 'He's never bitten anyone.'

Wanting to look friendly, Shakespeare opened his great panting jaws.

'He's a monster,' she said, putting a hesitant hand on his head.

That was all it took for the dog to slump, besotted, to the ground and offer her his tummy to scratch. Rebecca laughed like a child. Her fine fingers disappeared into Shakespeare's thick cream-and-brown fur, and I suddenly felt very jealous.

'You know how to handle males,' I said, helping her back up, earning a resentful glare from Shakespeare.

I guided Rebecca towards our dining area. An oval table had been set with the greatest care. Miguel, the caterer whose roly-poly frame and imperial dignity were trussed into a white uniform with silver buttons, had seen to that. Even Marcus couldn't match him in the art of table setting. The Cuban had gently overruled Marcus on the layout of the forks, a philosophical debate that left me unmoved, though I thought the result a triumph. The glasses sparkled and, in a cut-crystal decanter, the wine glowed like rubies on a tablecloth embroidered with gold thread. Miguel and Marcus had both insisted on putting my fine Bordeaux into decanters. I didn't want Rebecca to think I was serving her plonk, and would have preferred her to see the labels, but they'd assured me that was vulgar.

So that we could admire the sunset as we sipped our aperitifs, I'd borrowed a white wooden bench seat covered in velvet from Donna. Rebecca removed her boots and rolled her boy's pants up to mid-calf but didn't put on her shoes, which she abandoned along the way. Seeing her walk barefoot went straight to my head. She settled herself on the bench, sitting to one side with her feet tucked under her. I briefly pictured her naked, in this exact position, and I had a furious urge to take her ankle and slip her foot into my hand. Shakespeare came and sat facing her. He gazed at her for a long time, hoping to be petted again, but Rebecca discouraged him by laughing. She asked him to lie down. To my surprise I watched as my dog – who, like his master, didn't obey many people – lay down as close as he could get to us, with his head resting on crossed paws. Miguel opened a bottle of champagne and served us a glass each and some canapés. Rebecca clearly enjoyed them, and complimented Miguel on their delicacy. He accepted her kindness with a modest batting of eyelids. The moment was perfect.

The sun sank slowly behind skyscrapers, giving way to softer shades of pink, mauve and grey. Marcus was throwing himself into his piano playing, and my beauty beat her hand on the back of the bench in time to 'Take Five'. The conversation flowed lightly and easily, most likely helped by the glasses of champagne that we drained in quick succession. Rebecca told me about her forthcoming exhibition and the project she was now working on: a giant triptych that she sketched out in one of her notebooks for me. I didn't understand half the references or explanations, but my ignorance made her laugh. She asked me why I'd chosen this building and I explained that it was my second construction project, and would be followed by many more.

'My future is playing out here,' I added, looking directly into her eyes. 'I wanted you to be a part of it.'

Most women would have looked away; Rebecca didn't blink but simply smiled and asked, 'What sort of part?'

Wrong-footed by her candour and not yet ready to declare my feelings, I grabbed at the first idea that came to mind.

'I'd like you to design artworks for the two entrance lobbies. They'll be the first thing people see and the memory they take away with them.'

Now it was my beauty's turn to be surprised.

'You've never seen what I do!'

'I've seen your drawings and I've listened to what you've said . . . I'd like you to blow me away.'

I'd judged it right. Rebecca was a disconcerting combination of arrogance and self-doubt. Her family's standing may have spared her any concerns about her social status, but she still had to prove her own worth as a person and an artist. Her colour heightened and her eyes shining, she tried – unsuccessfully – to disguise her pleasure. She accepted my offer without even thanking me or discussing remuneration. I would later discover just how shameful and complicated a relationship she had with her father's fortune and money in general.

'Come on then,' I suggested. 'I should show you the rest.'

I helped her up, making the most of any opportunity to touch her. I kept an eye on the ground, afraid she might hurt her bare feet. Without heels, Rebecca only just reached my shoulder, but there was a density to her, a presence that went way beyond her slender form. As we leant side by side on the edge of the terrace which overlooked the whole site, I was acutely aware of her body only inches from me. To stop myself kissing her on the spot, I explained the difficulties we'd had to resolve in order to buy the plot and secure planning permission. I told her about the next stage, about a huge plot of land on the banks of the Hudson that I coveted and that would radically change the stakes. Using one of her notebooks, I drew the plans of the possible apartments. She teased me for my inadequate drawing skills.

'I'm not Frank Howard,' I protested and explained that he'd designed the buildings.

'Frank Howard? But I know him really well!' she exclaimed.

I told her that he was also the father of my best friend and business associate, who had been with me at Yale, but I didn't mention that the same friend was currently playing romantic ballads on the piano. Another barrier fell: with the magic of a name, I wasn't just a nobody. Having this mutual acquaintance was as good as being championed by Marcus's father. I was in the club of socially acceptable people. My studies at an Ivy League college further improved the picture, even though I was careful not to reveal I'd abandoned them after two years to embark on my first real-estate operation. The love of my life might have liked to see herself as a rebel and had, in fact, sloughed off many of the constraints of her caste, but her wariness still obeyed the perfectionist rules of those who have a great deal to lose.

Once we were seated, Miguel presented his feast with a lot of bowing and silver platters and cloches removed with a flourish. He went to all this trouble for scant reward: Rebecca and I were wrapped up in each other. She didn't finish her plate and I curbed my usual appetite. Not because I wasn't hungry – that never happened – but because I was trying to respect the rules Marcus had instilled in me, like not focusing on my plate and not loading the next forkful when I hadn't finished the first. Keeping a check on myself like that while maintaining conversation with my beauty, I didn't get around to eating. We were less half-hearted about the wine, and our laughter grew more frequent with each new glass. Rebecca, whose cheeks were flushed and whose speech was a little halting, became more relaxed. Miguel served a strawberry tart and, having left a pot of herbal infusion and some brandies and liqueurs on the sideboard, slipped away, as we'd agreed in advance, taking Shakespeare with him.

Marcus played on. He could go on like that for hours, carried off into his own world of pleasure. I invited Rebecca to dance to the notes of 'Moon River'. In her happy intoxicated state, she sang along while I twirled her slowly before taking her in my arms. I could smell her perfume, her hair brushed against my chin, we glided to the music, but still I hesitated. Don't be too keen too soon, don't miss the opportunity out of cowardice . . . I held her closer in my arms. She didn't resist so I put my mouth to her ear.

'We had a bet,' I whispered.

'I wondered when you'd mention that.'

'Now,' I said, lifting her into my arms.

I carried her to the bench seat and sat down with her on my lap. She kept her head on my shoulder. I lifted her chin with one hand, and held the back of her neck with the other. I saw a spark in her eye that surprised me: it was a glint of anxiety. I waited, so close to her, not moving. I felt her quiver. She half-closed her eyes and seemed to smell me for a long time, like an animal. I stayed half an inch from her lips when my own lips were burning. She opened her eyes wide and every trace of fear had gone. Her dilated pupils had almost obscured her violet irises. My fingers could feel the blood pumping in her neck. I kissed her. She was as soft as I was firm, as docile as I was pressing. Perhaps I became too eager because, out of nowhere, she gripped my lower lip between her teeth, not squeezing, just as a warning, before releasing me. I slowed myself and Rebecca broke away for a moment. She stood up and faced me, staring at me intently. Her face and eyes were ablaze. She took a deep breath then sat down, straddling me. She pressed herself shamelessly against me and, arching her back and rocking against me, she returned my kisses.

Germany, 1945

By the time they'd been travelling for five hours, Marthe had stopped letting anyone except for Anke touch the baby. When they reached Berlin station one of the train inspectors was amused by the sock on Werner's head, but when he took the liberty of lifting the makeshift hat and stroking the baby's hair, Marthe snatched his hand and bit it till she drew blood. This attack created quite a scene and the two women had a very difficult time extricating themselves from it. After a long wait, during which they made inroads into the bread, beans and dried sausages, they were allowed to board a train, but this mode of transport proved even more of an ordeal than the lorry. The train kept stopping for inspections, because of obstructions on the track or to make way for units of retreating troops. Forty kilometres from Peenemünde they were told the train could go no further.

The small straggle of passengers alighted at the deserted station of Züssow and stood there helplessly, watching the carriages head back to Berlin. Marthe decided to continue on foot, hoping they would find a vehicle to take them to the base. The cold burned their ears, noses, cheeks, chins and fingers. She and Anke took it in turns to carry Werner, strung to their fronts or their backs in a piece of netting they'd found on the verge. The child was lulled in this improvised sling, swaddled in several layers of towelling and the shawl as well as a thick pullover Marthe had put over the top. The few vehicles they saw were all heading south. They wanted to stop a Volkswagen driven by two soldiers to ask them if they would contact Dr von Braun and ask for someone to come and collect them, but the car skirted around them and sailed away, accompanied by insults from Marthe. They walked for hours, until every muscle ached. In the end Anke sat down by the side of the road and the two women stayed there, huddled side by side, as the sun dropped in the sky. A fine rain started to fall, but they no longer had the strength to look for a barn to spend the night in, or even a tree to give them some shelter. It was almost dark when an old farm labourer hoisted them onto his cart drawn by a horse as ancient as he was.

When the two passengers said they wanted to go to Peenemünde he gave a sceptical whistle.

'There's Russkies over there, my lovelies, y' sure that's where y' want to go?'

'Sure,' Marthe replied.

The old man told them that the grocery shop in Mölschow still had a delivery van. The grocer's wife, Gretel, had been running the shop single-handed since her husband was mobilised, and she welcomed the two women kindly while the old man continued on his way. It wasn't a good idea to be out and about at night in times like these, and Gretel's house was barricaded.

'I've stopped opening the shutters, even during the day,' she told them.

She was a redhead with a jolly face and doll-like colouring: white skin with a circle of pink on each cheek. She had such high, arched eyebrows that she constantly looked amazed, almost naive despite her forty years. Mölschow was just outside the military base, and Marthe wanted to go there straight away, but their hostess looked at her sadly.

'You've come a long way, haven't you?'

'From Dresden.'

Mention of the devastated city cast a shadow over Gretel's kitchen where the three women were sitting. There was a long silence.

'Did you know there's no one left at Peenemünde?' Gretel asked eventually.

'What do you mean, no one left?' Marthe said in a half-whisper.

'Over the last couple of days dozens of lorries have come past and there have been goods trains on the move too. They've been sent south, away from the Russians. They took everything with them.'

'That's impossible!' exclaimed Marthe.

'They left us with no protection but I don't intend to be pushed around,' Gretel said, pointing to two rifles on the sideboard.

Marthe thought two paltry popguns wouldn't protect the grocer's wife from the Russians for long. Anke meanwhile slumped onto the table with her head resting on her crossed arms. Little Werner started to cry and Gretel wanted to take him but before she was anywhere near him, Marthe stepped in.

'I'll take care of him,' she said tartly.

The threat in her voice made Gretel back away.

'You need to get some rest,' she said soothingly. 'We'll have some supper, then I'll put you in my little brother's room and tomorrow, if you like, I'll take you to Peenemünde. You'll see I'm not lying.'

'But where have they gone?'

'To the Alps. No one's meant to know, but everyone does . . .'

She fed them a wheat gruel with scraps of ham and cabbage, then helped them tend to their feet, washing them with black soap, smoothing them with oil and bandaging them. That night while the baby slept, the two women shared a bed and Marthe took Anke in her arms. The young woman was shivering with cold and anxiety, and Marthe soothed her as she so often had Luisa. When Anke's breathing settled into a regular rhythm Marthe stayed awake thinking of the sister-in-law she'd lost. It was only two days ago. A couple of days ago, Luisa had been a complete, warm, living body. Marthe couldn't come to terms with it. As soon as she was still for a moment, hideous images and thoughts filled her mind. Anke must be haunted by ghosts too. She never stopped thinking about her son, just as Marthe couldn't stop thinking about Luisa, but the two women didn't talk about them. So long as their very survival was in danger, there wasn't room for their grief. During the course of the night, their arms, legs, feet and hands became intertwined. Comforted by the shared warmth, they sometimes changed position but always found a new way of slotting together. Werner woke at regular intervals and Anke sleepily and mechanically got up to suckle him. Marthe changed him and the two women returned to bed, unabashedly pressed up against each other. Anke went back to sleep but Marthe still couldn't, until eventually her sorrows hazed over and she in turn sank into oblivion.

Anke and Werner were still asleep when Marthe wrote a little note and left the room the next morning. She and Gretel drank scalding cups of chicory and devoured a slice of bread each, with home-made ewe's-milk cheese. Once the washing up was done, Gretel agreed to take Marthe to the base. She'd stopped opening her shop since the troops and scientists had left the area, anyway. It was too dangerous. The two women climbed into her van, which was so old that the top of the gearstick had come off and been replaced with a lump of wood carved into a ball. The Baltic Sea soon appeared before them, and when they reached the base there was no one at the gate; the barrier hadn't even been lowered. The site had been dismantled, leaving only signs of a hasty departure. They saw metal crates full of partially burned papers, and piles of semi-destroyed plans that were picked up by gusts of wind and then sailed back to the ground nearby. Personal belongings lay scattered everywhere. The offices had been turned upside down, the production lines deserted, and tools thrown pell-mell into uncoupled trailers.

The last convoy of equipment had left the base two days earlier, according to the only man left on the premises, the oldest watchman at the base. He'd buried his wife a few months earlier and didn't want to leave her 'all on her own', as he said. He'd rather wait for the Russians and his own end. He invited Marthe and Gretel in for a hot drink. He had a few remaining tins of condensed milk, might as well put them to use. At least that was something the Russkies wouldn't get. It was warm in his tiny house and while the old man was busy heating their drinks, Marthe cornered Gretel: they needed to take the van and head south as soon as possible. Horrified, Gretel asked why on earth she would go to the Alps? Her husband was coming back any minute! And what about the shop! And her stock! But when Marthe wanted something she could be extremely persuasive. She described how inhuman the Russians were, how ferocious their attacks and how they tortured their victims. Poor Gretel went even whiter than her natural complexion. She stammered the occasional 'My God!' and 'Sweet Jesus!', breathing noisily and keeping her hand over her heart. Pushing her advantage, Marthe stepped up her vehemence and flights of imagination so that even the old watchman started to doubt his decision to stay. He almost gave in, then strengthened his resolve: he refused to abandon his wife's grave but, with tragic enthusiasm, he joined Marthe in convincing Gretel to flee. *He* was ready to die, but a young woman! Only just forty, so fit and well, and with her whole life ahead of her: she must get out. Especially as a man could hope for a quick death, one bullet and bang! – it would all be over. But Gretel . . . a woman like her . . . full of life, with glorious hair, Lord alone knew what the bastards would do to her before executing her . . .

The poor shopkeeper looked close to passing out, despite the charming compliments. She hastily thanked the old watchman and climbed back into her van with Marthe. Gretel had been apathetic on the way over but she now seemed to be at one with her van, which she manoeuvred at top speed along the country lanes. She talked non-stop as if words could offload her fears, at the forefront of which was the question of provisions and fuel. In her cellar she still had five jerrycans of synthetic fuel – which constituted a goldmine in such straitened times – but that wouldn't be enough to reach the Alps. They would have to find more along the way and, what with bombing and requisitioning, that would be a hard task. Back in Mölschow, they told Anke about their plan, and Anke mostly seemed grateful they wouldn't be travelling on foot. After their trek the previous day, her every step came at a price.

In her eagerness, Gretel started packing up half the house, and Marthe had to curb her ambitions.

'We don't have the time or the petrol for it,' she said.

It broke Gretel's heart that she couldn't take her furniture, or her wedding dress which she hadn't fitted into for years, or the collection of sentimental novels inherited from her mother, or the electric toaster her father had given her before he died, or her exquisite collection of porcelain figures. Still, she managed to persuade her fellow travellers to take provisions which they could use for bartering.

'But carrying your stock could also cause us trouble. It could be stolen, or worse . . . people get killed for the tiniest things in times like these,' Marthe warned.

Gretel brushed aside her objections. She might not know much about the Russians and their atrocities, but when it came to deliveries, no one could tell her how to do her own job. The van had a false floor and a false ceiling. Having been held up and robbed several times, Gretel had asked her younger brother, a mechanic, to make these modifications. That was a few weeks before he was sent to the front.

'Just a boy . . .' she sighed.

She was about to tell them the whole story but Marthe stopped her with a black look, and the potentially lengthy account was reduced to a single sentence: 'When I saw him leave, it broke my heart.'

Marthe loaded a bundle of blankets into her arms; now wasn't the time to become emotional. They stowed most of the important cargo in the two hidden traps at the front of the van: the petrol, several boxes of bottled beer, a case of schnapps, a bag of dried fish and a sack of potatoes, the two remaining hams from the storeroom, tins of tomatoes, beans, pickled vegetables, beetroots and artichokes, as well as sugar and her last boxes of biscuits. At the back they put soap, clothes and a quilt, along with scarves and hats. Marthe's descriptions of the terrible assaults that would be made on Gretel's virtue had made such an impression on her that she put on two pairs of her husband's trousers under her dress. She begged the other two women to do the same, and – anxious not to waste time on pointless discussions – Anke and Marthe each put on a pair of leather breeches that Gretel's husband used for game shooting. They also loaded up her arsenal: the rifles with all the ammunition, and a large knife each. Marthe was happier keeping her own knife which she still had strapped to her thigh. She'd thought she would get rid of it when she heard that Kasper was dead, but had changed her mind. As they were leaving, Gretel insisted on taking a fishing rod. Anke gave Werner a feed and then Marthe put him back in his basket and they all set off.

They followed in von Braun's footsteps, stopping in villages and asking which way the military convoy had gone. Such a major displacement of men and equipment hadn't passed unnoticed, and they had no trouble gathering information. Gretel and Marthe took turns at the wheel while Anke, who didn't drive, looked after the baby. Werner proved an exemplary passenger, and the only thing likely to make him angry was hunger. If Anke didn't put him to the breast within seconds of his letting it be known he was hungry, he filled the van with screams that achieved an astonishing volume for such a small creature. The group travelled as swiftly as the ancient engine would allow, avoiding frequent roadblocks. When they couldn't make a detour around a checkpoint, they settled for negotiating their way. These were extremely tense times: they had no travel warrants and had to appeal to the good nature of the checkpoint officers, saying they were fleeing the invasion and joining their husbands in the south. When the men had searched the van and found nothing, even the most obtuse of them revealed their military good nature when Gretel handed over her 'last bottle of beer' which she was keeping at her feet.

'Much more efficient than paperwork,' the shopkeeper said gleefully.

After the first 200 kilometres, with their waves of refugees, the roads were very quiet. They avoided major arterial routes which were more likely to be bombed, and in between the road-blocks, they felt almost like tourists. The first night, spooned together with loaded rifles within reach, the three of them slept on the floor of the van in an abandoned barn. On the second night, they took shelter in a forest where Gretel had a terrible time getting to sleep. She desperately needed to relieve herself, but daren't go out, and listened to noises in the trees, convinced the four of them would be eaten by wild beasts. After a long struggle she succumbed to a restless sleep populated by wolf-men in Red Army uniforms.

The little band took to the road once more, narrowly escaping a burst of gunfire from a source they failed to identify. One bullet cut through the bodywork and perforated their last jerrycan of petrol in the hidden compartment. They saved what they could, but were soon only ten kilometres from an empty tank. Gretel was frantic: they needed ration cards – which she didn't have – to fill up at the few remaining authorised petrol pumps. They were told where to find one of these pumps but the teenage attendant, a very good-looking boy, refused to serve them. They cajoled him and tried to soften him up, to no avail: no coupon, no fuel. Gretel started to think that – really, if she had to, because there was no other option – she would agree to sacrifice her virtue to this stubborn boy in exchange for a jerrycan of petrol, and she let this be known. But the young man was far more interested in taking the ham that Marthe produced from the van at that exact moment. He salivated just looking at it, and was thrilled to think how happy his mother would be when he brought such a trophy home. He was so pleased with his prize and his speedy abandonment of his principles, that he watched uncomplaining as the three women filled the tank and their four undamaged jerrycans to the brim.

Two days later, after another night in a forest during which wolf-men were replaced in Gretel's imagination by enterprising schoolboys, the three friends saw the blue-white outline of the Alps rear up in the distance ahead.

Marthe, Anke and Gretel scoured the area, but there was no sign of the scientists. After four days of fruitless searching they discovered the cause of this disappearance: a battle for authority had erupted at the highest level of what was left of the Reich, and the Peenemünde teams had eventually been dispatched to central Germany, near Nordhausen, where they were quartered in the V_2 construction factory. Marthe contemplated setting off north again, but this time she quickly realised they couldn't make the journey. Little Werner had contracted bronchitis which, for a baby only a few days old, ruled out any further travelling. Marthe was desperate, the child's fever was a catastrophe. Outwardly, she seemed calm, but the very thought that his condition could deteriorate threw her into a panic. She said there was no question of going anywhere. If the rumours circulating from village to village were to be believed, the end was drawing near, anyway.

Forced to stop and find a roof over their heads, the three

women offered their services at the Kaiserhof Inn in the village of Oberammergau, taking two rooms in exchange for work. Gretel was an excellent cook and ended up at the stove next to the woman who ran the inn. Marthe worked as a waitress and Anke did nothing except smile at customers and care for little Werner when Marthe was busy. The baby was very unwell. Marthe massaged his chest at length, using an unguent enriched with rosemary, and she patted him to help him cough and clear the mucus from his lungs. She brought his temperature down by bathing him in hot water and gradually cooling it with cold water, and by putting slices of potato to his temples and holding them in place by wrapping a damp cloth around his head. Werner wailed angrily, choked, grew furious all over again and eventually fell asleep, exhausted by his illness and the energy he put into resisting Marthe's ministrations. After four critical days, his condition improved, to the great relief of the inn's customers who were getting very little sleep. The moment he was well enough, he seemed to embark on a charm offensive of adorable yawns so that everyone immediately fell under the spell of this beautiful baby and new life.

'That littl'un's incredibly strong,' Gretel said.

'Oh, I could eat him!' added the manageress.

Werner became the inn's mascot, and five weeks went by. The news of the war that was doing the rounds was far from reassuring, but the women's work allowed them to forget their concerns. They were kept busy at the Kaiserhof, and yet, against the backdrop of this pastoral ski resort, they felt far removed from the ructions of the outside world. Being out in the country afforded them a pleasant life. For the time being, Marthe had abandoned her attempts to find Johann. She prayed that the Lord would spare him, just as she prayed for Werner to be protected. And for once the Almighty seemed to hear her prayers.

One afternoon, after they had finished serving lunch, the four women – Marthe, Gretel, Anke and the manageress – were eating their own lunch in a corner of the dining room when Marthe was astonished to see the towering but youthful form of von Braun appear in the doorway. The engineer was wearing a brown leather coat which did not disguise the fact that his left shoulder and arm were in plaster.

'Marthe, at last!' he exclaimed, spotting her and hurrying over. 'What a relief! Ever since the appalling news from Dresden, I've been sick with worry, then I heard that three women travelling with a baby were in the area asking everyone about me and Johann Zilch . . . but where's Luisa?'

The pain that pinched Marthe's face was all the reply he needed. Von Braun stood in silence for a long time and, as the news gradually sank in, he let himself drop onto the bench beside her.

'In the bombing?'

'Yes.'

'And the baby?'

'He's here,' said Marthe, taking the baby from Anke to show him to von Braun. 'His name's Werner.'

The engineer studied him, clearly moved.

'Luisa wanted me to be his godfather.'

He tried to take Werner with his good arm but Marthe ignored his attempts. Thwarted, von Braun made do with stroking the baby's foot with two fingers, which Marthe didn't like but she felt that, in his capacity as godfather, he couldn't be refused this privilege. Von Braun gazed at this brand-new life wriggling in front of him.

'Poor Johann, my poor friend,' he sighed, frowning. 'He's already in such a bad state.'

'What happened?'

'His captors beat him and left him for dead. At least that's what we thought must have happened when we found him. I didn't mention it in the telegram to avoid frightening Luisa. He recovered, slowly. But his memory's been badly affected . . .'

'How badly?'

'He's forgotten whole swathes of our research and events over the last few years. It's as if his life stopped seven years ago. Around the time he was married.'

Marthe listened in silence.

'I was banking on Luisa to help him,' von Braun admitted, then he added with another sigh, 'Such a beautiful couple, and so much in love . . . and now this child . . . What a tragedy!'

Devastated, he ordered a glass of brandy, and took it upon himself to order the same for the whole table. He asked the three women about their expedition and found it miraculous that they'd reached Bavaria safe and sound.

'When I think what you've been through!' he exclaimed, visibly distressed.

He drained his glass, and ordered another.

'And you?' Marthe asked, gesturing to the plaster on his arm.

'A car crash shortly after we evacuated Peenemünde. We'd driven all through the night and my driver fell asleep at the wheel . . . We were lucky to come out of it alive.'

'Why did you leave Nordhausen?' Marthe asked. 'I thought you were at the V2 factory there . . .'

'Three days ago, on orders from General Kammler, the scientific committee had to abandon the base where we were living. They keep moving us.' He leant closer to Marthe and, casting a wary eye around the room, whispered, 'I think what matters most to Kammler is keeping us close at hand in case events take a turn for the worse. We're his life insurance.'

Von Braun had been on his guard ever since Johann's arrest. A misinterpreted comment could cost him dear. Marthe nodded; she understood.

'Marthe, I wanted to say, about Kasper . . . Did you receive my telegram?'

'I did,' she said, her face unreadable.

'I'm so sorry . . .'

'I'm not,' she replied. 'I hated him and you didn't like him. It's because of him that Johann was in prison for so long, so it's because of him that Luisa's dead, not to mention what he subjected me to. There are millions of lost lives to be regretted in this war, but not Kasper Zilch's, believe me.'

Von Braun was struck by Marthe's steeliness. Although he'd been close to Johann for several years, he had not fully appreciated the loathing between the two brothers. He knew nothing of the perversities Kasper indulged in, and couldn't believe the man had deliberately aggravated the situation for his brother in prison. Shocked by the violence emanating from Marthe, he emptied his glass and stood up.

'Come, I'm taking you with me. We're only a few kilometres away.'

He paid the bill and lit a cigarette. Anke and Marthe didn't have many belongings to gather up. Gretel chose to stay at the inn, not wanting to let the manageress down at such short notice. The three women hugged each other goodbye, and even Marthe seemed emotional. In these turbulent times, when you parted, you couldn't know whether you would ever see each other again.

Von Braun's Mercedes was waiting for them outside the inn. With his chauffeur's help, von Braun removed his heavy leather coat. Marthe was shocked to see he was wearing an SS uniform and even the War Merit Cross that Hitler had given him a few months earlier. She was all the more confused because von Braun had never disguised his dislike of Himmler's henchmen. Poker-faced, she sat beside him in the back with the baby, while Anke sat in the front.

On that April evening in 1945, Marthe, Anke and little Werner moved into Haus Ingeborg Hotel, a luxurious establishment nestled in the Bavarian Alps, almost on the old Austrian border. The most sought-after minds of the Second World War had quickly settled into a routine there. Von Braun requisitioned two neighbouring rooms for Marthe and Anke, and naturally the baby slept with his aunt. Marthe was both anxious to introduce Werner to his father, and a little nervous about it. She felt Luisa would have been happy for them to meet, of course, but she was afraid Johann would want to take the baby from her. When Werner was sound asleep she decided to go and see her brother-in-law's condition for herself before showing him his son, and she left the baby with Anke while she followed von Braun.

The hotel was built entirely of wood and was a vast building with complicated architecture. They descended staircases, walked down long corridors whose walls were lined with a collection of cuckoo clocks, climbed a few steps and turned down another corridor. They came across two engineers from the team who greeted Marthe with great enthusiasm. One of them, a shy and awkward bachelor who answered to the name Friedrich, had had a soft spot for the nurse when she had come to spend a few months with Luisa and Johann. Luisa had encouraged Marthe to give him a chance, but Friedrich's powers of seduction were in inverse proportion to his intellectual abilities. He seemed especially happy to see her again now. Von Braun led her out onto the hotel's terrace and there, leaning on the balustrade with his back to her, was Johann. Marthe was horrified: his right calf and ankle were in plaster, and his hair had been shaved so that the wounds on his head could be treated. He held a cigarette in one hand and was drawing on it absent-mindedly.

Von Braun called to him and he turned around. He had bandaging over his left eye but his face broke into a smile when he saw von Braun. He had two teeth missing.

'Johann,' said von Braun, walking up to him, 'do you remember Marthe?'

'Of course,' he said with a tormented expression. 'How do you do?' he added, extending his hand to Marthe.

'Come on, Johann, you can kiss her, she's your sister-in-law!'

As Johann obediently leant towards her, Marthe took a hasty backward step and studied him. She was frightened. Johann smiled at her a little vacantly and opened his arms.

'That's wonderful, he recognises you,' von Braun whispered. 'I knew you'd do him good. And he hasn't seen the baby yet!'

Von Braun pushed Marthe into her brother-in-law's arms. They hugged for a moment, then the engineer patted them both affectionately on the back.

'Marthe, go and get Werner,' he said. 'He must meet his father.'

Manhattan, 1969

My angel was a woman. An explosion of contradictions that set me ablaze. Imperious and submissive, gentle and passionate, Rebecca gave of herself without reservation and without calculation. In the limousine taking us to the Pierre Hotel where I'd reserved a room for the night, I unbuttoned her blouse and buried my face in the silky vales of her neck and breasts. She was unfazed by the chauffeur who avoided looking in the rear-view mirror and appeared not to hear her sighs. She arched herself back against the door, offering herself up to my caresses. Her eyes glimmered hungrily through half-closed lids and she held me to her fiercely. Her skin had an amber smell that intoxicated me. When I slipped my hand inside her boy's slacks, her desire was palpable through her cotton panties. The feel of her drove me crazy. I was in the process of undressing her when the car slowed. We'd arrived.

I buttoned up her blouse over her breasts, which rose and fell at an accelerated rhythm. I tightened her tie, which was now almost undone, and stole another kiss in the process. We stepped out of the car, and Rebecca's hair was awry, her lips flushed and her eyes glazed. I carried my jacket over my arm to hide my erection as we walked through the lobby. I'd come by to pick up the keys before dinner: if the evening turned out well, I didn't want my beauty's enthusiasm to cool during the always tiresome delays necessitated by formalities at reception. I steered her towards the elevators and she seemed to come back to her senses.

'You had everything planned . . .' she said with a smile, as the elevator attendant pressed the button for the fifth floor.

In our room, Rebecca slipped off to the bathroom for a moment. I heard her turn on the faucets in the bathtub and the basin, and smiled at this subtle courtesy.

I got things back on track as soon as she reappeared.

'Don't worry,' she laughed. 'I won't change my mind.'

'You never can tell!' I protested, leading her to the bed.

I took off her jacket, her blouse and her bra, at last revealing her round breasts with tight, pink, perfectly centred nipples that seemed to point right at me. Despite her slender form, she exuded a sort of power, an animal quality. I removed her belt and pants. I took the time to admire her, almost naked, while I was still clothed. I knelt on the bed and kissed her feet, the first object of my attraction to her. Rebecca drew them away from me with a graceful scissor action of her legs which gave me a momentary glimpse of the ripe mound of her intimacy. She wanted to get up, but I put an authoritative hand on her stomach, making her lie back down. I ran my hand slowly down and slipped off her last vestige of clothing. I was beguiled by her blonde down, so fine and smooth it looked combed. It seemed almost profane to touch it. Rebecca, inflamed with passion, let me gaze at her and penetrate her with my finger. She was by turns avid and reticent, depending on the relative success with which I explored the geography of her pleasure. She made precise demands which irked me slightly, but the effect I achieved by respecting her requests rewarded me for complying with them. She made no effort to suppress herself, accepting that I could give her pleasure, and not worrying what I might think of her. I felt more and more relaxed. Rebecca was incredibly responsive and incredibly selfish. She liked me holding her, stroking her, shifting her around, but tried nothing on me. She was obliging, though; when I took her hand and put it on my erection, she toyed with me skilfully. Her expertise made me jealous; I didn't like imagining what she had done with other men, and learned from them. I wanted her to take me in her mouth but wasn't sure I could hold myself back. I took the upper hand again, exploring her body with my lips and hands, lingering between her legs and on the crease between her buttocks and thighs. She told me to take her and the words she used – clear, crude words – rang out in the silent room. I started a fierce battle with myself, listening to her desire and wary of my own. The sight of her ankles when she lay on her back with her knees bent and gave herself to me; the fiery look she shot me when I thrust into her; her on top of me with her blonde curls clothing her like a wrap and falling to stroke my knees when she arched backwards; the feel of her skin when I put my hand at the base of her neck . . . I tried to think about swimming in the sea, about snow and ice, to cool my ardour, but – just like her – I was caught up in a chain reaction that carried us away and left us exhausted and happy for a long while afterwards.

Our life together began that very first night. After making love she nestled up to me. With other girls I felt smothered as soon as my desire was satisfied; I was very happy to sleep with them, but definitely didn't want them clinging to me and putting their legs over me. But when Rebecca moved close, wedging her foot in the crook of my bent knee and putting her arms around me, I thought it charming. Her hair tickling my chin didn't bother me. It didn't occur to her for one moment to go home; the notion of sleeping apart when we'd just made love didn't cross her mind, and I was perturbed by the sudden tolerance I felt, having her so close. She was disconcertingly unaffected: after a long cuddle, she rolled onto her side, put her arms around her pillow with the same tenderness she'd shown me only moments before and said a soft 'good night' as if dismissing a servant. Then, utterly trusting, she succumbed to sleep. I watched her, fascinated that she was here, next to me, so alive and accessible. I was jealous of her dreams, of the distance they put between us, but I didn't dare touch her. There was a childish concentration on her face, as if she were achieving something of utmost importance. Her breathing was barely perceptible. I thought her magnificently beautiful.

The next morning she didn't stir when I got up and took a shower. Nor when I started hunting for my underpants and clothes around the bed. Her indifference started to bother me. I opened the door to the room, took the newspaper from the floor outside and opened it noisily. I read the whole thing without my beauty putting in an appearance. The sun had been up a long time when I eventually knelt next to her and called her name, stroking her cheek with one finger. Clearly displeased, she opened thunderous eyes, then smiled and reached her arms out to me.

'I have to go . . .' I said, hugging her.

She smelled good and was burning hot.

'Go where?' she asked indignantly, sitting up. 'We didn't even have breakfast!'

'Order whatever you want.'

'Nuh-uh! You're staying with me.'

She was like a young panther – it made me laugh.

'Are you just a tad bossy, ma'am?' I asked, mussing her hair.

'Please stay. Breakfast is important. We can't start the day abruptly like that . . . we need a transition. I hate suddenly being confronted with reality.'

'A princess,' I smiled. 'I *was* warned.'

'And by whom?' she asked playfully, pulling me close.

'The legions of broken hearts littered at your feet.'

'I think you give as good as you get in that department.'

'Did you do your research?'

She gave a little smile and reached for the room-service menu. She focused on it like a banker on stock-exchange prices.

'What would you like?' I asked, picking up the telephone.

The princess had an ogre's appetite, like me. She ordered a continental breakfast with pastries, buttered toast, scrambled eggs with smoked salmon, fruit salad, white coffee, orange juice and yoghurt. I asked for the same and added a plate of sautéed potatoes. We demolished our food enthusiastically with me managing to spill a bit of everything on the sheets whereas Rebecca, who like most artists had virtually lived in her bed for years, didn't drop a single crumb off the tray. This extensive menu sent us to sleep, then I wanted her and she wanted me, so we were tired all over again. When we woke we were hungry and went out for lunch, which – perfectly logically – required a siesta, but logic didn't get the last word.

Rebecca needed to change and work. I needed to work and change. We agreed to meet that evening in the same room, which I'd decided to keep for the weekend. We lived by this routine for two more days, we were indefatigable. The only thing plaguing me was the question of finances. Having money was a foregone conclusion for Rebecca, and she let me settle checks without even thanking me. Eventually the time came for us to leave the room. Thanks to further financial acrobatics and to pawning Marcus's cufflinks, I managed to pay the stiffest of bills, but we couldn't stay at the hotel any longer. I was worried Rebecca would be disappointed if I took her home: the apartment was tiny, half of it was set up as an office, and I shared it with Marcus and Shakespeare. It didn't seem worthy of her.

I couldn't turn up at her parents' place and I didn't want to be parted from her. I felt I needed only to take my eye off her for a moment and she would disappear around a street corner – an all-the-more-worrying concern now that I'd been witness to her talents as a seductress. Although she herself didn't seem aware of it, she spent her days charming the birds from the trees. She listened in wide-eyed wonder to the most insignificant information pronounced by the most insignificant people. She strolled through the world with a combination of innocence and selfishness that alarmed and fascinated me. Gifts and favours seemed to shower down on her. The moment she appeared, all eyes turned on her. I didn't go unnoticed myself, and I enjoyed the admiration we elicited together, but I was wary of the covetous looks she was bound to inspire the minute my back was turned. I would have liked to put her in a glass case to protect her from the weather and the assaults of the outside air, to keep her all to myself. On the Sunday evening, unable to pay for another night, I claimed I had a meeting early on the Monday morning.

We kissed in a corner set back from the street, a few doors from her parents' house. I wanted to ask her when I'd see her again. I think the same question was burning her lips, but we were too proud to ask it. I let her go. She refused to let me see her to the door.

Bavarian Alps, 1945

Marthe gave the excuse that the baby was asleep. The next day she said he was ill, as she did the day after. Von Braun wouldn't stand for it. He insisted on seeing Werner and, when Marthe showed him the baby, he simply took him with his good arm to introduce him to Johann himself. Marthe tried to intervene but the scientist lost his temper: she was ridiculously possessive with the child. He understood that she was concerned about Johann's condition, he also understood that she wasn't yet ready to hand the baby over to him, but Johann was Werner's father, while she was merely his aunt – and only by marriage, at that. There was no question of her stopping them meeting. They had weeks to catch up on, a connection had to be established between them, and that certainly wasn't going to happen if the baby was kept hidden.

'It's dangerous!' Marthe protested. 'Johann isn't himself and Werner's too young . . .'

'You won't even give him to *me*! Don't think I didn't notice at the inn. Am I dangerous too?'

'You have a broken arm, I was afraid you'd drop him,' she stammered.

'Well, see for yourself, I'm coping very well.'

It had to be said that Werner, who was lying on the scientist's forearm like a lion cub on a branch, with his head on one side in von Braun's large hand, didn't look unhappy.

'Well, I was wrong about you, I admit, but Johann . . . it's different,' Marthe still tried.

Von Braun's patience ran dry.

'I don't understand. What do you have against Johann? You're astonishingly ungrateful. You were perfectly happy to live in his house when you separated from your husband!'

'That's not it at all.'

'His imprisonment and what he's been through have affected him, I won't try to tell you they haven't, but you need to give him time to recover, to regain his strength. I hardly dare imagine what he endured, it chills me to the core just to think of it. A little compassion, Marthe! I'm amazed – outraged, even – that a woman like you, and a nurse to boot, doesn't show more kindness to the poor man.'

The young woman's protestations didn't weaken the scientist. He was now very angry.

'Marthe, if you're convinced that my entire team is set against this child, then you need only leave. I have no right to stop you, but I won't let you take my godson.'

This appeared to make Marthe back down. There was no question of her abandoning Werner, and von Braun kept tabs on her: he warned the SS officers guarding the hotel not to let her out alone with the child, and to be extra safe, he asked his chauffeur, Gunther, to follow her. That same evening, she couldn't walk ten paces without this clumsy forty-something in attendance. Friedrich, her devoted admirer, never left her either. Unable to throw off these two partners in crime, she reduced them to slavery: they carried her things, went to fetch her tea, her pullover if there was a draught, or Anke when it was time for a feed. They let her win at cards, even though Friedrich had an exceptional photographic memory, for fear she would be ill-tempered if she lost. They rocked Werner's basket for hours and when Werner cried, the nurse forced them to sing in rounds. Marthe was, therefore, treated very well, but the moment she had Werner in her arms, she was well and truly a prisoner.

Johann kept his distance. Von Braun insisted he took an interest in his son, but the moment he came near, the baby screamed. The abuse Johann had suffered had stripped him of personality and emotion. But he tried to do whatever his friend and boss told him. He conducted distant, courteous conversations with the other members of the team, but was still oddly absent. He spent whole days smoking, gazing blankly into the distance, on the hotel terrace. Von Braun, who was optimistic by nature, thought time would heal him.

Marthe, meanwhile, wasn't sleeping. Every evening she closed her shutters, locked her door and pulled the chest of drawers across to block the entrance. She had put Werner's cradle between her bed and the wall to keep him away from the window, and she rested in half-hour stints with her knife under her pillow. Anke was the first to criticise her friend's behaviour; she had immediately rallied to the new authority, and appeared prepared to do whatever it took to please von Braun and the men in his team. She joined the other women there in gossiping disapprovingly about 'Marthe's appalling attitude'. The scientists' wives had quickly established a preference: Anke had the advantage of being submissive and married while Marthe was a widow, free and unpredictable. They greeted the first condescendingly and the second with animosity. Marthe's character and, worse, her single status, had provoked almost instant dislike among them. Those who had known her when she lived with Johann and Luisa had bad memories of her – not very nice, they claimed. Not to mention the fact they'd thought Luisa rather blind to let her sister-in-law prowl around her husband like that. You only had to see the devotion Marthe inspired in Friedrich to know what the schemer was capable of. Oh, they knew all about seductresses like her, the ones who aren't much to look at and you don't look out for but they'll steal the most responsible and honourable of husbands and fathers from under your nose. Anke agreed wholeheartedly with them, and complained about how Marthe had treated her, describing how dictatorial and self-centred she was. She would sigh about her miserable fate, and take every opportunity to remove her socks and show the other women her damaged feet.

'And look what I got in return! If it weren't for me, Werner wouldn't have survived, and I can tell you, it was difficult feeding that child when my darling Thomas, my sweet, kind little Thomas had just joined the angels.'

The wives went even further: what a dreadful person this awful Marthe was; it was to Anke's credit that she'd sacrificed herself to such emotional pressure. The women exchanged meek, tear-filled, resolute glances. They delighted in their own generosity, their decorum and their shared suffering. With all the odious zeal of someone desperate to be accepted, Anke made the most of feed times to take Werner down to Johann, who tickled the baby self-consciously until a fuming Marthe came to reclaim him.

Apart from these tensions and the sword of Damocles that the SS kept dangling over their precious grey cells, the scientists' lives resembled an unlikely holiday. While the Germany they had known dragged slowly to an end, they spent their days playing cards and chess. They listened to the radio or sat on the hotel's terrace, looking out at the snow-capped Alps and enjoying the glorious spring sunshine. They wanted for nothing, but were conscious that the fate of the world, as well as their own fates, were being sealed at that very moment. Whenever they were alone, their conversation revolved around the best way to persuade the SS to give them up – instead of killing them; or they speculated about which of the enemy forces was likely to reach them first. The British, French and Americans were to the west, and the Soviets to the east; and all of them were searching avidly for this team. The British intelligence services had compiled a list of the Reich's 'brains' – people who must be identified and removed from the clutches of what was soon to become a Soviet empire. The scientists didn't know that their names featured high on this list, but they had all heard tell of colleagues who'd disappeared overnight, never to be seen again. Nor could the agents scouring Germany for von Braun, Johann Zilch and their team, ever have guessed their targets were only a few kilometres away.

Late at night on 1 May 1945, the whole group had gathered in the blue lounge and were drinking Jägermeister and listening to Bruckner's Seventh Symphony when the radio programme was brutally interrupted and the Führer's death was announced. The scientists and their wives jumped up to cluster around the radio. In a wavering voice, the journalist said that Adolf Hitler had perished in battle after bitter fighting against the Bolshevik hordes in the ruins of Berlin. It was a huge shock. Even though this answered the wishes they'd held for many weeks, they reeled at the uncertainty of the future. Some were openly exultant and were roundly reprimanded by the more law abiding among them: it was unpatriotic to celebrate the Führer's death. Anke broke down and wept; she felt like an orphan, abandoned, and bemoaned the death of the man who had led and guided them. Other women cried too, terrified of what lay in store.

When Marthe was in bed, she heard Anke sob for a long time through the wall, but, on this occasion, felt no compulsion to comfort her. Anke's true character had been revealed to Marthe in recent weeks. Shy and self-effacing people are often thought kind when they are in fact simply weak. They'd slit your throat as soon as they had a chance to avenge their own mediocrity. Luckily, Werner could cope without Anke; he was now eating solids. Marthe wanted to get as far as possible from her country and her past. She wanted to start again and build a better life somewhere else. She just had to work out how to leave, a problem that preoccupied her – as it did many other residents in the hotel – for much of the night. On the floor below, von Braun considered the best strategy for himself, his team and his thwarted dreams of a space rocket. He lay on his back with his uncomfortable plastered arm beside him, or sat on the edge of the bed or paced around his room, while his mind churned. He was restless, burning his way through three packets of cigarettes and twice as many ideas before he managed to reach the obvious decision.

The next morning he gathered his men together. Time was of the essence. Hitler's death had freed him from his remaining moral qualms and had thoroughly distracted their already chaotic guards. The important thing was to avoid falling into Soviet hands. Accounts of the torture inflicted on German prisoners by the Russians had made an impression on these scientists who had not been unduly concerned by the horrors of forced labour in the Dora factory – where slaves died by the thousand – only a few weeks earlier. Von Braun wanted to hand himself over to the Americans, and his team followed his lead, with the exception of two researchers who opted for the Russians. Marthe thought she would make the most of the general pandemonium to sneak away with the baby, on foot if need be, across the mountains that were less hostile now thanks to the spring. The opportunity never arose.

Only Marthe and Magnus von Braun, the boss's younger brother, spoke good English. Von Braun knew the Americans were geographically closest, and he sent Marthe and Magnus as scouts. Evading their jailors' surveillance, they bicycled at great speed down the steep slope that dropped away towards Austria. They felt they were risking their lives at every bend: if the SS had seen them leave the hotel without permission or if they saw them approach foreign soldiers, they wouldn't hesitate to shoot them. To make matters more perilous still, Magnus's brakes didn't work. When they reached the valley, they spotted an American anti-tank unit of the 44th Division, and Magnus staked everything on a daredevil exploit. He steered his bicycle towards them at frightening speed with no idea how he would stop it, and called to the Americans in halting English, 'My name is Magnus von Braun, my brother invented the V2. We want to surrender.'

When the Americans realised the couple were unarmed, they agreed to talk to them. Nonetheless, Magnus and Marthe had to use all their powers of persuasion to convince the Americans that the inventors of the V2 were somewhere in the mountains, and they asked to be heard by General Dwight Eisenhower immediately. Fred Schneikert, a short, dark-haired soldier from Wisconsin with a shrewd eye, decided to take them to the headquarters of the CIC, the American secret services, which had been set up in the town of Reutte. There, First Lieutenant Charles Stewart was incredulous but didn't want to risk losing one of the most sought-after brains of the conflict. He put four men and two cars at their disposal, and asked Magnus and Marthe to return with von Braun.

In the meantime, most of the SS guards at the hotel had thrown off their uniforms and fled. In the hope of saving their own lives, those who were still there let von Braun go to meet the Americans. The deal was agreed the next day in Charles Stewart's office over a breakfast of scrambled eggs, bacon, white bread with jam, and real coffee, luxuries the scientists had almost forgotten. That morning they had their first taste of toasted cereals that you ate in a bowl with milk and sugar – and thought them delicious.

Relieved and replete, von Braun and his men officially handed themselves over to the American authorities.

Manhattan, 1969

'But I already said I don't give a damn!' Rebecca protested, exasperated.

'Well, I do give a damn,' I replied defensively.

'Is it really that terrible? Are there roaches? Or rats?'

'No, of course not!'

'Well then, take me to your apartment.'

'No.'

'Or let me pay for the hotel.'

'No way,' I said categorically.

Rebecca, who had become aware of my financial difficulties, had invited me for a picnic in Central Park. From the kitchen at home she had brought a luxury hamper: white tablecloth, beautiful glasses, plates and cutlery, a bottle of champagne, fish terrine, slices of roast beef, a salad of grilled vegetables, speciality bread, cheese and of course sautéed potatoes which I demolished cold. On top of this there was chocolate cake.

'I bought it myself,' she boasted with a sardonic smile.

'Do you know how to cook?'

'Not at all. Not even an egg. When I was bored as a kid I'd go down to the kitchen and watch Patricia work, but I was totally banned from trying anything myself.'

'I'm sure you were very good at licking the bowls!' I teased, tipping her back onto the grass.

Her hair on the plaid blanket formed a sunny blonde halo around her face. I was fascinated that such a small head could contain so many thoughts and longings, such intelligence. She kissed me and then, when I was least expecting it, she stuffed a handful of grass down my shirt. I brushed it out, cursing her and promising I'd spank her if she did it again, then I laid her down again and held her prisoner.

'Make up your mind, Wern,' she complained.

'About what?'

'About where you're going to satisfy my desires! You're a tease, you think it's fun getting me worked up when you don't have a solution.'

'Are you worked up?'

'Yes.'

'Very worked up?'

'Yes.'

I sat up with a sigh.

'Don't you have a studio for your work?'

'Yes, of course I do! Why didn't I think of that! It's right under my father's office, I'm sure he'd be thrilled to meet you,' she quipped sarcastically; she knew I was making a big deal of meeting her parents. I'd been very careful not to talk to her about it, but this delicious nuisance of a girl saw right through me, no problem.

I was still resisting her request to come to the apartment so she deployed her full arsenal of charms to persuade me. Her overt sensuality amazed me, particularly as she was inversely expansive where emotions were concerned. I'd started mentioning my feelings for her, but she swept aside my declarations with a mocking remark or a laugh. She hadn't pronounced a single tender word about me, even though her eyes, her caresses and her kisses told me how she felt about me. In the end she made me capitulate: I agreed to take her home. She was hard to resist. She alternated emotional blackmail with childish pleading, humour with sulking, logical reasoning with pestering. Exactly the methods, according to Marcus, that I used on our clients, our suppliers and anyone who impeded my plans . . . I think she and I were as determined as each other.

In the taxi heading downtown I was nervous. She was delighted, determined to be enchanted by the most repulsive of dives. She described my street as 'cute', ignored the garbage cans for the restaurant downstairs, and thought the building itself 'very nice'. The metal stairs that swayed as soon as you set foot on them were deemed 'good for the heart' and she melted with joy when she was reunited with Shakespeare who greeted us as if he hadn't had company for weeks. After making a fuss of the dog and without asking me, she embarked on a tour of the property.

'You have running water!' she taunted in the bathroom.

She opened the window which looked onto a gloomy court-yard and the neighbouring ventilation system. 'Typical New York view, a real picture postcard,' she said with a realtor's intonations. She inspected the shower and Marcus's state-of-the-art shaving things, including the badger-bristle brush with an ebony handle edged with silver, and the matching razor and bowl, which looked out of place against the bottle-green tiles around the basin. Next Becca went into Marcus's impeccably tidy bedroom – 'Now, this, I bet, is your roommate's' – and then into mine which was a terrible mess – 'and this is yours!' she laughed. My beauty finished her inspection with the desk which was piled high with files – 'the headquarters of the great multinational' – and then the last room: 'Oh my! A fully equipped kitchen. With a refrigerator *and* a cooker! Mister Zilch, you do spoil yourself.'

I was mortified. My desire to prove to the world and this insolent creature what I was capable of ate away at my insides. Time passed so disgustingly slowly. If everything had gone according to plan, and without those corrupt officials delaying our work, I should already have had my first million in the bank. I had my eye on the next Z & H project, a huge seafront plot which would change my fortunes once and for all. She sensed my frustration and came over to kiss me.

'Honestly, Werner, your apartment's great.'

'Good enough for what I plan to do to you!' I retorted, leading her to my bedroom.

'Aren't you going to give me a drink first?'

'Nope.'

'You're not very polite, Mister Zilch.'

'Not polite at all,' I agreed, laying her down.

'Or very tidy,' she added, extracting one of my belts from the sheets because the buckle was digging into her back.

'Any other grievances from the princess with the pea?'

'Oh, plenty!'

'I shall do what I can to earn your forgiveness . . .' I told her, pinning down her wrists.

In lovemaking, Rebecca liked authority and I had a natural tendency to express mine; these intimate moments redressed the balance. The sight of her giving herself to me, the way she yielded to my hands and my orders, gave me a feeling of power I hadn't experienced with any other woman. She wanted vigorous onslaughts. This woman who could be so dominant took pleasure in being submissive. She liked to bite and scratch, and liked me to play-act suffocating her. She liked to get the feeling she was being forced because, she admitted one time, it was liberating for her. Rebecca forgave me three times in the next few hours. I was counting, even though she didn't like me to count, or to ask her about how it was.

'You don't need any extra compliments,' she said. 'You're arrogant enough already.'

I loved the way she could shrug off her upbringing. In the heat of the moment, she could ask clearly for what she wanted, and I liked the fact that afterwards she reverted to being refined and restrained. I felt she was giving me a part of herself that I alone got to see.

At around six in the evening, we heard Marcus come home and Shakespeare greet him noisily. Marcus came over to the door, heard us giggling and withdrew discreetly to his bedroom with his traditional end-of-the-day pot of tea. He'd adopted this habit during his years at an English boarding school, but had never succeeded in converting me. Still, I offered Rebecca a cup of tea.

'At last!' she exclaimed. 'I thought you were going to let me die of thirst.'

Marcus had taken the only teapot in the apartment, so I poured half the box of Twinings Earl Grey into a glass jug with lukewarm water so it didn't shatter. Rebecca swallowed a mouthful with a haughty cat-like displeasure and pronounced my concoction 'repulsive'. My beauty did not have the gift of subtlety, a consequence of her sensitivity that made her react to people and things with the responsiveness of a Ferrari. She borrowed a T-shirt and a pair of my underpants, and went into the kitchen to make her own tea, followed by Shakespeare who yelped and fussed around her like a puppy, because he was in love, naturally, but also because he was hungry. She called me a few seconds later. She couldn't light the gas cooker.

'Perhaps I can help?' Marcus said, popping his head around his door with a charming smile.

'Yes please,' Becca replied.

'Marcus,' I yelled, dragging myself out of bed. 'Stop checking her out!'

'For the moment all I am checking out is the state of the teapot,' he retorted.

We had tea together in the living room. Marcus had bought cookies, fresh milk and apples at the store. Rebecca half-lay on the sofa with her feet under my thighs to keep warm. She and Marcus fell into conversation easily, they had dozens of mutual friends and reeled through names I didn't know. They'd been to the same holiday camps and the same tennis club. They endured classes with the same dance teacher, and both mimicked him in turn, aping his extravagant mannerisms and his Russian accent.

It was strange they'd never met, and I was jealous of their complicity. Marcus tactfully avoided mentioning the two boys whose hearts Rebecca had reduced to ashes, and Rebecca complimented him on his father's work. They exchanged niceties like this until I decided we should all go out to dinner.

Rebecca had stained her white pants when we were rolling on the grass in Central Park so she borrowed a sweater as an improvised dress which she cinched at the waist with one of my ties. I plunged my hand into the deep V neckline to cup one of her breasts and then tried a similar operation from underneath. Her makeshift outfit gave me very satisfying access to her person. We went, as a sort of pilgrimage, to Gioccardi's where Paolo greeted us effusively. Happy to see I'd achieved my aims, he winked at me the moment Rebecca's back was turned, and offered us a bottle of prosecco to celebrate the occasion.

Afterwards Becca insisted we dropped by The Scene, the club where everybody who was anybody had to be. Jimi Hendrix, who was just back from London, was playing there that evening. She 'didn't want to miss it for anything in the world'. The Scene had a basement about the size of a shoebox on 46th Street between Eighth and Ninth Avenues. It had enjoyed unprecedented success since a blind-drunk Jim Morrison had caused a scandal on another night when Jimi Hendrix had played there. Morrison had climbed onto the stage, grabbed Hendrix around the waist and tried to perform fellatio on him in public. Hendrix had thrown him off fiercely but Morrison didn't want to let go and clung to him, roaring obscenities. Janis Joplin had brought an end to the Lizard King's performance with a smart blow to the head with a bottle, an initiative that earned cheers and applause from onlookers. In a city always hungry for excess, an incident like this could hardly fail to make a name for The Scene.

Getting into the place wasn't a foregone conclusion. Crowds thronged by the door, but very few people got to spend the evening there. First of all, out on the sidewalk, you had to sweet-talk Teddy, a tank dressed in a Mafioso's suit. When the club first opened, Marcus – who always knew where you had to be and with whom – had gotten on the good side of the guy. The odds were more random with Steve Paul, the club's owner. He was the same age as us, unbearably arrogant, and had developed a habit of greeting his customers with a raft of personalised insults. Marcus found this amusing, I did not. Steve must have sensed this because he never went too far with me, and that evening we didn't have a single unpleasant remark. Rebecca started by throwing her arms around Teddy, which gave me the first of several hot flashes, then she threw her arms around Steve who gave her a hug and rocked backwards and forwards with her for what felt to me like forever. After this effusive greeting, he proved almost friendly, shook my hand for the first time since we'd been visiting his establishment, and found us a table right by the stage.

Everything was tiny: the room, the tables, and particularly the chairs which were a struggle for my large frame. Smoke from cigarettes and firecrackers along with the body heat of tightly packed people created a fug that blurred your eyesight and your mind. Rebecca was euphoric: she moved her hands expansively as she talked and couldn't sit still, too busy saying hello to friends. She fell into the arms of Linda Eastman, a pretty young photographer everyone was talking about since her marriage to Paul McCartney; and then the arms of Deering Howe, a regular at the club and the millionaire heir to the tractor company of the same name. Next Becca cried 'Andy!' and gave a big hug to Andy Warhol who had just arrived with his full court in attendance, and not one of them failed to grope the love of my life. Lastly, she pressed herself to Allen Ginsberg's chest. I hadn't read any of his books, as I was quick to tell him glumly when she introduced me to him. Rebecca praised his work with a tirade that I interrupted, grabbing her hand and bringing her back to our table. Then I sat her on my lap to make it very clear to these international-grade gropers that this woman was taken. She laughed at my disgruntled expression.

'Don't be jealous.'

'I'm not jealous.'

'They're all gay.'

'So what? Do you think that's an excuse?'

'We were just saying hi, that's all. Already possessive after one week . . .' she sighed.

'I was possessive from the first day.'

'Probably because you have stuff to be ashamed of . . .'

'What's the connection?' I asked, twisting my head back to see her more clearly.

'When people spread their affections wide, they tend to believe others do the same.'

'I don't believe anything at all. I just see you spending more time in strangers' arms than in mine.'

Rebecca wasn't in an argumentative mood. She laughed and pressed herself close to me, but she didn't stay there long. She was already back on her feet a few minutes later when we heard cheering. Hendrix appeared on the stage and the tension in the room rocketed. He gave the crowd a silent greeting and played a few chords. The audience was as tightly wound as the strings on his guitar and he skilfully made the anticipation last. His fans were on tenterhooks. His guitar howled like an animal, he produced sounds with it I've never heard before or since. He gave his all and the room went wild. Rebecca was sensuous and abandoned, at one with the music and the crowd. I watched the scene but couldn't let myself go. I always have a sort of split personality: I live my life and watch myself at the same time. I don't like losing control. Rebecca, I would soon learn, liked nothing more. She wanted to follow her instincts and urges, push back the limits of her mind and break the locks that shackled social behaviour. It was her job as an artist, she said, and in those days that's what people believed. Rebecca had a vitality and strength that made her unsinkable, but I suspected there was a fault line in her, a fragility she couldn't entirely disguise. A well-brought-up young lady by morning and a wild child possessed by guitar music by night, uptown and conventional one minute, downtown and free-spirited the next, she was everywoman. I watched her succumb to the feverish atmosphere that night. She had taken a pill and had offered me one, but I wasn't ready to let go of my moorings in among that unruly clan. Neither was Marcus. My beauty was very funny on acid, giving long mystic speeches, dazzled by the lights, colours and sounds, as if every inch of her skin had highly sensitive receptors. She charmed us with her poetic brilliance and the virtuosity of her thinking.

Dawn was breaking when the three of us returned to the apartment. She walked through the streets singing, and took off her shoes. Afraid she would hurt her feet, I told her to ride on my back. She let her head drop on my shoulder. I could feel the skin of her thighs in my hands, her stomach against my spine, her breath on my neck. Her feet swung with every step I took. I was enveloped in her perfume. I wanted her so furiously.

Manhattan, 1970

It was one of the happiest periods of my life. Rebecca loved me and I loved Rebecca. The money was finally rolling in, and Z & H had just acquired the seafront plot that should seal our fortune. The day Marcus and I received the cheque that really changed the stakes, we returned to the dive in Queens with three bottles of champagne each in our arms, and Shakespeare on our heels. I put my father's Patek back on my wrist, Marcus reclaimed his cufflinks and tie-pin, and – both of us drunk on the American dream – we offered champagne to everyone who'd come to drop off something precious.

'You're just going through a bad phase,' we told them. 'It won't last. Everything's possible, you know.'

Some dubious, others buying the dream, customers accepted the champagne and drank to the future. Two men hung back and seemed less good-natured. They'd read the piece about us in *Village Press* so they knew we'd just made millions, and they thought it ostentatious of Zilch and Howard to come parading their good luck. When I offered them a drink, they emptied their paper cups onto the floor, spitting out their resentment of the 'daddy's boys' they took us to be. Shakespeare, who'd requisitioned the kindly hand of one of the cashiers to scratch his stomach, leapt to his feet at the first sign of raised voices and growled, drawing back his lips and raising his hackles all down his back. I made super-human efforts to control myself, but the dam broke when the bigger of the two men ran out of arguments and was reduced to calling me a 'double-crossing asshole'. I grabbed him by the collar and Marcus grasped me around the waist.

'Good Lord!' – (that was Marcus's most obscene curse) – 'you're having dinner with Rebecca's parents this evening, you don't want to arrive with a tooth missing or a broken nose!'

'It won't be me who has the broken nose, I can guarantee that,' I yelled.

I stepped around Marcus who snatched at my shirt, making the buttons fly all over the room. Shakespeare barked dementedly and nearly everyone else had fled. My partner managed to get me to back away, and a bystander did the same with the man challenging me. Marcus dragged me towards the stairs, followed by Shakespeare. I heard the second moron call me 'filthy vermin' and 'little capitalist', and I spun around, my fist ready. Marcus caught me by the belt and hauled me back towards the exit.

'Well, the little capitalist will get bigger!' I exploded. 'I'll be the one giving you and your kids a life, if there's a woman dumb enough to give you any.'

'Leave it, Wern,' Marcus said, still restraining me. 'We don't want to ruin the day.'

Out on the street, I gave a resounding kick to a garbage can and yelled for a few more minutes, then I gathered up Shakespeare and sat at the wheel of our Chrysler, which was anything but the incarnation of triumphant capitalism.

The prospect of dinner with Rebecca's parents wasn't helping me keep my cool. I was strung out. Nathan Lynch had insisted on meeting me, and to make this first encounter easier, at Rebecca's request, he'd also invited Marcus and his father, Frank. Being on close terms with 'both parties', as Marcus put it, the Howards could act as a 'binder'. For the last week Marcus had been telling me all the things 'one does' and all those 'one doesn't do'. My head was stuffed full of these illogical rules known as manners. Rebecca herself seemed no calmer than I was. However much she insisted that her parents were 'adorable' and 'everything would be fine', her brightness seemed forced. In fact, she'd said she would prefer not to arrive with me, but before me to 'pave the way', which led me to understand that the 'way' wasn't favourable to me. Mostly I felt that by refusing to come with me, she was already choosing the other camp. Marcus reminded me that, until it was proved otherwise, 'the two camps were not enemies', and he would be there to support me, but by then I had a bad feeling about it.

Standing at the door of 4 East 80th Street with a huge bouquet of flowers in my arms, I didn't feel at all confident. Frank, on my right, patted my shoulder. To my left, Marcus was wearing a perfunctory smile. I thought that once I'd stepped over that threshold there would be no going back, but Rebecca lived in that world, on the other side of this door, and I wanted to join her. I rang the bell.

A butler in blue-and-yellow livery opened the door to us. He took my bouquet, handed it to a young woman and led us to the library. Nathan Lynch appeared before we'd had time to sit down. He was a man of about sixty with white hair and ruddy cheeks. He had small grey eyes, tightly clamped jaws and thin lips set into an impatient curve. He studied me with mild hostility. A gnawing anger emanated from this man who reached only armpit height on me: in order to stare at my face he had to tilt his head noticeably upwards. He proved scarcely any friendlier with Frank and Marcus and then, with an irritable circling motion of his hand, he indicated the chairs we should sit on. He offered us Scotch and raised a displeased eyebrow when I accepted. He and I eyed each other briefly. I found it hard to believe that a creation as magical as Rebecca could have been fathered by him. And he couldn't get used to the idea that his only daughter might have any form of contact, least of all physical, with a great tall thing like me.

I was, in fact, beginning to wonder what on earth his daughter was up to while Marcus engaged our host in a bibliophilic conversation that meant absolutely nothing to me. I hadn't read the classics; I felt little attraction for books in general and none for novels in particular. I couldn't see the point, when life itself was so rich and diverse, in wasting your time in a parallel world. I was interested only in books about economics or politics. I had not yet developed a taste for art and, let's face it, I was boorishly ignorant in most fields that interested my possible father-in-law. As a demanding philanthropist and patron, Nathan Lynch granted only a small window of attention to people who were introduced to him. He formed an opinion in a matter of seconds and did not go back on it. A few unfortunate words or an attitude he deemed 'not quite above board' would be enough to seal the fate of an individual or project. He was always in demand and so dealt only with 'efficient, competent' people. He loathed waiting, loathed being crossed and loathed being disappointed. His entourage of lawyers, assistants, advisers and childhood friends rigorously filtered the human race to bring only 'the cream' before him. He spoke with politicians, businessmen, famous artists: in other words, people who had proved themselves. Nathan Lynch didn't waste his time on unknown quantities.

By dint of the reason that had brought me to his house, his daughter, I was already suspect. My hazy origins, my early endeavours in real estate, my youth, my physique, everything about me must have irked him. He would have loved a great intellectual, accepted the heir to a fortune, tolerated an older and already recognised banker, but he was in no mood to see any good qualities in me. He didn't ask me anything and spoke only to Marcus and his father. Trying to be friendly, I asked him about a painting of a dwarf with his hand on a huge dog.

'Can't you see it's a Velázquez?' he asked, apparently shocked.

'I'm too far away to read the signature,' I said defensively.

'You shouldn't need to see the signature. It's blindingly obvious!' he snapped, turning his back on me.

I didn't give up: a few minutes later, when there was a brief silence, I made another attempt.

'Rebecca tells me you're having a museum built for your art collection. I'm passionate about architecture, thanks to Frank and Marcus,' I explained, smiling at my two allies who nodded encouragingly. 'I was wondering what sort of building you—'

'Rebecca tells you too much,' he interrupted. 'That project is confidential. As for the work, thank you for offering your services, but I already have contractors.'

'I wasn't hoping to offer my "services", I only develop my own projects,' I replied, irritated. 'And I didn't know that the museum about which you gave an interview for the *New York Times* was confidential.'

For a split second, Nathan Lynch seemed astonished that I'd shown signs of resistance, then he parried with bad faith worthy of his daughter: 'If you believe everything journalists say . . .'

I wriggled deeper into my chair and shut myself away in disgruntled silence. Frank and Marcus tried to get me to join the conversation several times but Nathan Lynch invariably interrupted them. He had a habit of talking over anyone trying to speak, and I was gripped by a violent dislike for him. The butler came over and offered me another glass of whisky which I accepted.

'At the rate you're draining your glass,' Nathan Lynch said with exasperation, 'keep the decanter.'

'Excellent idea,' I acquiesced, taking the elegant vessel from the butler's tray and putting it on the side table next to me.

The butler flinched and rushed to put a square of red felt between the decanter and the inlaid wood. Marcus sent me a discreet, understanding look to help me keep calm. I looked down and concentrated on the pattern on the carpet. Not a single word came from my mouth in the twenty minutes it took Rebecca to come downstairs. I resented her terribly for abandoning me in enemy territory. I felt I'd been separated from the world by a thick layer of solitude. Only the sound of the ice cubes clinking against my glass with each mouthful of Scotch reminded me that my existence was more than virtual. With fingers white from the pressure, I angrily clutched the arms of my chair. By the time Rebecca appeared, I wanted to stand up, throw my glass against the wall and leave the room.

She was pale, visibly nervous. She greeted Frank and Marcus with excessive enthusiasm and I was hurt when she gave me a peck on the cheek, as she had done them. I glowered at her and she reciprocated as if to say, 'I can't exactly French kiss you in front of my father.' She aggravated her case by sitting on the sofa, miles from me, and chatting as if everything was fine. Unlike her father, she included me in conversation, but in a detached, urbane tone that infuriated me. I descended into gloomy silence. Marcus was giving me his pinched look which meant 'Make an effort!', but I was overcome with disgust for this hypocrisy, and a paralysing inability to pretend.

Rebecca's mother appeared to complete the nightmare. She made a theatrical entrance, paused briefly, stared at me unsettlingly, and then advanced into the room. Judith Lynch must once have been glorious. She was extremely thin and wore a hard expression on her face, neither of which promised sensuality, but her tall figure – she was taller than her husband – and her narrow waist and hips, clothed in an austere black evening dress, along with her spectacular blue eyes and her opulent Titian-coloured chignon, were still striking. She wore too much jewellery, as if wanting to protect herself with it. Her décolletage was hidden by a heavy Queen of Egypt necklace, and her left forearm was almost entirely covered by a stack of gold cuffs. Nathan, Frank and Marcus rose to their feet as one man, and one after the other they graciously air-kissed her hand. I wanted to do the same, and tried to remember Marcus's instructions (don't raise her hand, bend over but not too much, barely touch her skin with your lips), but when it was my turn, Judith Lynch froze. We saw her sway. Marcus, who was closest to her, took her arm to help her sit down. This reaction made me very ill at ease. I went over to Judith but she gestured to me to stay away.

'Forgive me,' she muttered. 'I don't feel very well. Probably the new drug the doctor prescribed for me.'

'What did that charlatan give you now!' her husband said irritably. 'You shouldn't trust him, we already talked about this. You'd do better to call Dr Nars.'

'Your beloved Dr Nars refuses to prescribe me sleeping pills,' Judith retorted in a muted voice. 'And I need to sleep, Nathan. Sleep! Do you understand?'

We didn't know what to do with ourselves now. Marcus and his father hovered awkwardly, trying to find a diverting subject of conversation, while I fumed inwardly. Not only was Rebecca's father proving intolerably rude – considering that Marcus had harped on at me for the last week or so about the courtesies that were allegedly so important to this man – but his wife almost fainted at the sight of me. As for Rebecca herself, she seemed panic-stricken. Nathan Lynch asked his wife if she'd like to go back up to her room, but Judith seemed to be recovering gradually. To gloss over this unpleasant incident, they cut short the aperitifs and we went through for dinner.

The meal was excruciating. The mistress of the house hardly spoke a word, and I made no more effort than she did. Frank and Marcus battled to break the ice with a succession of anecdotes, historical and literary quotations, amusing stories and forced laughter. I kept my head down, finishing one plateful of food after another. My girlfriend's mother couldn't help staring at me while Rebecca talked too much, moved too much and laughed too much. By the time we had dessert, the atmosphere had eased a little thanks to Frank Howard who, struck by how little attention Nathan Lynch was paying me, spent the latter part of the meal talking to me.

When we rose to move to the living room, something strange happened: after everyone else had already gone through and I hung back behind Judith Lynch to let her walk ahead of me, as Marcus had taught me to, she stopped in her tracks, snapped shut the door between the two rooms and locked it so that she was alone with me. I heard Nathan Lynch call his wife several times. She quickly locked the other door which led to the kitchen, and came over to me. There was a disturbing feverish glint in her eyes. It implied vast pain or a type of madness: her face shone with violent distress. Mrs Lynch came over to me and, keeping her eyes pinned on me, removed her heavy necklace and dropped it unceremoniously on the floor.

'Mrs Lynch, I don't understand,' I stammered.

She put one finger to my lips and with the other showed me a fine pale scar around her neck, just above her collarbones.

'Mrs Lynch, please let me through,' I said firmly. After the evening I'd just had, I was in no mood to watch this old nutcase strip in the middle of her dining room.

She pressed herself up against the door on which her husband was thumping and, trembling from head to foot, she removed one of her wide gold cuffs. The entire length of her right arm was criss-crossed with regular white lines. While she revealed her stigmata, a terrifying distillation of contradictory emotions flitted across her face: shame, pride, exhibitionism, pain, but mostly a sort of demented, determined provocation.

'Why are you showing me this?' I asked several times.

The handle on the other door rattled vigorously. Nathan Lynch had walked around to get into the room, and was calling his wife again. She didn't reply, her eyes still locked on mine. As a final flourish in this strange ritual, she removed the last large cuff on her left arm and held out her wrist to show me tattooed numbers and a small triangle.

'Does this still mean nothing to you?' Judith asked.

'I know what the numbers mean. I learned that in high school, Mrs Lynch. I'm so sorry.'

'In high school,' she said with a stifled laugh. 'Just in high school?'

'Yes, ma'am. I don't know what you were expecting.'

'Nothing,' she said. 'I expected nothing else.'

She gathered up her jewellery and, with her hands full, she withdrew slowly, as if sleepwalking, through the door to the kitchen, where Rebecca, the butler and one of the housemaids were waiting for her.

'Mom, what's going on?' Rebecca asked, putting her arms around her mother. 'Mommy darling, talk to me.'

They disappeared upstairs while, still reeling from the scene, I unlocked the other door where Nathan Lynch was now waiting again.

'I think Mrs Lynch's not feeling well,' I explained tersely.

The man looked at me as if I'd attacked his wife and was now claiming responsibility for the assault. Frank Howard used the excuse of a meeting early the following day to curtail the evening, and he turned down the coffee and liqueurs that the butler had just brought in.

I asked to speak to Rebecca, and the butler went upstairs but returned without her.

'Miss Lynch sends her apologies, but she needs to look after her mother,' he said.

I was very hurt that she didn't come down to kiss me goodbye, and as I walked through the door I was none too sure what sort of fate had been sealed that evening, but I knew the real trouble was about to start.

Once we were in Frank's car he turned to me.

'Nathan behaved despicably this evening,' he said, hoping to ease the humiliation that was consuming me. 'But you mustn't take it personally, Werner. He can be like that with me sometimes.'

'It's very kind of you to try to apologise for him, Frank, but I take it very personally. He can't stand anything about who I am, and even less about where I come from. Take him out of his fish bowl of highborn connections, and he can't breathe.'

'He's a difficult man,' Frank admitted.

Marcus had been more struck by Judith's erratic behaviour.

'Had you met Mrs Lynch before?' he asked.

'Never,' I growled, still feeling very bruised by Rebecca's attitude. I resented her for spoiling everything. I'd thought she was a free spirit, I thought I was dealing with an artist, and I'd found a conformist heiress. I was sad and disappointed. I felt she'd been disloyal. She'd disowned me.

'I don't know who you reminded her of, but it was like Mrs Lynch had seen a ghost!' Marcus said.

'You must be the dead spit of someone she loved long ago,' suggested Frank, to lighten my mood.

'He obviously didn't treat her well because it definitely wasn't love she was giving off this evening.'

'What did she say after she locked the door? To treat Rebecca well?' asked Marcus.

'She didn't say anything. And her daughter's the least of her problems. I mean, she half-undressed in front of me.'

'Excuse me? She undressed?' father and son asked almost in unison.

'Well, she took off her jewellery piece by piece and showed me her scars. She was in the camps.'

'The camps? Which camps?' asked Marcus.

'The extermination camps,' I explained wearily.

'I didn't know that!' Frank exclaimed several times, horrified. 'I've known her twenty years and she's never mentioned it to me. How do you know that? Did she tell you?'

'She has tattoos on her left arm . . . there's no mistaking those numbers. And she has scars all over her.'

'So that's why she always wears so much jewellery . . .' Frank murmured. Absorbed in thought, he realigned all the information he had about Judith Lynch to see her in an entirely new light.

We sat in silence for a while.

'What I don't understand,' I said eventually, 'is why she showed her scars to me, and me alone.'

Bavarian Alps, August 1945

Wernher von Braun was extremely tense. The harsh crease of his furrowed brows carved a line across his face. He smoked two packets of cigarettes a day and drank as many bottles of brandy, but still couldn't raise his spirits. He was afraid of reprisals from Nazi hardliners, kidnap by the Soviets, an ultimatum from the British wanting the inventors of the V2 to pay the price for the devastation of the London bombings, a shift of opinion in the United States that would preclude them emigrating there, and plenty of other eventualities. The British government insisted they be tried, and Washington refused entry to anyone implicated in Nazi organisations. In other words, he wasn't welcome in the land of the free, and neither was most of his team.

Von Braun would have liked to leave Germany immediately, but his American partners seemed in far less of a hurry than he was. He also wanted to know what would happen to his ageing parents. He had asked to take them with him, and the American authorities had not yet replied; he had even been refused permission to visit them, which was making him ill with worry. His new allies were putting him to the test and savouring the capture of their prize. During the surrender negotiations with his future employers, he had revealed the secret location of fourteen tonnes of plans and drawings that his team had compiled while they designed and developed the V2. The GIs managed to recover this precious documentation from a disused tunnel at the very last moment. The Russians were furious to have been outplayed in territory that they had identified as theirs since the Yalta Conference, and the Americans, proud of this coup, ensured that news of their agreement with von Braun was broadcast far and wide. Press correspondents of every nationality arrived in the picture-postcard Bavarian village. Belted into a black mackintosh, von Braun, the most sought-after scientist of the now-defunct Third Reich, still had his arm held out in front of him in plaster so that, with unintentional irony, he permanently appeared to be in the process of making a Nazi salute. The journalists photographed his tall figure, fattened by weeks of forced inactivity. He smoked with his free hand and never stopped smiling. Beside him was Johann Zilch and a dark-haired young woman with mistrustful eyes, tightly clasping a chubby-cheeked baby.

Some members of the team took the Reich's humiliation very badly, but not von Braun. He swept about the place like a carefree and affable celebrity. He might have been Rita Hayworth visiting the troops on the front. He shook hands, posed for photographs, and exchanged niceties. He boasted about the significance of his inventions, and already talked of flying to the moon. Some people struggled to believe that this thirty-three-year-old Prussian with his Hollywood-idol looks and his overfondness for food could have created the most feared weapon of the war. The British soldiers were ashen-faced, probably recalling the Blitz. Some had lost friends and family, buried beneath the rubble of their capital which had been crushed by missiles. Those events were years ago, but was it because he could sense this animosity that the scientist was so fretful? He tried everything in his power to be well disposed towards the soldiers on whom his future, and the future of those close to him, depended. But he didn't succeed.

After the team's surrender, its relationship with the American authorities cooled. For three months von Braun, Zilch and their colleagues were duly interrogated by a committee of Allied experts. Military engineers rushed to Bavaria took on the task of transferring the technology to the Texan base where the scientists were to be sent, while senior-ranking officers evaluated the extent of their Nazi convictions, the gravity of their crimes and their potential compatibility with the American way of life. The wives were also interviewed in their husbands' presence. There was no question of allowing fanatics to raise budding Hitlers in the home of the brave. Still less of allowing 'reds' to contaminate Uncle Sam. Very many were called forward but only a few were chosen, and each case had to be negotiated.

Von Braun wanted to take Marthe with him: she was his interpreter, and he trusted her judgement and appreciated her candour. She might prove useful in their new life. Besides, Marthe was passionately attached to Werner. Von Braun thought of the child as his godson and had misgivings about separating him from his aunt, given how little affection Johann showed him. After giving the matter careful thought, he decided that, thanks to the administrative mayhem caused by the war, he could pass her off as Johann's wife. None of the Allies would guess that Luisa had been killed in Dresden, and von Braun knew the team wouldn't betray him – out of loyalty but also because they liked Marthe. They had thought it very brave of her to set off by bicycle with Magnus to make first contact with the Americans, and several of them were also susceptible to her charms. The women in the group were less kindly disposed towards her, but von Braun had worked on bringing them to heel. The nurse was now called Luisa, and anyone who did not comply would fall foul of him. The message was clear. Only Friedrich, still besotted with Marthe alias Luisa, continued to stumble over her name. He had proposed marriage to her and she had considered it, but the possibility that the Allies might not allow the marriage and could then forbid her from travelling to the United States had dissuaded her. What she really feared was that, if she accepted Friedrich's proposal, Johann might want to take his son. She felt it safer to pass herself off as Luisa.

Von Braun made an official request to include Marthe in the first group heading for the United States. She was summoned with Johann, and Marthe scored several points during the hearing. She put on quite a performance to woo the Texan officer and the regular soldier, of Mexican origins, who questioned them. Apparently instinctively aware of who was in a position of authority, Werner joined her in shamelessly charming Captain Flickson, showering him with smiles and ecstatic eye contact as if this grim man were the holiest man alive. Meanwhile, Marthe hypnotised him with her topaz eyes. She said she'd dreamed of living in America since she was a little girl. As a teenager she'd listened to jazz all day – Billie Holiday, Louis Armstrong, Duke Ellington – and she confessed how she despaired the day Goebbels banned this 'degenerate' music. She'd buried her record collection in her parents' garden – alas, her parents were now dead – in the hope that one day she could take this precious stash back out of hiding. She claimed to be crazy about Coca-Cola, that there was no vacuum cleaner more efficient than a Hoover nor any car more beautiful than a Ford. She hoped she would soon be able to take her son to see Walt Disney's *Snow White* 'at the movies'. She continued her declaration of love for the American dream by singing, in a pretty voice but with a strong German accent, a few bars from *Jezebel*, Bette Davis's last film which she had seen before the war. This questionable rendition provoked a peal of laughter from Werner and consternation from Johann.

Next, Marthe gazed lovingly at the baby, and said she wanted a wonderful future for her son, far from the violence and hatred that were ripping the Old Continent apart. She wanted him to grow up in a country where ambition was encouraged and hard work rewarded. A land of tolerance that gave the same opportunities to people, whatever their origins . . . Hearing this, the Latin American soldier recording the meeting nearly choked. He who was lumbered with all the regiment's thankless tasks and whom the others called 'Sergeant Garcia' because they claimed he looked like Zorro's enemy, he could have told her a few downsides, but his coughing fit didn't stop Marthe's enthusiastic tirade.

Captain Flickson seemed to be won over. The other scientists in the group showed themselves off in their best light, but their efforts were far from enough. Welcoming Nazis onto American soil was no simple feat. If President Roosevelt or the Senate had been informed of a project which consisted of bringing von Braun's team to the United States, they would most likely have flatly refused to take in these refugee scientists. But the American secret services were not prepared to hand such a catch over to the Soviets. They arranged an extensive rewrite of the scientists' career histories. In a few weeks these valuable brains would no longer have anything to be ashamed of.

Von Braun left first, with Johann and a small entourage. After this, came two further groups. Under cover of extreme secrecy, one hundred and seventeen scientists, accompanied by close family, took planes and then boats to the North American continent. Eisenhower may have broadcast the inventors' surrender, but on this occasion journalists were painstakingly kept away from the transfer. And so it was that without visas and mostly without passports, the V2 team embarked for Texas, their only guarantee a one-year work contract with no specific remit or mission. Marthe and Werner were among the passengers.

Manhattan, 1970

Naturally, I avenged myself. I slept with one of Rebecca's cousins to be sure she heard about it; with a girl I didn't even like just because she'd been a schoolfriend of hers; and, most importantly, with a Mexican-born folk singer who was a big hit. I wanted every family gathering to remind her I existed, every social occasion to make her run the risk of bumping into me on another woman's arm, every magazine to be a bomb ready to explode in her face. I was in the headlines of everything that mattered in New York with a picture of me kissing Joan full on the lips taken after one of her concerts. On paper we looked very much in love. The businessman – as I was now called – and the singer, the blond giant and the beautiful brunette: people liked the story. The paparazzi called me by my name, and didn't bother to hide. My mother, Armande, was in heaven, collecting every scrap of newspaper that mentioned me, and her friends in Hawthorne took it upon themselves to give her any she might have missed. Although more discreet, my father was just as proud. Even my sister, a virtual recluse in the depths of a hippie commune in California, called me. She'd come across an article all about me when using an old newspaper to wrap the carrots she was going to sell in the market with her long-haired friends and, although she deemed my life too materialistic, she'd felt the need to call.

All anyone could talk about was me but I was still invisible as far as the Lynches were concerned. None of my provocations produced a reaction from Rebecca. I didn't come across her once in eleven months. No one knew where she was; the love of my life had evaporated. When I wasn't trying to forget her in other women's arms, I worked day and night, tortured by bitterness, prepared to do whatever it took to equal the Lynches and show Rebecca what she'd lost.

Outwardly I was fine, but the distress I managed to dispel by day came back to haunt me at night. I started having the same dream that had hounded me for years as a child, one that always left me feeling terribly sad. It was a dream of two halves that didn't appear to be linked. First I saw a very beautiful blonde woman running and, some fifty strides later, I saw her fall. She was thrown to the ground by an invisible force and then flipped savagely onto her back. I went over to her and she spoke to me. Her huge, ethereal, dark-blue eyes seemed to absorb me. She looked at me very tenderly and said things that I understood in the dream but couldn't put into words once I woke. Then I was in a completely different place, tearing myself away from the world to watch it disintegrate. I had no physical sensations: I could see fire but not feel its heat, see people screaming but not hear their cries. I watched buildings collapse but their dust didn't fill my mouth. Fragments of masonry flew in every direction but never struck me. I couldn't say how old I was in the dream, nor whether I was sitting, standing or lying down. Still less whether I was alive or already dead. After a while a noise grew louder, and I realised that the appalling clamour of the apocalypse wasn't reaching me because it was smothered by this whirling, thumping sound all around me. A noise circling me. At some points it pulsed and raced, completely deafening me. I didn't panic, I became conscious of myself. I was completely surrounded by red, as if the blood of all those victims was spattered over the whole world, as if I were deep inside their organs. Through the membranes I could see orangey lights, veils being torn, then a vast vault, splashes of red and white. The swirling sound dropped away and I was sad to leave it behind. Screams pierced my ears. Something burned my lungs like acid or toxic fumes. I heard explosions. The earth opened up and humanity seemed to disappear into it, swallowed up. It was when all life had ceased to be, when every bird, river, breath of wind, animal and human had fallen silent that I understood the absolute solitude of my situation. And that was when I would wake with a cry.

When we slept together Joan would soothe me as best she could. She helped me understand my feelings. The sense of abandonment drove me almost to distraction, and she listened to me talk about Rebecca for hours. She worried about my problems as if we were long-standing friends, as if my obsession with Rebecca were just another topic among many that didn't affect her. She never showed it, but I know it hurt her to be in competition with a ghost she could never fight. She was right. Everything I did was aimed at or against Rebecca. Joan was a great girl: intelligent, sexy, tender, funny . . . I should have been crazy about her, but Rebecca had made me lose the old me. I slept with other women without feeling any emotion or passion, at best momentary relief.

One weekend I tried to take refuge at my parents' house, hoping to find some calm and peace of mind in my childhood home. I felt even worse there than in the tumult of Manhattan. I loved Armande and Andrew, but I didn't understand them. They always seemed to be apologising for being alive. I had kept a spectacular downtown apartment for them in one of our construction projects but they refused to live in it and chose instead to rent it out. I suspected my mother was responsible for this decision: she was a jealous woman, and was most likely afraid my father would use it for romantic assignations. She had spent so many years supporting him and watching over him that she couldn't let go. They claimed that they had their friends and their garden in Hawthorne. I gave them an annuity which my mother scrupulously ensured my father didn't spend. Still, he had managed to buy himself a beautiful car, his little weakness.

He may have placed slightly larger stakes on the rummy, had a few fine suits, but Armande still rationed him. She refused to have a cleaner, claiming that the upkeep of the house kept her figure trim. I told her that with the money I gave them she could afford gym classes but she thought it would be 'ridiculous' at her age to 'waggle her legs in her living room and jiggle about to young people's music'. I would have liked them to discover luxuries, to come and move in near me and shake up their old habits. Joan told me that in trying to be generous, I was being selfish. They liked their day-to-day life, the house they'd spent years paying off, their garden where Lauren and I grew up.

'You want to make them happy,' she said, 'but you're invalidating what they've built up. You're trying to write off a life's work with one cheque.'

Their modesty produced mixed emotions in me. I felt guilty for moving away from them when they'd given me everything with such generosity, but at the same time I couldn't help feeling a sort of resentment.

By leaving me, Rebecca had shown she thought me unworthy of her, and had sent me back to my social class, my inadequate education, my ignorance of the codes that so ably protected her world. I was angry with her, with myself and, although I knew how unfair this was, I was also angry with my parents for not making me Rebecca's equal. I illogically felt it was their fault, and their unwillingness to change the little habits that anchored them so firmly in the humdrum life that I was struggling to leave behind sickened me. I couldn't help pointing this out to them and, the next minute, I couldn't help hating myself for being so ungrateful. Then I would try to redeem myself by arranging surprises for them. Having sent them on a trip to visit my sister in California, I took their house in hand: no fewer than ten workmen came over in their absence. I had an automatic gate installed and an electric door for the garage so my father no longer had to get out of the car and hurt his back turning the crank handle. I had the bathroom and kitchen renovated, and the living room and dining room repainted. I bought them a water bed, again for my father's back, then I created a laundry room – something my mother had wanted for a long time – in the old lean-to next to the house. Transformed into a proper room with two windows, it now housed a brand-new washing machine, a tumble-dryer, a professional pressing iron for sheets and a real sewing workroom. One whole wall was filled with a rainbow of cotton reels, and another with shelves of fabrics arranged by colour. A desk acted as a stand for the very latest Singer sewing machine. In drawers divided into sections by wooden partitions were braids, elastic, buttons, lace, ribbons, scissors and everything a seamstress could wish for. Donna, who helped me with the project, had even bought a dressmaker's dummy, and a large table for pattern-cutting.

I couldn't wait to see their reaction and went to pick them up at the airport. They were quite surprised to see me there, and I insisted on driving them home myself. Thrown by the new gateway, my father thought I'd taken them to the wrong address for a moment. He was delighted with this innovation and even more enthusiastic when he saw the garage door. My mother's first reaction, on the other hand, was to fly into a temper.

'You're crazy to spend all that money! You're completely out of your mind!'

She didn't stop complaining the whole time we looked around the house. She couldn't understand the new cooker at all, a fridge like that for two people, honestly, it was too big . . . And where would they store the wood in winter now they didn't have the lean-to? Her comments put me in a terrible mood. I wanted her to throw her arms around me and show me how happy she was, but she was too embarrassed to do that.

However many times I told her I had money enough to live my life twice over, and if I sold the buildings that Z & H owned, my assets turned into dollar bills could fill her whole house, she still didn't believe me. She thought I was making it all up or the buildings wouldn't sell, or that it was Marcus's money, not mine. My father had tried to explain to her, no more successfully than me. He was not much more expansive than my mother, but he didn't lecture me.

'Thanks, son, it's very good of you to take care of us,' he reassured me. 'But you're very busy, don't worry about us, we have everything we need, you know.'

His modesty stung me. I wished he was flamboyant and asked me for more. I wished I wasn't building on a vacuum, for no one but myself, for nothing.

I trailed my anger and melancholy around like a ball and chain. Nothing felt the same since Rebecca had left me. I was sickened by the way she'd treated me. A year of perfect love, a year of tender words and plans had evaporated in one evening. I'd called her parents' house the very next day after that dinner, but the housekeeper picked up. I took to calling a hundred times a day. Literally. It was always the same woman who replied. I yelled at her the way I'd learned to ball out site managers. It reduced her to tears. Her professional conscience forced her to pick up, and I just kept on calling. She told me the Lynches were not in New York, she didn't know where Miss Rebecca had gone, she begged me to stop. After two weeks of this treatment, she eventually abandoned her principles and unplugged the telephone.

Then I turned up at the Lynches' front door and rang the bell a hundred times too, but the butler spotted me through the window and was careful not to open up. Furious, I destroyed my fists and my shoes pounding on the thick wood of the door. When I started vandalising the hedges around the house with my bare hands and breaking ground-floor windows with my elbows, he called the police. I refused to leave and it took four officers to haul me away. Assaulting a police officer, refusal to comply with a police officer, violation of property . . . If it weren't for Marcus, they'd have been only too happy to keep me in a cell for three days. With his characteristic intuition, my friend had the excellent idea of telling Lieutenant O'Leary about my broken heart. The big softie had been dumped by his wife only weeks earlier. Without even realising it, he found he was telling Marcus his life story over a bottle of Redbreast. Whenever one of his underlings knocked at the door to his office, he sent him away with a torrent of abuse so rude it would make his inmates blush. Heartache, the real sort, not just bruised egos or a rush of possessiveness, that was something O'Leary knew all about. The man secretly admired me for daring to do what he had forbidden himself. He too wanted to smash his mother-in-law's windows. She was a bitch and had done everything she could to separate him from Maggie right from the start. Marcus depicted me as a young man with a great future, hopelessly in love and sneered at by a powerful family. An unspoken sympathy trickled my way. When the bottle and the reminiscences were finished, a slurred and bleary O'Leary agreed to release me on condition that Marcus promised not to let me go anywhere near the Lynches' home.

Marcus asked to see me and, poker-faced, he gave me a lecture that was addressed more to the police officer than to me. I promised Marcus I wouldn't go back to Rebecca's house if he agreed to ask his father to call all the Lynch residences to locate them. He agreed and I walked free with a hearty pat on the shoulder from an emotional O'Leary.

'Away you go, young'un,' he growled. 'You hang tough. And don't do anything dumb again.'

I watched my step and, as agreed, Marcus asked his father to investigate Rebecca's and her parents' disappearance. Frank Howard left messages in all their properties, but he came up against the same silence as I had. The family had left the country and no one could understand why. All of New York was filled with cold and loneliness.

I wondered whether Rebecca was still alive. A month after she vanished I went to The Factory: when we'd been together she went there a lot for her work, to see what Andy was doing, feature in his films, show her paintings, see other people's art and discuss techniques. I'd always refused to go with her, the place was full of weirdos. I found them slightly ridiculous and was jealous of the close connection she had with them. I wanted her all to myself. If I could, I'd have put her under lock and key. Warhol's studio was a strange, almost disturbing place: you got up to higher floors on a freight elevator with rusted grating and a floor of patched, graffitied metal that didn't inspire confidence. Shakespeare and I opted to take the stairs. An insistent trumpet and shrill piano notes tumbled down through the floors. I reached the fifth floor which was one huge space; the brick walls were painted silver, and the supporting iron columns as well as any pipework were covered in aluminium foil. The floor was plain grey concrete.

I was greeted by a blonde drag queen in hot-pants. Intrigued by this woman with a man's voice, Shakespeare wanted to know what he was dealing with and unceremoniously poked his nose between the creature's buttocks. She was startled but then turned to stroke him.

'So, cutie-pie,' she cooed in a husky voice, 'getting your facts straight?'

I turned about as red as the sprawling sofa dominating the middle of the studio. I pulled on Shakespeare's collar and mumbled my apologies. The drag queen, who had more make-up on than a stolen car, looked me up and down languidly.

'Don't you worry. He was very gentle . . . and I like gentleness . . .' she said meaningfully.

'I'm looking for Rebecca,' I said almost apologetically.

'The beautiful Rebecca! She's not here, gorgeous, but if you want another blonde as consolation, I can suggest . . .'

I went from red to scarlet and didn't answer.

'You're the shy type, I can tell. Would you like a drink? I have coffee or tequila.'

I accepted the offer of coffee and she went to make it in a corner of the room. Half of a chrome-coloured fashion mannequin leant up against a rack of warehouse shelving that was used as a wardrobe. In front of the sofa a lamp shaped like a wide-brimmed hat and inlaid with flashing reflective glass served as a coffee table. Easels spattered with paint were dotted about among rickety wooden tables covered with drawings, fragments of canvas, pieces of cardboard and broken toys. Large paintings of stylised flowers in childish colours were laid out over the floor. The space was divided into sections by sheets hanging over ropes and the look was completed by metal and Formica chairs and sagging armchairs.

The drag queen handed me my coffee in an old mustard jar and showed me the corner where Rebecca used to work. Her paintbrushes had dried out in the dregs of some turpentine. Dozens of canvases leant against the wall. Her paint-spattered denim overall lay over a wooden chair splashed with myriad flecks of colour. On the easel stood one unfinished work. My heart constricted when I recognised myself, seen from behind, standing naked looking out over the city, with my arms spread out to welcome the rising sun, a stance she had often teased me about. After taking my shower in the morning and before getting dressed, I had a habit of opening the curtains wide and greeting the cityscape with a resounding 'Good morning, world', which amused her. It was troubling to see that she'd painted this scene.

I wanted to buy Rebecca's paintings. Warhol himself wasn't there: he'd launched into a tour of Europe to paint portraits of anyone on the Old Continent who could sign a fat cheque. The drag queen who'd played host to me and was 'holding the fort' didn't put up any resistance to the acquisition. She sold these items that didn't really belong to her and pocketed a wedge of bills without negotiating or counting, too glad that, the moment

I'd left, she could go down and buy herself an instant trip to a world of augmented reality. Drugs were the fuel for New York in general and The Factory in particular. The luckiest of Andy's guests left his studio in limousines, the others in ambulances.

I arrived home with about twenty paintings and two boxes bulging with drawings, and crammed them into my small bedroom. Marcus thought it showed a lack of consideration for Joan, and I told him she would never know. She rarely came to the apartment, anyway – I found it difficult seeing her where Rebecca had once been, and preferred her lovely house full of flowers and herbs, only a few streets away. Marcus couldn't understand why I was so fixated on Rebecca. For so long I'd displayed total cynicism about the fairer sex, so he hadn't given up hope of seeing me revert to this mindset. He introduced me to ravishing replacements, and I made good use of them but never formed any attachment. For the first time in my life I felt guilty: as I suffered from Rebecca's absence, I understood Joan's unvoiced hurt, Joan who was so kind to me and complained so little. She was very astute and knew perfectly well I wasn't faithful to her in body or in spirit. I was ashamed that I wasn't capable of loving her as she deserved to be loved. She should probably have been tougher with me, given me a bit of a hard time . . . A woman's indulgence cements habits, but it's not a powerful foundation for love.

I hated myself for being obsessed with Rebecca. I wished I could stamp out my feelings but they seemed to be indestructible. The city had become a hostile place for me: at any time, a place, a song or an image could pierce my heart and leave me gasping alone in the street, waiting for the wave of pain to change frequency so that I could continue on my way. I was appalled by my impotence: I'd tried everything in my power to wipe this woman from the map of my life, but she had marked it with indelible ink.

*

Only dogged work allowed me to forget her. The energy I put into it paid out beyond my hopes: the first seafront buildings were nearing completion and Z & H was now raking in a fortune. After celebrating our first million, then our second, we'd progressed to tens of millions. The knock-on effect was incredible, with every profit reinvested thanks to state-set zero interest rates. As Frank Howard had said, to make a large fortune you have to steal the first million. We were now making our fortune thanks to the city council, and it was perfectly legal. In this rapidly expanding market, public authority guarantees meant we could finance our reckless real-estate ventures with no costs and almost no risk. Of course, our work was helping to regenerate the city, bring neighbourhoods back to life and offer solutions to the housing shortage, but we were pocketing staggering profits.

We restricted ourselves essentially to Manhattan and the safer neighbourhoods in its immediate vicinity. We carefully avoided Mafia territory but still had to grease the palms of countless minor administrators and pen-pushers. In order to reign you have to share, which is always easier when your 'gifts' don't eat into your own lifestyle. There was only one town councillor for whom I still bore a grudge: the Brooklyn Borough president. He'd come all too willingly to enjoy the sound of his own voice at the inauguration of our first building, the place where I'd kissed Rebecca for the first time. He'd cut the red ribbon, drunk my champagne and then still he'd had the nerve to ask for further sweeteners. The moron. He should have guessed I wouldn't let him humiliate me without retaliating after the way he'd treated us.

When, a few days later, he came to claim the apartment he'd extorted from us, I took no small pleasure in personally escorting him on a visit of the property. I took him to the top floor and, as we stood outside the reinforced door, I handed him the key to his asset on a length of ribbon. Oh, his face when he opened the door and found he was . . . out on the roof! It took him a while to understand. I had to ram his contract in his face: his front-man was unquestionably in possession of a plot *to be constructed* on the top floor of the building. Marcus had adroitly omitted the clause concerning the completion date for the apartment and, playing on this nuance, I had simply shaved one floor off our build. Yes, co-ownership laws meant it would be possible to add another floor, but on condition of achieving a majority vote at the next owners' meeting. Realising he'd been played, he succumbed to a very gratifying outburst, and I did nothing to appease his anger. Quite the opposite, in fact: I told him that his deputy, to whom I was not in the least kindly disposed, had been given the keys to his studio that same morning. This priceless satisfaction totally compromised Z & H's chances of securing public contracts in Brooklyn, but Marcus circumvented the problem by setting up a buffer company. Meanwhile, I dug the knife deeper into my enemy by giving massive financial support to his adversary's political campaign. He lost his mandate at the next election. I was there on the day that power was handed over and it gave me extra satisfaction seeing his face fall when he had to be civil to me.

Success breeds success, and we were now handling about fifteen sites at once. The city was covered with tarpaulins imprinted with the name Z & H. We'd taken over handsome offices on Broadway, not far from the apartment, and Donna now presided over a small team of three secretaries, an architect and five project managers. Frank Howard still helped us on the more prestigious buildings, but we'd made a name for ourselves and established our independence. Even so, I still refused to move out of the apartment, and although Marcus was tired of being 'cramped in this hovel', he couldn't bring himself to leave me there on my own. I still clung to the idea that Rebecca would want to see me again.

'She can just call the office! The name Z & H is plastered all over town on our scaffolding. You might as well have a poster campaign saying "Rebecca, call me".'

'It's very important for work . . .' I said defensively.

'I'm not denying that,' Marcus conceded, 'but I know you, Wern. I know why you were so keen to have all those tarpaulins printed with our address and phone number . . .'

Marcus was right. I still hoped Rebecca would turn up one day unannounced. With a hell of a good excuse which would make it easy for me to forgive her betrayal and pick up our relationship exactly where we'd left off. I think I'd have found an actual break-up easier; I'd have been able to hate her without a hidden agenda. But her disappearance left room for doubt and for that bastard – hope – which chains us to the past and won't let us move on.

After months with no news, I played my last card. We'd decided to celebrate the completion of our most substantial project. The great and the good of New York were invited to the inauguration of the Z & H Center. The highlight of the evening was that Joan had agreed to perform. I signed a very fat cheque for her charity which helped destitute children in Mexico. She would have sung anyway, but I needed to get myself off the hook, because the event revolved entirely around Rebecca. The invitation card, sent to 1,500 people, featured one of her works: the triptych she had painted for the lobby of our first buildings in Brooklyn. It was a view of Manhattan bay in a poetic, abstract mist – a cruel reminder of our first dinner together. Inside the card, Marcus Howard and Werner Zilch hoped 'Mr and Mrs X would do them the honour of attending the inauguration of the Z & H Center and the opening night of an exhibition of works by Rebecca Lynch'. An exclusive concert by Joan, at 9.30, would be followed by a 'violet reception', with a dress code to match. The colour of Rebecca's eyes had inspired the theme for the party. For the first time since she'd disappeared, the twenty-odd paintings and the drawings I'd bought at The Factory would be shown in public.

The two weeks leading up to the event were difficult for me. Every day I hoped to receive a call from my missing artist, even if only to hurl insults at me for organising an exhibition without her permission. I'd envisaged every possible reaction from Rebecca: angry but touched; angry and shrouded in silence; happy and showing up; happy but too proud to call me; still somewhere abroad and unaware; now amnesiac; married and pregnant; having a mystic crisis and recovering in an ashram; kidnapped by white-slave traders . . . and a hundred other hypotheses, each one followed by a thousand outlandish ramifications that tested Marcus and Donna's tolerance levels. Marcus no longer recognised me. He'd got along very well with Rebecca and, like me, was concerned about her inexplicable disappearance, but he was also very fond of Joan, and his fatalistic attitude didn't sit comfortably with my obsession. Marcus called Lauren to come to his aid.

My sister had started studying at Berkeley four years earlier, only to abandon university to live in a commune. Along with about twenty friends, she had bought a ranch near Novato, an hour from San Francisco. They raised hens, goats and sheep, practised yoga and meditation, and all cooked and made love together. They tended their vegetables, washed their clothes in the river and, the rest of the time, smoked cannabis that they grew themselves. This cultivation had started with two plants that one member of the commune had brought back from Mexico, hidden in a bag of dirty laundry with such a horrifying smell that the customs officer had been dissuaded from sniffing through it. The male plant was baptised 'Robert' and the female 'Bertha', before they were solemnly planted on the edge of the chicken coop out of reach of the goats. Robert and Bertha brought forth an abundance of offspring, and the members of the commune – inveterate smokers every one – attributed a name to each new seedling to express their gratitude to these divine plants. They now had the complete genealogy of this cannabis family, which was embellished with psychedelic drawings and pinned up in the kitchen.

Their experimenting didn't stop there. One member of the group had studied chemistry at Berkeley and had briefly worked in the pharmaceuticals industry before feeling the need – when he was fired for making too liberal use of the company's products – to build a life full of meaning, in harmony with nature. Thanks to his inventiveness, the commune tried out all sorts of concoctions, produced using a variety of stills in an old larder next to the kitchen. 'Gateways to Light' were meant to help them reach new heights of wisdom and understanding of the world. Once a substance was approved by the commune, it was then sold to young executives in San Francisco as the best way to open their minds to the world and, by giving them access to full consciousness, prepare them for the Love Revolution. The first two generations of Gateways to Light were very successful and pleasingly subsidised the commune's income, but things soured with the third generation. These concoctions were undeniably potent but they had side effects: paranoid episodes and bouts of aggression. The group felt that everyone needed to be purged of his or her latent violence; this was indispensable to the Love Revolution, so they increased their consumption of the new Gateways to Light so that they could get through this difficult but salutary phase more quickly.

Lauren thought her final hour had come when the chemist, on a headlong downer, tried to strangle her. Her experience of imminent death proved revelatory, and she no longer felt she had the strength to be a soldier of Love. Ashamed but determined, she acknowledged her mystic failure before the whole commune, assembled under the sequoia that presided over their weekly meetings. The other members of the group were afraid her lack of faith and courage might contaminate them and voted unanimously for her to leave.

My sister had given herself, body and soul, to the group which she thought of as her family, and she felt they were disowning her at the first sign of weakness. She was very depressed and was contemplating calling our parents to go back home to Hawthorne and reinvent herself. She didn't contact me. I'd financed her share of the ranch, and she knew what it had cost me at a time when I had almost nothing, so she didn't dare admit to me that her experiment had come to an abrupt end.

When Marcus called her for help, giving her an alarming description of my mental state, her reluctance evaporated. My sister, a genuinely generous soul, liked nothing better than helping other people, and me in particular. She was broke so Marcus sent her a postal order for a substantial sum to pay for her journey. The commune got wind of this, and asked for financial compensation for her 'unforgivable desertion'. Lauren didn't dare claim back the money she'd invested in buying this ranch from which she was being expelled, and was fleeced out of what Marcus had sent her into the bargain. They left her with the bare minimum to pay for her travel by bus and for food during this cross-continental trip.

Lauren, who never bothered with practical or material considerations, didn't let anyone know when she would arrive. It must have been six in the morning when I heard the doorbell. Instantly awake and fired by a huge feeling of hope, I didn't even take the time to put on a T-shirt, and leapt down to the door in just four strides, ready to take Rebecca in a passionate embrace. When I saw my sister in her clumsily dyed dress, with an embroidered headband in her hair and filthy sandals on her feet, my disappointment must have been clear to see.

'Expecting someone?' she asked.

I muttered a 'Not at all' and took my sister in my arms, an affectionate impulse that I soon cut dead.

'Lauren, you stink! You smell like an old goat!' I protested. Shakespeare didn't appear to be so disgusted and, after he'd made a ridiculous fuss of Lauren, he conscientiously sniffed her feet and, if I hadn't held him back by the collar, would have done the same between her legs. Instead he made do with Lauren's bags which he inspected thoroughly.

'Perfumes are full of harmful chemicals,' Lauren told me when I reiterated my complaint.

'Just wash with soap and water for a start, and that'll be enough for me,' I said.

I picked up her two huge canvas bags, and wondered how she'd managed to carry such a heavy load of junk by herself. Marcus, who'd taken the time to get dressed, appeared at this point. He wanted to hug Lauren but I dissuaded him.

'Believe me, you'd do better to wait till she's showered.'

I didn't give my sister time to sit down and have a coffee but bundled her straight into the bathroom.

'Pass me your clothes, I'll take your stuff down to the cleaner. He opens at seven.'

Lauren did as she was told and while Marcus made breakfast, I took all my sister's things to the Chinese man we used for our laundry. Although very professional, he seemed staggered by how dirty it all was. I came back with still-warm cinnamon rolls and blueberry muffins. Lauren emerged from her shower, draped in a large towel and with her hair still wet.

'I can kiss you now!' said Marcus, and he gave her a long hug.

'That's enough, you two!' I said, going off to get a shirt for Lauren from my closet.

Marcus completed the outfit with a pair of thermals he used for skiing in Aspen. We had a slow breakfast during which Lauren told us about what had happened to her. When I heard how she'd been treated, I got on my high horse, but she persuaded me against launching into a punitive expedition in California.

Marcus insisted that, while Lauren looked for somewhere to live, she should move into our old office and our new lives.

My sister had hard-and-fast ideas about pretty much everything. I told her about my broken heart and, seeing me so devastated by losing Rebecca when I had 'every reason to be happy', she decided to take me in hand. My happiness and mental balance became her mission and her purpose in life, a way of transforming her doubts into certainties. In three weeks she reorganised our day-to-day lives, starting with the food we ate. When we didn't eat in restaurants, Marcus and I fed ourselves on pasta, pizzas, hamburgers, fries or bagels – both sweet and savoury. Lauren was horrified by our diet, which delighted me: I'd watched my mother cook as a child and thought of cooking as being an innate female quality. I was distinctly less enthusiastic when she decided to ban meat, and replaced it with a sort of tasteless paste called tofu. Then she embarked on a merciless campaign to convert us to vegetarianism. Animal protein 'polluted our bodies and minds', and she rebelled against the cruel and pointless slaughter necessitated by the 'debauched Western diet'. She even wanted to convert Shakespeare to the soya-based brew, but the dog went on hunger strike for a week.

Lauren also changed the apartment. She bought flowers every day and burned incense that made me feel sick. She put Indian shawls over the sofas, transformed the living room into a Buddhist temple and the kitchen into a plant nursery for strange vegetables and a storeroom for grains and spices from all over the world. When we came home we were greeted by a smell of curry, and we ate so much of the stuff I even felt my skin was impregnated with the smell. Joan confirmed that yes, I did have a little whiff of cumin and turmeric, which wasn't at all unpleasant. She seemed to be very happy about these changes and endlessly discussed menus and politics with Lauren.

Claiming that we were tense and 'in conflict with our emotions', Lauren introduced us to yoga. She put on music by a monk who worried away at the solitary string of his instrument for hours on end. Marcus appeared more receptive than me to this internal adventure, and I thought him shamefully indulgent towards Lauren. Once a day, she made us lie down in the living room, and we had to shut Shakespeare away because he found this very amusing and kept coming and licking our faces. I was particularly unsusceptible to meditation. The slow sibilant voice Lauren affected to encourage us to listen to our breeeeathing, release the muscles in our faaaaaaces, toooooongues, aaaaarms, leeeeegs and our whooooole booooodies made me laugh helplessly. This didn't bother Lauren: she claimed laughter was a therapy in itself. She ended these sessions by striking a Tibetan bowl several times to make it ring and then putting it onto one of our stomachs. When the last reverberation had died away I jumped up to get back to the telephone and pester our builders who never worked fast enough for my tastes. Lauren didn't seem put out by how little impact her methods had on my behaviour and took consolation from Marcus's progress. He bought all the treatises on spirituality she recommended and was soon very knowledgeable on the subject.

This literature may have inspired indifference in me but I quickly got a taste for my sister's massages. A Japanese girlfriend had introduced me to this pleasure a few years earlier but I'd never surrendered myself to professional hands. Lauren had a real gift. She detected painful areas and could ease the knots as if by magic. She was unexpectedly strong and was particularly effective on feet which she claimed could heal almost every part of the body. I didn't understand much about the principles of Chinese medicine that she tried to explain to me, but I went into a blissful state the moment she started work on my toes. Sadly, she also insisted on coating us in a preparation of Ayurvedic herbs that stained clothes and yellowed the enamel in the shower in a single session. I adored my sister but, apart from my parents, there wasn't a person on the planet further removed from me. Happily, there were moments of respite: Lauren regularly disappeared for a day or two to go and play music in squats or to sleep in Central Park. Marcus always worried about these 'eclipses', but Shakespeare and I made the most of them to have a carnivorous blow-out.

New York was full of Flower Power that summer. Young people from all over the country congregated there to thwart the society their parents had built. They summarily rejected capitalism, individualism and the criminal contempt with which we treated our planet. Lauren was an idealist, she rebelled; in other words, she was perfectly in tune with her time, while Marcus and I coped very well with this society which had granted us such a generous existence in such a short space of time.

We glided from one success to the next. The launch party for the Z & H Center brought together the chic, the sexy and the powerful of New York. Lauren kept criticising my 'materialism' and the people I saw: awful influential capitalists, horrible bankers, ambitious upstarts, powerful egotists – in other words, people like me. Only Joan, whose music and militancy she admired, found favour with her. The singer was her idol, an example of the sort of success that could be achieved and how it could be used for good in the world. Despite her criticisms, my sister had a fantastic time at our party. In a lilac-coloured sari, with her brown hair coiled up on her head and her very dark eyes heavily made-up, she looked genuinely Indian. All the guests were dressed in different shades of purple; it was quite a sight. Photographers snapped away constantly, and asked Marcus, Shakespeare and me to pose at the top of the escalators. For the first time in his life, I'd had my dog cleaned in a pet parlour. He was wearing a wide collar in mauve leather, which was actually a woman's belt adapted by Lauren. He greeted new arrivals with a friendly eye and a wag of his tail as if he were hosting the event.

'I have the most sociable dog in New York,' I commented.

'Which compensates a little for your boorishness,' Marcus retorted.

Joan brought the house down. We'd set up a stage in the covered atrium in the centre of the building. Knowing how gentle and shy she was by nature, I was always amazed by the transformation in her when she gave concerts. She could suddenly own the space, be the focus of every eye, hold the crowd. She exuded almost mystic energy and happiness. At the end of the set, performing without the band, she sang an Irish ballad, accompanied only by her own guitar. She created such a sense of intimacy that it felt as if there were only five or six people in the room, when there was a crowd of over a thousand listening to her. For the brief spell of that illusion, we all became friends. Captivated, transported, we all shared in her raw emotion. Joan ended the song with a sustained note that went on for a lifetime, its last reverberations fading into a momentary silence, immediately followed by thunderous applause. I loved those moments of triumph, and almost managed to believe I was in love, but once she had stepped down from her pedestal, Joan reverted to a frank, straightforward woman, and my admiration descended along with her. I hated myself for failing to enjoy my good luck. In her white lace blouse and her bell-bottom pants, with the soft halo of her hair neatly parted, she was a luminously gentle creature. Lauren congratulated her with touching enthusiasm. They could have been sisters; they had the same oval face, big round dark eyes and amber skin. Most of all, they had the same vision of life and of the world.

An acquaintance asked to buy some of Rebecca's paintings, but I refused. Her works seemed a little lost in the vast space and, apart from the occasional art enthusiast, our guests looked at them only half-heartedly. I was nervous. I'd promised Marcus that if Rebecca didn't show up I would erase her from my thoughts once and for all. I'd made up my mind: if this failed,

I would find a new apartment. And I'd made the significant decision to ask Joan if she'd like to move in with me. I admired her, I respected her, and love had done me more harm than good. The sensual brand of friendship I had with Joan seemed like a better way to improve my life. I liked being with her and I persuaded myself that, if I spent more time with her, I'd end up believing in us and really loving her.

While our company enjoyed its triumph that evening, I privately felt that time was ticking by unbearably slowly. Every blonde girl I saw from behind made my heart leap, but not one of them was the girl I was waiting for. I couldn't disguise my impatience or my disappointment. A few minutes before midnight, when our guests started dancing, I gave up and left Marcus to play host alone. Joan didn't want to stay on without me, so I didn't even say goodbye to anyone but simply left with Shakespeare and her. I dropped her outside her house and felt a pang of regret when I saw how hard she was trying to disguise her sadness. Her smile was shaky and her upbeat voice sounded forced. I could have stayed with her but I wouldn't have been able to pretend on that particular evening. I kissed her, told her she was beautiful and that she'd made the evening the success that it was. When she closed the door behind her, I swore to myself that I'd buy her a gorgeous piece of jewellery the next day. It was almost a proposal, after all: I was going to suggest she came to live with me, that was quite something. I should have been over the moon, but all I could think about was my pain. I knew it well, this old wound that had been reopened. I hadn't felt it since I was a teenager, since the times when I'd stay awake all night wondering why my 'real parents' had abandoned me. I was alone and I was lost.

Hawthorne, New Jersey, 1948

Little Werner didn't speak English. Armande, who had waited months for this moment, was in tears. Andrew hugged his wife to him, he was in a state himself. The director of the adoption agency, an abrupt woman with greying chestnut hair, had dropped the child off with them like a parcel.

'I wish you the best of luck,' she'd announced. 'He doesn't understand a thing and he's poisonous.'

The little three-year-old had not displayed the least regret to see the woman leave, but when Andrew tried to take him in his arms with a 'come on, little man', Werner started screaming with such terrifying fervour that Andrew beat a retreat.

'You should try first,' Andrew said. 'A woman's more reassuring.'

Armande had no better success. The child kept calling for his 'mama' with harrowing sobs. It broke her heart. For all those years when she'd hoped for the miracle of birth, Armande had forgotten how absolute a child's despair can be. She felt all the more helpless because the woman from the agency hadn't taken the time to tell them about Werner. She knew nothing of what he liked or what his routine had been. The Goodmans stood outside the Tudor-style house they had bought just after they were married, and the child wouldn't let them touch him. He didn't want them to come near him. To avoid frightening him any further, the apprentice parents left him sitting where he was on the lawn and sat down to watch him. They talked calmly to each other while Werner – tired-looking, red-faced and his chest still shuddering with sobs – toyed distractedly with his feet and peered at them with his pale, mistrustful eyes. They waited for hours. Probably exhausted by the journey and his emotion, the child's eyes drooped and his head nodded. He was on the verge of falling asleep but wouldn't let down his guard.

'He must be hungry, and thirsty,' Armande said. 'I'll get something for him.'

She came back a few minutes later with a tray that she set down between them and the child. When she moved closer to him with a bottle of fruit juice, Werner screamed again.

'Don't be frightened, my baby,' Armande said, backing away. 'Look, I won't come near.'

She went back and sat down next to Andrew.

'How are we going to cope?' she fretted.

'Don't worry, he looks strong.'

This wasn't how he'd pictured their son: this child with his very blond hair and his almost transparent eyes that bore right through them. They'd been warned that the early days would be difficult, but it was only now that Andrew appreciated that. He studied the child. Werner was sturdy and there was an extraordinary intensity to his eyes, as if, inside the young rudiments of his body, his personality was already fully formed and infinitely larger than his outward appearance. The way the little boy could keep them, two adults, at a respectful distance impressed him, moved him. Andrew liked the child. He glanced at Armande who was studying Werner with almost disturbing passion, and he thought everything would be fine.

'Let's try having a taste of your cake. He may want to copy us . . .' he suggested.

They cut slices from the pound cake that Armande had lovingly made the day before, and demonstrated their enjoyment of it with loud exclamations. Werner watched them wide-eyed. They couldn't work out whether he was amazed by their performance or in fact hungry. Armande moved closer to him on all fours. She put the bottle of juice and a plate with a slice of cake next to him. Head lowered, he turned his attention back to his right foot which he was holding in both hands. For several long minutes he didn't make a single move. Andrew had an idea.

'Turn away,' he said. 'If we don't watch him maybe he won't be so shy.'

Andrew turned round and pulled Armande into his arms. They heard a slight sound behind them and Armande wanted to look, but Andrew told her not to.

'Wait, we need to give him time. Everything's going to be fine, darling, relax. He has to get to know us.'

Using the Patek that he had bought in 1943, shortly before he left for Europe, Andrew showed her when she would be allowed to take her first peek. She put her head on her husband's shoulder. After these months of waiting, every minute felt to her like another hour.

Shadows lengthened across the garden until they converged and the last pools of sunlight disappeared from the lawn. There was not a sound from the child now. The hands of the Patek on Andrew's wrist said it was a quarter to seven, and the Goodmans turned round at last: with the empty bottle still in his hands and the teat in his mouth, Werner was lying on his side asleep. The cake had gone.

'Poor baby. He's had it,' whispered Armande.

'Come, let's take him up to his room,' said Andrew, his voice full of emotion.

He picked up the child whose head lolled back in his arms. Werner didn't wake, not even when they undressed him and changed him, shocked to see how soiled he was. They would soon discover that Werner was perfectly potty trained but the woman from the agency had either not wanted or not had the time to worry about his needs, and had put him in a nappy. Werner's skin was very raw, and Armande cleaned him carefully. She'd practised on her neighbours' children so she worked deftly and confidently. She'd been preparing for her son's arrival for a long time, asking for advice from all the best mothers in Hawthorne and reading every book on the subject including Benjamin Spock's *Baby and Child Care*.

There was a whole medicine cabinet devoted to children's ailments, along with baby shampoo that didn't sting eyes, and Palmolive's 'children's' soap, a bottle of sweet almond oil with a picture of a bear on it, talcum powder and plenty of barrier cream. She had it all. A chest of drawers full of bath towels, sheets and embroidered blankets. A hairbrush with very soft bristles, nail clippers with a blue plastic guard. A quantity of nappies and nappy pins that Andrew thought unreasonable. Over the white cot hung a wooden mobile that Armande had made, painted and varnished herself, and in the cot there were already five soft toys: a bear, a rabbit, a felt tortoise, a cat and a pony. She would happily have bought more over the last few weeks to fill the unbearable void, but Andrew had stopped her.

'The place looks like Noah's ark! Leave some room for him. He *will* come. We won't be let down this time.'

Their friends' children were aged between seven and fourteen so they had inherited whole suitcases of clothes. She'd filled two sets of shelves with them. She planned to sew new clothes for her son too, but was pleased she hadn't started before he arrived: Werner looked very big for his age. Andrew had painted the room yellow, and Armande had put two rattan armchairs in there. She could have spent hours watching her little boy sleep. The possessive pronoun had come to her immediately. He was *her* son. *Hers*. She'd waited so long for him!

She wanted to stroke Werner's blond curls which seemed to have a life of their own. To kiss him on his cheeks and the crook of his neck. Squeeze his arms and calves. Tickle him, hear him laugh, take great lungfuls of his child smell and memorise it. Armande had so much love to give him it was stifling her. She was afraid Werner wouldn't let himself be loved. He would have to be won over, of course . . . they would have to earn the first glance, the first word, the first thank you, the first kiss. And so the mother in her stayed walled up and silent. Almost not daring to move for fear of waking him, she savoured the child's sleep which at least allowed her the freedom to feast on him with her eyes.

'He's so beautiful . . .' she murmured.

'Wonderful,' agreed her husband.

Andrew had to be quite high-handed to get Armande downstairs for dinner. She went back upstairs between the quiche and the chicken to check that 'everything was alright', again between the chicken and the remains of the pound cake, then between her cup of tea and tidying the kitchen. As she embarked on her umpteenth trip up the stairs, Andrew caught her arm.

'Leave him to sleep! Everything's fine . . .'

Armande laughed and slipped into her husband's arms.

'I can't believe it . . . He's perfect.'

'Yes, a good strong boy.'

'I can't wait to show him to the Spencers and the Parsons!'

'The person you really want to show him to is that pest Mabel Campbell, go on, admit it . . .' Andrew teased.

'You're not wrong there . . . The look on her face when she sees Werner!'

'She'll be furious. Our boy's so much more beautiful than hers,' Andrew agreed.

They were already feeling more confident. From now on he would be a father and she a mother. They wouldn't be given any more commiserating looks. They wouldn't be asked those questions that cut them like knife wounds: 'So, when are you going to get on with it?' 'Any good news for us at last?' 'Are you pregnant, then?' And she would no longer suffer the disappointment visited on her every month, the indelible stain and indelible condemnation. He would no longer endure his friends' laughter and jokes when they met to play rummy: 'We'll have to teach you how to aim!' 'You don't know what you're doing!'

'I thought they said those French girls know how to go about it . . .' There would be no more fights when, fired up by alcohol and the tension of the game, one of them went too far and Andrew demonstrated his virility by punching him in the face. There would be no more ribbing, no more whispering, or the word they dreaded, the word that snuck along walls and followed them, spreading on the lips of their acquaintances, the word that poisoned their existence: Sterile . . . 'The Goodmans are sterile, you know. It's her of course, it must be! He should never have married a Frenchwoman. No one knew her. God knows what sort of life she had before the war . . . An abortion! Who told you that? No one? Oh, so you're just assuming? But you're bound to be right. Mind you, she's a Catholic . . . and why would you be Catholic unless you have something serious to be forgiven? And that poor man doesn't suspect a thing . . . I thought there was something wrong about her when I first set eyes on her.'

Andrew and Armande sat in the living room that evening and their television – the first in the neighbourhood – stayed off. They drank port and teased each other about how they would bring up Werner. He would be polite and intelligent. He would be sporty and confident. He would do great things . . . They slipped some 45s in the record player and listened to Benny Goodman's 'Memories of You' and Danielle Darrieux's 'Une Charade', the music to which they had had their first kiss, in Lisieux. They danced in each other's arms, slowly, on tiptoe. Before going to bed, they very carefully opened the door to the yellow room where the child who had already changed their lives in the space of a few hours now slept. The Goodmans were the happiest couple in the world that evening.

Manhattan, 1971

Marcus and Lauren came home arm in arm and blind drunk at about four in the morning. In no fit state to find their keys, they rang the doorbell non-stop to drag me out of bed. Having reached my decision about Rebecca, I didn't rush. Shakespeare started barking wildly which made the neighbours yell. After they'd rung about twenty times, I arrived at the door, scowling furiously. My sister was wearing Marcus's jacket and he was hugging her to him and rubbing her back. I unloaded some of my frustration onto them, but they just laughed.

'Exactly as I said!' Lauren trilled to Marcus.

They were completely out of it. I had hardly got back into bed before the idiots thought it very funny to go out and start ringing the bell again. I stormed out of my room like a hurricane, knocking over a chair that Shakespeare narrowly avoided. In my anger, I flung open the door which banged noisily against the wall, but my curses died in my throat when I saw who was standing on my doorstep. It took me a few seconds to understand that this pale tomboy with short purple hair was none other than Rebecca. I recognised her eyes when she turned them on me.

'Come in,' I whispered, shocked.

'Thank you,' she said, slinking along the wall.

Lauren and Marcus, who'd been chatting rowdily in the kitchen, appeared. Their laughter died away when they saw the slight figure with me.

'Rebecca . . .' Marcus stammered.

She gave a smile but said nothing. Shakespeare danced around her, giving her a heartbreaking welcome, then sat on her feet. She stroked his head, her fingers looked translucent. Lauren kissed Rebecca exuberantly and said meaningfully that she'd 'heard a lot about her'. Rebecca smiled again. She looked like a featherless baby bird next to Lauren with her abundant brown hair and generous breasts. I offered her something to eat. She refused. To drink. She refused that too.

'Actually, I'd like to sleep,' she said.

Without miring myself in complications, I showed her to my room.

'Would you like to borrow a nightshirt from Lauren?' I asked.

'I'll stay as I am.'

She simply removed her loafers and curled up on the bed, facing the wall. I lay down too, but didn't dare move close to her.

'Could you take me in your arms please?' she asked.

I drew her to me. She seemed so fragile, as if her every bone might break. There was nothing left of the sumptuous animal I once so loved to dominate. I became aware of her warmth, and breathed in her smell of sweet almond. At least her skin hadn't changed. I tried, slowly, to recognise her, to find the Rebecca I had known. I wanted to ask her questions, ask for an explanation, but she stopped me.

'Please, I'd rather not talk.'

I twisted impatiently but she seemed too frail for me to pressure her.

'We'll do whatever you want, Rebecca,' I said, my voice husky.

'Then hold me,' she asked again, 'and don't let me go.'

'I promise I won't.'

She didn't move all night. She was so silent that several times I put my hand in front of her face to check she was still breathing. My arms were stiff, my neck sore and my legs full of pins and needles, but I didn't change my position. The sun broke over the horizon and the light allowed me to have a better look at her. She was thin, and tired. Dark rings under her eyes carved into her cheeks; and her short, dyed hair accentuated her delicate neck. I lifted her up to extricate my arm and she felt alarmingly light. My comings and goings in the room didn't stir her. I came and lay down next to her again to say goodbye but got no reaction. When I left the room, she moved across the bed into the space I'd left warm, and put her arms lovingly around my pillow.

Following on from the launch of the Z & H Center and the reception — which headlined in a good many newspapers — Marcus and I had scheduled meetings and interviews for the whole day. In the kitchen Lauren was already squeezing oranges and making toast. Despite everything she'd had to drink, she was the picture of health. Compared to the effects of her commune's Gateways to Light, a hangover felt perfectly painless to her. Marcus, on the other hand, was grimacing as he sipped his third cup of black coffee. Pasty-faced and clutching his head, he struggled to regain possession of his faculties. He pushed aside a lock of hair lolling over his eyes.

'My hair hurts,' he complained. 'It sounds weird, but my hair literally hurts . . . it's so painful.'

'Let me do something,' Lauren offered.

She took Marcus's head in her hands and started slowly massaging his temples and scalp. I watched them for a moment then asked for my turn.

'What about me?'

Lauren finished her treatment by touching pressure points on Marcus's face, but when she turned to me, he held her back by the belt of her jeans.

'More, please, I need it more than he does.'

I wasn't feeling that fresh either. I'd spent the night watching Rebecca for fear she would escape while I slept. Lauren bombarded me with questions, but as my sleeping beauty had said no more than twenty words to me between arriving at the apartment and falling into her nocturnal semi-coma, my sister's curiosity wasn't satisfied. Afraid that TLOML – 'The love of his life,' Marcus explained sleepily to Lauren who wasn't familiar with the acronym – might evaporate all over again, I asked Lauren not to let her out of her sight.

'Really. Don't go out without her, even for five minutes, or if you do, lock the apartment . . .'

'Wern! You can't imprison her!' Marcus protested with a burst of energy that drained all his resources. He reached his empty cup towards Lauren as if his life depended on it, and she topped it up with coffee.

'But she asked me not to let her go!' I countered, determined to legitimise my abuses of power over the next twenty years thanks to these unfortunate words Rebecca had uttered in a moment of weakness when we were reunited.

'Don't worry, either of you,' Lauren said, biting into a slice of toast. 'Go make the most of your triumph and your despicable millions. I'll take care of the young lady.'

Marcus muttered indignantly and I retorted we'd more than earned our millions. Unlike some people, we didn't spend our time with a flower between our teeth flirting with people who recited poetry while strumming on a guitar. Marcus agreed with me and Lauren laughed out loud.

'Guys, come on. It's official: you have no sense of humour!' she cried, but her face grew more serious as she added, 'What do I tell Joan if she calls?'

'Say nothing! Nothing at all!' I almost yelled while at the same time Marcus was quite the attorney again with, 'Deny everything!'

'What am I denying?'

'That Rebecca came back. She mustn't know. I'll call her when the time's right.'

'Poor Joan,' Lauren sighed. 'It's sad, I really like her.'

I pretended I didn't hear that.

'Yes, it's terrible. Poor girl, she loves you so much,' Marcus added thoughtfully.

'That's enough, you two! It's not as if I hit her, or killed her!'

They didn't dare reply but their silence hurt me as much as their criticism. We left the apartment unwillingly, Marcus because his every movement was torture and me, because I was afraid Rebecca would use the opportunity to flee. From the very first interviews, with *Village Press* and then the *New York Times*, we were back in the saddle, and the day went by as if in a dream. All my grey matter was absorbed in a succession of calls, interviews and meetings, and the energy I invested in them was a form of armour to stop my feelings diverting my thoughts. At times like that, Z & H proved such a well-oiled machine that I had a strong feeling of perfection and power. We had invented this machine and it worked; and that thought gave me a sense of paternal pride. The success of it made us hungry for more success.

I called Joan when we broke for lunch, and apologised that I wouldn't be seeing her that day. I had a lot to do for Z & H as a follow-on from the reception. Things would soon calm down, I reassured her, and I'd come by to see her the next day or the day after that at the latest. I could hear her concern over the telephone. She was astute and sensitive. My heart constricted when she asked me, not for the first time, whether I would travel to France with her for her European tour. She wanted to be with me when I explored my mother Armande's native country. We'd discussed it several times previously but I'd lost any urge to make the trip. I was as evasive as I could be before saying goodbye. Donna, who came into my office at this point, made an instant diagnosis.

'Now there's a man who feels bad about something.'

I told her that Rebecca was back and she looked terribly sad.

'Poor Joan,' she said. 'She's been dreading this for months . . .'

I took Donna to Tiffany's so she could help me choose a gift. I decided on a pendant of a treble clef in white gold and diamonds with a stone the size of my thumbnail in the middle.

'Poor Joan,' Donna sighed again as she watched me write the last few zeros on the cheque, which totally ruined the effect.

Meanwhile, she nervously fingered the bracelet I'd just given her, 'to buy her approval' as she had said, laughing. That was exactly the case but it was also because I felt it would be tactless to take her to a jeweller without giving her something. I left Tiffany's feeling as guilty as when I went in. The reaction from 'Poor Joan', as everyone had decided to call her that morning, was no more cheerful: the gesture worried her. She revealed the fact under cover of a joke when she called to thank me.

'It's not the first time you've given me a beautiful gift, but I get the feeling this one's all about the past rather than the future . . .'

Joan was right. Rebecca had already reclaimed all her rights over me. I wished I could admit it to her straight away, but I didn't know how. I said the loving words she needed to hear and put off the painful confrontation until another time.

When we arrived home at the end of the day, 'our faces glowed with self-satisfaction', to quote Lauren. I paled when I realised Rebecca was nowhere to be seen, but Lauren didn't give me time to start worrying.

'Your darling's in your room. She's asleep.'

'Still!'

'She got up for an hour, had something to eat, had a shower and went back to bed.'

I half-opened the door to the bedroom and saw Rebecca in the exact position in which I'd left her twelve hours earlier. She'd taken off her T-shirt and jeans in favour of a romantic white nightdress of Lauren's. The oversized garment revealed the delicate bones of one shoulder, and one thin, toned arm. I desperately wanted to wake her, but Lauren stopped me with angry miming, a silent shake of her head reinforced by emphatic finger-wagging, so I withdrew unwillingly. I tried to call the Lynches several times. It was now many weeks since I'd stopped pestering them, and the housekeeper picked up. The halfwit trotted out her usual spiel: The Lynches weren't in New York, she didn't know how to contact Rebecca or where Rebecca was. I replied tartly that *I* knew where Rebecca was.

'If her parents would like to know, they mustn't hesitate to call me,' I added before hanging up.

Lauren and Marcus calmed me with a bottle of wine, some sunflower seeds and grilled peppers that Lauren had made to keep us going before she served up a vegetable-and-cashew nut curry with coconut milk. I was in dire need of meat and potatoes but I'd given up that fight. We ate and drank to our projects and to our friendship, and we also decided not to wait a moment longer before moving out of the apartment.

'At last! It's the high life for us now!' Marcus exclaimed, jumping to his feet in his enthusiasm, grabbing up my sister in his arms and twirling her around.

Lauren struggled, laughing, and he put her back down. He'd clearly forgotten the headache he'd had that morning, and cracked open a second bottle of wine to celebrate this news he'd been waiting months to hear. As happy and carefree as they'd been the night before, he and Lauren went out to see what the city and the night had to offer them.

When I went into my bedroom I made far more noise than was necessary as I got ready for bed. Becca didn't even seem to notice I was there, but the moment I lay down in bed she nestled up against me, fitting between my arms and my legs. My side was framed between her breasts, my hips pressed up to her stomach. She rested against me so trustingly that, again, I didn't dare wake her. I listened to her barely perceptible breathing and drank in the smell of her. She'd washed her hair and it smelled of oats and flowers. Every inch of my body that was in contact with her seemed to have an intensity all its own, an acute presence. My desire for her was a searing pain through my pelvis. A few hours later I was on my back with my eyes wide open. I'd laid Rebecca on my stomach to free up my tired arm. Her legs were either side of me and I could feel the jut of her pubis just above mine. My erection felt like a raised fist.

Hawthorne, New Jersey, 1950

It wasn't love, it was adoration, and Werner made the most of it. Showered with boundless affection, attention and encouragement from the Goodmans, he flourished like an extraordinarily vigorous plant. It took him only a few weeks to understand English perfectly, a few months to speak it. He took possession of the house and garden, and romped exuberantly from one end of his kingdom to another. His parents weren't in their home, they were in his. Nothing could be denied him, and nothing could be out of his reach: he opened cupboards, doors and gates, climbed up to the attic and down to the cellar, and pushed all the boundaries that Andrew and Armande tried to impose on him. The little man was a force of nature: a series of pencil lines on the aquamarine wall facing his parents' bed bore witness to his impressive growth spurts. Armande's gleaming white Singer Featherweight sewing machine whirred away every evening. She took pride in making her son's clothes herself, and his growth rate and adventurous nature meant she had little respite.

Werner's first major show of strength came when he was four years old: he launched into a fight with the neighbours' dog, a temperamental, smelly old mastiff. One day when Werner was trying to expand his play area by exploring bordering territories, the dog bit him. It wasn't a serious bite but it left a clearly defined red semicircle on the child's forearm. In full sight of the astonished neighbour running to help him, Werner Zilch didn't burst into tears or scream for his mother, but looked at his bitten arm in disbelief and threw himself at the dog's head.

'Incredible little guy,' the neighbour would relate later. 'Not only did he attack Roxy who was twice his size, but he bit off part of his ear, just like that, with a snap of his teeth' – and the man would mime the action with his jaw – 'I've never seen anything like it in my life! You don't forget a kid like that. I have to say his mother's quite a number too . . .'

When she saw her darling treasure's arm, already disinfected by the neighbour, Armande gave a scream as terrifying as the roar her son had given moments earlier. She insulted the dog's owner, embracing all the linguistic nuance of her native tongue, and threatened to throttle the dog with her own hands. When the neighbour pointed out a little awkwardly that he'd seen the child bite Roxy, tear off the end of his ear and swallow this scrap of skin whole, Armande reeled. She hurtled off to take her son to the doctor, who tried unsuccessfully to reason with her. He refused to give Werner an emetic, carefully disinfected the wound, gave the child an anti-rabies injection and sent him home. For a whole month, Armande scrutinised her son more closely than a scientist studying bacilli with a microscope. Werner, meanwhile, was in perfect health and far from being 'once bitten, twice shy', he continued his geographical explorations with the neighbour's blessing. As for the dog, whose ear had scarred over but the fur had not grown back, he lay on the ground submissively as soon as the child came into sight.

This victory served only to reinforce Werner's imperious nature. He could be extremely ill-tempered: when his parents or plain reality didn't comply instantly with his wishes, he flew into rages that left Armande speechless. Andrew brought him firmly to heel but secretly took pride in his son's temperament. When father and son were alone, Andrew often picked Werner up under the armpits, raised him above his head, looked him right in the eye and said, 'Be fierce, my son! Be fierce!'

Werner often had to be punished, but he was never resentful. After spending half an hour or an hour locked in his room, he would go back to his activities as if nothing had happened. He didn't apologise but made subtle reparatory gestures: picking flowers for his mother, finding a gleaming crow's feather so black it was almost purple, or a beautiful pebble from the garden for his father. Werner was prepared to go to considerable lengths so long as his pride remained intact. Some parents would have wanted to quell him, but the Goodmans immediately knew that unconditional love would be the key to allowing their son to thrive, and having him in their lives had already brought them such joy that they were inclined to indulge him in every way. One sign of their boundless affection was that it was Werner who changed their name rather than the other way around.

The day after Werner arrived, Armande looked through the one small bag of clothes that the agency had dropped off with him, and noticed that embroidered on every item of clothing were the words: 'This child's name is Werner Zilch. Don't change his name, he's the last of our kind.' This mysterious discovery perplexed Andrew and Armande. They speculated endlessly about it, and tried many times to glean more information from the agency. Battle weary and with a sort of reverence for the extraordinary gift of this child that life had given them, they didn't change his first name. His family name was more problematic. Armande was furious with herself when she realised she'd washed a jacket of Werner's without noticing there was a letter in the lining. All that was left of it was a magma of paper covered in barely discernible traces of blue ink. Andrew tried yet again to call the agency to find out more, but had to accept that any explanations about their son's origins had now been lost forever. So the child was registered under the name Werner Zilch-Goodman and, as his adoptive parents didn't want to have a different name to their son, they also called themselves Zilch-Goodman.

Any other man might have thought this a huge sacrifice, but Andrew was quite unique; he invested none of his ego in such outward signs of virility, and the happiness that this little boy had brought into their lives erased any doubts he may have had. The transformation in the couple was there for all to see: Armande had filled out and was serenely busy from morning till night, cooking, cleaning, ironing, washing, scrubbing, hair-brushing, scolding, cuddling and telling stories. Andrew had changed too: he stood taller, no longer kept his clenched fists in his pockets or his shoulders hunched in the compact stance of a boxer anticipating an assault. He moved nonchalantly and his voice was deep and assured. Armande found him more and more attractive and he adored his wife's new curvaceous figure. Their nocturnal embraces – which had become so strained with their repeated disappointments – were happy and carefree once more. A year after Werner arrived, his mother's curves were no longer simply the result of her *gratins dauphinoises*, her sautéed potatoes and her roast legs of lamb. Nor were they due to the crumbles and creamy lemon pies to which she treated her husband and son. Her breasts doubled in size, she was radiant, and the little emperor Werner could tell something was afoot. He kept lifting her blouse to inspect her growing stomach. They told him he would soon have a little brother or sister and that for now the baby was safe and warm, cooking in mommy's oven. The young tyrant refused to share his kingdom. A brother? No, he didn't want a brother. And he decided from the start that the baby would be a girl.

Werner was about to turn five when Lauren was born. Fate had granted his wish, and Andrew and Armande were relieved. To ensure that Werner wasn't unsettled, Armande lavished even more attention on him, but he didn't appear to be jealous. In fact, he adored the baby, kissing her, talking to her at length and offering her his toys. He wanted to carry her the whole time, which worried Armande. He also became Lauren's official translator: when the couple seemed powerless in the face of their daughter's crying, Werner would explain to them in his childish language how best to calm her or give her what she needed. Lauren was *his*: a new being which he felt he owned and for which he was responsible.

Physically, the baby was the exact opposite of him, with dark hair, amber skin and big apprehensive eyes. Werner was her own personal living god. The moment she caught sight of him her face lit up, her chin puckered to form a delicate dimple and her laughter rang out. He meant everything to her and she would have followed him to the ends of the earth. So much so that, a few years later, she narrowly escaped breaking her neck when she climbed a tree where Werner was building a treehouse, and she almost drowned when she joined him in testing out rafts of badly roped-together logs. Luckily, Lauren survived all her brother's inventions and moods.

Manhattan, 1971

Lauren, Marcus and I were concerned. In three days Rebecca had been awake for no more than four hours, and always while I was out. Only Lauren had exchanged a few words with her. Even when she was awake, Rebecca didn't really seem to be there. My sister had tried talking to her, putting on cheerful music and getting her to breathe invigorating essential oils of nutmeg, lemon and Scotch pine. She'd even set up a burner in a corner of my bedroom to diffuse these essences continuously, with no other result than to make me sneeze compulsively and to burn a few hairs on Shakespeare's flank when he sat on the thing by mistake.

On the evening of the fourth day, I shook Rebecca gently. My beauty muttered that she wanted to sleep and to be left in peace. When I persisted she became aggressive, roaring like a big cat and paddling furiously at the air to bat away my hands. When I picked her up to put her forcibly on her feet, she bit me fiercely and in my surprise, I let her go. Marcus and Lauren heard me slam the door to my bedroom, making the whole floor of the building shake. I burst into the kitchen and insisted my sister disinfect the wound.

'It's nothing, you'll just have a bruise,' Lauren said.

This indifference didn't stop me emptying the ice bucket from the refrigerator with a thunderous noise. I dropped most of the ice cubes on the floor, which, along with a whole pile of dish-cloths, I then used to make myself an unnecessarily large armband before going to die a slow death on the living-room sofa. I'd had enough of Rebecca ignoring me like this. She'd been using me as a hot-water bottle for days, sliding her hands and feet onto my stomach or my buttocks when the need arose, and pushing me away as soon as I'd warmed her up. Lauren glanced into my bedroom: smiling happily, Rebecca was in a deep sleep again, alongside Shakespeare who had taken to lying next to her the moment my back was turned. She had the nerve to replace me with my own dog! I was all the more put out because the sofa was too short for me. I spent an appalling night going over our relationship with every possible interpretation, and planning my revenge on the Lynches and their daughter.

The following morning nothing had changed.

'Sleeping beauty!' Marcus concluded, when the three of us stood staring at the bed where Rebecca still lay asleep. 'Did you try kissing her?'

'Seeing how she can bite, I won't risk it,' I grumbled. 'She could chop off my tongue.'

'Well, if it's only your tongue . . .' Lauren teased. We both turned on her in horror and she just sighed, 'You guys have no sense of humour.'

We went off to work again. We were preparing an offer to purchase three new large plots that we would divide into lots. Our team had worked on the budget and the development plans, and various architects were due to come back to us with their drawings to bid for the contract. We spent the day in meetings and when we arrived home the situation hadn't changed. Then it got worse.

Rebecca decided to take a bath one evening and I only just avoided the whole apartment being flooded: she'd forgotten to turn off the taps. At three o'clock the following morning she set about cooking everything she could lay her hands on from the kitchen cupboards. After a week without sleep I'd collapsed in a heap and didn't hear her get up. When Lauren and Marcus woke they found neatly lined up on the table two dishes of lasagne, one of macaroni cheese, a tabbouleh, a fruit cake, industrial quantities of cheesecake on which she'd drawn strange geometrical shapes, a tomato salad, and five bowls of a sort of fish pâté that she'd put together using soured cream and all the cans of sardines meant for Shakespeare. This strange whim of Rebecca's proved to me that, contrary to what she had said during our first picnic in the park, she was an accomplished cook. I rather liked this, a sentiment Lauren condemned as 'simplistic male chauvinism'.

'A woman's place isn't necessarily in the kitchen, would you believe,' she lectured.

I was much less pleased a few days later when I discovered the fresco that Rebecca had painted in ketchup with her fingers on the kitchen wall. Marcus was very taken with this depiction of a forest overlaid with geometric designs identical to those she'd inscribed on the cheesecakes.

'Sadly,' he said thoughtfully, 'given the nature of the pigments, this work doesn't have a long life expectancy.'

He was quite right: Shakespeare sealed the fate of this short-lived work by licking the walls up to a height of four feet.

'She's not a woman, she's a three-year-old child!' I railed every time I discovered another of her misdeeds.

Next, she sewed together every single one of my spare socks to make a sort of flower-shaped pouf – a really nice one, according to Lauren. In order to avoid the same fate befalling the replacements that Donna bought for me, I had to put a padlock on the dresser where I kept them. I was frustrated and disgruntled, I even found myself thinking wistfully of Joan. And while all this was going on, I found I could no longer talk to Joan. I'd often behaved towards women in an offhand way, but Joan deserved to be treated properly. After ten days of avoiding her, egged on by admonishments from Lauren, Marcus and Donna, all of whom spoke to her regularly on the telephone, I made up my mind to tell her that Rebecca was back.

It was cowardly but I invited her for lunch in the latest cool restaurant very close to Radio City Music Hall. I thought a public place would spare me a scene. I started with a lengthy tirade about Nixon's policies and then talked her through our new real-estate projects. I said I was worried about Marcus's love life because he hadn't introduced us to any girlfriends for ages, and had stopped his usual habit of disappearing when he had a new squeeze. I gave an extensive commentary on the menu, and ordered a steak, sautéed potatoes and a bloody Mary to give me some Dutch courage, before expounding indignantly about the country's latest murderous operations in Vietnam where so many of our boys were still dying every week.

Joan, who was perceptive and braver than me, interrupted.

'So did she come back?'

'Yes,' I said piteously.

'And you're leaving me, then?'

'I didn't say that.'

'But do you still love her?' she kept going, her voice as professional as a doctor's.

'I don't know, I'm lost . . .'

Joan admitted that she'd hoped to make me forget Rebecca, but she understood. I'd never lied to her; she couldn't hold this against me. She told me tenderly that she would miss me, but she was too sad and overwhelmed to finish her lunch. I offered to walk her home but she shook her head.

'Don't let's drag out the goodbyes. It would be as difficult for you as it is for me.'

I felt sad too. I admired her. She was a dear friend and, deep down, I was sorry she was in love with me. The disparity in our feelings for each other was forcing us apart, when her indifference would have guaranteed our friendship. I paid the check. We hadn't eaten a thing. She planted a kiss on each of my cheeks, not allowing me time to hug her.

'Stop, you'll make me crack,' she warned.

Out on the street, Joan looked me right in the eye one last time.

'You'd better be happy, Wern!' she said. 'If you mess up this thing with Rebecca, I won't forgive you.'

She gave me a pat on the shoulder and turned away. I watched with a heavy heart as she walked off. She hadn't shed a single tear. She walked straight and fast, without turning around.

Peenemünde, Germany, October 1944

Johann had been locked in the interrogation room for five hours now. He was hungry and thirsty. The memory of Luisa's face clutched at his insides, but once the initial terror of the arrest was over, he had realised he was the victim of an intimidation tactic. The Gestapo were sending a message to von Braun; they wanted to frighten him, and Johann happened to be their pawn. He couldn't think of any other explanation. Their accusations were preposterous . . . Obviously he shouldn't have complained about the war effort, and he regretted being so careless, but he'd been demoralised that evening and had had too much to drink. It took all the paranoia of the SS to see a plot or sabotage in that one moment of weariness. Johann was annoyed with himself but he was gradually gaining ground: the interrogators were weakening and were less vigorous than they had been when they started questioning him.

What hurt him most wasn't the fact he'd ended up here, but that he'd been denounced by one of his colleagues. He'd always thought of the Peenemünde team as a family. He just couldn't understand it, and mentally ran through everyone who had been there that evening: Hermann? No, Hermann was terrified of the Gestapo, he would never have dared speak to an SS officer. Konstantine? Impossible, they got along so well, shared the same office and lunched together almost every day. Konstantine's wife Christin, on the other hand, was plausible. A real nuisance, and she was jealous of Luisa . . . except Johann couldn't remember whether she was still there when he uttered those wretched words. Friedrich had definitely been there, though, but he would never have done a thing like that. He was shy and had clearly fallen in love with Marthe since she'd come to live with them a few weeks earlier. He would never have done anything to harm the family.

Johann was tired, he rubbed his face. Elfriede was a no. So was Guillem. But then who could it have been? Who? Andrei? Even less likely. Yes, there'd been some friction between them, but it was quite a leap from minor disagreements to sending in the Gestapo . . . Johann had every intention of getting to the bottom of this once he was back at the base, and could rely on von Braun to help him. This unpleasant incident would soon be resolved. The Führer himself had made the V2s an absolute priority so the SS would eventually have to see sense. Johann stood up and walked around the table three times, then froze when he heard a key clink in the lock.

'What are *you* doing here?' he asked icily of the man in SS uniform who appeared.

Kasper took his time, studying his brother in silence with a sardonic smile before stepping further into the room.

'Hello, Johann. You don't look very pleased to see me . . .'

It was disconcerting to see the two men together. They were so similar that if one hadn't been wearing military uniform and the other civilian dress, they could have been mistaken for each other.

'I thought we'd agreed to have no further communication,' Johann replied.

'That was before you stole my wife. I've come to take her back,' snarled the older brother.

'I haven't "stolen" your wife, Kasper. Marthe has taken refuge with us to escape the hell you were putting her through.'

'Poor darling, and you believe her?'

'I believe her because I know you. You're mad, Kasper. Mad and dangerous. Our parents should have had you locked up.'

'For now, you're the one who's locked up. And I can choose whether you're released.'

Kasper drew up a chair and lit a cigarette.

'What do you want?' Johann snapped from where he was standing by the window.

'I told you, Johann. Do try to use this great brain of yours. I've come for my wife. I heard you'd been arrested and I told my colleagues I would try to reason with you. They thought you'd trust me . . .'

'If there's one person on the planet I don't trust, it's you. Don't waste your time.'

'I'm in no hurry,' Kasper said slowly. 'And I only want to help you.'

'I don't need your help, I'll be out in a few hours.'

'You're dreaming, dear boy! They're convinced you're an agent who's infiltrated the team. I didn't contradict them . . . you've always had questionable friends.'

Kasper had tipped his chair back and was rocking on it. The stripes on his uniform indicated that he'd been promoted.

'You know very well I'd never betray my country,' Johann replied.

'Oh, I don't know anything. Well, yes, I do. I heard your bitch is going to whelp . . .'

'Which bitch?'

'Isn't Luisa in pup?'

'I won't let you talk about my wife like that!'

Kasper crushed out the end of his cigarette in the small tin bowl that acted as an ashtray. He leant forward, his eyes glittering.

'I know exactly what I'm talking about with Luisa. I had her before you did and she couldn't get enough of it.'

'Shut up!' Johann roared. 'You can't bear the fact she chose me.'

He clenched his fists and instinctively hunched his back, ready for a fight.

'If you're so confident why did you run away with her like a thief when our parents died?'

'I left,' Johann said quietly, 'because you'd turned our neighbours against Luisa with all the rumours you put about. They treated her despicably. I didn't have a choice.'

'Your problem is, you always want to take what's mine: first Luisa, and now Marthe . . .'

'Luisa wasn't yours.'

'We were engaged!' Kasper exploded, a glimmer of pain in his eyes.

'What you call an engagement wasn't official, and Luisa would never have married you,' Johann retorted.

'She would have married me if you hadn't terrorised her with all your stories about me. And then our parents took your side. You all ganged up together to take her from me.'

'All I did was tell her the truth, and the way you treated Marthe confirmed my worst fears.'

'I loved Luisa. You had no right!'

'She's a human being, free to make her own choice,' Johann said, unbuttoning his shirt collar. He was suffocating.

There was a cruel light in Kasper's eyes as he lit another cigarette.

'I've never understood what she saw in you. You're so hopelessly ill equipped for this world with your mathematical scribblings and your head in the clouds, like a retarded child.'

'What she saw in me? She saw right through you and she knows I love her more than anything in the world.'

'I'm surprised you're interested in my left-overs.'

'Don't start that again,' Johann said irritably.

'If you knew what I did to her you'd go right off the idea . . .'

'Stop it!' Johann cried, thumping the table with his fist.

'I made the most of her, really made the most of everything she had to offer, and you just tagged along afterwards . . .'

'I told you to shut up!'

'Or maybe I carried on seeing her behind your back? How do you know I didn't carry on seeing her?'

Johann's fist flew. His clenched fingers thudded against Kasper's nose which snapped like a piece of wood. Johann wanted to carry on fighting but instead of retaliating, Kasper grabbed one of the chairs and, calling for help all the while, threw it against the window, which shattered.

The noise brought two SS officers racing into the room.

Kasper was holding his nose, his face covered in blood.

'I confronted him and he attacked me! He tried to escape by breaking the window . . .'

The two men grasped Johann savagely.

'Don't listen to him,' he tried to defend himself. '*He* threw the chair at the window . . .'

Johann struggled but the officers wouldn't hear his protestations. They dragged him towards the cells and failed to see the triumphant smile and sarcastic goodbye wave that Kasper addressed to his younger brother.

Donna asked for news of Rebecca every day, as worried as the rest of us by her constant sleeping. She took things in hand by calling her doctor, in whom she had every faith since he'd saved her daughter from a serious infection. I'd never met Dr Bonnett, but he came to our apartment that same evening. He was a short, slight, dark-haired man who had spent the early years of his career in Africa and had a slight limp because a Malian, showing little gratitude for the care the doctor had administered, had damaged his calf muscle with a slash of his machete. Dr Bonnett had recovered thanks to a concoction applied to the wound by the witch from the neighbouring village. This balm had proved so effective that afterwards he spent his free time trying to reproduce it using the plants the old woman had shown him and that he'd carefully catalogued.

He was boundlessly inquisitive and looked barely fifty years old but, as he told me later, he was in fact sixty-four. At one time he had worked in a research laboratory in Boston and had then returned to New York where he was born, and thrown himself passionately into alternative medicines, particularly acupuncture, a detail which very much impressed Lauren. In fact, the doctor had to be dragged away from the thorough interrogations to which my sister submitted him, in order to attend to Rebecca.

She was asleep. The new sleepwalking phase of her illness made her very obedient. I didn't need to touch her to wake her up; I simply had to call her name three times, and she sat up in bed. Once in this semi-wakeful state, she need only be given an order and she would instantly obey, a symptom that was much more to my taste. Despite certain ideas that came to me, I did not abuse this newfound power, except in thought. I even respected her nakedness. As for washing, Lauren had reported that Rebecca regularly locked herself in the bathroom, spent thirty minutes in there and re-emerged wearing a pair of pyjamas I'd bought her.

I brought Rebecca to the living room and Dr Bonnett started by studying her very intently. When he asked her to, she undressed. I didn't want to leave her alone with him and was shocked by the sight of her body which was covered in bumps and bruises. I was consumed by a surge of anger. Whoever had done this to her, I wished I could beat them to death with a metal rod. I gently asked Rebecca to put her clothes back on, which she did.

'Is this your wife?' Dr Bonnett asked, turning to me.

'Not yet,' I said in a muted voice.

'Does she take drugs?'

'I don't know,' I admitted, remembering that, before she disappeared, she often smoked weed. 'Not in the last few days, anyway.'

'Do you know whether she has recently returned from a tropical country?'

'No, I don't know where she was before she came here.'

I realised I wouldn't get away with so little explanation: the marks on Rebecca's body were quite something, and I didn't want him to think I was responsible for them. I summarised how I had met her, our first months of happiness, the dinner at her parents' house, her disappearance for nearly a year and her sudden reappearance. Dr Bonnett seemed reassured by my openness, and conscientiously noted each detail in an elastic-bound notebook. He diagnosed a possible case of narcolepsy, an acute sleep disorder whose causes were little understood. He took bloods using a syringe and a series of small tubes that he stowed in his black leather case.

'I'll have these analysed,' he said. 'She may have developed a pathology of the sort produced by the tsetse fly, but I can't see any infected bites and she has no fever . . . Still, we shouldn't take any risks. That illness is a real bastard.'

'Is it fatal?' I asked, horrified.

'Eventually yes, unfortunately. Does she make no sense when she speaks?'

'It's worse than that, she doesn't talk at all. She must have said fifty words to me since she came back, and not many more to my sister Lauren who's here with her all through the day.'

'Does she have hallucinations or cry out in distress?'

'No, she's very calm. And she cooks at night.'

'She cooks?' he asked, surprised by this bizarre manifestation of her condition.

'As if preparing a banquet. We had to empty the cupboards, or she'd be feeding the whole neighbourhood. She makes art too. And she sews socks . . .'

'She sews socks?' Dr Bonnett asked in amazement. He was like a child with a completely new object, examining it from every angle to understand what it was and how it worked.

I showed him the pouf Rebecca had made and the remains of a fresco in mustard. He studied them with his characteristic intensity and made a note of his thoughts without sharing them with me.

As we went back into the living room I asked whether a tropical disease could be communicated by biting.

'Does she have aggressive outbursts, then?'

'Only if you try to wake her. Otherwise she's pretty affectionate.'

I showed him my arm and he told me it was 'nothing', which piqued me. He went back to examining Rebecca's eyes and the colour on the inside of her eyelids.

'There are no worrying clinical signs,' he said, reassuringly. 'She's just anaemic. I'd incline more towards some sort of post-traumatic disorder. In some cases of violence or extreme shock, a person can heal themselves with sleep.'

'So it's a good thing, then?'

'It's a good thing, unless this recuperation becomes a permanent evasion of reality. Some sufferers gradually return to their normal lives, others never come back, happier to remain in the reassuring cocoon of their dreams.'

'When will we know if she'll come back?'

Dr Bonnett couldn't say. Narcolepsy required a great deal of patience; sufferers needed time. Given the wounds Rebecca had, God alone knew what her unconscious was trying to forget. He wrote out a prescription for all sorts of tonics, and would add to it once he had the blood analyses back from the laboratory. When he left he asked me to call him regularly to keep him up to date with any changes in her behaviour. While we talked, Rebecca had curled up into a ball on the sofa, and was now fast asleep again.

Her eclipse seemed to go on forever. I burned with desire for her, and she seemed barely conscious I was there. I'd visited three former girlfriends in rapid succession, girls who were happy to see me without any complications. I'd indulged in all my favourite positions and practices, but their bodies had felt lifeless to me, their pleasure mechanical. These failed attempts only frustrated me further. Ever since Lou and that first kiss she had stolen from me in the school gym, I'd worked my way through women as if they were delicious fruits, revelling in their individual quirks, their smell, the texture of their skin, their tempers and their weaknesses. But now, when I came away from these girls with whom I would once have relished making love, I felt no more emotion or satisfaction than if I'd shaken their hands. The most humiliating part of it was, the moment I lay down next to Rebecca's sleeping form at night, the blade seared through my loins again.

I confided in Marcus with my troubles.

'You have to admit, it's kind of funny that you, the don Juan of Manhattan, have suddenly ended up monogamous!' he teased.

'I don't find it funny at all, actually.'

'Your cock is in love and faithful, you'll have to get used to it.'

'My cock is masochistic. It's fixated on the one girl in this place who doesn't give a damn about me.'

I was strung out and unbearable.

'Just call Joan back!' Lauren yelled at me one morning, exasperated. 'At least you got to sleep with her!'

'You *were* more relaxed . . .' agreed Marcus, softly dabbing a forgotten toast crumb from the corner of Lauren's mouth.

Seeing the colour drain dangerously from my face – a warning sign of one of those rages that neither of them had any desire to endure – the pair of them changed the subject to our new home. We were due to move at the end of the week, and I was hoping this change of scene would have a positive effect on Becca. It had taken Marcus only a few days to find a gorgeous house in the Village. It was brick-built, four storeys high and had been completely renovated, and it was on a quiet street that appealed to me as much as the house itself. In the basement, lit with skylights in the courtyard, there was a kitchen, a utility room and a separate studio apartment with a small yard. On the first floor was a large living room and a dining room, and there was another living room on the second floor. The four bedrooms were arranged on the second and third floors. The roof space contained a terrace and another huge room. It was a good investment: the Village was evolving all the time, and I was sure my acquisition would increase in value. Our last projects had been so profitable that I could buy it without a mortgage, which meant I could get an even better price than the one Marcus had negotiated. He offered to pay a share, but even though it was clear we would both live there, having a place of my own was a long-held dream of mine. Besides, his father would have taken that badly because he owned half a block on Central Park and regularly invited Marcus to move in there.

Donna took care of the removal company with her usual efficiency, and on D-Day five Poles with bodybuilder muscles turned up at our apartment and started emptying the place. In among all the boxes, Marcus and I were chained to our telephones by a new project. We had submitted a bid for a plot near Grand Central Station, and we'd just discovered that the dice for the bidding were loaded. We had only a few hours to outmanoeuvre the scam. The removal men followed Donna's and Lauren's instructions, and loaded the truck with everything except for the bed where Rebecca was sleeping. She didn't seem at all disturbed by the disruption. Meanwhile I raised my voice on the telephone, and Marcus pandered or threatened. It was a tight negotiation.

When the apartment was empty and the removal men stopped for a snack, Marcus and I stayed on for another hour, sitting on the floor to make more and more calls in our attempts to swing the deal in our favour. When we finally hung up, I took Rebecca in my arms and carried her to our good old Chrysler. I was struck by her pallor in the July sunshine; she hardly ever saw the light of day and her skin looked translucent. On the other hand, she was now blonde again; the purple dye that I'd loathed had faded in the space of four weeks, and her short hair, perhaps stimulated by so many hours of sleep, had grown a lot. It now fell in a curly bob that softened her face, making her look more as I had once known her. I propped her between Shakespeare and Lauren on the back seat, and my beauty used Shakespeare as a pillow – and he took the opportunity to lick her arm gently, which she didn't appear to mind. Marcus and I sat in the front and, with its rear axle slung low, the car dragged itself to our new home.

The removal men set up a bed in a ground-floor room so that I could lay Rebecca on it; she was still sleeping blissfully. I didn't even bother to do a quick tour of the premises but, almost before the door was closed, sat myself down on a box in the living room, plugged in a telephone and resumed my campaign (the perfect Donna had already had lines installed). Two hours later I granted myself a few minutes to call my parents. I wanted them to come down the next weekend to see my first house. I was sure they'd be proud of me.

That evening a suffocating heat descended on the city. A storm was brewing. I put Rebecca in the room next to mine, with Shakespeare because he – the traitor – followed her around like a shadow and had almost forgotten me. I locked them in, an assault on Rebecca's liberty that Marcus had stopped criticising since the night when the incomparable artist had sewn all his neckties together to make a carpet six feet long. Lauren, thinking this creation 'sublime', had instantly requisitioned it for her bedroom and Marcus had been forced to rebuild his collection with no hope of compensation.

At night the house was wonderfully quiet, far from the racket I'd grown used to. It was so hot, I slept naked and at about 1 a.m. I felt an animal sneak into my bed. I cried out and leapt to my feet, wrapped in a sheet toga and ready to defend myself. When I realised it was Rebecca I was still shocked and angry; I grabbed her by the collar of her pyjamas and shoved her off my bed.

'You said you wouldn't let me go,' she said reproachfully, her eyes flashing with accusation.

'So you're talking to me now?' I glowered.

'I've always talked to you,' she said defensively.

'In a whole month you haven't talked to me more than ten times . . .'

'I didn't have anything to say,' she replied with a shrug.

I was about to give her two or three ideas for topics of conversation when something struck me.

'Wait, how did you get out? I locked you in.'

'I know. And actually, don't do that again. I don't like being locked in.'

'How did you open the door?'

Rebecca tilted her chin towards the window.

'Don't tell me you climbed across the outside of the building!'

'I only stepped from one balcony to the other.'

'You're crazy!' I said. 'This woman is crazy!'

'I'm not crazy.'

'Well, you're dangerous, then.'

'Not dangerous enough,' she said, her face darkening. 'I thought I was dangerous, but not enough.'

'I'm in no mood for riddles, Rebecca. You gatecrash into my life, then disappear for months on end, then reappear, you don't talk to me, you sleep twenty-three hours a day, you cook at night, you jump across balconies, you're covered in bruises . . .'

'Excuse me?' she said, surprised.

'Don't you know you're covered in bruises?' I said.

I sat down on the bed and pulled down the pants of her pyjamas. I was so angry that the soft swell of her blonde pubis didn't even hold my attention.

'Doesn't this mean anything to you?'

I looked at her skin and the brown-and-blue patterns that were beginning to fade. Rebecca gazed down at her legs without a word, then looked up, disconcerted.

'Look!' I said again, running my hand over her thighs.

Her skin shuddered into goosebumps. I'd been holding back my desire for weeks and was surprised by this. Her eyes looked opaque, her face intent; I sensed in her expression the fever that used to take hold of her before she left me. I withdrew my hand from her thighs – I hadn't forgiven her for disappearing, or for not speaking, or for biting me.

'Where were you all that time?'

'Are you sure you want to talk?' she asked, sitting on my lap.

'Yes, I want to talk!'

She put her arm around my neck and wanted to press herself up to me, to crush her breasts against my chest, but I held her hips firmly to keep her at a distance.

'Stop it, darling,' she said, kissing me softly on the lips.

I tried to protest but she kept going.

'You see, you *don't* want to talk,' she said, pressing the cleft between her thighs against my penis.

I pulled her against me more firmly and she rolled gently back and forth.

'Take off your T-shirt,' I ordered.

She removed it gracefully. Her smooth hairless armpits implied she'd premeditated this. In her clothes she looked thin, but once naked she had exactly what was needed where it was needed. Her firm round breasts pointed directly forward, I liked her long neck, her resolute shoulders. I caught sight of our reflection in the window: Rebecca, arching backwards, was wickedly beautiful. She leant forward, and her back and waist curved downwards to exaggerate the swell of her buttocks.

'If you think you can have me with a crude trick like that . . .' I protested, forcibly holding her still.

'*You* can have *me*, if that's what you want.'

'You seem very awake all of a sudden,' I said, slipping one finger close to but not quite inside her.

Rebecca half-closed her eyes, absorbed in her pleasure, almost conscientiously so. The effect I was having on her ramped up my own arousal. She didn't seem in the least awkward or embarrassed.

'You see,' she insisted when she opened her eyes again. 'There's no point talking.'

'You're a pain in the ass, Rebecca,' I said, flipping her over like a judoka.

I pinned her to the bed, holding her wrists behind her. She tried half-heartedly to break free, but the writhing of her hips only helped me extricate myself from the sheet and slip between her thighs.

'You're a pain in the ass,' I said again, kissing her and thrusting inside her.

Her protestations almost immediately metamorphosed into sighs. I released her wrists and buried my face in the crook of her neck and shoulder. Our bodies rediscovered each other with clumsy eagerness. I crushed her and manhandled her but my brusqueness seemed only to fan the flames of her desire. I muttered quiet orders to her, saying 'please' for convention's sake, and she obeyed. I lifted her up, and bent her over with disconcerting ease. I'd forgotten how incredibly soft her skin was. She wanted me in the very depths of her; she loved my power, how hard my body was, and how that justified her own softness and curves. When I took her like this I understood the meaning of the expression 'made for each other'.

The day after this reunion, she got up at dawn when I did. I rarely slept for more than five hours, and liked that time when the city was resting and I was awake. Rebecca dressed and then came and stood in front of me with one hand held out.

'Could you give me some money, please?'

The thought that she was asking for payment for the night before crossed my mind. Almost before I'd had time to formulate this idea, she swept it aside with a peal of laughter.

'Not that, you moron! I have plenty of money, just not on me. I need to go buy materials.'

'Materials?'

'To work, to paint! I don't have any.'

For the first time in weeks I saw the 'old' Rebecca, the independent, determined, mocking Rebecca. I took a thick wad of bills from my wallet, counted out four hundred dollars and handed them to her questioningly. She rolled her hands around each other, and I doubled the sum.

'Don't worry, I'll pay you back,' she said, pocketing the money as nonchalantly as if she'd given it to me the day before.

'I'm not worried, and you don't have to pay me back,' I retorted, amused by the cheek and determination of this little female animal who planted an absent-minded kiss on my lips, her eyes already straying towards her own imaginary worlds, before skipping off goodness only knew where without a by-your-leave, or even any breakfast.

Manhattan, 1971

Rebecca and Lauren decided they would share the large top room on the roof to make a studio and an area for practising yoga that made the most of the sunlight. When Marcus and I came home that evening we found one doing a headstand and the other up a stepladder with a scarf over her hair, her face daubed with paint, four paintbrushes in her hands and one in her mouth. She was perfecting the shading on a composition that turned out to be a giant-sized erect penis.

'Is that yours?' Marcus teased.

'Nothing like it!' I said indignantly.

'Yesh, it is,' Rebecca announced, still with a paintbrush between her teeth.

'Well, that's a big beautiful way to say you like someone,' Marcus laughed and then turned to me and added, 'I didn't know you were so well endowed.'

'When he was little, it fascinated mom,' Lauren said, still in her upside-down position. 'He's got a huge one.'

'That's enough!' I begged.

'Oh, no, we won't stop,' Rebecca announced, taking the brush from her mouth and coming to give me a kiss.

'No PDAs!' wailed Lauren, dropping down to her feet, her face as red as mine but for purely mechanical reasons. 'Please don't torment us with that.'

'PDAs?' Marcus asked.

'Public Displays of Affection,' she replied, smoothing down her long dark hair.

That evening we went out onto the terrace for a dinner of

olive bread, tomatoes and cheese washed down with several bottles of Chianti. For dessert, Lauren whipped some cream and folded in strawberries. I was still desperately hoping for a rib of beef with sautéed potatoes but Lauren insisted firmly on the 'vegetarian only' directive.

While we ate our strawberries, she told us she was going back to college to study psychology and hypnosis. Dr Bonnett had recommended she also take an interest in acupuncture, a discipline that was not yet the subject of university curricula but he had offered to pass on his knowledge to her and she could go on from there. She intended eventually to open a well-being centre. When I asked whether her massages for men would include more intimate parts of the body – which, out of pure provocation, Lauren promised they would – I announced that I was prepared to invest in her future establishment. We spent quite a while coming up with improbable names for the place: it had to combine the notion of personal fulfilment and sexual pleasure, and we eventually agreed on 'Eden's'. I asked whether it would be for members only, or could clients simply pay at the time, and Lauren said she wanted to 'make people feel good, not make money'. I bit my lip to stop myself saying it might also be an opportunity for her to take responsibility for herself. Our parents had paid for her studies in San Francisco, which she hadn't finished. I'd financed her share of the ranch, which she didn't dare claim back when she left the commune, and I'd been supporting her for several months. I adored Lauren, but I was less taken with the moralising tirades about finances, materialism and profit that she served up more and more frequently.

Marcus and I were working on securing our most ambitious build, a tower block on Fifth Avenue, right in the heart of Manhattan. It was going to be a tough fight: not only were a lot of people interested in the project, but the city council had just changed administrations. Grants offered by the city were under review, and without this fiscal advantage the venture became far less profitable. Another challenge was the small size of the plot. To stand up to high winds and possible seismic activity, a tower of that proposed height should have been anchored on a much larger base in order to secure planning permission. Frank Howard had resolved these structural difficulties, but if the building's small footprint meant we had to shave off several floors at the top, the project would no longer be financially viable. We pulled a lot of strings, and Lauren disapproved of this lobbying. Even when I told her our competitors didn't have the same qualms and wouldn't think twice before going much further than Marcus and I did, she simply said I shouldn't 'stoop to their level'. Marcus, who was an old hand at such peace negotiations, had banned the subject but with a brother and sister, there's no need for words to know what the other is thinking and trying to hide.

The next day all of us were up at dawn. Only Marcus, who definitely had the least resistance to drink, appeared to be suffering from our excesses. It was an especially tough day at work and we came home from the office hoping to sit down to a meal but found the girls up on the roof, Rebecca completely absorbed in painting and Lauren equally focused on making notes from a hypnosis manual. Meanwhile Shakespeare was patrolling the studio and the terrace, busily following a precise but mysterious itinerary that no one but he understood. He sniffed in corners, reared up on his hind legs to look down at the street, and barked at pigeons like a general at recalcitrant troops. We took Rebecca and Lauren for dinner at Chez Marcel, a French bistro two blocks away that allowed dogs. In fact, they even gave Shakespeare a helping of beef bourguignon, and we had a very enjoyable evening.

Marcus gave an amusing description of the weeks and weeks when I'd exhausted him by talking about Rebecca day and night. It made me laugh but was also embarrassing. With each successive anecdote, I sank a little lower in my chair, and

Marcus, eventually realising my sense of humour was wearing thin, stopped his teasing. I took advantage of the fact we were discussing that period, though, and started questioning Rebecca again. I wanted her to tell us once and for all what she'd done for all those months. She succeeded in evading the issue and moments later we were laughing at her stories about Andy Warhol and The Factory.

'Wouldn't you like to go see them again?' Marcus asked her.

'Not yet. Right now, I want to get on with my work. It's been so long since I painted, too long . . .'

She reminded us all of how she and I had first met and the reciprocal car-denting episodes. I hadn't told Lauren the story, and she loved it. I watched Rebecca out of the corner of my eye during this conversation: she seemed completely normal, as if one night of lovemaking had brought her back. Here was the girl I'd known, sure of herself, astute and unbelievably attractive. Her lust for life, her impertinence and her almost childish tenderness when we were alone together, captured my heart all over again. We were happy that evening, and perhaps I should have settled for that happiness, but I had so many burning questions. I needed to understand, I couldn't just leave it at that and live with the thought that Rebecca might vanish again for no apparent reason. If I was going to trust her I needed her to trust me.

Before leaving Chez Marcel we bought French bread and some milk from them for breakfast the next morning. It was balmy as we walked home and we didn't feel like going to bed. Lauren and Marcus went off to their own bedrooms and Rebecca and I stayed out on the terrace for a while. She went to stand by the balustrade and asked if I'd join her. Very soon we were entwined in each other's arms. She was wearing a blue dress, rather like the one from the first time I saw her, and she was naked underneath it. I caressed her, and took her slowly from behind, by the light of the moon and the streetlamps below. It was unsettling how easily our bodies reacquainted themselves.

Rebecca's narcolepsy went into reverse: my beauty woke at five and worked relentlessly. According to Lauren, who I asked to continue to keep an eye on her, she stopped only for a few minutes at about eleven in the morning and then again at three in the afternoon. She would sit facing her work in progress, her face tormented and hair awry, and would eat on the hop: crackers with Philadelphia cheese, a beer, a coffee, maybe a banana. She went on painting right up until we came home. Then she would take off her paint-spattered blue apron and a checked shirt of mine she'd taken to cover her arms, and slip on a white T-shirt. She did this right in front of us and this lack of discretion exasperated me but she laughed it off, taunting me for being 'conventional'. Next she went down to shower and put on an outfit for the evening borrowed from Lauren, telling me yes, yes, she'd go buy some clothes soon, she just didn't have the time right now. Jealousy scalded my heart and, despite my sister's reassurances, I couldn't believe this overloaded schedule was due only to an urgent burst of creativity.

The four of us always had a drink before dinner, and after dinner Rebecca and I would make love. Sometimes she woke in the night and I found her out on the roof. She liked standing there on beautiful summer nights, watching the city and letting her mind stray. She encouraged me to join her and I resisted for a while. Then she let me plead a little before eventually coming back downstairs and curling up beside me. Rebecca was a cat.

Manhattan, 1971

Now that she was awake, Rebecca charmed the whole household. She had irresistible vitality and a combination of candour and exuberance that won over anyone she spoke to. She could transform ordinary things into a party, the smallest anecdote of our day-to-day lives into a novel, and the simplest things into great pleasures. She named us the 'gang of four' and introduced our sacrosanct 'schnicks', a word she conjured up from goodness knows where as a nickname for our pre-dinner drinks. Rebecca, who took pride in the fact that she'd been a barmaid in the Hamptons one summer, much to her parents' displeasure, made us a different cocktail every evening, and we discussed how our days had been over this drink. From the simple noun form of 'Shall we have a schnick?', the word progressed to a verb that even our friends adopted: 'Can we come and schnick at your place this evening?' There were often ten or even twenty of us congregating to share wine accompanied by cheese, olives or Rebecca's particular weakness, cashew nuts.

Through those summer months, she also converted us to the *paseo*, the pleasure of going out for an after-dinner stroll, breathing in the life of the city, delighting in its teeming energy, snatches of conversation, laughter or disagreements, and the juxtaposition of incongruous scenes and lit windows. We looked at apartments and imagined the lives of the people who lived there. We went to Washington Square where Marcus and I sat down at the stone chess tables with old guys from the neighbourhood while Rebecca and Lauren met up with friends or sat on the grass listening to music. Every evening young bands came to play their very best in the hope of being noticed. Young actors also performed short comedies and sketches. Some made us laugh till we cried.

Sometimes we chose to avoid the crowds and set off at random through the city's streets, led only by the olfactory preferences of my dog who had an unbounded sense of adventure. We put the world to rights as we walked the streets either in tandem or shoulder to shoulder in a line like musketeers. We often stopped at a sidewalk restaurant for a late-night snack or one last drink. Marcus was always first to call it a day and Lauren, who was the most indefatigable of us, would protest. Rebecca and I would go along with whichever one of them prevailed.

Even if we were home very late, I never tired of Rebecca's skin, the glow of it. When we were alone together, I needed to look at her as if feeding off her vital energy. When I caressed her, my fingers didn't skim over her absently but became inhabited, magnetised. I concentrated all my thoughts into them. I gradually re-explored her sensitive spots, gently nibbling the nape of her neck to make her shudder or softly stroking the curve of her buttocks at the very tops of her thighs, a feather-light touch that made her freeze, hold her breath and dissolve with pleasure. She loved my penis, saying 'he' was her best friend. She made me laugh by making affectionate or cheeky speeches to him, and she kissed him at every opportunity. I was passionate about the most intimate smell of her, laughing as I drank in this smell with my head between her legs, even sometimes falling asleep with my head resting on one of her thighs, a possessive hand on her stomach and her fingers still buried in my tousled hair.

My beauty loved to dance and would turn the music up to full volume. Sometimes when Marcus and I came home we found the girls carried away with their dancing in the living room or on the terrace. Pink-faced and wild-haired, they leapt about like savages and sang at the top of their lungs – Lauren very out of tune and Becca with a pretty voice. They asked if we'd like to join them, and they had to beg because we were tired and didn't really understand this craze. Their eyes sparkled with sheer fun, their enthusiasm was unflagging and soon all four of us were dancing in pairs. Rebecca liked acrobatic rock and roll and I proved inept at it, but Marcus twirled her around him like a hula hoop. He offered to teach Lauren and she let herself be persuaded, so they took to practising every evening. Lauren bit her lip as she counted out the steps with great concentration, and she squealed with fear or delight during the lifts.

We also became regulars on Wednesday and Friday evenings at the Electric Circus, a hip club set up in the former Arlington Hall on St Marks Place in the heart of East Village. Warhol had used the space for a while before selling it to an investor who put 300,000 dollars on the table to renovate the huge premises and install spotlights, projection screens and stages with massively powerful speakers. We collapsed into sofas, ordered whiskies or 'bananas', and met up with friends. We came across the local hippies, Tom Wolfe, Truman Capote and Warren Beatty – whom I loathed because Rebecca was susceptible to his charms. I was even more exasperated by a guy named Dane whom my girlfriend introduced to me as 'her best friend'. He said he was an artists' agent, but I didn't believe that for a moment. He was average height, thin, with pale skin, eyes as black and lustreless as his hair, a tormented expression, a constant note of sarcasm in his voice and endless insidious questions on his lips. He looked at me as if I were an assassin and took every opportunity to take Rebecca to one side whispering I don't know what into her ear. He was clearly crazy about her and her innocent denials of this infuriated me. She told me friendship between men and women was possible and that her relationship with Dane proved the fact. I told her that was a joke: friendship is what people settle for when they can't hope for anything better from someone more attractive than themselves. Unless they've previously dealt with the question of sex, which isn't always enough. My relationship with Joan was a prime example; I would have loved to call her, talk to her and have lunch with her from time to time, but I knew she wouldn't accept that. Because of her feelings.

At the Electric Circus, evening gowns mingled with flowery sundresses, men with slicked-back hair talked with guys covered in tattoos, and a man dressed as a Roman emperor could come on to a model in a sequinned minidress. There was experimental theatre and sets by people like Velvet Underground, the Grateful Dead or Cat Mother & the All Night Newsboys. Fire-breathers and trapeze artists came on between the musicians' sets, all the arts combined perfectly randomly. A few months later Rebecca would exhibit her 'phallus' series on the premises, and it would cause quite a stir there and in the press.

On Thursdays we went to the Bitter End on Bleecker Street where the new manager, Paul Colby, had some pretty wild programming. He'd worked for Frank Sinatra and Duke Ellington before launching a range of furniture. He also painted and had a 'nose' for new talent; the best of his finds ended up on the red-brick stage that would soon be legendary. Over the years, through our separations and reunions, we listened to Frank Zappa, Nina Simone and Bob Dylan there, and also roared with laughter at jokes from Woody Allen and Bill Cosby.

We stayed in on the weekends to avoid the suburbanites who flocked to Manhattan. We preferred to read, work, spend time together or occasionally tidy the house. The place was an indescribable mess, breakfast cups left lying around, melted packets of butter open on the kitchen table, crumbs, empty jam jars, dirty plates piling up in the sink, unmade beds (except for Marcus's, of course), dirty clothes waiting to go to the cleaners and towels left in heaps on the bathroom floor. One evening when I came home and couldn't even find a scrap of ham or cheese to eat, I protested, and the girls said I could just do the shopping myself. Since Lauren had started studying again she didn't have a minute to spare, but Rebecca had a shakier excuse.

'I'm not a homemaker,' she announced. 'I can't even boil an egg.'

'Are you kidding!' I snapped a little tartly. 'I had to put padlocks on all the cupboards in our old kitchen to stop you cooking meals for twenty people when you were sleepwalking. If you can cook lasagne and cheesecake in your sleep, you must be able to boil an egg when you're awake!'

'Well, not only do I not know how to, but given the mood you're in, I certainly don't want to learn.'

She stalked sulkily out of the room and went to take a shower. She took a long time to come down and we were all waiting for her before going out for dinner, so I went upstairs. I found her curled up in a ball in our bed, fast asleep. I shook her gingerly – I had no desire to be bitten again – but she didn't wake.

'Oh no!' I wailed and then succumbed to some more belligerent language which drew Marcus and Lauren up to our room.

They looked at Rebecca.

'Seriously? She's impossible! I can't say anything to her . . . the smallest criticism and we're meant to endure another month in a coma? I'm done,' I said angrily.

'She did a lot of work today, maybe she's tired,' Lauren suggested with little conviction.

She tried to wake Rebecca by wafting phials of essential oils under her nose, and Marcus sang a piece from *Betulia Liberata* in his fine baritone voice. Rebecca didn't stir.

'This is too much! It's blackmail!' I exploded, pacing around the bed. 'I warn you, the minute she wakes up, I'm leaving her.'

'You can learn a lot just by taking a little nap . . .' the bed announced.

I froze, and so did Marcus and Lauren. Rebecca chose that moment to jump out of bed already dressed for dinner and, looking triumphantly happy, she bowed to me like an actress to an audience. Lauren and Marcus burst out laughing.

'So, you want to leave me, then?' she asked, which made the other two laugh even more.

'Exactly right, I'm leaving you! As far as I'm concerned, you no longer exist!' I countered furiously.

'Come on, honey, don't be a bad sport.'

'Honey, is that what she calls you?' Marcus asked with one eyebrow raised in amazement.

'Don't *you* start now!' I said indignantly and, not knowing what to say or what to do with myself, I stormed out of the room.

They followed me, chuckling among themselves, all the way to Chez Marcel. A half-bottle of claret later, I'd forgotten my anger but had decided to go ahead and deal with the problem of housework: I hadn't bought my first house to see the place turned into a garbage dump. The next morning, I called Miguel, our Cuban caterer friend who was having financial difficulties. He'd accepted a job organising two big parties in the Hamptons for a crook who vanished without paying him, and Miguel was now being hounded by his suppliers. Even though he'd helped make them rich over the last three years, the human animal has a short memory and a whining wallet. I contacted him to ask whether he could recommend someone, and he recommended himself.

'What about your company, Miguel? I thought you liked being independent . . .'

'Working for anyone other than you doesn't suit me, Mr Werner.'

The deal was settled in a matter of minutes, and a whole new life started for us. With his generous figure poured into an impeccable uniform, Miguel was going to be the best housewife in Manhattan. He was passionate about a well-run household: he sewed, darned, washed, ironed and starched, he made sumptuous flower arrangements and cooked like a great chef. He liked a well-stocked larder full of fresh vegetables and pots of jam with handwritten labels, he put plate covers over food, folded napkins in old-fashioned ways and appreciated fine glasses and silverware. He liked inspecting his closets filled with piles of starched tablecloths and sheets. He'd spent many years working in luxury hotels before being taken on by one of New York's high-ranking society families. The experience ended badly: his employers' eldest son, then aged about twenty, had fallen hopelessly in love with Miguel and had pursued him assiduously for eighteen months. Their passionate relationship saw Miguel fired, and this professional trauma was made infinitely worse by his inconsolable heartbreak.

When I triumphantly announced this new appointment, Lauren was shocked that we could pay someone to take care of our dirty washing. She thought it immoral to exploit a human being to do our lowliest tasks. We told her there was no question of 'exploiting' anyone, but giving work to someone who desperately wanted it . . . and who had offered his services entirely spontaneously.

'Capitalism is the syphilis of our society,' Lauren declared portentously. 'I refuse to stay in this house if you intend to martyr a housemaid.'

'Capitalism suits you very well when it lends you money to open your centre.'

'That's the least you could do! By helping me heal people, you're giving back a little of what you owe to society!'

'And what do you suggest if neither you nor Rebecca nor Marcus nor I have the time to deal with these things?' I countered, struggling to keep my cool.

'If we share the chores, the four of us can manage perfectly well.'

'Last time you tried sharing chores with your gang of hairy star-gazers, it didn't exactly work out . . . so, be nice and let me arrange this,' I said irritably.

'Oh my God, listen to yourself, talking to me like that! Just because you have a sausage between your thighs, that doesn't mean you get everything your way!'

'In this instance, it's not about the sausage, it's the cheque-book.'

'Oh, cheques, money! Your god! The key word!' Lauren barked exasperatedly. 'Is that all that matters, then?'

'Well, I don't see why that's a problem.'

'So materialistic!' sighed Rebecca, rolling her eyes.

This was too much for Marcus who cut in with, 'You haven't made any complaints about our materialism up till now!'

'When you're born with a silver spoon in your mouth and you don't know how to boil an egg, it's easy to criticise other people's materialism,' I added specifically for Rebecca.

The doorbell rang at just the right time to stop us getting too heated. It was Miguel coming to see the house and his studio. He greeted us all amicably but could feel the tension, and when he and I were alone I explained the conversation I'd had with my sister. To ease Lauren's qualms, Miguel asked to have a private conversation with her in what he called the 'library'. This was in fact the second-floor living room where the shelves were mostly empty except for the *Encyclopædia Britannica*, some piles of magazines, a few dirty glasses and the beginnings of one of Rebecca's plaster sculptures. I don't know what they discussed but when Lauren left the room she seemed completely won over.

It wasn't long before Miguel had his bearings. In his rolling, sibilant Hispanic accent, he gave us ceremonial names: Mister Werner, Miss Rebecca, Mister Marcus and Miss Lauren. However many times we told him there was no need for such solemnity, he insisted on it. Etiquette was not an obligation for him but part of the art of living and one that he took pleasure in applying, accepting that – like most of humanity – he didn't have an equal share in power and wealth. Our butler, as he described himself, gave a very bleak diagnosis of our home. We had been rather glibly camping there while the battered, outdated furniture from our old apartment looked lost in its large rooms. Even Marcus had been overwhelmed by negotiations for our tower block and had hardly moved into his bedroom.

Miguel turned out to be a homemaking genius. I gave him carte blanche to equip the house, and he presented me with a ten-page list and made several suggestions for improvements. He took extraordinary pleasure in choosing curtain fabric, making lamps out of cheap vases, bargain hunting for old armchairs and reupholstering them himself. Rebecca contributed to the improvements: she made a coffee table out of an empty reel for industrial cable which she found on one of our construction sites and covered with beaten metal, and a bench seat for the terrace built out of painted wooden pallets. On the chimney breast she hung one of the huge phalluses from the series dedicated to me. Miguel swooned with admiration when he saw this 'magnificent painting, absolutely magnificent'. He then asked Rebecca in a very convoluted way whether he could see the other paintings in the series. She showed them to him and from that point on he looked at me with the rapturous gaze of a convert seeing the figure of Christ in a halo of light.

Marcus arranged for his books and furniture to be delivered, and this included his grand piano which made our evenings even more fun. My house was turning into a palace: Miguel's classical taste was brought to life by Rebecca's flights of fancy and Lauren's exotic leanings. My sister relocated her collection of Indian drapes and Mexican carpets that the members of her former commune had eventually sent along with the money they owed her – money that had been politely and then not so politely asked for by the excellent attorney I'd hired near their ranch.

My stormy relationship with Rebecca sometimes thwarted these collective efforts. Her inclination for secrecy and her fierce refusal to answer my questions set my nerves jangling. I still hadn't had an explanation for her disappearance and I couldn't get used to this. We had gotten into a bad habit of slamming doors, and soon there wasn't a single one left in the house that wasn't cracked, or didn't have a damaged lintel. Lauren, who liked opening up minds as well as spaces, recommended that Miguel remove any doors that weren't vital and store them in the basement. He had to restrain himself from doing anything about the others, particularly the door to our bedroom and the one to Becca's studio.

Our relationship was a constant succession of explosions and passionate reconciliations followed by equally fiery couplings. We couldn't stand to be apart and couldn't seem to understand each other. It was exhausting. Four months after Miguel joined us, I came home from work one evening without Marcus, who had gone to have dinner with his father, only to discover Dane sitting on the same sofa as my girlfriend: Dane, the so-called artists' agent, her 'best friend'. They were alone together and were only inches apart, peering at a document. Without saying a word, I charged towards him, grabbed him by his jacket and dragged him out of the room. Shocked and surprised, he tried to defend himself but I chucked him out of the house. The whole scene lasted a few seconds. I was shaking with rage.

Inside, Rebecca was waiting for me, beside herself. She slapped me, hurled insults at me, said I was sick and she refused to spend another minute with me. I raced after her up the stairs, but she took refuge in our bedroom and locked the door. I started kicking the door down which brought Lauren running from the rooftop studio. Miguel emerged from the kitchen, armed with a carving knife, and watched the scene in horror. I got into the room at last but, true to form, Rebecca had slipped out through the window. She was currently climbing down the outside of the building. Seeing her taking such a terrible risk frightened me enough to calm me down a little. I flew downstairs but Lauren stopped me running after Becca in the street.

'That's right!' I yelled at her from the living-room window. 'You go to him! Go on! But don't think you can come back. You can cross me off your list.'

She scowled at me furiously, tapped her index finger to her temple three times to show how crazy she thought I was, and then brandished another single finger high in the air before disappearing, barefoot, around the end of the street.

Lauren spent the evening reasoning with me: I really needed to learn to control my temper and tone down my jealousy. Wanting to own another person was illusory and abusive, she told me. I didn't share these fashionable hare-brained theories which said you could be loyal without being faithful. Even when I was a bachelor in search of easy company, I hadn't liked my lovers sharing themselves with another man. I won't say they were faithful to me, but they had the tact to let me believe they were. Now that I was in love, the thought that someone else might even look at Rebecca made me lose all reason. It was as if she had a chemical effect on my organism. She'd intoxicated me. Weary of talking me around, Lauren tried to calm me with a forced meditation session, and Miguel brought me an infusion 'to help me sleep'.

After calling on a girlfriend who'd lent her a too-big pair of Converse, Rebecca had called Frank Howard's house to get hold of Marcus. She'd described my fit of jealousy and asked for his advice. She was wrung out by our rowing and didn't know how to cope with me.

'Put yourself in his shoes,' Marcus said, wanting to open her eyes on the origins of my anger. 'You have this perfect love together, he comes for dinner with your parents, it doesn't go well, and you disappear into thin air. He spends months desperately looking for you and a year later you turn up with no explanation. He's convinced you're going to vanish again at the least opportunity. Honestly, knowing him as I do, he must really love you to accept this situation.'

'He can't deal with it, though.'

'Well, why don't you talk to him then?' Marcus asked heatedly.

Rebecca was sufficiently shaken to listen attentively to this suggestion.

'I wish I could talk to him, Marcus, but I'm afraid it'll be worse afterward . . .'

'What do you have to say that's so tragic? Were you unfaithful?'

'No, it's not that . . . It's much worse.'

'So tell us. We're your friends and we're here to help you.'

Frank Howard asked his chauffeur to drop them both home, and they arrived solemn-faced. Rebecca walked into the living room which was lit by two candles and where Lauren and I were lying in the relaxing Savasana position.

'OK,' my girlfriend said, switching on the light. 'Seeing as I don't have a choice, I'll tell you everything. But you need to know, Werner, the reason I haven't said anything before was to protect you.'

Manhattan, 1971

We made ourselves comfortable in Rebecca's studio. She was very pale and teetered a little longer on the brink of the abyss of her secrets, before, sitting cross-legged on the floor, she dived in.

'I was around fifteen when I started to understand where my mother was from, and to guess at what she'd been through. She tried to protect me from it for as long as possible. She's a very private person, and rarely confides in people.'

'Like mother, like daughter . . .' Lauren said with a smile.

I shot my sister a black look to shut her up. Rebecca paused and then seemed to come at her story from another direction.

'I've never known my mother happy,' she said. 'She's always been on medication, bought a lot of stuff, travelled a lot on the spur of the moment, spent a lot of time in clinics, and left my father a lot, even though she always came back. I can count the number of times she's thrown her head back and laughed on the fingers of one hand. Even then her laughter was forced and over the top, like it was a performance or a smokescreen. I've never seen her go with the flow and be cheerful without there being a false note, as if her laugh were a cracked bell. Sometimes she's calm but the rest of the time she's constantly negotiating with her ghosts. She doesn't feel right in her bedroom, or in the living room, or on her own, or with other people.

'I gradually put together the pieces of the puzzle: a clue she gave inadvertently one evening when she'd had too much to drink; half-admitted facts from my father who definitely didn't want to know any more; things that her body betrayed even when her lips were sealed. Of course there was her personal diary. She'd hardly written anything at the time, it would have cost her her life, but she still keeps going back to it now. Her past crashes into her present, destroying what she's tried to create. It only takes a smell, an image, a single word. She freezes, her eyes go blank, and I know she's reliving something she should never have lived. It's the same with her diary. She's describing a party or a lunch and then this banal description breaks off thanks to some mysterious association, and she's back in her hell. I stole those books, or maybe she left them around for me to see, I'm not really sure. I sometimes think she wanted me to know. In terrifying flashes and elliptical references, they describe what no one could imagine.

'I'd been working at piecing together her past for several years when we met a woman on Fifth Avenue. My mother and I were shopping. I don't really like buying clothes – I guess you noticed that,' she added with small smile, 'but it's one of her drugs and her way of showing me affection. We were just coming out of Saks when my mother saw her. The crowd seemed to part. They stopped right in front of each other, paralysed, then threw themselves into each other's arms. They cried and hugged and stroked each other's faces and hair. They kept saying, "You're alive!" The woman called my mother Lyne and my mom called her Edwige. I didn't understand any of it. My mother introduced me to her and Edwige said, "You're so lucky, Lyne. So lucky to have such a beautiful daughter. Such a perfect daughter. I . . . couldn't." I asked whether Edwige would like to join us for lunch and they both almost flinched. They looked at each other and reached some understanding. Edwige was dressed modestly, she worked as a saleswoman in a store on Fifth Avenue. My mother removed her diamond earrings, her bracelets and the gold necklace she never took off, even in bed, because it hid the scar on her throat. She put the earrings on Edwige, who tried to protest, and forcibly put the bracelets in her pockets. Then she took Edwige's hand, put the necklace into it and closed her fingers, saying, "It's nothing. You're helping me by taking them. Please . . ."

'They hugged each other close one more time and my mother said, "If you ever need anything, come see me. I live east of Central Park on 80th Street." She tore a page from her appointments diary and scribbled our address. They parted very briskly. When we were in the car my mother couldn't stop crying. "Don't worry, sweetheart," she said, "please don't worry, I'm happy," but I could tell she was much more sad than happy. The years she'd buried had just come spilling back into her life, more real than ever. That woman had made such an impression on her that I moved heaven and earth to find her. I stopped at every building on Fifth Avenue until I eventually found the place where she'd worked for a few weeks under a different name. Then it took me months to talk her round. She didn't want to betray a friend. I won't describe what my mother suffered, it's indescribable. And so is everything that happened back there. I'm just trying to give you the facts.'

I was struck by how tormented Rebecca was. Equally shocked, Marcus and Lauren sat in silence. Rebecca couldn't look us in the eye; her gaze drifted somewhere beyond us. When she started talking again, tears rolled down her cheeks but the factual monotone of her voice didn't change, as if she weren't even aware she was crying. As if someone else was crying for her.

'My mother was born in Budapest in 1929,' she said. 'She was arrested along with her father on 30 March 1944, a few days after the Nazis invaded Hungary and formed a new government. She was sent to Auschwitz-Birkenau and arrived on 17 May 1944 after four days' travelling with no food or water. When they reached the station, there were men waiting to help them off the train because they were in cattle wagons with no running boards. One of these men took my mother under her armpits and, as he lifted her to the ground, whispered, "Whatever you do, don't get in the truck."

'She didn't think, she just obeyed. She wished she could take her father with her but he could hardly walk and the SS bundled him into the crammed truck. She couldn't even kiss him goodbye and never saw him again. The people getting into that truck were the weak, the exhausted, anyone too young or too old, or already sick. I have no illusions about what happened to them. My mother walked a couple of miles to the camp, along a road that was a narrow tongue of mud and frost edged on either side with barbed wire. Every colour seemed to have been drained from this filthy snowy landscape, with a tide of devastated figures trudging through it. It was a black-and-white world. She saw squalid huts with cadaverous faces at the windows. Their haunted eyes gave her a glimpse of the horrors to come. At fifteen, my mother looked like a seventeen-year-old, she was well developed and very beautiful. At the gates to the camp the SS officer dividing the deportees into groups didn't realise how young she was, or he'd have sent her to her death. Once inside, they were ordered to strip. My mother hadn't undressed in front of anyone since she was six years old when her nursemaid still helped her. And now she found herself naked. In the snow of a Polish winter. In front of hundreds of other women . . . and men too. Her back hunched with shame and cold, she didn't have enough hands to cover herself. In front of her, guards had started shaving her fellow deportees of all their hair. Others were standing in line, waiting to be tattooed. My mother was tattooed with a dirty needle pierced carelessly into her skin at least thirty times. The ink spread, swallowing up her number and a triangle representing a star of David. She was frightened. They told her she had to learn this number by heart, but it was illegible. When they started shaving her pubic hair, just before getting to the hair on her head, an SS officer intervened. She didn't understand what he said but he grabbed her hair in one hand, tipped her head back and opened her mouth to inspect her teeth. Like a horse. Then he said, "Block 24." Only one other girl had the same luck, if you can call it luck. A pretty Polish Jew who would go by the name Edwige and who I would meet years later on Fifth Avenue.

'A guard gave my mother a yard of brown felt to cover herself and led her, still barefoot, to the first building. She was washed once, disinfected, then washed again with a coarse brush. She was taken into a separate room where a female doctor subjected her to various examinations, including a gynaecological examination. The doctor checked that she was a virgin and informed the guard who'd brought her. She was trailed over to a small red-brick building near the camp gates. There were about twenty other women there, and she learned that the place was called the "Joy Division".

'An SS guard gave them new names: my mother would be Lyne and her friend Edwige.

'She talked to some of the other women, trying to understand what to expect. They didn't have the heart to explain. Meanwhile, the washing and vigorous scrubbing had cleaned her tattoo and revealed the triangle that betrayed her Jewish origins. The other women warned her that this symbol could put her in serious danger. Her life depended on how much pleasure she could give the SS guards but their racist laws forbade them having relations with a Jewish woman. One girl told her she should fill out the triangle with ink every day, and gave her a small pot and a pointed stick left by another woman. When my mother asked what had happened to this woman, one of the girls told her that she'd started coughing and was sent to join the other prisoners. "Just don't ever forget to black out that triangle," the girl said. A black triangle was the mark of "social outcasts", which meant prostitutes or common criminals. With this tattooed onto her, she wouldn't risk being summarily executed as some prisoners were.

'There was high demand for sex workers. In the spring of 1944, the SS took to choosing them according to aesthetic criteria or to meet some perversion, not worrying about Himmler's codes which dictated that "only women who no longer have anything to offer the German people may be selected". They put about rumours that this work was voluntary – even the other prisoners believed it was. My mother very quickly realised what would happen to her.

'Whatever the season, the camp was subjected to falls of dirty snow, an acrid grey cloud that veiled the sun. A shower of human ashes. Anyone in Block 24 who rebelled was threatened with the ovens. If she rebelled a second time, she was sent there. The building was officially meant to be reserved for Aryan and more deserving prisoners, but in 1944 two sections of it had been set aside to satisfy the needs of the SS. If the men stuck to the guidelines, they were allowed to commit the sexual act – condoned purely for reasons of physical and mental health – but only in the missionary position. A guard watched through a hole in the door to check the correct procedure was observed. It was easy to arrange for this overseer to close his eyes. If the man wanted to take a girl on all fours, it cost him extra. If he wanted to beat her, it cost a little more. After each session, the women had to wash, use anti-bacterial and spermicidal lotions, hide their bruises with make-up, and wipe away traces of tears or blood before going back to work. They weren't allowed to speak all day. If a guard was put in a difficult position by one of the women because she'd confided in someone about how he treated her, he would kill her on the spot. In everyone else's opinion these girls were lucky: they had endless supplies of soap, they wore clean underwear all day long, seven days a week, they had make-up, they didn't go hungry because the SS didn't like them too thin, and they lived a few extra months if they didn't get sick or pregnant. A pregnancy signed their death warrant.

'The SS chose whatever appealed to them. Some had favourites and could reserve these girls, unless they'd been claimed already by a higher-ranking officer. Unfortunately for my mother, she caught the eye of one of the most senior officers, who also proved to be one of the most violent. He was a very tall and particularly muscular man. He could have broken a girl's neck with one hand. He had dark-blond hair and ice-coloured eyes. He was beautiful but that only made his cruelty even more unbearable. My mother had never been with a man, but shortly after she arrived in Block 24, he savagely deflowered her. She was used by five other men on that first day. Her "master", as he liked to be called, bragged that he wasn't jealous. In fact, he liked sharing. He had a perverse weakness for scars. My mother was only fifteen and still had skin like a child. He took great pleasure in damaging it, and used a number of scalpels, which he kept in a small red case. It was as if purity was an insult to him, freshness a condemnation. He needed to drag her innocence down to his own degraded level. He enjoyed games, like strangulation, that diced with death. This man chose my mother's friend, Edwige, only once but all those years later she still described him as the devil incarnate. He'd studied chemistry to quite a high level and could have made a career in that field, but he'd found true fulfilment in the SS.

'My mother wasn't released after three months, as the guards had told her she would be. She had miraculously escaped illness and hadn't fallen pregnant, but the traumas, despair and shame of her life had drained her. Her period stopped the very first month. Edwige envied her: unlike my mother, she had to undergo a "curettage" administered by one of the other girls. It saved her life but left her unable to have children. I think it was her thwarted maternal feelings that drew her to me and allowed her to tell me their story, even though that meant breaking the pact she had with my mother . . .' Rebecca's voice trailed off, and she seemed lost in thought for a moment.

'My mother arrived at Auschwitz at one of the worst points in its history,' she went on. 'The SS were "liquidating" the Romany camp. I found tiny pieces of paper in her diary: cooking recipes that the women exchanged in what little spare time they had. In among these slips of paper was a brief account of camp life. It described how the Romanies were told to dig a deep pit and once it was finished, they had to stand on the edge of the pit while the SS shot them. Then another wave of prisoners would come and line up, shots rang out, the victims fell and covered the first layer of bodies. The human tide continued to flow and disappear until the pit was full and was covered over.

'Edwige also told me about one early-summer day when, for once, there was no ash falling from the sky. The Germans brought together a Jewish orchestra – some of the best musicians in the world were in that camp. For an hour they played the most sublime melodies, and people sang. The beauty of it had a more profound effect on my mother than many forms of torture. It broke through her armour and touched her soul which was huddled in some uncharted part of her. She wasn't the same after that. She stopped talking to people and hardly ate, and then one evening in August, when the SS were overwhelmed by a huge pile of bodies produced by more shootings, my mother escaped. Edwige didn't understand how she did it, or who helped her. Her private diary helped me piece the facts together: one of her guards had fallen in love with her, and he knocked out her tormentor . . . *in flagrante*, as they say. Then he put on the other man's uniform and helped my mother. I'll probably never know how she got out of the camp. Even a high-ranking SS officer would have had trouble smuggling out a captive . . . but this guard managed it.'

Rebecca came to a stop again. She seemed to be flagging.

'The evening you came to dinner, Werner,' she said, still not looking at me, 'was the only time she really confided in me, but she didn't tell me how she escaped. Fear made the words stick in her throat. My mother's a very gifted linguist, she speaks eight languages fluently. In a few months Edwige had taught her enough Polish for her to get by. In the first days after she and the guard escaped, she found support among the locals. Peasant farmers fed them and put them in touch with the resistance in Krakow. Once they were over the Slovak border my mother managed to give the love-struck guard the slip. She travelled on false papers, going as fast as she could and as far as she could. She didn't try to find out what had happened to her father, or the rest of her family. She travelled hundreds of miles until she eventually found a way to get to the States.'

We were stunned. Rebecca wept silently. I got up to take her in my arms, but she stopped me.

'Wait!' she said. 'Please wait.'

She was shaking now, and hunched over, apparently digging into her very depths to find the strength to go on.

'I haven't told you everything. I haven't told you the most important thing.'

We waited, hanging on her words.

'My mother's torturer had a name . . .'

For the first time since she started talking, Rebecca turned her reddened face towards me and peered right at me with her violet eyes. I stood up to go over to her, but she put up her hand again and said flatly, 'His name was Zilch. Captain Zilch.'

The words reverberated around the room. The three of us were in shock. This revelation had so many possible ramifications that we couldn't grasp its full weight. It drove into my mind and my body, blocking my ability to move or think.

'His name was Zilch,' she said again, 'and I have proof that he was your father.'

The first thing I did was yell at her. I told her she was crazy, that this whole story was nothing to do with me. She saw evil in everything. She had no right. She was sick to hate me that much. What did she want? To destroy me? Drag me into hell with her? I hadn't done anything to deserve being treated like this. How did she come up with this stuff? She knew how much it upset me that I didn't know anything about my biological parents, it was a dirty trick to get at me on that front. To play on my weaknesses and fears. What she was telling me was a despicable form of attack. It was cruel and unfounded. I couldn't even find the words to describe it. Or actually, yes, I could, just one: perverse.

Marcus and Lauren seemed to have been turned into pillars of salt. Stranded between the two of us, they didn't react in any way. Their silence just made my shouting ring out all the louder. Lauren tried to stop me pacing furiously, but I dodged her. I didn't want her to touch me, and she started to cry. On I talked, and on. I said everything I wanted to say and then fell silent and looked into Rebecca's face. She looked away, and I knew then that she was telling the truth. My anger subsided instantly and I was left feeling tormented, drained.

To know. I had always so badly wanted to know . . . but this! To be branded with a red iron, guilty of the worst a man can do. To be born of that infamy. I felt dirty. Trapped. Repulsive. The others didn't say anything but eyed me fearfully. The room started to spin and my ears to buzz. Something I'd buried inside me for years suddenly surfaced: a volcanic eruption.

I leant against the wall and beat my head against it, until Rebecca stopped me. I pushed her aside harshly and then felt bad and reached for her. But my anger gained the upper hand again and I said she had to prove what she was saying, I couldn't believe her, it was impossible.

'Do you hear me? It's impossible that out of all four billion people who live on this planet we managed to meet when we're both stained by the same blood. Blood that connects us but will keep us apart forever.'

She had to tell me everything, right then, right there. How could she have spent all those months without talking to me? And I couldn't see why she'd come back to me, anyway. If I really was fathered by this man she was describing, she shouldn't have. Or come anywhere near me, or kissed me, and certainly not claimed she loved me. You can't love the son of a man who's done things like that.

Rebecca took my head in her hands. I was crying and tried to turn away but she forced me to look at her.

'I came back, Wern, because I can't live without you. You're my love, my man, my life. I don't know what will happen to us, but I know I can't be with anyone else. I can't deal with everything all the time, sometimes I can't take any more. I didn't tell you anything because I knew what all this would do to you. It nearly destroyed me. For months I was broken but when I pulled myself together I came to find you as soon as I could. I tried to ignore this stuff, I thought we could pretend, go back to how it was before, when we had no idea what was drawing us so violently to each other. But it's there now, crouching between us. However hard I tried to hide it, you could feel it stirring inside me. I tried to sidestep the issue again and again, and then this evening I realised this pain is a part of our love. When we manage to go beyond it, no one will have a more wonderful love than ours. Werner, the very fact that our paths crossed is because of this wrong that was done and that we, you and I, have to atone for.'

Manhattan, 1971

Marcus and Lauren joined our hug, along with Shakespeare. We were fragile, tortured; it felt like the smallest draught of air would blow me over. We tried to hold each other close despite the chasm that had opened up between us. I tried to get a grip on myself, but I needed Rebecca to talk, to tell me everything. I couldn't go on with this waiting stringing out my heart and my stomach. She promised she would hide nothing from me.

Marcus went down to fetch a bottle of vodka and I drained two glasses one after the other without the usual comforting glow. It left me bleary and nauseous. My eyes filled with tears again for no particular reason. My old childhood anxieties and the images associated with them were resurfacing. I urged Rebecca to tell us more, and so she started to talk again.

'From the age of fifteen to seventeen, I became obsessed with my mother's story. I was consumed with these ghosts of hers. I was appalled, powerless, haunted. I lost a lot of weight, and started having sleeping problems . . . I could spend almost a week without waking and then one when I didn't sleep at all . . . You've seen that for yourselves. The doctor couldn't find any physiological problem. My father sent me to my mother's analyst, Dr Nars. Without even knowing him, I loathed this uptown guru. I blamed him for ruining our family by taking my mom from us for months on end. At every opportunity he shut her away in his clinic, knocked her out with drugs and wouldn't let me see her on the grounds I exhausted her – me, her own little girl.

'When my father took me to Dr Nars's office for the first

time as a teenager, the "good doctor" didn't see any conflict in treating mother and daughter at the same time. In a situation in which any analyst with even the rudiments of an ethical code would have sent me to see a different practitioner, he insisted that, no, this would give him a "better overall picture". What this definitely did give him was control over one of the richest and most powerful men in the US – my father. I disliked Nars from that very first meeting. He listened to me for ten minutes, then listened to the sound of his own voice for a half-hour, diagnosing me with pathological feelings of guilt, hysterical tendencies and an inability to face up to reality. These mental disorders explained my artistic aspirations: painting was just a form of escape. He advised me not to draw, to give my body clock a chance to reset. He dealt out his theories with such arrogance, such conviction, that he discredited himself in my eyes. I couldn't see what harm there was in running away. Reality is terrible. My mother knows all about that. And anyone born this century has seen it unmasked. It sets limits on us, humiliates us. Meaning we're constantly sacrificing our dreams and our endless possibilities. How could I respect a psychiatrist who stubbornly saw art as neurosis? And labelled me hysterical because I was a woman he was trying to shoehorn into his simplistic schemes? I was outside the box. I came out at the top, the sides and the bottom. After about ten sessions I spoke my mind: if he'd studied psychoanalysis and written so much about it, that was because he personally didn't have the basic tools to make connections with other people and be loved by them, starting with listening and empathising. And his contempt for art was an admission of his own impotence, his blinkered imagination and his terror of appearing abnormal when he was someone who should really have embraced and celebrated abnormality.

'Despite my father's protestations, I never set foot in Dr Nars's office again. I painted more than ever and I left home, moving in with friends and then with Andy. I had my first exhibition at eighteen, and several more followed . . . In the end, Daddy begged me to come home, and I gave in for my mother's sake. And as for reality, I decided to tackle it in my own way. I kept on piecing together the jigsaw puzzle, listening to other victims describing the things my mother couldn't tell me. She was ashamed, you see. Confessions from the Block 24 girls never produced a good outcome. They weren't protected by the aura associated with victims and martyrs because everybody thought they'd been "willing". Willing to be raped?

'It was while I was looking into all this that I met Dane at a meeting for former deportees. He's about ten years older than me, his parents were Polish Jews and his family was almost completely wiped out in the war. Eighty-nine people in all. He just has one aunt left, and he was living with her in Brooklyn. As soon as we met, we knew we were carrying the same burden. Just like me, he couldn't bear how powerless we were. Just like me, he had a great crater of hatred seething inside him because thousands of torturers had acted with impunity. Every ounce of him clamoured for justice, and for blood. I was enthralled. He planted this idea in my mind that I could cleanse my mother of the agonies she'd suffered and the burning shame she still felt. I couldn't help believing it would soothe her. She had to know what had happened to her tormentor; he had to be tracked down and punished. Dane is part of a network of camp survivors and their close relatives, a network that centralises information from all over the world. Hundreds of letters come in each week from victims and from ageing Nazis betraying former friends.

'A few months before I met Dane, he and his group had come across a very valuable document: an official register of the SS. They bought it in Austria, from a former member of the Gestapo who was crippled with debts. The guy realised that the men at the top of the Nazi party had made a lot of money during the

war. They had beautiful cars, gold bars, soft manicured hands
. . . but he hadn't put anything aside so he denounced his fellow
officers. The network had several copies made of the register,
adding notes to it and handing it on to other organisations.
They had no state support because at the time everyone was
trying to forget, the subject was meant to be closed after the
Nuremberg trials, but they believed the victims should reclaim
their right to see justice done.

'Dane offered to enrol me. He'd give me access to his network
to shed light on my mother's past and I could do him some
small favours. "A pretty girl like you," he said, "a known artist,
from a respectable family," could be very useful in his hunt for
information and maybe in other operations, but he was mysterious about what those might be. I soon realised why he needed
me – most of the former criminals were protected and there was
no way the authorities wanted to open that Pandora's box. Even
evil individuals with the most heavily documented crimes felt
perfectly safe. We could bring all the proof we liked before the
Justice Department, nobody was going to think it was a good
idea to pursue these cases. So Dane and his network started
using more . . . robust methods. I took part in three operations.
Once we located the criminals, I got to know them, I charmed
them and they tried to seduce me. We went out for dinner, then
they took me to their place or a hotel for a nightcap—'

That was too much. I broke away from the tight circle we'd
formed.

'You're completely out of your mind . . .'

'Nothing happened,' Rebecca said calmly. 'I put a sleeping
pill in their drink and opened the door to let Dane in. That's
where my part stopped.'

Marcus also stood up and asked what happened to the men
she'd drugged.

'We tried to hand the first one over to the American authorities anonymously, but he was released the next day without

even being interrogated. There's no way of bringing these monsters to trial in the United States because their crimes were committed abroad.'

'And the others?' Marcus persisted.

'Dane sent them to Israel where they *can* be tried. We got them over the Mexican border and from there it was child's play.'

I could feel my anger rising again.

'But who finances this, the flights?'

'Thousands of victims are prepared to pay dearly to see these bastards judged,' she said coolly.

'But what if you made a mistake?' Marcus asked.

'We didn't make mistakes,' Rebecca replied tartly. 'We had more proof than we needed. If this country weren't rotten to the core, those men would already have been sent to the electric chair.'

She paused to avoid getting too carried away, and poured herself a glass of vodka before picking up the thread of her thoughts.

'On these missions, I met a lot of researchers and historians who tracked Nazi criminals. Armed with the details my mother gave me that evening you came for dinner at my parents' house, I contacted them. I needed to know about this SS officer who answered to the name of Zilch. I went to Germany and spent several weeks gathering information. A history professor in Berlin, who's been helping us for several years, found some photos in Nazi archives.'

She rummaged through her muddle of painting materials and from under a pile of papers she produced a brown folder tied with red ribbon. She opened it and took out photos of various sizes. She handed the first one to me and I snatched it from her. Lauren and Marcus peered over my shoulder.

'It was taken when the inventors of the V2 surrendered to the American authorities. The event was a big deal at the time. This guy's the major brain of the team, Wernher von Braun,' she said, pointing to a good-looking dark-haired man with a broad frame.

'Hey, he's the Disney guy! I loved those space films!' Marcus exclaimed.

'More importantly,' Rebecca snapped, 'he's the guy from the Dora work camp. He ran a missile factory where thousands of prisoners were reduced to slavery. The "workers" were subjected to inhuman routines. That man killed more people *making* bombs than blowing them up.'

'We watched those films too, Werner, remember?' Lauren said in a shocked voice. '*Man in Space* and *Man and the Moon* . . .'

I nodded, tight-lipped.

'He's a hero to a whole generation! Millions of little Americans dreamed of going into space and to the moon because of him!' Lauren half-whispered, turning to Rebecca with a horrified expression.

'I know, but he's also a former SS officer.'

'And can I ask what the connection is with my supposed father?'

Rebecca handed us another photo.

'This one's older. It's from after war was declared, when Himmler inspected the base in Peenemünde.'

I grabbed the photograph: one man stood out from the group of scientists that included von Braun. He was a head taller than the other men, and was so like me it looked as if the picture had been skilfully edited. Beside him stood a young woman, a ravishing blonde who set my heart beating. They were referred to in the caption as 'Professor Johann Zilch and his wife Luisa'.

I sat on one of the crates that served as chairs in the studio, rubbing my face but failing to eradicate what I'd just seen. I took the photo again to have a closer look at it, and was swamped by a tide of contradictory emotions. The room span again and my ears buzzing. Things I'd kept buried for years were still surfacing. Everything scrolled through my mind: Armande, Andrew, my constant feelings of otherness, difference, loneliness; the black hole of my early childhood and my terrible teenage years. The time spent searching, endlessly but hopelessly trying to imagine why my parents had abandoned me. I'd tried to picture their faces countless times, and wondered whether I looked like them. Seeing them at last, recognising myself so clearly in their features made me feel sickeningly light-headed. I couldn't reconcile these young people with the monsters Rebecca had just described . . .

She handed me another picture showing four men in swimming trunks and Johann Zilch in a shirt. He was standing beside a swimming pool, idle and happy. I was struck again by the resemblance: it was as if I'd had a previous life but had no recollection of it.

'This was taken at Fort Bliss, just after the war when the scientists had moved to the States,' Rebecca told us.

'What are you talking about!' Marcus exclaimed, taking the photo. 'How can you think the United States would take in Nazis! Scientists, yes, but definitely not Nazis!'

'That's what happened,' Rebecca retorted. 'Their background was carefully edited by our friends in the secret service, with the help of NASA. Why do you think the authorities are so uncooperative?'

Marcus fell silent. He couldn't believe the military would have hidden such momentous information from the American people. I took the photo back from him and studied the face of Judith's torturer in minute detail.

'Now I understand your mother's reaction when I came to your house . . .' I sighed.

'She was traumatised,' Rebecca said. 'When I went upstairs with her after dinner, mom talked and talked and talked. She told me more in one evening than she had since I'd started asking her about her past . . . I didn't tell her what I already knew, she'd have been too hurt. But she described her tormentor, this terrible Captain Zilch. When she came into the library where you were waiting for us, she thought she was seeing him.'

'But I can't help any of this! I'm American, my parents are called Armande and Andrew Goodman, I have nothing to do with this insane guy who cut up unfortunate women in hell months before I was even born!'

I paused and looked right into Rebecca's eyes so that she couldn't possibly lie.

'Does your mother know we're together?' I asked.

My beauty flushed and admitted her mother didn't know.

'She's in hospital. She's completely lost her mind. Dr Nars won't let me visit her. My father's devoted to that psychiatrist, as if he's a saint. He's very unstable too, my dad, I mean . . . some days I understand him, but other times I don't get him at all. In his shoes, I'd have put my whole fortune on the table to track down this Nazi and make him pay for his crimes. Instead, he spends hours at my mother's bedside, reading to her and calming her when she's delirious. I don't want to fight with him, so I wait till he's gone and figure out my own way to see her.'

'How?' Lauren asked, amazed.

'I go on evenings when there are baseball matches. The watchman at the clinic is glued to his TV and doesn't notice anything. I climb over the garden gate and go in on the third floor.'

'By scaling the front of the building, I suppose . . .' I said.

'Yes. I really scared myself last time I went. The gutter suddenly gave way and I would probably have broken my neck if the awning outside the day room hadn't broken my fall. I managed to get up and run away before security found me. After that accident, when I thought my time had come, I wanted to see you . . . And I came knocking at your door,' Rebecca admitted with a sad smile. 'You wondered how I got my bruises, now you know.'

I could feel the blood draining from my face.

'From now on I forbid you to climb anything higher than a footstool! You scared the life out of me just this evening . . .'

Lauren handed me the photos, which she'd just looked at in more detail. I tried to dredge up some meaning from them, some sign that would help me extricate myself from the fog that had closed in around me.

'I'm trying to understand this, but I just can't . . . How did you get these photos of Fort Bliss?'

'Dane helped me when I returned from Germany. He activated his network. We found out there was a Johann Zilch in Operation Paperclip.'

'What's Operation Paperclip?' Marcus asked.

'That was the code name for the mission that brought fifteen hundred Nazi scholars and engineers to the States in complete secrecy – and completely illegally. One hundred and seventeen of them spent several years in Fort Bliss in Texas. I went there with Dane. The base was impenetrable, but we hung around a lot at Ella's Diner where soldiers and staff from the base liked to go, and we started offering them drinks and asking them questions, then we established contact with a woman who'd been secretary to Commander James Hamill who oversaw the scientists back in the day. She still worked at Fort Bliss and we hinted that she could make money out of helping us get our hands on specific information. She lived alone and was about to retire, so she took the bait. First of all, we wanted the list of scientists and their wives, and we supplied her with false names and a phone number where she could contact us.

'A few weeks later, she sold us this precious list and, most importantly, gave us a key to our investigations. I'd asked her whether she remembered a Johann Zilch and she described an especially interesting incident. She admitted that she'd taken an immediate dislike to Zilch, and – after a few tequilas – she was more explicit: in 1946, she and Johann Zilch's wife Luisa had become friendly. She remembered them very well and the story about them that created a scandal at the time. She told us the Zilches had had a child, an adorable boy about eighteen months old. She said he was a really tough kid, big, blond and determined, with blue eyes.'

'What was his name?' I asked, sitting up from my slumped position on the sofa.

'His name was Werner, darling . . . that little boy must have been you. I've cross-checked on the list of scientists. Johann Zilch arrived with von Braun in September 1945. They landed in New York and spent a while in a base in Massachusetts before being posted to Fort Bliss. Then Johann brought over his wife, Luisa, and his son, Werner.'

A tidal wave of questions, memories and rebellion washed over me again.

'Then the secretary told me this strange story. Johann was a troubled man, and had a difficult relationship with his co-workers; von Braun was the only one who seemed to protect him. He spent very little time with his son. From what the secretary gathered, he hadn't recovered from a serious accident during the war. One day, he beat his wife so violently he almost killed her. Luisa asked to leave the base with her son but at the time the scientists and their wives didn't have residence cards or passports. They weren't allowed to leave the military base or have any contact with the general population. So Luisa said she wanted to return to Germany with you, Werner, but Commander Hamill refused to let her. The secretary got married two weeks later and took a month's vacation. When she returned, Johann, Luisa and the baby had disappeared with no forwarding address.'

'I don't understand any of this,' I said, rubbing my head.

'I don't understand all of it, either. There are lots of missing pieces. I have only one more thing to tell you and then you'll all know as much as I do: I asked the secretary in Fort Bliss if she had a photo of Luisa, so that I could try to trace her. In the end she sold me one.'

Rebecca handed me a snap of a plump young woman carrying a blond child. I found it immensely moving to see myself in my mother's arms, to see the face that I'd imagined a thousand times and had tried in vain to retrieve from the limbo of my earliest years, as I had her voice, her smell, the things she did and the tenderness she showed me. It brought tears to my eyes. I devoured that photo with all the avid passion I'd been holding back for years. I tried, just by looking at her, to bring this woman to life, and recognise her. I wanted to reawaken my memories, to record the child I once was, to make this image a part of me, a founding stone on which to start rebuilding myself. I looked, and looked again, but suddenly all the illusory power of the photo collapsed, and I felt my face harden.

'You've noticed, haven't you?' Rebecca asked.

'Yes,' I answered, knowing instantly what she meant. 'In the picture from Germany, Luisa Zilch was very blonde, with a triangular-shaped face and light-coloured eyes. The woman holding me in this picture has a round face and dark hair and eyes . . .'

'That's the question . . . Which is the real Luisa?'

'And which is my real mother?'

Manhattan, 1971

Rebecca had opened Pandora's box. I felt like someone picking themselves up after an earthquake. The questions that had haunted me as a teenager and taken me years to bury, were resurfacing from the dark depths of my mind. It seemed impossible to ignore them now. I wanted to meet von Braun as soon as was feasible. During the year that Rebecca had devoted to understanding her mother's past and mine, she'd learned that he was now Director of Strategies at NASA; naturally, she'd considered visiting him, but had felt I was more likely to succeed in getting him to talk. My name and my face were bound to bring back memories for him. Von Braun was too important a witness to risk provoking his mistrust with a botched conversation. He alone could unravel the mystery of my origins or, if he didn't have all the answers, he could put us in touch with other witnesses.

Donna's legendary efficiency was set in motion. She persuaded von Braun's assistant, Bonnie, to mention me to the great scientist, and my name did all the work: von Braun would see me late morning the following Friday at the NASA headquarters.

I flew to Washington early on the morning of the meeting. I refused to let Rebecca come with me, she wouldn't have been able to disguise her anger, and putting von Braun in the dock didn't strike me as the best way to get him to talk. I was nervous. I imagined the worst possible outcomes, and tried to prepare myself for them. If von Braun confirmed that my father was a sadistic pervert who had committed war crimes, how could I wash myself clean of that poison? Could I be the product of evil without being evil myself? Marcus and Lauren could go on and on telling me children weren't responsible for their parents' crimes, but it seemed to me my blood was contaminated. I had discovered an unknown beast lurking deep inside me, ready to pounce at any moment. Wasn't I brutal and irascible, prepared to go to great lengths to get what I wanted? Hadn't I been criticised for being cynical and hard? In the space of an evening I'd become my own enemy, and what von Braun could tell me threatened to make me despise myself.

NASA occupied an impressive glass-and-concrete building. I was greeted on the first floor by Bonnie, a round little woman with tight auburn curls tumbling over her red glasses. She was professionalism personified.

'The director's just finishing a meeting, he'll be here any minute,' she told me, showing me into a room with dark wood panelling.

She asked whether I'd like anything to drink and I asked for a glass of water. She closed the door behind her and I studied the room: thick carpeting muffled footsteps, lined up along a low sideboard along one wall were three-foot-high models of Saturn rockets. The room was dominated by an imposing elm-wood desk. Beside the telephone on its polished surface stood the prizes awarded to von Braun by the most prestigious civic and scientific American institutions. On the other side of the room, next to bookshelves filled with historical and technical volumes, a series of wooden frames displayed photographs of the scientist with President Kennedy, President Johnson, President Eisenhower and other major figures. A pleated chestnut-brown curtain was partly drawn across the window, subduing the bright late-morning light.

I was standing facing the desk when von Braun came in. He looked a lot older than in the photographs or in my childhood memories of his television programmes about the moon, the cosmos and the solar system. His thick brown hair was streaked with grey. He was wearing a dark suit with a small checked pattern, a white shirt and a blue tie.

'Good morning, young man, I'm delighted to meet you,' he announced, shaking my hand and giving my shoulder a fatherly pat. He still had a strong German accent.

He peered at my face and said, 'It's incredible how like them you are! I hope you don't mind if I call you Werner?'

'Of course,' I consented.

'You know we have the same first name,' he said.

'Yes, I think there's just an "h" between us.'

'That's right. Your mother liked the name better without the "h". Did you know I'm your godfather?'

I felt my heart accelerate to hear him mention my mother, but tried to remain outwardly calm.

'No, I didn't.'

'Well, godfather . . . at least, that's what your mother said when she was pregnant with you. And she did give you my name . . . I imagine you're here to talk about her,' he added, gesturing for me to sit in an armchair in the more comfortable corner of his office.

'I am. I hope you can help me answer some questions.'

He nodded and, smiling warmly, asked, 'Tell me, how's your father?'

'What do you mean?' I asked rather abruptly.

'Johann, your father, how is he? I haven't seen him for twenty years . . .'

'I'm not sure I understand . . .' I ventured, unsettled.

We looked at each other in some confusion.

'My father's name is Andrew Goodman,' I said. After a fraught silence, I added, 'I was adopted.'

I could have broken the glass coffee table with one hand and he wouldn't have been more surprised.

'How do you mean, adopted?' von Braun asked.

'When I was three. By Armande and Andrew Goodman, a couple from New Jersey.'

'But what happened to Johann?'

'Johann Zilch? So was he my father?'

'Well, yes . . .'

'I never knew Johann Zilch, and until last week I didn't even know he existed. He's why I'm here.'

'I can't believe it,' von Braun said, so perplexed that he took a handkerchief from his pocket and mopped his brow. 'Would you like a coffee?'

'No, thank you.'

Von Braun didn't have time to go out: Bonnie came in with a tray. She handed me the glass of water I'd asked for and gave von Braun a cup of coffee with two sugars, treating him with deference and admiration.

'So you don't speak German?' he asked me once she'd left the room.

'Not a word.'

'I just can't understand what happened . . .'

He fell silent for a moment and drummed on the armrest of the sofa, then looked at his watch and stood up.

'You don't have a lunch appointment, do you?' he asked.

I shook my head. He called Bonnie on the intercom and asked her to list his meetings for the rest of the day. He cancelled them all until four in the afternoon and came back to sit down.

'Great, I can keep you, then. We're going to need some time.'

I wasn't expecting to meet such a benevolent man. Rebecca had painted a picture of this man's crimes, but his charm and the intelligence shining in his eyes threw me. Von Braun was warm and empathetic.

'Given what you've just told me, I'm not sure I can help you, but at least tell me what you came here for,' he said.

'I wanted to know about my birth parents. I've managed to trace them back to Fort Bliss and therefore to you, but the trail gets confused before they came to the US . . .'

I reached for my bag and took out the file with the photographs. I selected two and laid them on the table in front of him.

'You mentioned my mother earlier and you even said you were my godfather, so maybe you can help me by telling me which of these two women is Luisa Zilch.'

Von Braun took the photos and, with a solemn nostalgic expression, pointed to the young blonde.

'That's Luisa. We look so young . . .' he sighed. 'Just children . . . This picture was taken before the war. We were still at Peenemünde.'

'Do you know what happened to Luisa?' I probed.

He paused for a moment and looked at me with a mixture of concern and compassion.

'My poor friend,' he said, putting his hand on my shoulder again. 'She died years ago . . . before we came to the States.'

This came as a terrible blow. From the bar under the bookshelves, von Braun took a decanter of whisky and two glasses, and filled them generously.

'I think you'll need something more comforting than what you have there. And so will I.'

'How did she die?'

Dr von Braun chose his words carefully.

'She was critically injured in the Dresden bombings.'

He grasped from my expression that I had no idea where Dresden was.

'It's a German city, it was one of the most beautiful. During the war the British razed it to the ground. The building your mother lived in was destroyed. Soldiers managed to extricate her from the rubble, but she couldn't be saved. She only lived long enough to give birth to you . . .'

He was still telling me what he knew of Luisa's death when I was knocked sideways by a powerful realisation. The dream that had haunted me for years came back to me in a flash, and

I instantly understood that this dream was my first memory. An event so monstrous, it had been imprinted on my mind before I was even born.

First I saw a very beautiful blonde woman running and, some fifty strides later, I saw her fall. She was thrown to the ground by an invisible force and then flipped savagely onto her back. I went over to her and she spoke to me. Her huge, almost super-naturally dark-blue eyes seemed to draw me in. She looked at me very tenderly and said things that I understood in the dream but couldn't put into words once I woke. Then I was in a completely different place, tearing myself away from the world to watch it disintegrate. I had no physical sensations: I could see fire but not feel its heat, see people screaming but not hear their cries. I watched buildings collapse but their dust didn't fill my mouth. Fragments of masonry flew in every direction but never struck me. I couldn't say how old I was in the dream, nor whether I was sitting, standing or lying down. Still less whether I was alive or already dead. After a while a noise grew louder, and I realised that the appalling clamour of the apocalypse wasn't reaching me because it was smothered by this whirling, thumping sound all around me. A noise circling me. At some points it pulsed and raced, completely deafening me. I didn't panic, I became conscious of myself. I was completely surrounded by red, as if the blood of all those victims was spattered over the whole world, as if I were deep inside their organs. Through the membranes I could see orangey lights, veils being torn, then a vast vault, splashes of red and white. The swirling sound dropped away and I was sad to leave it behind. Screams pierced my ears. Something burned my lungs like acid or toxic fumes. I heard explosions. The earth opened up and humanity seemed to disappear into it, swallowed up. It was when all life had ceased to be, when every bird, river, breath of wind, animal and human had fallen silent that I understood the absolute solitude of my situation.

Myriad factors realigned themselves in my memory. I'd probably been sitting there, glass in hand, staring into space for several long seconds when von Braun's hand on my arm brought me back to reality.

'I'm so sorry to have to give you this terrible news. It's a big shock,' he said, squeezing my arm with one hand and topping up our glasses with the other.

He told me what he knew of my mother's final moments, the doctor who'd helped her, and my birth in the church in Dresden just before it collapsed. He talked at length about what a wonderful woman she'd been. Irresistibly attractive, he told me.

'She adored your father. They were a golden couple. Your mother married very early. She was only about twenty-five when she died. She was a gorgeous woman, an excellent musician, always cheerful. She adored nature and plants, and she tended them avidly. She was the one who looked after our flowerbeds in Peenemünde. She made them look glorious . . .'

His voice trailed off and he sat in pained silence for a moment before adding, 'And to think we thought she'd be safe in Dresden . . . Johann was never the same after she died.'

'Why did she leave the military base?'

'Your father had been arrested. We hadn't had news for several months. The Gestapo were breathing down our necks the whole time . . .'

'I don't understand. Was he opposed to the regime?'

'He had some defeatist opinions and had voiced thoughts we'd all had privately. Including me. You have to try to picture what Germany was like at the time, we had to make difficult choices.'

Von Braun looked me in the eye. He waited for some sort of acknowledgement from me, but I didn't give it.

'Your father's so-called friends,' he went on, 'denounced him to the Gestapo. He was arrested for sabotage within hours.'

'What exactly had he said?'

'That he wanted to make rockets, not missiles equipped with bombs. That he couldn't bear having all that blood on his hands.'

The picture von Braun was painting contradicted Rebecca's accounts. From what he was saying, Johann and Luisa were a delightful couple who lived on love, daisies and scientific research. Was von Braun defending his generation in the silent trial to which mine subjected it? Even if I'd had all Rebecca's anger in my heart, I'd refuse to condemn anyone without a fair hearing.

'Who's the dark-haired young woman, then?' I asked, pointing to the other photo. 'My father's second wife?'

'Not at all,' he said with a smile. 'She's your aunt.'

'My father had a brother?'

'An older brother, Kasper Zilch.'

I paused while, in my mind, all the scenarios I'd envisaged took on different shapes, and new questions vied for attention.

'Why's my aunt referred to as Luisa in the lists from Fort Bliss?'

Von Braun fidgeted slightly in his seat.

'You can trust me,' I told him.

He hesitated again, trying to understand my intentions.

'I want to know where I'm from.'

Von Braun took the plunge: 'When we surrendered to the Americans, once their initial enthusiasm abated, our relationship with them was . . . complicated. We'd reached an agreement about our exfiltration and clapped cheerfully, but hadn't gone into the finer details. It was a painful wake-up call. At first, they gave us only one-year work contracts, and even refused to allow our families to join us in the States. In the end they agreed to wives and children, period. Parents were not allowed, neither were brothers and sisters. Johann had been badly injured a few weeks before the end of the war, he was weak and disturbed, in no state to look after a baby. Marthe was desperate to come to the States to take care of you. She adored you. To cut a long story short, the only way to get all three of you here was to claim that Marthe was Johann's wife and therefore your mother. She had to be passed off as Luisa.'

'Did you falsify her papers?'

'Europe was in complete chaos, you know . . . we didn't have any trouble muddling the facts. Millions of people had died and disappeared, no public registers were up to date. No one noticed the deception.'

I thanked him for confiding in me, and assured him I wouldn't betray him.

'It could cost me a great deal,' he said emphatically. 'Even three decades later. This place is very political. You can't imagine what a stickler for rules this country is. Not to mention the authorisations and counter-authorisations, and forms in every colour under the sun. It's quite dispiriting . . . I know I have it in me to defy gravity, but not paperwork.'

This declaration made me sit up and listen. Did von Braun miss the Third Reich's efficiency? Did he have less 'paperwork' to worry about when he could dispose of other people's lives as he saw fit? I suddenly remembered the images of bodies in the Dora work camp that Rebecca had shown me. How could a man who appeared so affable, attentive and cultured have contributed to that carnage? How could he live with that burden? I was seeing him in his handsome office with its thick carpet, a new American hero, a benign describer of stars for the children of the land of the free, and I wanted to smack him full in the face with his own past. Von Braun could feel the tension now buzzing between us, and stopped talking.

'You mentioned my father's brother . . .' I said eventually.

'Kasper.'

'Did you know him?'

'Very little. I met him a couple of times.'

'Did he look like Johann?'

'In every way!' he said. 'Plenty of people actually thought they were twins.'

'Dr von Braun, I have a question for you. I know Johann was your friend, but a lot of water has flowed under the bridge and I need to know . . .'

The great scientist crossed his arms defensively.

'Do you think that during the war my father could have been guilty of crimes against humanity? Was he that kind of man?'

'Of course not!' he protested immediately.

'But during the long months when he was gone, could he possibly have gone to Auschwitz?'

Von Braun looked at me in total surprise. Perhaps he'd expected me to talk to him of Dora, the London bombings or other dark chapters of his own past, but not Auschwitz.

'I can't imagine how he could have ended up there. And beside the fact that Johann was a very gentle man, if the Gestapo had sent him there, it would have been as a prisoner. Certainly not in a position to harm anyone at all.'

'Could he have been forced to?'

'Frankly, this makes no sense at all, Werner. When Johann came back he'd been beaten so badly that his torturers had left him for dead. He'd lost his memory, he was a broken man. I can see how, twenty-five years later, you have a hard time understanding what we did and the inextricable situation we were in, but we were scientists, Werner, scientists focused on a single goal – to explore space as sixteenth-century sailors had explored the oceans. To see the earth reduced to a blue pearl through the portholes of our rockets. We were scientists, not politicians, or warriors.'

'But you *were* Nazis.'

He sighed. He must have learned to live with this accusation, this constant suspicion that tainted his greatest achievements and would tarnish his image for all eternity.

'We would never have been able to do our research without the Nazi party's backing. We were patriots at the time, we wanted to work for our country. The government put extraordinary funds at our disposal. We had to play the game. I was never a Nazi out of personal conviction.'

'How about Johann Zilch?'

'Not a single ounce of him. In fact his idealism made him less compliant than I was. He found it harder to stay blinkered, to focus solely on our research.'

'And what about this Kasper Zilch?'

'I don't know. The brothers didn't get along. Johann said Kasper was troubled and jealous. He and Luisa had even taken in his sister-in-law, Marthe, when she separated from her husband. The Zilches were fairly private about their family affairs, but I gathered that Kasper wasn't an easy husband.'

'Could Kasper have been in Auschwitz? On the camp staff?'

'I'm very sorry but I have absolutely no idea,' von Braun admitted. Every time I said the word 'Auschwitz', his face flinched slightly.

'When did Johann leave Fort Bliss?'

'Almost two years after we arrived. For the first few months we just twiddled our thumbs. The government had requisitioned our documents, our plans, our machines and our best engineers, but wasn't using them at all. The Americans had brought us to the States to keep us out of the clutches of other enemies rather than for us to pursue our research. Different military corps fought over our team. Administrative bodies battled it out. In those days the Department of Defense was obsessed with "the bomb". They opted for boats and planes to transport it, so the endless possibilities of our missiles had been put on a back-burner.'

Von Braun paused and looked at me before saying pointedly, 'Don't go thinking I have any particular liking for armed conflict, but no government is prepared to invest money in capturing the moon and stars. Arms have always been the driving force behind our discoveries and I knew that, with no immediate defence-related application, we'd never secure the funds to realise my lifelong dream.'

'Does that dream justify everything, then?' I asked.

We exchanged another look, heavy with unspoken words.

'That's a complicated question, Werner . . .' he sighed, looking away. 'When I look back now at how things happened, I think we should have behaved differently. I was dedicated to a goal. It blinded me. I didn't see what I should have seen and fought against. Would I have had the courage to do that? I don't know. The Reich was a brutal and dangerous machine. And it had not only spared me, but brought me closer to what mattered most to me. Werner, your generation can't understand the circumstances we lived in. Now that everyone knows the outcome, it's easy to judge. We were walking through the swamps of a disturbing reality. History is written by the conquerors, and from where I am now, of course I regret the past, but I am and always have been a scientist.'

I maintained a condemning silence, but von Braun side-stepped the issue and went on with his account of events.

'We were peacetime prisoners in Fort Bliss. We weren't allowed to leave the base without an escort. We lived in cramped, poorly maintained shacks. Their zinc roofs weren't insulated and in summer the heat soared to well over 110 degrees. We'd been pampered in Peenemünde, but in the States we had to count every cent. All the projects we suggested were rejected. I was reduced to doing astronomy demonstrations for the local Rotary Club or in schools. I worked on my English which was very poor, and made a lot of progress in chess. They gradually granted us residence permits and my team broke up: those who could went to work for private companies where their talent would be useful and the salaries high. They were the worst years of my life,' he confided.

This admission reignited my indignation. The worst years of von Braun's life, or at least the worst months, should have been when he was exploiting and killing thousands of slaves in his underground factory in Dora, certainly not this prolonged vacation in Texas. There was an uncomfortable silence, but von Braun kept going.

'The army were happy to gather all the information they could on the V2s and appropriate our technology. We launched a few rockets in White Sands Desert in New Mexico. The Americans brought the press along and took us out of our hovels like fairground animals. Our scientific antics were extensively relayed to the international press to frighten the Russians in the new war that was brewing. We lost a lot of time before the Department of Defense finally gave us permission to look into the possible applications for our rockets – although this work was only theoretical, and we were given no credit for it. That was when we fully understood what had happened to Johann: the blows to the head that he'd suffered during the war had almost completely wiped out his scientific knowledge. This man who'd been one of our most brilliant minds had forgotten everything.'

'Did you ask him to leave?'

'He *wanted* to go. He couldn't bear the situation. Our work had been the most important thing left to him. He'd lost the wife he loved, his family, his country. Now he could no longer do his job. Life had no meaning for him any more. Of course, there was you, but I think he was too broken to make room for you in his world.'

'Do you think he may have killed himself?' I asked slowly.

'He left Fort Bliss with Marthe two years after we arrived. He'd found work in a factory that made agricultural fertiliser and pesticides. I had no reason to stop them leaving. And anyway, he wasn't the only one to go . . . At the time I had nothing to offer all those men who'd trustingly followed me to a foreign country.'

'You didn't have any further contact with him?'

'I tried to call him at work several times. He never called back. I asked for news from the receptionist and she told me

"Mr Zilch is fine". I thought he must associate me with too many painful memories – Luisa, the war, his amnesia . . .'

Von Braun suggested we went to have some lunch. Unusually for me, I wasn't hungry and I wanted to pursue our conversation. I still had a thousand questions for him. He took me to the restaurant reserved for NASA directors. It was a huge space lit by a large sheet-glass window, and there were about ten tables covered with white tablecloths and sumptuous place settings. There wasn't a woman in sight, not even serving. Von Braun greeted a few colleagues. Everyone looked respectfully, almost shyly at this man who, as I saw it, had an astonishing ability to adapt: having been adulated by the Nazi regime, he now enjoyed the same treatment from the most powerful country in the world and – putting all moral considerations aside – I couldn't help admiring such a *tour de force*. Von Braun had a hearty appetite, and the prospect of lunch revived his good mood.

'And Marthe,' I said, trying another angle. 'What can you tell me about her?'

'She was a wilful young woman with a strong character. When she wanted something, it was difficult to make her give it up.'

'Did you get along with her?'

'Yes and no. She took very good care of you, there's no question about that. Marthe was intelligent, instinctive. She was brave, and she proved that when we surrendered to the Americans. When she separated from her husband and came to live with us on the base for a few months, she studied to be a nurse, so she could support herself. Other women might have been happy to live under their brother-in-law's protection, but Marthe was independent. She wanted to be mistress of her own destiny. Luisa, your mother, adored her.'

'Why didn't you get along with her, then?'

'I liked her but the other women in our circle weren't taken with her. There were endless stories. Marthe didn't pull her weight. She was a loner, kept herself to herself. And the main thing was her capriciousness, she'd sometimes react to things so irrationally.'

'What sort of "capriciousness"?'

'As soon as she joined us in Bavaria, Marthe took against Johann. She thought he was dangerous to have around a child, she didn't want to let him near you. You can't stop a father taking his son in his arms! True, Johann was disturbed, his memory was failing, but she should have been more under-standing, more patient. Helped you and him form a bond. She did the exact opposite. She even tried to run away and take you with her. Marthe wasn't your mother and there was something out of proportion about the way she protected you.'

The head waiter came to take our order. Relaxing in antici-pation of the meal, von Braun drank two large mouthfuls of red wine and generously buttered his bread before turning his attention back to me.

'Do you have any idea what may have happened to Marthe?' I asked.

'Sadly not,' he replied, looking very apologetic. 'I'm sorry I haven't been much help to you. The only thing I can tell you is that Marthe would never have allowed you to be adopted. Ever! All she wanted was to take care of you. Virtually no one could lay a finger on you in her presence. She'd so loved your mother . . . how can I put this? It was a passionate, sometimes worrying love, and she transferred it to you. I'm tempted to say that would have been the root of the tensions between her and your father. While Luisa was alive, she'd made the friendship work, but without Luisa there you were the high-stakes prize they wrestled over. Did Johann move away from her, tired of not having you to himself? But then why did you end up in an orphanage? Did Marthe have some kind of accident? I can't think what might have happened.'

'Do you think she would have kept the name Luisa Zilch or could she have changed it?'

'That's a good question. I don't know what sort of red tape she'd have to go through to do that. Now, what was her maiden name . . . let me think . . . Oh, it's coming back: it was Engerer. She was born Marthe Engerer. That might be a lead worth following.'

I kept on asking him questions while we made the most of our lavish lunch. Even though I knew the darker side of von Braun, and even though Rebecca's voice in my head and my own conscience warned me against him, I found it hard not to like the man. I couldn't understand how intelligent, educated men had succeeded in ignoring or even actively participating in such barbarity during the war.

After the meal, von Braun took me to the area of the building devoted to plans and models on which a whole army of engineers were working. Then he asked his driver to take me back to the airport. He was very sorry not to have been able to help me more and would happily oblige if any more questions came to me. He made me promise to come back and see him – the next time we would have dinner at his home, I would meet his wife and children. In short, he'd adopted me. Of course, he suggested I should come with my girlfriend, but I didn't have the heart to tell him that this meeting was unlikely to take place, unless he was keen to find himself bound and gagged in a plane heading for Israel where he would be judged. He said goodbye to me in true American fashion, hugging me to him warmly.

'I really loved your parents, you know,' he said when he released his grip, and then gave a great peal of laughter.

At the end of the day, as I fastened my seat belt and absent-mindedly reciprocated the smile from a pretty fellow passenger, I was agitated and ill at ease. The frontiers between good and evil seemed hazier than ever. Life was slipping through my fingers. I wondered whether I would ever have it under control again.

Soviet occupation zone, October 1944

Johann was transferred to Sachsenhausen-Oranienburg, the Nazi regime's camp for political prisoners, and from the moment he arrived was subjected to many of the tortures that the SS enjoyed inflicting on their inmates. He was ordered to undress and was given coarse cotton clothes covered in grey and white stripes and a pair of wooden-soled clogs. He also had to sew a triangle of fabric to the chest to indicate his status as a traitor to his nation.

When he failed to make his bed properly – and it was a straw mattress, impossible to fold neatly – he was first sent for a month's solitary confinement in a cell with no light where he could neither sit nor lie down for twelve out of every twenty-four hours. In this tiny, cramped space, there wasn't room to take a single step in any direction. He was reduced to shuffling from one foot to the other and raising his knees to help the blood circulate and stop his legs freezing. He tried not to lose track of time, and guessed that the guard's three visits represented a day and the long period when no one came was a night. After twenty-eight days in the dark he made the mistake of rebelling: for the last four meals the only food he'd been offered was a dead rat, and when the guard brought this verminous offering back for the fifth time, Johann threw himself at his tormentor and tried to ram the dead animal into his mouth. He was strung up, in front of all the other inmates, on the 'Bock', a form of torture rack. A guard beat him with a wooden rod until his buttocks were reduced to a bloodied pulp.

Ernst, a communist who had been in the camp for three years, helped him tend to his wounds with carefully preserved margarine wrappers.

'You must be under some kind of protection,' Ernst told him. 'I'd have been shot for less. Beatings are their most lenient punishment . . .'

Johann did indeed seem to be the subject of special instructions because after this thrashing he was not returned to solitary confinement, but sent to a workshop. He had to spend sixteen hours a day unpicking seams on clothes and shoes in search of possible hidden treasure. Johann realised these things had been taken from prisoners who had been stripped or perhaps executed, and the sheer quantity of them made him feel nauseous. In the pockets of coats, jackets and trousers he often found photographs of women and children smiling out at him, and his heart constricted at the thought of all these ruined lives. He thought of Luisa, and their baby . . . and prayed they were safe and well. Sometimes, hidden in a lining or the sole of a shoe, he felt a ring or a gold chain, a small gemstone or banknotes. Intimate items such as lockets of hair or love letters brought home for him the horrors his country had engendered and that he, safely sheltered in Peenemünde, hadn't suspected. Yes, he'd been privileged. The war had been only an abstract reality for him, a vague justification for his research, not this monster destroying his flesh, his soul and his mind, turning him into a dazed and damaged animal.

'You think you've hit bottom,' Ernst had told him. 'You think it can't get any worse, but it's just the beginning. With them, there's always something worse.'

Ernst had been right, Johann could see this now. He understood it still more cruelly when, a few weeks later, the exhausted inmates had to evacuate the camp and over twelve days, suffered all the savage power the SS exerted over them. The prisoners were gathered together on the camp's main thoroughfare one morning, and the guards announced they were to be transferred.

They were not allowed to take any belongings. The barriers were raised, the gates opened, and soon there was not a living soul left in the camp. Within hours of starting the journey, prisoners who couldn't keep up were being shot in the back of the head, and their bodies abandoned. This happened in Nassenheide and Sommerfeld. The abomination was repeated in Herzberg, Alt Ruppin and Neuruppin where eighty-five people were executed, and then in Herzsprung where there were as many victims again. Johann doggedly supported Ernst, but his friend who had resisted the unspeakable conditions in the camp for so long, was suffering from dysentery. After about six miles, with nothing left to give, he begged to be left there. Johann wanted to drag him along forcibly, but his friend released his grip and gave up the fight. The report of a gunshot a few minutes later told Johann it was over. He trudged on, choking on a combination of anger and sadness. His shame for failing to save Ernst and his doubts as to whether he'd done all he could gnawed at him like acid.

Throughout this twelve-day misery, generous gestures and surges of determination allowed some to withstand the ordeal, keep walking, and stay on their feet even when they were beaten. The prisoners formed clusters of humanity, a single unified flesh suffering the same pain and gathering protectively around the weakest, as they all tried to keep going, slowly and painfully, but keep going all the same, to cling to life a little longer. The verges were dotted with huddled corpses. Thirst was even more punishing than hunger or the cold which was aggravated by the prisoners' soaking rags. After four days they reached a temporary camp in the middle of a field. It was surrounded by barbed wire but even more surely marked out by the SS's 'shoot on sight' policy. Inside this hellish thirty-hectare square, all-consuming hunger and the desperate will to survive eventually drove the miserable prisoners to sordid fights and acts of lunacy. Human dignity was trampled underfoot. Cases of cannibalism multiplied along the edges of vast communal graves, while some resorted to eating grass, dandelions and nettles. The leaves on trees that were within reach were all eaten, the bark ripped off up to eight feet from the ground – both to provide food and to fuel fires – and then the wood itself was gouged out to make a sort of paste to chew on. The river which would have allowed the prisoners to quench their thirst was so polluted with excrement that those who succumbed to the temptation died of it. A single well provided drinking water because it drew directly from the groundwater table. It was guarded by the SS, and merely to approach it was to risk death.

One evening a miracle came about in the shape of ten Red Cross trucks. They were greeted with cries of joy, but they had enough food parcels for only one in three of the men, and the distribution of rations produced further scenes of barbarity. The lucky ones slunk off with a few crackers or biscuits but, in their exhausted, dehydrated state, they still had to find a way of slowly ingesting this dry food which stuck to their tongues and the roofs of their mouths.

The next day, the long march was resumed. Once again, the prisoners left behind many of their number, people who had rolled themselves up in their blankets on the ground and never risen again. Every footstep the survivors took caused appalling suffering, and yet on they went, in the certainty that at the end of this journey two options awaited them: death or liberation. Two days later came another miracle, a real one this time, when the convoy met with Soviet forces in the forest of Raben Steinfeld. The prisoners' hellish endurance test came to an end in silence; they were so worn down and starved, they didn't even have the strength to celebrate. And their boundless unspoken relief was haunted by the thousands of ghosts of their lost brothers. At this point, Johann finally dared to sit down without fear of a murderous bullet coming his way. He privately thanked Luisa for sustaining and protecting him – he had survived only in the hope of being reunited with her and seeing his baby.

They spent a week in the forest. Johann never knew how the Soviets managed to identify him; there were thousands of prisoners wearing the same ragged clothes, with the same emaciated face and the same concave stomach and jutting ribs, and yet their liberators found him. The Russian secret services had most likely drawn up a list of the scientists at Peenemünde, and when the Red Army took in victims who had escaped the camps, their first job was to take a census. Names, dates of birth and professions were noted on a never-ending list. Johann settled for describing himself as an engineer, saying nothing more specific, but this was probably enough to alert the Russian officers who were actively looking for the creators of the V2 missiles.

He was questioned by several high-ranking officers and was then brought before Sergei Korolev, a prodigiously talented scientist whom Stalin had sent to Germany to gather all information and equipment relating to the V2. Like von Braun, Korolev had been very young when he grasped the huge potential of liquid fuel for space travel. He had seen himself swiftly promoted to directing the Russian centre for rocket research, but his work was reduced to nothing by political purges. Korolev had recently been released after seven years in prison and, although only thirty-eight, he looked almost fifty. He was a colossus of a man with an affable demeanour despite the fact he never smiled. He had lost half his teeth when his jaw was broken during an interrogation, and scurvy – which he developed in Kolyma, the Soviet Union's toughest penal colony – took the other half. Although he was officially seen as an enemy of the Russian people, Korolev was now back in work; Stalin had recently launched an ambitious programme developing ballistic missiles, and couldn't manage without Korolev's priceless expertise. The Germans were ten years ahead of the Soviets, and their V2 fascinated scientists and armies the world over. Stalin wanted to get his hands on this technology whatever the cost, but so far Korolev had drawn a blank.

Finding Johann Zilch, one of von Braun's closest collaborators, in a Red Army-controlled zone was an extraordinary godsend. Zilch had been on the German team when it launched its very first missiles. Affectionately nicknamed Max and Moritz, these five-foot 160-pound toys had travelled only 11,500 feet off the ground, but they were destined for greatness. Johann had been involved in every stage of development and every version of the rockets, which had later proved sufficiently effective to bomb London from the European continent. He was a valuable asset, and Korolev – who, like von Braun, was obsessed with reaching the stars – made him a proposition that the prisoner was in no position to refuse. When Johann fell into Russian hands, his communist friend Ernst's words rang in his ears: 'With them, there's always something worse.'

He wasn't sure that his fate would be any better now that he had different captors.

Manhattan, 1971

I had to get out of this psychological trap as soon as possible. Donna set about contacting the country's best private detective agencies, and I took on five agents to report to a sixth, Tom Exley, an ex-con who'd opened an investigations bureau and had been recommended to me by the head of the New York Police Department.

I also got back in touch with Dane because Rebecca had convinced me that he and his network were best placed to unravel the brain-teaser of my origins. Our meeting was frosty but effective. I couldn't care less whether he liked me and did nothing to be agreeable, except make out a 100,000-dollar cheque to his organisation for the children of deportees. He took the piece of paper between two fingers with some disgust and pocketed it without a thank you. Rebecca noticed the colour draining from my face and hastily saw her friend to the door while Marcus poured me a Scotch. Marcus wasn't at all convinced by Dane's methods; he was horrified by the crimes committed during the war and the American state's complicity in erasing them, but he thought it dangerous to give an individual – even if he or she was closely related to a victim of the Holocaust – the right to judge and punish another person. I, meanwhile, understood Dane and Rebecca: vengeance is still the surest form of justice. Until then, I had indulged in it only in our business affairs, and I'd never been sufficiently wronged to cross the line, but I couldn't have been sure how I'd react if anyone had harmed Rebecca, Lauren, Marcus or my parents.

'You act like you've dealt with the shock and like you've moved on, but you now have your very own way of handling the problem. They often say that an instant outburst of anger is easier to cope with.'

Ten days after Rebecca's revelations I was woken in the middle of the night by such a blinding realisation that I woke her gently. I forced her to sit up, kissing her eyes and face to help her wake up – little demonstrations of affection that she rejected.

'What's going on?' she asked huskily. 'The sun isn't even up yet . . . Did you have a nightmare?'

'My darling,' I said, beaming. 'I want to have a baby with you.'

Rebecca sat in stunned silence and asked me to repeat what I'd said.

'I want to have a baby with you.'

'But it's too soon to talk about stuff like that! And anyway, I'm not sure it's such a good idea . . .'

She yawned, dropped back down onto the bed and turned her back on me.

'Of course it's a good idea. It's the best idea we could possibly have.'

'Look, this isn't the time,' she said conclusively.

'This is important, Rebecca! I'm talking about a baby, our baby.'

Rebecca realised her night's sleep was over. I was too much of a monomaniac to leave the subject and talk about it sensibly over breakfast in the morning. Frowning, she listened as I developed an ambitious theory that started with reconciling people and forgiving crimes, moved on to how the fusion of two people into a single person was the most beautiful act of love there was, and ended with 'I want us to have a baby with gorgeous soft creases in its skin and tiny hands and feet. A girl with eyes like yours and your adorable face . . .'

'You worry me sometimes, Wern . . . Are you feeling OK?' she said, studying me intently.

'I'm absolutely fine. Better than ever. I want us to have a baby.'

'But where's this sudden urge come from? Why now?'

'Because I love you and because our baby won't just be very beautiful, it'll also be incredibly intelligent!'

'This isn't, by any chance, just a really good way of keeping me here?' she asked.

'Definitely not, I know you'll never be able to leave me, anyway,' I said with my usual aplomb. 'But it's the most positive and beautiful thing we can do about this horrible situation that is not of our making. What do you think?'

I was putting the pressure on, ready to make the baby there and then.

'I need to paint . . . Creativity and procreation have never made good partners. If we have a baby now, that would be the end of my painting and I'll be shackled for the rest of my life.'

'That's not true! I'm not thinking about me but about you. Look at your beautiful hips,' I said, stroking them. 'And your stomach . . . you're made to bring life into the world, and you'll never be a complete woman, or artist, until you've done that.'

'The macho garbage you just spouted leaves me speechless.'

'And feminist theory is so cerebral it makes you forget what really matters,' I countered.

We fought for the rest of the night. Rebecca was furious, and so was I. In the end she took a blanket and her pillow off to her studio to be alone. I wanted to follow her but she slammed the door in my face and locked herself in. I went back to bed but couldn't sleep: my idea had taken possession of me. For a whole week I couldn't shake it off. I told Rebecca fifty times a day that I wanted us to have a baby, and without even realising I was doing it, I took to cupping my hands proprietorially over her stomach. She pushed me off unceremoniously. Pregnant women suddenly seemed amazingly graceful, and I gazed at them, dazzled, as if watching the Virgin Mary herself. This behaviour piqued Rebecca's jealousy.

Marcus didn't want to take sides, and Lauren didn't dare intervene either, but couldn't understand Rebecca's reticence. Lauren longed for a man to love her enough to give her a child but no one had lasted long enough for her to broach the subject. She went through a succession of flings but none of them stayed around. At best her lovers agreed to give her pleasure, if and when they weren't simply taking their own. Lauren was incapable of calculation or scheming. However many times I told her she could do better and that, to attract the right sort of man, she needed to be more tricky and not give of herself without asking anything in return, she was still a generous soul. I'd told her my theory about the state of affairs: the more time and money a man invests in a woman, the more he stands to lose in leaving her. Lauren thought this a monstrous view of emotions, and Marcus agreed. In fact, in his opinion, the men who made advances on Lauren were losers who didn't deserve her, and not one of our friends found favour in his eyes when I tried to matchmake for her.

Lauren's honesty caused problems again when Rebecca turned to her for support and asked her opinion. Lauren shared her enthusiasm for the idea: a baby was such a wonderful thing! How could Rebecca hesitate for a moment? Lauren would be godmother and Marcus godfather. And of course she would look after the little one so Rebecca could keep painting . . . and babies are so cute and adorable and soft. And, anyway, with parents like us, this baby was going to be amazing. To be honest, it was all she could think about. It would fill the house with laughter and life. We'd take it everywhere, it would play with Shakespeare . . . Confronted with Lauren's ecstatic proclamation, Rebecca fell apart. It seemed the whole world was in league against her. Feeling misunderstood, she took refuge in her work and embarked on a series of paintings featuring women in the clutches of vampires. A few days later she flew into a wild temper when Lauren looked at the canvases and had the misfortune of asking whether that was how Rebecca saw children, as sucking the lifeblood out of women. Rebecca stormed out, disappeared for the whole day and didn't speak a word over dinner. The last straw was when Miguel, quivering with anticipation, came to give Rebecca an embroidered alphabet sampler he'd sewn himself that week.

'Mr Zilch told me the big news,' he said. 'Congratulations, Miss Rebecca!'

She handed the book back abruptly and told him a child wasn't on the cards. I had, she pointed out, an infuriating tendency to view my own wishes as realities, even if that meant ignoring the fact that it takes two to make a baby, and the baby therefore has to be wanted by both people, which, in the current circumstances, was not the case. That same day, I came home from the office triumphant, my arms brimming with cuddly toys in anticipation of the happy event which Rebecca hadn't even started to contemplate. She skewered me with an icy stare, put down her paintbrush without a word, took off her overall, went downstairs to bed and woke for no more than one hour a day for the next fortnight.

In my disappointment, I worked twice as hard, leaving before breakfast and arriving home after dinner, which meant Marcus and Lauren were left alone together for two weeks. I interpreted Rebecca's attitude not as a refusal to have a baby in general, but a refusal to have one *with me*, and this made me very unhappy. I was branded with suspicion, as if a serious illness or criminal insanity was hidden somewhere in my healthy-looking body. Over the last few years, I'd succeeded in persuading myself I was writing on a blank page, that my unknowable origins allowed me to write a completely new, completely free story for myself. In the space of a few hours, a past I didn't want had come and destroyed this patiently constructed edifice. What's more, it was the woman I loved who'd struck the first blow, and ever since then she'd been doggedly destroying what little confidence I had left.

Manhattan, 1972

Shakespeare was deeply traumatised when Rebecca left. Her mother had finally come home from Dr Nars's institute and, to support Judith for a few weeks during her convalescence, Nathan Lynch had asked his daughter to 'come home', an expression that struck a blow to me when Rebecca said it. She reassured me that it was only temporary and promised to call me every evening, which she did, but this separation reminded me too much of her disappearance for me to come to terms with it. Her absence compounded our recent conflicts, further widening the fault line that was gradually opening up between us. My dog was also well aware that Becca's decision wasn't as innocent as she claimed. She walked out one morning, leaving her belongings here, but I knew this paltry token wouldn't be enough to bring her back if the situation got worse. Shakespeare turned his back to her on the doorstep and refused to be stroked.

Lauren and Marcus were worried too; our quartet was broken, and much as we tried to pretend nothing had changed, the balance of our household had taken a knock. Shakespeare lost his appetite, he stopped chasing pigeons on the terrace, and gave up barking at the neighbour's cat that had outrageously granted itself right of passage through our basement courtyard. He no longer offered his tummy to be tickled to every stranger who took an interest in him. This dog who once loved nothing better than taking long walks with us, now preferred to hang around the house with his head held low. One day, Miguel noticed Shakespeare had stolen a sweater of Rebecca's and taken it to his basket. Miguel tried to reclaim it but Shakespeare proved so dissuasive that he gave up. When Marcus and Lauren came home, instead of the exuberant greetings he'd taught them to expect, Shakespeare wagged his tail wanly and went back to bed. Meanwhile, I was in disgrace: he didn't even come when I called. When I made a show of authority, he eventually obeyed my orders, his eyes full of reproach.

'I did what I could, boy!' I tried to defend myself. 'She doesn't want to be with us, that's all there is to it. Do you think this is easy for me? I'm sad too, but I couldn't lock her up. And if she doesn't love me enough to have a child, what can I say?'

Shakespeare slunk back to bed, cutting short what I was saying, like a wife avoiding a conversation with her husband. No one liked me much at that time. Becca was distant on the phone. Every evening I asked her to come home, and she gave Judith's condition as an excuse not to.

The recurring nightmare of my birth came back to ruin my nights. After von Braun's revelations, I thought I'd gotten rid of it, but it was more insistent than ever. I see this very beautiful young blonde woman, whom I now know to be my mother; she runs and then falls, is thrown over violently. I'm drawn in to her eyes. The bottomless love I can see in them soothes me and terrifies me because I can sense I'm going to lose it. The scene changes now, and the red substance and that swirling sound are back. Along with the noise and the shouting. I'm one of the soldiers who tried to save her. I cry. I don't know how to help her. My mother's lying on a table, her distended stomach covered with a blood-drenched sheet. Her head is turned to the wall. I come closer, to kiss her one last time. I put my fingers on her forehead, turn her ice-cold face towards me and cry out in shock when I recognise Rebecca.

Rebecca had been living with her parents for two weeks when we met for lunch at the Tavern on the Green in Central Park on a bright mild day. Rebecca was wearing a long pearl-grey coat with a belt that accentuated her waist, a beige dress and boots with high red heels. Her mane of blonde hair wafted with her every footstep, and she'd emphasised her cat-like eyes with eyeliner. It was a long time since I'd seen her so feminine and sophisticated. It was as if she wanted to win me back, when I'd never stopped being utterly won over. She was stunning. She pressed herself up to me and said she'd missed me, showing that she loved me with a hundred little signs, but refusing once again to come home.

'Is this new?' I asked, opening her coat to caress her waist and hips through the fine soft wool of her dress.

'Yes, mom and I went shopping.'

Over lunch we chatted about everything and nothing, carefully avoiding incendiary topics. We wanted to be happy, not to fight. We spotted Ernie, her father's right-hand man, which made us laugh and reminded us of our first meeting. Ernie gave me a sour look, unlike David Minett one of New York's most successful entrepreneurs and renowned ladies' man, who accosted us with an enthusiastic exclamation.

'And here's the prettiest girl in Manhattan! Aren't you a lucky guy,' he said, kissing Rebecca's hand and eyeing her greedily.

He invited us to dinner the following week. Rebecca said she was going away to the country for a few days with her mother, news that instantly wiped away my good mood. Minett didn't notice this, and walked on to his table where a blonde creature was waiting for him.

'That's not exactly a nice way to find out you're leaving the city.'

Becca rolled her eyes.

'I'm not "leaving the city", I'm just going to the country for a few days.'

'How many days?'

'I don't know . . . maybe ten, maybe two weeks, nothing's decided . . .' she replied a little awkwardly.

'But when exactly are you planning to come back?'

'As soon as my mother's better.'

'Your mother's not been well for more than twenty years, there's nothing to say she *will* get better,' I said sharply. 'Why do you have to spend time with her *now*?'

She sat in silence, wearing the sad, tired expression that had a way of making me angry. I got the feeling she was lying, and told her so.

'You're not the only human being on the planet, Wern! My family needs me. That shouldn't be a problem . . .'

I reminded her tartly why it was a problem. Had she forgotten how they treated me? Her unbearable disappearance? The uncertainty about my true father? The fact she refused to have a baby with me?

'Here we go again!' she sighed angrily.

We didn't touch our food. I left a wad of money on the table so we didn't have to wait for the check. I didn't want to argue with Rebecca in front of witnesses, least of all David Minett and Ernie. Once we were outside, the row escalated rapidly, and we parted on angry terms.

I headed down Fifth Avenue in an intolerably jumpy state. At the office people scattered at the sight of me, and back at home Marcus, Lauren and Miguel also avoided me, tired of my moods and obsessions. I went out without the others that evening, met up with a gang of partygoers and stayed up all night with them. Like the last time Rebecca wasn't there, I tried to take consolation in new conquests. I couldn't bear being dumped or sleeping alone. Over the ensuing days I made sure my bed was filled. These young ladies, charming though they were, were not given a warm welcome by Lauren and Shakespeare. My dog proved intransigent, growling at each of my guests, and I had to shut him away because he was so aggressive towards a dark-haired book editor who kept me busy for a while. Even Marcus, who could have made conversation with a houseplant if decorum required it, was not very receptive.

'Your determination to replace her is as pathetic as it's

pointless,' he retorted when I commented on this. 'At least have the decency not to inflict your ersatz girls on us. Rebecca's not only your ex, she's also our friend.'

I thought their attitude indefensible. Rebecca was the one who left, after all! The woman was impossible to keep happy . . . If one of them had the instruction manual, I'd have been delighted to be informed. In the meantime, I was looking for a nice kind partner who made normal demands like going to restaurants, seeing friends, going away for weekends and buying jewellery. A woman who would have time for me, who wouldn't need to be sleepwalking to cook me an egg, who wouldn't torment my friends with her complicated past, devastating revelations, existential interrogations and artist's demons.

'Basically, you want an employee, then?' Lauren snapped. 'A woman you pay to take care of you?'

'The advantage with women who love you for your money is, you know how to keep them,' I said sadly.

I gave up on securing my sister's or my best friend's blessing, and resolved to meet my consolations away from home. The fact that I often slept somewhere else and didn't take Shakespeare with me was the final blow for him. He abandoned non-violent resistance in favour of action: when I came home at dawn from a night with a ravishing Venezuelan model, I found a declaration of war in my room. Not only had Shakespeare urinated on my bed, but because he had no trouble opening my closet, he had methodically shredded all my shoes. The guilty party was nowhere to be found, and I woke the whole household in my rabid search for him. Lauren, who had an important acupuncture exam a few hours later, came out of her room like a fury and threw a book at my head, yelling that my selfishness knew no bounds.

'You're not the only person on the planet,' she snarled, a refrain I'd already heard from Rebecca, and that instantly enraged me.

Marcus appeared in striped navy-blue-and-white pyjamas.

'This constant song and dance is extremely tiresome,' he announced with one eyebrow raised and a clenched jaw.

Meanwhile Miguel was giving refuge to the rebel, who was lying silent and resolute with his head between his paws under the butler's iron bed, not daring to come out of his hiding place.

This canine assault on my authority got me thinking: I attributed Shakespeare's depression to the fact that he didn't have a partner and wanted to be a father. He's four years old, I reasoned, that's the equivalent of thirty for a human. He needs to have children.

Manhattan, 1972

Rebecca had been gone eight interminable weeks when Tom Exley, the private detective I'd hired, called me with good news. With the help of his team he'd traced Marthe Engerer. My aunt was alive and living in the United States, in Louisiana to be more precise, about twenty-five miles from New Orleans. She was working as a district nurse and lived with a woman psychiatrist. Tom didn't know the exact nature of their relationship but guessed that the two ageing spinsters had decided to cheat loneliness by moving in together.

Memories of all the years I'd spent trying to trace my real family came flooding back. At the time, I'd thought the key to my birth would be somewhere in Germany, a place whose language and customs I didn't know. To think that all this time the answer to my questions, far from being lost in the foreignness of Europe, was waiting for me right here, just an internal flight away!

Tom had discovered Marthe's address, had gone there himself and successfully identified her. He had chosen not to contact her directly without me, for fear she might flee. We had no idea of the part she had played in the war, and she might not want to dig up the past now. I was having lunch with Lauren and Marcus when I took the call, and when I told them the news, they both wanted to let Rebecca know. I was against the idea: there was no way I would grovel at her feet to get her to come with me. It was up to her to make the first move, I wasn't going to give an inch.

'Marthe Engerer doesn't belong to you, Wern,' Lauren

protested. 'Sure, she can give you information about your real father, but she can also shed some light on Rebecca's mother's past. You can't exclude her like that.'

'She's the one who excluded herself, I'd like to point out,' I replied, handing a big piece of chicken to Shakespeare.

I couldn't forgive Rebecca for choosing her family over me again. And I understood her silence even less. After her year-long disappearance, after her professions of love and loyalty, how could she do this to me? Since our failed lunch date, I'd had no news of her, at least no direct news. Marcus, Lauren and Miguel had all spoken to her on the phone about various practical matters, which made me all the more resentful. She spoke to everyone in the house but me! My sister and best friend were more lenient with her than with me. In fact they saw everything from her point of view and I thought this favouritism unforgivable. They should have been on my side instead of observing this pseudo-neutrality; they should have refused to speak to Rebecca, left her in a vacuum, made her miss the whole household – to force her to come back. I was hurt by their disloyalty, but if I complained, Lauren got on her high horse.

'You can't force us to stop liking Rebecca overnight,' she railed, 'just because the two of you are incapable of behaving like adults!'

'Lauren's right, Wern,' Marcus agreed. 'The fact we care for her doesn't in any way contradict how we feel for you . . .'

It took them forty-eight hours to convince me to let Rebecca come to Louisiana with us. Even then, I refused to call her, so Lauren did it while Donna organised the trip. The four of us would go to Marthe's address with Tom Exley. A week before we left, Tom called Marthe, passed himself off as a rep for medical supplies, and arranged a meeting with her to ensure she would be at home the day we were coming.

Tom, Marcus, Lauren and I set out together while Rebecca travelled to the airport independently. Judging by the way she

scowled at me when she arrived, she was furious, but I couldn't
see what she had to hold against me. We greeted each other
distantly with a brief wave, not even a peck on the cheek.
Disappointed, I stalked off to find a newspaper and did the
rounds of the airport boutiques in search of a present for Marthe
Engerer. I chose a huge tin of biscuits.

On the plane I sat next to Marcus, took refuge behind the
Financial Times and didn't utter a single word. The three and
a half hours of the flight seemed to go on forever. Rebecca and
Lauren nattered away behind me in a way that made me angrier
still. I wanted Rebecca to talk to me, to explain things to me,
even curse at me, but definitely not behave as if I didn't exist.
Marcus tried to cheer me up but I responded to his attempts
with a series of grunts. He eventually gave up and threw himself
back into Erich Segal's *Love Story* with what looked like great
concentration. It was high time he found himself a girlfriend.

The stewardesses served us a meal, and I was hungry so I
asked the prettiest of them for a second meal. She brought it
over, pink-cheeked, and leant close to me.

'I gave you some chocolate cookies,' she whispered. 'Don't
hesitate to ask if there's anything else you need.'

In the row behind, the girls' conversation stopped dead.
Rebecca's irritation was palpable. I stepped up my charm offensive on the hostess, but my ex soon went back to her chatting
with Lauren and ruined the short-lived pleasure I'd derived from
making her jealous.

When the plane landed, we were greeted by a moist, almost
tropical heat. We had no bags in the hold, and in a matter of
minutes were out of the airport where a small red bus was
waiting for us. We looked like tourists. Behind me, Marcus,
Lauren and Rebecca burst out laughing about something they
didn't share with me. I couldn't understand how they could be
so cheerful and relaxed. Marthe Engerer was going to give me
answers to questions that had been tormenting me for years.

My future and my past depended on this conversation. My heart was in my mouth and my friends were making jokes.

'I can't see what you're laughing about,' I exploded. 'There's nothing funny about today.'

This pronouncement established the chilly silence I'd been hoping for. Tom walked off, claiming he had to check the rental agreement for the bus with the agency, and left us to sort out our differences.

'We were laughing because we're happy to be together, Wern,' Rebecca said.

'The fact we're not together is your choice.'

'You know it's not that simple,' she said. 'And you've made good use of your time and my absence . . .'

I shot a suspicious look at Lauren and Marcus to see which of them had betrayed me. They looked away quickly.

'What were you expecting, then? For me to wait meekly until you deigned to explain your disappearance?' I asked irritably.

'You started cheating on me a week after I left! No one can say you went to any effort to understand or show some patience. And don't go accusing them,' she added because I was glowering threateningly at my sister and so-called best friend . . . 'You wanted me to know, and I knew.'

'I'm not at your beck and call, Rebecca. I don't have to wait like a dog in its kennel without even an explanation to chew on.'

She opened her mouth to reply, but I interrupted her, 'I have no desire to have this same conversation with you for the umpteenth time. You left, you have to deal with the consequences.'

I turned to the others and snapped, 'Right, let's get in the bus and go!'

I sat at the front and the others split themselves between the next two rows. Tom drove, and a deathly silence hung over us the whole way. The air was suffocating. Looking out at the streets of New Orleans, I felt as if I were in a foreign country. There was something exotic about the awnings, the passageways, the plants spilling over balconies and the low-slung buildings. Outside the city, the road plunged into a jungle then skirted along a swampland. Those muddy waters must have been teeming with life, we could have been in South America, perhaps Brazil. Only the radio and its commercials reminded us we were in the United States.

It took us half an hour to reach our destination. Marthe lived in a small town halfway between New Orleans and Baton Rouge. In front of the white wooden façade of her house was a long porch with columns. On it were two rattan chairs and a cast-iron coffee table. Flower pots hung from the porch roof, brightening the scene with touches of pink and white. The impeccably kept lawn completed this elegant look. We were right on time. I waited in the bus for a few minutes to gather my courage. My companions sat in silence.

'Come on, Wern,' Marcus said, sensing my nerves. 'Let's just the two of us go first.'

I must have given him a helpless look because he put a hand on my back and added, 'Don't worry . . . come on . . .'

I gathered my strength and, with Marcus by my side, covered the few strides that lay between me and my fate.

I rang the doorbell.

'Coming!' called a woman's voice.

A woman of about sixty opened the door. She had long wavy light-brown hair, streaked with grey, red glasses and brown eyes. She peered at me inquisitively.

'We have a meeting with Marthe Engerer.'

'Ah! The medical supplies? Is that right? I'm Abigail,' she introduced herself, extending her hand. 'Marthe's inside. Come in . . . I'll tell her to come down.'

She led us into the living room and offered us lemonade, which we accepted.

'Marthe, your meeting!' she called towards the stairs, before going off to the kitchen.

A few minutes later Marthe appeared in the doorway. I recognised her immediately. She'd aged, of course, but was still the woman I'd studied at length in the photo. Marthe saw Marcus first because he was sitting facing her, then she noticed me. She reeled visibly.

'Oh my God!' she breathed with a stifled cry.

She leant against the doorframe and brought her hand to her chest. Abigail, who was coming in with a tray of glasses, thought she was about to collapse. She put down the tray and rushed to support Marthe.

'What is it, darling?'

'It's Werner,' Marthe explained. 'Luisa's son.'

She turned to look at me again, and said, 'I can't tell you how like her you are. Everything about you is her.'

'Everything about me is who?' I asked to be sure.

'Your mother.'

She came over hesitantly and sat next to me on the sofa. Her knees touched mine. This proximity made me uncomfortable, and so did the intense way she stared at me. She ran a hand through my hair. I didn't dare move.

'I'm so happy you're alive. You're so big, so gorgeous . . . You're so like her!'

'In the pictures, I feel like I look more like Johann,' I said, as if we'd known each other forever.

'Yes, a bit . . . the general impression, but your nose, your eyes, your cheekbones, it's her.'

She took my face in her hands and felt it, like a blind woman wanting to memorise my features. The touch of her hands made me shiver.

'I thought I'd never see you again. If you knew how long I've spent trying to find you. Months, years . . .'

'She talks about you every day,' Abigail added.

'I was frightened he'd killed you . . .'

'Who wanted to kill me?'

'Kasper, your uncle.'

'Why did he want me dead?'

'It's a long story, my darling,' Marthe replied, leap-frogging the boundaries of courtesy with every word she spoke, to establish an intimacy between us that felt obvious to her but less so to me. 'I'll tell you everything. I guess that's why you came . . . As for Kasper, believe me, that man is, or was, capable of anything.'

Haus Ingeborg Hotel, Bavarian Alps, 1945

Von Braun and a few of his colleagues were playing cards in the hotel lounge. Since they had handed themselves over to the Americans their life hadn't changed; they simply had different jailors, replacing the SS with GIs who were just as punctilious and disciplined. Marthe was tired and went up to bed. It was already dark, her bedroom curtains were drawn and the lights out, but as she stepped into the room she was immediately aware of a presence. Panic-stricken, she tried to go back out, but it took him only a fraction of a second to catch her by the arm and throw her on the bed.

'Stop your play-acting, Marthe, I want to talk to you.'

She'd always been terrified by the speed with which he moved. Even with an ankle in plaster he was frightening. Marthe shuffled to a sitting position on one side of the bed. She wanted to stay calm but an icy chill ran through her. She thought of the knife she kept bound to her thigh. She had to be sure . . . was she capable of that? The man claiming to be Johann sat in the armchair, facing her. He had reverted to his true voice, the voice she heard every night in her nightmares.

'Look at me, you idiot.'

Marthe looked up. In two weeks, the man's swollen eyelids had gone down, and half an inch of hair was starting to cover the scars on his scalp.

'Now you listen to me. I know that you know. We're not going to lie to each other. Not between a husband and wife,' he taunted ironically, stretching out his good leg to lift Marthe's skirt with his foot. She ducked aside quickly.

'You're still a wild little bitch,' he said, eyeing her lecherously, and this sent a new wave of panic through her.

'What do you want, Kasper?'

'Stop arousing suspicion. Von Braun's started looking at me strangely. I want to get out of Germany as soon as possible. The Americans are my best ticket out and von Braun's going to be my travel agent.'

'Or . . . ?'

'Or I'll take Werner away from you and you'll never see him again. I'm his uncle, and you're no one to him. Even von Braun would admit it, if it comes to that. Family is sacred.'

Marthe digested this. Kasper knew how attached she was to Werner. He knew that was the best way to get to her.

'And if I agree?' she asked.

'You have no choice. And if you can manage a single valid thought process in your empty little head, you'll realise you have everything to gain from it. Now that I'm officially Johann Zilch, you'll just have to become Luisa. You speak English, you've always dreamed of going to that degenerate country, a nurse can find work anywhere. Then I'm sure you'll dig out some old fool to marry you and look after you and the boy. I'm not interested in Werner. If you do as I say, I'll leave him alone . . .'

Marthe took a moment to reply and Kasper's jaw twisted irritably. He waved a threatening fist at her.

'Do you understand?' he asked in a voice strangled with anger.

'I understand,' she replied.

Kasper stood up. Marthe was still frozen with fear but he walked around the bed and headed for the door. Marthe moved in time with her husband to keep as much distance between them as she could in the small space. When he put his hand on the door handle, she finally challenged him.

'Everyone thinks you're dead . . .' she started.

'Being dead is my best chance of survival.'

Marthe's heart was slamming against her ribs, but she found the courage to keep going.

'What did you do to Johann?'

'I sent him back to where he should have been all along.'

'What do you mean?'

'You know exactly what I mean.'

He was hardly out of the room before Marthe threw herself on the key to lock the door. She pushed the chest of drawers across the doorway, leant against the wall and slipped to the floor, drained of all her strength. She didn't know how to escape Kasper's malevolent grasp. She found it excruciatingly difficult not to succumb to panic and yet now she had to calculate her every move carefully to protect herself and the baby. After thinking for a long time, a very long time, she moved aside the chest of drawers, went out into the corridor, and went to fetch Werner from Anke's room. She stayed awake the rest of the night, watching the child sleep.

From that moment on, a pale and drawn Marthe played the part of reconciliation. She kept Werner as far as she could from his 'father', but behaved charmingly with 'Johann' whenever they were in company. Von Braun seemed delighted with this encouraging development, and made no attempt to understand why it had come about.

Between New Orleans and Baton Rouge, 1972

Rebecca and Lauren had joined us, and in the house alive with birdsong from the garden, we sat in tense silence, listening to Marthe's story. She explained how Luisa, my mother, had died, and how a young soldier had saved me. Then how she'd found me in the arms of a stranger on the banks of the Elbe where thousands of survivors had gathered. She told us about her desperate race across Germany in search of my father, Johann. She described Peenemünde, the grocer's wife who'd helped her and my wet nurse, the journey to the Alps . . . her story filled the gaps left by von Braun during our lunch at NASA. The pieces of the puzzle were suddenly slotting into place, and I drank in Marthe's words, but I was waiting for the killer blow, the sins that would brand my family with a red iron.

Rebecca, Marcus and Lauren were as nervous as I was, and Marthe's friend, Abigail, tried to lighten the atmosphere, serving us lemonade that we didn't drink and handing out blueberry shortcakes that we didn't eat. During the saddest episodes of this odyssey through war-torn Germany, she nervously adjusted her glasses and mournfully shook her head with its soft waves of hair. She watched Marthe anxiously, but Marthe could see no one but me. She had reached the point where she was reunited with von Braun when, unable to wait any longer, I interrupted her.

'Was Johann ever at Auschwitz?' I blurted.

'At Auschwitz?' Marthe asked. 'But what would he have been there for?'

'As part of the camp staff, overseeing . . . prisoners,' I said, avoiding mention of gas chambers, torture, rape and other crimes that spooled through my mind.

'My darling, your father would never have hurt a fly, it wasn't in his nature. He was a thinker, a scientist. He wasn't fit for the real world. Still less for combat . . .'

'But he did disappear for a good part of the war . . .' Rebecca interjected.

Marthe turned to Rebecca as if only just noticing her. She studied her for a moment, her face unreadable.

'Johann was arrested by the Gestapo,' she said. 'And if he was ever at Auschwitz – and I'd be very surprised if he was – he would have been a prisoner. I don't have any proof to show you, but I can tell you what I believe in my heart. Johann is dead. He never joined von Braun's team at the end of the war. I, of all people, can confirm that the man who came to the United States with us was Kasper and no one else. He managed to pass himself off as his brother and to leave Germany before the Allies had a chance to hold him to account. I know that. And I'm telling you. As for Johann, may he rest in peace, I never heard of him again.'

This declaration was greeted with silence. My true father was not the monster that Rebecca had depicted. Along with the relief, I felt very strange now that I finally had a solution to the enigma that had been torturing me for years. Marcus was first to shake himself out of our dazed state. He came over and gave me a hearty slap on the back.

'That sure is good news, Wern,' he said.

'What a relief!' exclaimed Lauren, throwing her arms around my neck and hugging me. She released her grip for a moment, then hugged me again.

Marthe and Abigail watched us in amazement. They must have had trouble working out the reason for this sudden enthusiasm.

I turned to Rebecca, watching for her reaction. She gave me

a look I couldn't read. Was she still in any doubt? I couldn't see what she was thinking. My beauty was still out of reach, mysterious, locked down. She didn't move at all, and this filled me with a deep sadness that I worked hard to disguise. I'd hoped that those few words from Marthe would have been enough to prove my innocence, to stop the tectonic shift that kept driving Rebecca and me apart. I now realised that, as ever with her, it was more complicated than that.

'We came to Fort Bliss in January 1946,' Marthe said, picking up her account. 'I was in a group with about a hundred Nazi scientists. Very few of them were able to bring their families, who would join them later. I slipped into that first group which was made up almost entirely of men because von Braun thought of himself as your godfather. He didn't want to leave you in Germany. He'd agreed to pass me off as your mother, and arranged for me to travel with them. You were so good on the crossing, exemplary. The sea was rough but you weren't seasick, unlike most of the adults. You ate happily, you slept well, even when the waves were as tall as buildings and I thought we'd come to our final hour. When we reached Texas the heat didn't seem to bother you. You were incredibly resilient for such a young child.

'At Fort Bliss we were put in temporary housing which turned out to be permanent. You and I lived in the same bungalow as von Braun because it had two bedrooms instead of one. It had a simple corrugated iron roof. With no insulation except for that sheet of metal, which heated up like the element in a toaster, the Texas sun drove the temperature up to 110 degrees. You spent most of the day in a bathtub, under the lazy creaking of an ineffective fan. We had to be self-sufficient and we had no legal status. The men had no work, and felt pointless. It was like in Bavaria when they were waiting for the end of the war, they just played cards and chess, they smoked, listened to music and did what they could to get through those monotonous days.

'Kasper was the only one who made use of the situation. So long as the team was idle, so long as they couldn't get to work, his imposture went unnoticed. But the day von Braun could start his research again, it would become clear that Kasper knew nothing about aeronautics or V2s. His co-workers would immediately know he wasn't Johann. In other words, Kasper was in no hurry for that day to dawn. He had nearly a year's respite. He may have been frustrated that he couldn't leave the camp but was very happy to be safely sheltered from reprisals. The Nuremberg trials were going on in Europe, and we followed them in the American press. Most of the scientists didn't speak English so they asked me to translate. Kasper put on a solemn expression when he listened to those articles. I didn't know what he'd done in the war, we separated right at the start, just after the invasion of Poland. But I knew how sadistic he was and when the American press described the executions of those found guilty in October 1946, I saw the horror in his eyes and knew he had a lot to hide.

'Meanwhile, I made the most of those months of forced inactivity for the team and, in anticipation of eventually being given my freedom, I qualified as a nurse in the American military system. Unfortunately, the German qualification I already had wasn't recognised in Texas.

'At the beginning of 1947 von Braun was allowed to return to Germany with a military escort to marry his cousin, Maria-Luise von Quirstop. He came back to Fort Bliss with his young wife and her parents. I had to move out and von Braun couldn't find a way to explain to the American camp commandant why I shouldn't live with my "husband". Your uncle and I were given a one-bedroom apartment in one of the administrative buildings. It was more comfortable than the shacks, but we – you and I, Werner – were no longer protected from Kasper. I was right back in the depths of hell. I had to hide the bruises from his blows, the cuts and the sprains. I did what I'd done in the early days of our marriage: pretended everything was fine. I thought of leaving several times, and asked if I could go home to Germany with you, but neither von Braun nor the Americans would let me.

'I finally saw an opportunity to get out when von Braun was given the go-ahead to start working on his rocket projects again. Of course he didn't have the funds to build the machine he'd always dreamed of, but he could get on with his design concept. Rather than being found out as a complete ignoramus, Kasper pre-empted disaster and asked to leave the camp. Obviously, there was no question of my staying with von Braun, still less of my keeping you without your uncle. Yet again, to avoid being separated from you, I had to submit to Kasper. He justified his decision to leave by claiming how badly he was affected by amnesia, telling his co-workers that his scientific knowledge had been wiped out by the torture he'd suffered. With tears in his eyes – because he was a very good actor – he told von Braun he couldn't bear the shame and suffering of his own incompetence, and asked for permission to look for work and leave.

'Von Braun helped him secure papers for the three of us, and found him a job in Sanomoth, a company that specialised in plant-protection products. Fate seemed to be smiling on me at last, it was the start of a new life. Kasper would go his way, and I mine – with you. That's what he'd promised in Germany and he'd often reiterated that promise. I had no reason to doubt it. He quite openly despised you – you were his brother's son, in other words the child of his oldest, most sworn enemy – and his only feeling for me was contempt. But I didn't let my guard down. I was frightened of everything. As a precaution, I'd embroidered Luisa's dying wish on all your clothes: "This child is called Werner Zilch, don't change his name, he's the last of our kind." I also wrote your story on two pages and sewed copies of it into the linings of your jackets. In case, perish the thought, Kasper managed to separate us, I also put my name and how to contact me through the nurse who trained me at Fort Bliss, along with contact details for von Braun and Major Hamill's secretary, who'd become my friend. I don't know what instinct drove me to take these precautions because at the time I was convinced Kasper would be only too pleased to get out and get away from us without a backward glance. All I had to do now was find work. There was no shortage of jobs in Texas. The country was booming. And you'd be old enough to go to school soon . . . The two of us could start our life together at last. I knew it would be tricky to manage sometimes, but I couldn't wait. Sadly, things didn't happen the way I'd hoped.'

Marthe paused to drink a glass of lemonade.

'I'm sorry to ask you this,' Rebecca ventured, 'but why didn't you denounce him? Once you were in the States, you could have told everyone that Kasper had stolen his brother's identity.'

Marthe took a while to reply.

'Because I was frightened,' she said eventually. 'Frightened of Kasper physically, frightened of him morally, frightened of what his co-workers would say. Times have changed, you know. Twenty-five years ago, it wasn't a good idea for a woman to stand up to a man. It would have been my word against his, and my word wasn't worth very much. That would also have been the best way for him to take Werner from me. I was absolutely devoted to you,' she added, turning to me. 'And even though Luisa had said she wanted me to look after you, I had no legal claim to you. Kasper could have separated us on a whim . . .'

Marthe's voice trailed off, then she looked at Rebecca again and said, 'You know, it's easy to find solutions years later, but it's in the heat of the moment that decisions have to be made.'

'When did you finally leave Fort Bliss?' I asked.

'In May 1948. Von Braun and his team thought I'd move in with you and Kasper near Sanomoth's headquarters, but we were actually going our separate ways that first day. I'd found a job in El Paso in a hospital run by the Protestant community. The director had offered me a room on site while I sorted out my life with you and looked for accommodation. I'd told him I was a widow and lived with my young son, and he was very understanding. I didn't want Kasper to know where we were going so I asked him to drop us at a false address in the city centre, far enough from the hospital so he wouldn't be able to trace us. I'd thought of everything but I made the mistake of believing Kasper would look after his own best interests when, in fact, he had it in him to put himself in danger in order to enjoy making me suffer. I'd underestimated his visceral need to destroy me. There is evil in the world, and there are sadists too. There is no point in looking for excuses for them, there are none. It's the way they are, deep inside. They take pleasure in the wounds they inflict. You have to escape them or, if you can, kill them because you have limits that they just don't have. I knew I wasn't up to fighting.

'I decided to disappear with you, Werner, but he couldn't suspect a thing so, when he offered, I didn't turn down his invitation to lunch, "our last meal together", he said with that persuasive look that always used to win me over in the early days of our marriage. We went to the Riviera, a Mexican restaurant that had just opened on Doniphan Drive. I said the food might be too spicy for a child of two and a half, but Kasper ignored my reservations. We sat down at one of the bare wooden tables, close to the door. On the radio mariachis were singing "Aye Paloma", "Viva Mexico" and "Cielito Lindo". We placed our order and I remember the waitress who brought our meals. I remember we chatted almost playfully. Then I was suddenly too hot, I felt terrible. I could see Kasper smiling, this strange expression on his face. He was watching me with obvious pleasure. My temples pounded as if my skull was going to split in two. I drained my glass of orange juice in one and the room started to spin. I felt I'd lost control of my body. I saw my own hand grab the steak knife from the next table. I remember feeling amazed that I was doing this, independently of my own will. Then nothing. A total blank. A void . . .'

Marthe paused again. She was pale.

'Would you rather I told them?' Abigail asked, running her hand over Marthe's forehead.

I was struck by the harmony between the two women, the obvious tenderness they felt for each other. Marthe gave Abigail a slightly shaky smile and stood up.

'No, it's OK,' she said. 'I just need to get some air . . . I'll be back.'

We could see her through the living-room window: she headed for the circular bench around the trunk of an imposing tree that was covered in fleshy white flowers. She sat down and I got up to go and join her but Abigail stopped me.

'Leave her for a while. She'll be back. In the meantime, maybe you're hungry?' she asked.

We nodded, and Lauren offered to help Abigail. Marcus and Tom also wanted to be involved but Abigail said the kitchen was too small for four people. Needless to say, Rebecca didn't lift a finger. We sat in silence. Without her realising it, I watched her reflection in one of the windows. She seemed thoughtful. And I thought she looked beautiful, of course. But her unfailing gorgeousness wasn't enough to override everything else. I was angry with her. I wasn't sure I would ever be able to forgive her.

Between New Orleans and Baton Rouge, 1972

Marthe sat in her garden and tried to regain control of her emotions. There was joy, of course, at seeing the magnificent young man Werner had become. There were regrets too. It was all so long ago! Germany, Silesia, their youth, the war . . . She remembered family lunches in the Zilches' large dining room where the brothers would start by discussing politics and soon came to blows.

Kasper had been a Nazi from the very beginning; she remembered his vehement words, his loathing of Jews, blacks, women, the bourgeoisie, the poor, anyone who was different to him. No one escaped his criticism. His face taut with anger, he would get carried away by his zeal, intoxicated by his own harshness which made him feel strong and clear-minded. He prided himself on saying out loud what others thought privately, spitting out his degrading comparisons and Darwinian tirades. He delighted in these transgressions, gauging his power by his ability for destruction. There was even violence in his least significant habits: he had an infuriating way of cutting corks into tiny pieces and reducing paper to confetti. The moment he met someone he would look for their weak point, some detail about which he could bully them. For Kasper, life was just a permanent appraisal of strength.

If Johann talked of goodness or benevolence, Kasper sneered scornfully and trotted out the only quote from Nietzsche that he knew: 'For the strong, there is no greater danger than pity.' At other times, Kasper cited Hegel, whom he had never read, and caricatured his dialectics on masters and slaves. A less complex man than Johann would have rebelled more actively against the Nazi regime, but he was absorbed in his scientific research and took only a distant interest in the events rocking his country. Ever since childhood, his dreams of a space rocket had protected him from Kasper and the world. Safe among the archives on the second floor of the house, he transformed the realities of the world into equations so that he felt he had mastered it. When Hitler began his meteoric rise, Johann's only resistance was to his own brother. Luisa took even less interest in such questions than her husband. She was in love, and that kept every part of her busy. She 'knew nothing about politics' and was quick to attempt a diversion when the brothers started to talk. Kasper would then snub her with astonishing brutality. Johann would defend his wife and the meal would end in a fist-fight.

Marthe had been the only one to take a stand against Hitler's power from the start. She also harboured an instinctive feminism – not that she identified it as such until many years later – and baulked at the patronising image of German women glorified in Nazi propaganda. Her opinions were very definitely not shared, and her only attempt to contribute to a debate, one Sunday lunchtime, was pulverised by Kasper with a violent slap that scandalised the whole Zilch family. Marthe was amazed by their protests: did they genuinely not know what went on once their bedroom door was closed? Could the thick granite walls of this manor house really have been enough to stifle the sounds of her pain and despair? Granted, a sense of shame stopped her complaining or confiding in anyone, and Kasper was always careful when he struck her not to mark exposed areas, but she couldn't believe her parents-in-law weren't aware of her purgatory. In this loving, wealthy family, descended from a long line of dignitaries and industrialists, no character as tormented as Kasper's had ever been spawned. His aggressiveness constituted a mystery, even for his own parents. How to explain the disparity between their boys? The brothers had always been given everything: a carefully protected upbringing, robust good health, fine looks and remarkable intelligence.

Kasper used these assets to the worst ends and drew a despotic sense of superiority from his privileges. Every glance in a mirror confirmed his convictions: the Aryan race, of which he considered himself a perfect example, was bigger, stronger, faster and more beautiful. He felt like a giant surrounded by dwarves. His arrogance was coupled with obsessive jealousy of anyone who had any grounds to outshine him, starting with his brother. This despised younger sibling who, simply by being born, had dethroned him, provoked his appetite for punishment more than anyone else. Kasper liked to reign, he would have liked to be the only man on earth, and it so happened that Johann had the impudence to be more academically brilliant. He was also more loved. Johann had been a gentle child, given to reading and construction toys, then later mathematics and physics. Kasper had been a restless boy. His father, disliking conflict, avoided him so Kasper diverted his attention to his mother. He constantly tormented her, perhaps because she struggled to disguise her preference for her younger son. Who could resist Johann? He had neither his brother's narcissism nor his tempestuous nature.

The disagreements between the brothers were all the more surprising because, seen side by side, they looked like twins. They had the same build, the same graceful movements, the same eyes like limpid water, and the same boundless charm. Kasper had perhaps a suggestion of roundness to his features, greediness in his mouth and negligence in his general appearance that allowed those closest to them, with more practised eyes, to distinguish them. Despite these small differences, their likeness was striking, and the joking comparisons people made – an understandable reflex when confronted with such an original trick of nature – only aggravated the elder's resentment for his younger brother.

As a little boy, Johann had kept away from Kasper as much as he could, but as soon as he caught up with Kasper's height when they were teenagers, he trained himself up so that he could match him blow for blow. Having been Kasper's whipping boy for many years, he was rebelling. Kasper thought of Johann as an extension of himself, and Johann's demonstrations of independence sent him into blind rages. The Zilch household became the theatre of an open war for an imaginary throne that existed only in Kasper's mind. This bullying reached an intolerable level of violence when their parents died. The neighbours became involved, there were all sorts of rumours circulating about Luisa, most significantly that she had been Kasper's mistress before marrying Johann. Marthe, who had lived in Berlin at the time that this presumed liaison had taken place, asked Luisa about it.

The young bride acknowledged that Kasper had courted her – this had been a few months before she'd met Johann – but she vehemently denied there had been any physical contact. Their relationship, she stated categorically, had been purely platonic. Marthe was surprised by her own reaction: she should have been jealous that her husband had wanted Luisa, she should have been hurt not to be in on the secret, but instead she experienced an inexplicable pleasure at the thought of this proximity between Luisa and Kasper. The idea of sharing a man with Luisa even afforded her a strange satisfaction. The neighbourhood proved less magnanimous: the rumours and humiliations that followed created an unbearable atmosphere. Taking Luisa with him, Johann left the family home to join the young Professor von Braun's research team, and with their departure, Marthe had to say goodbye to her only sources of joy, the one thing that had stopped her foundering in that cold hostile manor house.

Oh Lord, these memories were hard to bear! The years should have healed the wound, but there it was, just the same. A magnolia flower fell at her feet. She picked it up absent-mindedly, cradling its fragile petals in her cupped hand. She stayed under the tree a while longer before going back in. Werner was waiting for her in the living room; now wasn't the time to weaken.

Between New Orleans and Baton Rouge, 1972

Marthe came back to her place on the sofa and picked up exactly where she'd left off.

'I must have lost consciousness at the Mexican restaurant where Kasper and I were having lunch. When I came around I was in a spotless bedroom. For a moment I thought I'd died, light seemingly filtering down on me from heaven. I tried to gather my wits: the light actually came from a tiny, barred window very high up in the wall. Then I realised I was attached to the bed. I couldn't sit up or even turn onto my side. I panicked, screamed for help. Two nurses came and told me brusquely to calm down. I asked where I was, asked to be untied, asked to see you. Who'd taken you? Who was looking after you? Why was I locked up? When they didn't answer my questions I became hysterical. They gave me an injection and I went under again.

'I slept for hours, days, weeks, I couldn't say. I was knocked out by their drugs. In my rare moments of consciousness, I begged to see you. The nurses told me you were with your father and you were fine. I knew that you could only be in terrible danger with Kasper, but no one listened to my protestations. Worse than that, my anxieties confirmed the medical team's diagnosis that I was paranoid. I was completely adrift, purposeless and lost. Time was just a huge blank and my heart was empty.

'One morning a member of the nursing staff told me that Professor Lesner would be seeing me. I was now very careful what I said, I knew my every word could be used against me. The professor proved kinder than his staff, and explained – at last – why I'd been locked up. He told me I'd had a manic outburst while having lunch in a Mexican restaurant with my husband. I'd threatened him with a knife, right in front of my son, and had also threatened the waiters who tried to intervene. It had been extremely difficult to bring me under control, and my husband had had to make the decision to have me sectioned. To support his account, he showed me witness statements written by customers at the Riviera. I read them and knew for sure that Kasper had drugged me. Right back in the early days of our marriage he'd amused himself by testing out all sorts of compounds on his family, which made his father furious. Kasper stopped his experiments only when his father threatened to disinherit him. I kept this version of events to myself – trying to explain myself to Professor Lesner would only have aggravated my situation. I settled instead for sowing the seeds of doubt by avoiding the temptation to be bitter or sarcastic.

'I asked whether my husband had been to see me since I'd been in the unit, and the professor admitted with an embarrassed smile that he had not. Had he called to ask how I was? No again. Then I asked whether my husband was paying the bills for my treatment, and the professor said that he was and I really mustn't worry about that.

'When I told him I was anxious about you and wanted to know when I could see you again, the professor played for time – he was a kind man. He said he wanted to be sure my condition had stabilised and I no longer represented a threat to my husband, my son or society. I made sure I was contrite and undemanding, I was prepared to do anything to be allowed out. He told me I had to have therapy with a very talented and understanding therapist, the first woman psychiatrist in the hospital. He hoped the two of us would get along. I said I was sure we would, the most important thing was for me to make the progress he expected of me. He seemed very satisfied and on the strength of this first meeting asked for me to be moved to a new room. I could also join other patients in their daily activities: walks, creative arts, household tasks and so on.

'I met the psychiatrist the next day. I didn't know it at the time, but she would save my life,' Marthe said, turning to look at Abigail.

'The psychiatrist was me,' her partner explained. 'I immediately knew something didn't hold together in Marthe's story. It took me a while to gain her confidence. She told me what any doctor would want to hear in the circumstances but didn't open up. I knew she was hiding the truth and I could tell she was frightened. In the end we got along, we understood each other so well that we ended up loving each other. We had to be cautious, clever. I managed to get her out but when, I don't know how, the team realised months later that we were living together, I was dismissed. Some of my former co-workers tried to have Marthe sectioned again on the grounds that I'd been seduced and had lost my professional objectivity. We left El Paso overnight and moved to Louisiana, hoping we'd be safe in Texas if anyone tried to pursue us. We had to start all over again. I started my own practice and Marthe found work with a nursing agency. We bought this house, planted this garden and built a life we love. Everything would have been perfect if we'd known what had happened to you, Werner . . .'

'I looked for you everywhere,' Marthe said. She jumped to her feet and went into the next room, which appeared to be her study. She took a thick file from a cupboard.

'These are the small ads I ran in the papers with a photo of you, also the letters I wrote and the replies I received. Nothing that I tried had any result. You'd evaporated. And so had Kasper. I ended up thinking he'd killed you and buried you somewhere before running away to Argentina, Chile or one of those countries where they took people like him in. It was terrible not knowing, but on your fifteenth birthday I gave up the search. Abigail had been encouraging me to let go for a long time. Your disappearance was preventing me getting on with my life, putting myself back together. I had to accept it. Part of me refused to, but I did stop searching.'

Abigail could see Marthe was faltering so she suggested we had something to eat. She'd made a big salad of tomatoes, corn and cucumber mixed with cold roast chicken. She gave us chilled beers which did us all good. It was my turn to talk now, and I told Marthe and Abigail about my childhood, my adoptive parents, Lauren's birth, meeting Marcus and our first real-estate projects. Lauren contributed her share of recollections, digging up funny anecdotes about my stubbornness and childhood mishaps that made Marthe and Abigail laugh. She also told them how much Armande and Andrew 'adored' me. I reminded her that my mother spent her whole time yelling at me, but Lauren wouldn't hear a word of it.

'Stop it! You know she'd do anything in the world for you.'

Rebecca didn't speak at all. She watched, grim and intense, and passed around plates of food. I couldn't work out what was going on inside her beautiful head. Her thoughts were tucked away behind the unbreakable glass of her amethyst eyes.

Abigail brought in a bowl of whipped cream and another full of strawberries. Marthe didn't touch her food; she wanted to know everything about me, about us. Her questions were never-ending.

'Why didn't your parents give you their name . . . did they find my letters?'

'No, sadly the only letter they found was in the lining of a jacket that my mother had just washed.'

'In water? What was your mother thinking!' Marthe wailed as if this blunder had happened only hours earlier.

'She realised her mistake when she unpicked the lining. She was furious with herself . . .' I paused before adding, 'and I resented her for it too, all those years when I tried to understand what had happened. But my parents did see the words you'd embroidered on my clothes . . . Why did it say I was "the last of our kind"?'

A veil of sadness fell over Marthe's face.

'Luisa was convinced – and it seems she was right – that Johann was dead. She knew she herself wouldn't survive. Your grandparents had died. Once she'd realised how Kasper had treated me and had discovered that he'd abused his status as the eldest to sell the family home without telling Johann, she thought of him as a monster not worthy to be considered part of the family. I'd claimed my freedom and taken back my maiden name. So she felt you really were the last of the Zilches . . .'

I sat deep in thought. Clearly, my family had had some standing in that distant country I knew nothing about, but it made me feel strange to think I was connected to it. Until now, my name had invited teasing and questions I couldn't answer, but it had been mine alone. I'd wanted to give it some significance by sheer force of will, to assert myself, prove my worth and be admired . . . Now I suddenly had to share it with other people. I didn't like being associated with this family which had once meant something. Deep down, I didn't like being descended from anyone, I didn't like being deprived of the complete freedom I'd had so far, the freedom to become whoever I wanted to be.

'If you had to find Kasper, how would you go about it?' Rebecca asked Marthe.

'Now that you're here,' Marthe said, looking at me, 'and I know you're unharmed, I have no reason at all to find Kasper. And if I'd had any sort of lead, I'd have followed it up long ago . . . In the early days, I went to Sanomoth where Kasper was meant to be working, but he'd been transferred. I didn't get anywhere from that. Maybe you'll have better luck than me, Rebecca,' Marthe added with a note of irony.

'I sincerely hope so,' Rebecca retorted.

'Why are you so interested in Kasper?' Marthe asked, helping herself to strawberries and cream. 'There's nothing to be gained from going anywhere near that man, you know . . .'

'An SS officer named Zilch was my mother's torturer in Auschwitz. You may have abandoned any thought of having your revenge, but I won't give up on seeing justice done. After the crimes that sadist committed, he can't be left to enjoy the sunshine in Chile or wherever he is. So long as there's the tiniest chance that the bastard is still alive, I won't give up,' Rebecca announced with a shudder.

'I didn't know he'd been in Auschwitz,' Marthe murmured.

'You said earlier he clearly had things to be ashamed of,' Marcus reminded her.

'Yes, you're right . . . I daren't imagine what he would have inflicted on a woman he had completely in his power. I'm so sorry for your mother,' Marthe said to Rebecca. 'Really terribly sorry.'

Rebecca didn't reply but thanked her with a nod of her head.

JFK Airport, 1972

It was already dark when we landed. The return journey was better than the outward one. The heat, the travelling and the emotional rollercoaster we'd just experienced had drained us of energy, and we slept on the flight. As we alighted from the plane, I could feel the tension mount. Rebecca and I hadn't talked to each other all day. She would head her way and I mine. It seemed unimaginable to leave it at that, and yet off she walked with her bag on her shoulder, without even a wave to me.

I'd thought that our estrangement had been due solely to the sword of Damocles that had hung over us for months. We now knew everything about my origins, and my father was absolved, but Rebecca was behaving as if nothing had changed, as if I were still presumed guilty, the son of a recognised criminal. Had the moments of respite we'd shared been just a ploy? Had I been the only one to believe in our relationship while she had been pursuing a quite different trajectory without my realising it? Her silence was eating me up. It was starting to make me doubt myself, my instincts, my perceptiveness. If she'd never loved me, had she been there only for the pleasure? Even in our most intimate moments when I'd thought of her as mine alone, I was now suddenly afraid she'd always slipped through my fingers . . .

I walked three paces behind her on the travelator at the terminal which took us – at double speed – towards the moment when we would part. Our reflections glided along the windows turned into mirrors by the darkness outside. Not for a moment did she slow down, not for a moment did she think of stopping, turning around and telling me she'd had enough, that we were made to be together and it would never be over.

'Shall we take you home, Rebecca?' Lauren asked chirpily – she was sometimes as subtle as a Labrador chasing a ball in a glassware shop.

'It's fine, don't worry. There's a car waiting for me,' replied the ex-love of my life. 'But maybe you'd like to come home with me?' she offered my sister.

Lauren must have been cursing herself. She seemed to have fallen right into the trap she'd set for herself.

'You can go, Lauren, if you like,' I said, tight-lipped.

'No, stay with them,' Rebecca insisted with a smile that said, 'if you ditch me now, consider this the end of our friendship.'

By the time this exchange was over we'd reached the parking area for private chauffeurs. There was an awkward pause that Marcus handled with an authority and impatience that we weren't used to.

'Lauren,' he said, steering her with a hand around her waist, 'you're coming with me. And you two are going home together, because we have had it up to here with your problems. It's been going on for months, and we've had enough of this crap!'

'This crap, Marcus? Where did that vulgarity come from?' I teased, delighted that this interjection of his was winning me some time.

'It doesn't suit you to be vulgar,' Rebecca said.

'If I have at least got you to agree on that one point, that has made my day. Meanwhile, we won't be hostages to your rows any longer. *Basta!* Enough! And I can say it in another half-dozen languages if need be. Come on, Lauren, we're out of here.'

He bundled my sister into the first reserved car, jumped in next to her and waved the driver off, cheerfully stranding us there. I opened the door to the second car for Rebecca, a gallant gesture that wasn't my usual style. She stepped in with a muttered

'Thank you' that didn't bode well. I sat beside her and asked our driver to raise the window between him and us so that he didn't hear our conversation.

'There's no point,' said Rebecca, wanting to bring all hostilities to an end. 'There's nothing to say.'

'What do you mean, there's nothing to say?'

'We've done all this, you know we have.'

'I don't know anything of the sort! *I* haven't "done all this", anyway. There's no way you can disappear into thin air again, shrouded in your mysteries and esoteric reasonings. You owe me an explanation at least.'

'You know very well why this – why we – can never work.'

'I don't. I don't know,' I answered flatly. 'I may just be a poor, short-sighted male, but I can't see. My real father had nothing to be ashamed of. He did no harm at all to your mother. I can't see what's stopping us from being happy together now.'

'You're so dishonest with yourself, I can't believe it!' Rebecca snapped. 'The problem was never your father, your uncle or God knows what past crimes you're not responsible for, but what *you* did. And your temperament, which I'll never be able to change. It's the way you are. You can't help it.'

'What the hell are you talking about?' I asked angrily.

'You cheated on me. And cheated on me again. And then again.'

'But I never cheated on you!' I exclaimed, stunned by the accusation.

'Joan doesn't ring any bells, then? Or Vanessa Javel, the editor? Eve Mankevitch, the psychiatrist? Annabel, my schoolfriend? And Sibyl? That really took the biscuit – the dumbest of my Lynch cousins. A proper blunderbuss. You wouldn't have the nerve to tell me it was a coincidence or you were in love! Not to mention the waitresses, the stewardesses, the married women! You'd make love to a club chair if someone put a wig on it. It's outrageous!'

I was so flabbergasted that I sat in silence for a moment. Rebecca had never given me reason to believe she was jealous. Quite the opposite, in fact: her apparent indifference had often exasperated me.

'But, Rebecca, why didn't you say anything?'

'If you weren't kind enough and sensitive enough to know for yourself, I can't live with you.'

'How do you expect me to know what's on your mind if you don't talk to me about it?'

'I did talk to you yesterday.'

'Rebecca!' I protested. 'It's weeks since you left me without a word of explanation and you vaguely mentioned the problem for the first time yesterday! I didn't understand.'

'You knew perfectly well.'

'I didn't have the least inkling. I thought you'd left because of Kasper, because of Johann, because of all this stuff going around inside our heads.'

'I left you because you cheated on me.'

'No, I cheated on you because you left me. Those names you listed, those girls I couldn't give a damn about, I only saw them when I was single, because you'd abandoned me. Even Joan, who's a wonderful woman, a woman who really deserved to be loved and respected, I dropped the moment you came back. How could I know? You seemed so detached . . .'

'What did you want me to do?' she asked. 'Break all the plates and roll on the floor? I wouldn't give you the satisfaction.'

Her eyes were sparkling and her cheeks pink. Her chest rose and fell feverishly under her white top. On her neck I could see the throbbing of a vein that I'd so often fixated on when we made love. Her hair was swept up to reveal the childish tendrils at the nape of her neck. Her hands were toying nervously with the strap of her bag. She was making my head spin.

'Even when you're angry, I can't manage not to love you . . .' I said almost in a whisper.

I felt her weaken. She glanced at me and the anger in her eyes was now diluted, but the chauffeur chose this moment to open the privacy window and ask a stupid question.

'Should I drop madam at the same address as sir?'

'Right now you're not dropping anyone anywhere, just drive,' I told him curtly.

I absolutely had to have more time . . . Talk and talk until she came back to me. Tie her up with my words, drown her in tenderness, demolish her with caresses. Take all of her back.

'Drive where?' asked the chauffeur.

'Just keep driving and don't stop, and don't interrupt us again!' I said, raising the glass and drawing the curtain.

'Don't take it out on him, it's not his fault,' protested Rebecca.

'Well, it's not my fault either, and it makes me feel better.'

'You can't make other people pay for our problems. You terrorised him!'

'There you go, straight to the big words again! Please don't change the subject.'

It was dark. We were alone, at last, and free to confront each other. We carried on in the same vein for hours. There was shouting. There was laughter. There were tears. There were kisses. There were accusations and there was forgiveness. There were punishments and pleasures. Shared equally. We were Rebecca and Werner together again in a car, like the first time I'd made love to her, the evening of our rooftop dinner in Brooklyn. The car drove on with no other aim than to keep driving. The movement was enough to silence our questions. We belonged to each other, were close to each other, with each other. Completely lost in the moment. Spellbound to be spellbound once more. The alchemy we'd thought lost, the alchemy we'd sought out in every recess of our battered hearts and then in the silent bodies of other women and perhaps other men, had taken hold of us again. Naked and wrapped in a coarse woollen blanket that we'd found under the armrest, we were happy and – as we were every time happiness smiled on us – ravenously hungry.

I was about to direct the driver towards a twenty-four-hour diner near the Rockefeller Center when the car stuttered and stopped with a suspect lurch. We waited about ten minutes, giggling like schoolchildren, then because nothing was happening, I drew back the curtain. The front of the car was empty. I pulled on my jeans and T-shirt, and stepped out of the car. We were right out in the country. The greyish light of dawn was paired with a cool, fragrant dampness.

The driver was leaning against a tree on the verge, smoking. A huge slumped figure. He threw away his cigarette when he saw me.

'Where are we?' I asked.

'Long Island.'

'In the Hamptons?'

'Yes,' he said as if this was the most natural thing in the world.

'But why?'

'You told me to keep driving.'

Rebecca had dressed, and she came out to join us. She'd put on my jacket, and she huddled up close to me.

'Did we break down?' she asked innocently.

'We ran out of gas, madam,' replied the driver.

Rebecca and I exchanged bewildered looks.

'Why didn't you get any along the way?' I asked as amiably as possible even though I could feel an eruption simmering inside me.

'You told me not to stop.'

'So you kept going till the tank was empty?'

'Yes, sir.'

'I don't believe it!' I exploded, pacing in circles while Rebecca tried to calm me. 'Why didn't you ask to stop?'

'Sir had told me not to interrupt you.'

The sun was just starting to come up and there wasn't a house or a phone booth in sight. I set off along the road, followed by Rebecca who was laughing so much she was crying – as she did every time I lost my temper – and the driver who was grumbling to himself. He'd done what I'd asked of him. It wasn't his fault. He didn't deserve to be treated like this. And, anyway, he was hungry and tired. He'd been driving all night. That's not what he'd been booked for . . . He hadn't even had a break and now look at the thanks he got. His complaints made me angry all over again. I spun around so that my nose was only inches from his and ordered him to head in the opposite direction. I didn't want to see him any more and I didn't want to listen to him any more. I gave him a wad of cash that covered twice the trip, and advised him never to cross paths with me again if he valued his pathetic existence. The guy was twice my weight and could probably have given me a thrashing, but he turned on his heel with a hangdog expression and trailed off in the other direction.

'Now what do we do?' Rebecca asked, still amused.

'Walk,' I said grumpily.

And that's what we did till we came to the deserted beach. Rebecca took off her socks and we carried on walking along the shore. The rising sun tinted the sea, the sand and our faces with ochre and pink. We saw a house, but it was locked up. Three hundred yards further along we had the good luck to come across a man of about sixty out for his morning walk. A small, slight man, he was impeccably chic and courteously melancholy. When we explained our misadventures he peered at us pensively, then a twinkle lit up his grey eyes and, with a surge of enthusiasm, he invited us to get some rest at his house. We were tired and hungry, he didn't have to ask twice.

Mr Van der Guilt had a beautiful house which went by the name of Sandmanor. He kindly showed us around, and Rebecca was very taken with it. The main building was of pale brick and had the feel of an English castle. It was built in a horse-shoe shape, and was dominated by a tower that housed the master bedroom. Its majesty was accentuated by the two wings flanked by covered walkways. It was nestled among an artful arrangement of box hedges, waterfalls, roses and cypress trees. Further from the house, the discipline of French-style parterres gave way to large trees spreading their limbs in more whimsical clusters.

'My wife had a passion for gardens,' our host said with a sad smile.

Cutting short the tour, Mr Van der Guilt invited us to join him for a substantial breakfast that he didn't touch. He watched us eat with the indulgence of those who are already on the path of renouncement but still admire the appetite of the living. He must have enjoyed our conversation because he offered to put his cabin at our disposal, a 'cabin' which turned out to be a very pretty house positioned near an Olympic-size swimming pool that he no longer used. He kept it filled and ready for use for aesthetic reasons.

'An empty pool is a sorry sight,' he explained.

It was sometimes used by the children of his staff. Seeing these brand-new little lives revelling in such a simple pleasure afforded him a modicum of joy.

He took us to our 'cabin' for us to freshen up, invited us to join him for lunch later and disappeared. What was meant to be a day's rest was followed by a night and another day, until we spent almost a week's honeymoon with Mr Van der Guilt. We'd found clothes and toothbrushes in Wainscott, the nearest town. We didn't go out so we didn't need anything. Our dirty clothes disappeared and reappeared a few hours later, washed and ironed. There was little to make them dirty again because we spent most of our time naked in bed. Life in the Hamptons was incredibly easy. Before visiting I'd imagined a cloistered little world where the rich lived airless lives in sterile villas. Instead I found a simple, almost village-like existence. If you didn't join the circus of cocktails, dinners and charity galas, you could spend your days barefoot with colonies of birds and the sound of the ocean as your only company. We gladly took refuge in this enchanted bubble.

I called Marcus and Lauren to let them know we were away, and they clearly didn't miss us. Marcus hung up after two minutes, having encouraged me to 'get some rest'. I was slightly anxious about this and told Rebecca about it. She pulled me close to her on the sofa that stood outside the cabin looking out over the swimming pool and the sea.

'They must be happy to be alone together too . . .' she reassured me.

'Why?' I asked with some surprise, kissing her neck. 'We're delightful company . . .'

'Don't tell me you don't know . . .' Rebecca said, checking me out with a sideways glance.

'Don't know what?'

'You *don't* know!' Rebecca confirmed, sitting up and smiling with a mixture of contempt and disbelief. She stared at me insistently and maintained a knowing silence that encouraged me to make an improbable supposition.

'Lauren and Marcus?' I gasped. 'That's not possible!'

I studied Becca, convinced she was joking, but she seemed utterly serious and utterly amused.

'But since when?' I asked heatedly.

'At least four months! It's about time you woke up!' she said.

A real conspiracy had been brewing behind my back.

'The bastard! Sleeping with my sister! And without telling me! Without even asking me!'

My indignation made Rebecca laugh. She spent the rest of the day teasing me.

'Your sister doesn't belong to you, and your reaction was so predictable that Marcus didn't tell you anything. They adore each other. Only you could refuse to see that.'

Marcus and Lauren . . . I hadn't seen their relationship evolve.

It has to be said he *was* unhealthily discreet. He and I had never had the swaggering conversations that men are said to have. He didn't tell me about his girlfriends, described none of their particular qualities and didn't confide how attached he was to them. I heard him mention a few, and we'd even met some of them together. He would contact them a few days later without talking to me about it. He entered into his relationships with total discretion, and I would find out by chance, or through a third party, that he'd been going out with such and such a girl for weeks, or perhaps months. We only ever knew the strict minimum about them; his chosen one was never invited to have so much as lunch with us at the house. My vanity had blinded me: I'd thought that he kept his conquests away for fear they would transfer their interest to me. I now realised he had in fact been keeping them away from Lauren, and I had a clearer understanding of why he flew into such a rage when a guy was offhand with my sister.

'They weren't offhand!' protested Rebecca. 'They all cleared off because of you! You doggedly drove them out. Every time she invited one of her admirers to the house, you carried out a total demolition exercise. Marcus didn't do a bad job either, but he had good reason . . . From what you said, no one was good enough for Lauren. At least this time you can't claim her new boyfriend isn't worthy of her.'

We met our host only for meals during which he described his colourful life with humour and a great gift as a raconteur. Mr Van der Guilt had been around the world ten times. He knew the most obscure countries, the most isolated peoples. He spoke six languages and had a very distinctive way of analysing geo-political situations. Having inherited a fortune, he had never really worked. He had been a diplomat for a while, notably in Paris, Istanbul and Vienna, but I suspected he had had other activities that he couldn't divulge. Van der Guilt was a charming man, a thousand times more cultured than I would ever be, and as wealthy as I hoped to become. He had lost his wife, Kate, two years earlier to an extremely rare hereditary form of brittle bone disease. She had been his great love and he couldn't get over her absence. Rebecca and I probably reminded him of his own happiness because on the evening of the fifth day, when we were meant to be returning to New York the following morning, he asked us a blunt question out of nowhere:

'You wouldn't like to buy Sandmanor, would you?'

We were having dinner on the terrace of the main house. Torches lit up the slightly cool summer night.

'You're planning to sell this magical place?' Rebecca asked, amazed.

He sat in thought for a moment, sipping at the grappa he had served.

'It reminds me too much of Kate. She chose everything here. The chair I'm sitting on, the glass you're drinking from, this plate, that silver torch that we brought back from India . . . As soon as I open my eyes in the morning, I see the pillow that she no longer creases, her closet that I haven't yet managed to empty, her beauty products. It's as if she's just gone out for a few minutes, as if she'll be back . . . Sandmanor was her life's work, and you've seen what a beautiful, detailed job she did. I can't go on living here, I don't want to destroy what she created, and I can't abandon it to just anyone. I have no children. Kate and I loved each other passionately, I lived the best years of my life here. I should leave, but I'd like Sandmanor still to be filled with love and perhaps with the children we didn't have. Things can't always be easy for you two, but your feelings for each other are strong and genuine, that's clear for anyone to see.'

Later, when Rebecca had already gone to bed and I was about to join her, Mr Van der Guilt put a hand on my shoulder, and said, 'I've always had a sort of admiration for people like you. People who make their way up all on their own, who fight their corner and build their own lives. I would never have had your energy . . . I'll find buyers for Sandmanor, there's no doubt about that, but, for the reasons I've explained, I'd rather it was you. There . . . that's a declaration of sorts . . .' he said with a joking smile. 'And your girlfriend will be happy here. She's the sort of woman who can follow in Kate's footsteps. She has Kate's class and generosity . . . OK, I won't go on.'

With that, he headed off towards the house. Before disappearing behind the laurels that edged the path, he couldn't help himself adding, 'I'm counting on you, Werner! You're an instinctive man. Make a quick decision, and make the right decision.'

Manhattan, 1972

Rebecca buzzed with excitement, she thought about Sandmanor morning, noon and night. And I was equally obsessed. This project meant the two of us could move forward and create something together that wasn't a child. Rebecca was frightened of becoming a mother. As for me, Sandmanor saved me from mulling over the shadowy areas and frustrations that Marthe Engerer hadn't been able to elucidate.

I'd invited Marthe to New York and to my parents' house. I liked her almost brutal frankness and her affection, and I called her regularly. We chatted about this and that or I'd ask for details for Dane, who was still doing his research. I hadn't given up hope of finding Kasper Zilch: I needed to know whether he was still alive, to know for sure. During the day I felt as if I was over the worst of the trauma, but at night the unresolved equations horribly disrupted my sleep. I dreamed of my mother, and my father. They kept changing faces, their features metamorphosing between Armande, Andrew, Marthe, Luisa, Johann and Kasper. I dreamed I was asleep in a lake of blood, or that a suppurating black mark appeared on my thumbnail, then contaminated my whole thumb, my hand, and stole on up my arm until it reached my shoulder, my neck, my jaw. The mark gnawed at my flesh, my teeth, skin and eyes. It was an ultraviolet poison destroying me, and there was no antidote for it. I woke with a roar of terror, sweating, but never seemed to wake Rebecca who retreated into her dense, imperturbable sleep. Then I would get up and put myself to work until the household woke, too afraid to return to the nightmare.

And circumstances didn't help me regain my serenity: the investigation into Kasper had stalled and our real-estate projects were being held up by a tax audit. I had the odd sensation that someone had implemented this inspection deliberately. Having a dozen tax inspectors on our premises the whole time created an unbearable atmosphere, but I refused to let them get to me. We had nothing to hide. When it came to organisation and record-keeping, Donna was a finely tuned machine – I doubted any agent could catch her out on the teeniest receipt. Marcus appeared far less relaxed about the audit than I was, and it came at a bad time when we needed to free up the funds to buy Sandmanor. Till then my investments had mostly been self-financed. With the exception of my house in the Village, anything I bought paid for itself. I was virtually very wealthy but had no liquid assets. Neither Rebecca nor Lauren wanted to move uptown, so Marcus and I tried to sell the top two floors of our tower block, but buyers with the means to snap up the sort of duplexes we were proposing were few and far between.

Sandmanor was worth a fortune. Mr Van der Guilt avoided mixing friendship with negotiations, and sent his lawyer to name the asking price. I wasn't surprised by the figure, but I had only about one third of the necessary sum to hand. Rebecca was in a similar position to me: she earned money with her exhibitions and someday would inherit one of America's greatest fortunes, but her relationship with her father was complicated. Sure, he gave her a generous allowance which she used reluctantly when the income from her painting wasn't enough. But there was a world of difference between that and asking him to sign a cheque for several million dollars. I didn't think Nathan Lynch would have refused his little darling anything, but I felt sure he would have used this lever to insist on something in return from her, and this suspicion was swiftly confirmed. Very much the artist and spoilt daughter, my beauty didn't handle things herself: she asked for a statement of her accounts from Ernie, who duly provided one. And the snooper took the opportunity to question her. She told him about our project with a candour that amazed me, and Ernie was quick to inform his employer about what was 'being cooked up'. Within two hours, Nathan Lynch's secretary called Donna to summon me.

I didn't like the tone of this summons and had excruciating memories of our only meeting. I asked Donna to say my diary was full for the next two months. If Nathan Lynch's secretary wouldn't take no for an answer, Donna was to decline appointment after appointment until the man who wasn't keen to be my father-in-law eventually gave up. I didn't give a damn about pleasing him – as far as I could see, that was a lost cause. Donna followed my instructions. Mr Lynch, to whom no one ever said no, must have been fuming because Ernie turned up at Z & H the very next morning. I made him wait outside my office for two hours before seeing him. Next, Nathan used Frank Howard as an intermediary, and Frank spoke to Marcus who lectured me without conviction, or success. I thought I'd sufficiently humiliated Rebecca's father to discourage him but that was underestimating his nasty character and his affection for his daughter.

It was while I was having lunch at the Phoenix with Michael Wilmatt, a respected architect who was working on one of our new projects, that I saw Nathan Lynch appear with Ernie by his side. He'd aged a lot in eighteen months: his complexion was a far cry from the ruddy glow I'd seen before, he now looked pale, almost powdered. I was struck again by how short he was, and he must have been conscious of his stature because he straightened his neck, puffed out his chest and powered towards me. He didn't even say hello before asking to speak to me in private. I was tempted to refuse, but was curious to know what he wanted of me, and didn't feel like creating a scene in front of Michael Wilmatt. I apologised to Michael and followed Rebecca's father into a separate lounge. Ernie wanted to come with us, but I made my feelings on the subject clear to Nathan.

'He's not joining us.'

'Of course I am!' Ernie protested.

I didn't waste my time responding to him but turned directly to his employer.

'He stays here or I leave,' I said.

Nathan Lynch dismissed Ernie with a curt wave. The lounge was very small and its décor stiflingly busy. Nathan sat in a plush blue velvet sofa, and I sat facing him, in one of three armchairs covered in the same fabric.

'What are you trying to do with my daughter?' was his opening gambit.

'I'm not doing anything with your daughter that she herself doesn't want.'

'You know I won't let you marry her without a contract, don't you?'

'Well, that works out just fine because we don't plan to get married,' I said airily.

'So on top of everything else you're just having fun with her?'

'Rebecca doesn't want to get married. Not to me or to anyone. Perhaps your idyllic relationship with Mrs Lynch hasn't set her the best example . . .'

'I don't need your insolence.'

'And *I* don't need your rudeness.'

Nathan Lynch paused for a moment. He would have liked to pulverise me with three well-chosen sentences but wasn't sure he could achieve that.

'So, you want to buy a house with her?'

'That's right.'

'Don't expect me to sign a blank cheque. If I pay for my daughter to make this acquisition, I intend to ensure she's protected. From what I've heard, you have an unfortunate habit of . . . diversifying your interests.'

'I don't know what sort of gossip you base your assumptions on, but I won't go into the details of our private life. As for your financial help, I'd prefer to cope without it.'

'I've done some research into your sandcastle. You won't be able to buy a property like that with your little wheeling and dealing efforts in real estate . . . Nevertheless, I wouldn't want my daughter to be deprived of something she longs for simply because she made a bad choice of man with whom to . . . associate herself. I'll be frank with you,' he went on, leaning towards me, tight-jawed and steely-eyed, 'you have no family, no proper upbringing and no fortune. An unremarkable physique. Very average intelligence and absolutely no morals. There's no justification for the time she's spending with you.'

The veneer that stood in for an upbringing cracked.

'I think it's because I make her come,' I replied with a smile.

He flinched as if I'd slapped him. After a moment of speechless suffocation, he started spitting out all the things he thought about me. I rose to my feet.

'You see why I wasn't in favour of this meeting. For the sake of your daughter's happiness, and yours and mine, the best thing would be for us to continue ignoring each other. We've managed very well until today.'

'You filthy little shit! I won't ignore you. I'll scupper any contracts you try to secure one by one, I'll stake my honour on ruining you and ruining your friends. Don't go hoping you can wriggle away from the inspectors who are currently scouring your accounts. There'll be twice as many of them by tomorrow morning. You won't be able to take a single step without bumping into me somewhere along the line. I'll make the very air around you unbreathable.'

'Shame you didn't put this much energy into avenging your wife instead of having her locked away. You're not very good at prioritising,' I countered.

He threatened me with his fists, bellowing with rage. Afraid I couldn't keep my calm much longer, I left. In the hallway Ernie was waiting, his face as white as the table napkins. I thought I could make out a glint of fear or admiration in his expression; he probably didn't see many people stand up to Nathan Lynch. I walked away without a word and, having found Michael Wilmatt, suggested we change restaurants to have some peace, which we promptly did. I was quite proud of how I'd put the old man in his place, even though I was worried about the personal consequences that my outburst might have. I couldn't hide the incident from Rebecca: a journalist from the *New York Gossips* had been in the Phoenix when Nathan first approached me. He'd witnessed the start of the exchange, watched us slip away and seen my rapid departure. He must have slipped a few dollar bills to the staff and, from what they told him, put together the bare bones of our exchange. The next morning the paper's 'society' pages ran the headline: *Nathan Lynch Lynched*. The first lines set the scene:

> *'I don't want your millions, I'd rather have your daughter . . . and she likes it,' Werner Zilch announced to the millionaire during a violent altercation at the Phoenix.*

I was very dismayed. Rebecca never read that sort of paper, but well-intentioned friends were eager to call her and let her know. I was working at home that morning, and she came and stood in front of me with a copy of the rag.

'Please don't tell me you said that . . .'

'Said what?' I asked sheepishly.

'"I'd rather have your daughter . . . and she likes it."'

'No, I didn't say that,' I confirmed in a steady voice.

'And when were you planning to tell me about this?'

'I didn't want to upset you . . .'

'Did you really have to provoke him?'

'But I didn't provoke him! He's been hounding me since you called Ernie and told him about our plans. He threw himself at me like a wild animal at the restaurant.'

'That's ridiculous!' Rebecca exclaimed.

I described the scene in more detail – tilting things fractionally in my favour, it goes without saying. She flushed with anger, hurled down the *New York Gossips* and launched herself at the telephone.

'Hello, Esther, I'd like to speak with my father . . . No, right now . . . I don't care if he's busy, if he ever wants to see his daughter again, he'll come out of his meeting . . . Exactly . . . I'll wait.'

She sat down on my desk, her legs dangling, and asked me to leave. When I took my time about it, she shot me a furious look and for the first time I could see a slight resemblance to Nathan. I took the liberty of standing just outside the door and spent a few delectable minutes getting the full benefit of their heated exchange before I heard Rebecca jump down from my desk. I scrammed. Still arguing energetically with her father, she strained the telephone lead as she came to check I wasn't listening. I only just escaped her surveillance.

The other telephone line rang. It was Mr Van der Guilt inviting me to lunch.

'I believe you're having trouble financing the purchase of Sandmanor which I'm trying to sell you by force,' he said with some amusement. 'I may have a solution. Shall we talk?'

'I'd be delighted. When are you free?'

'Today, does that work for you?'

'Absolutely.'

'May I suggest the Mayfair Hotel? But do come without Rebecca. I'll explain why . . .'

I met him at one o'clock. He was already waiting for me and was chatting to a very elegant Italian couple who had come over from their table to talk to him. I thought I'd developed a respectable network in the space of a few years, but I was a nobody compared to him. All through our lunch, a wide range of people came to say hello to him. Every time, he got to his feet to chat warmly and enthusiastically with his acquaintances, often in their own language. I heard him speak Italian, French and even Arabic. Courteous towards me, he introduced me with a flattering word or two and, when he sat back down, made a point of explaining how he knew these friends. All the same, he managed to outline his plan to me. His idea was simple, but it hadn't occurred to me he might be interested: he was offering me a swap. The sum I had available – in other words, one third of the price – plus the top two floors of Z & H Tower that we couldn't sell.

'Given the sort of house you live in, I would never have thought such a contemporary apartment would appeal to you . . .' I said, amazed.

'But it was you who gave me the idea. When you were at Sandmanor and you were trying to persuade Rebecca to move into the duplex, you said you liked the idea of sleeping somewhere where no one had ever lived. I realised that's exactly what I need. Somewhere new, where I have no memories of Kate. I went, I saw, I was conquered. And, at my age, it's just as well to get a little closer to heaven . . .' he concluded with half a smile.

I needed to discuss this suggestion with Marcus. Through Z & H, he owned fifty per cent of this asset. We would have to see whether our company could give me a personal loan. If Marcus agreed to it, which I felt sure he would, the solution was perfect. Into the bargain, Mr Van der Guilt would leave one year's salary for five of his employees in the Sandmanor accounts, and this would give me time to decide whether I wanted to keep them. On the other hand, he would take with him the couple who ran the household.

'They know me better than anyone and they were very fond of Kate, but I'm sure you'll be able to replace them.'

I reassured him on that point: Miguel, whom he hadn't yet met, would take possessive pride in presiding over Sandmanor.

At the end of our lunch, Mr Van der Guilt did me another, far more surprising favour: he took from his briefcase a thick green file and handed it to me.

'I thought long and hard about giving you these documents. I'm not the sort to get embroiled in other people's affairs, but I happened to read an article that touched on the tricky relationship you have with your fiancée's father and I thought these papers might be of help to you. They also concern Rebecca. I thought it important for her to know, but it would be indelicate for me to tell her myself. Look through them this afternoon,' he said, stopping me as I was about to read through the contents of the folder. 'And if you need any explanations, don't hesitate . . .'

Back at the office, I took a moment to skim through the file Mr Van der Guilt had entrusted to me. In it I found bank statements for a smokescreen company in the Cayman Islands, as well as transfer orders into the company from Rebecca, her mother Judith and even her father. Colossal sums had been transferred. At first I couldn't understand what this movement of funds was for, but this became clear when I reached the last wad of documents. By some subterfuge I couldn't understand, Mr Van der Guilt had found the name of this front company's owner-stakeholder: it was Ernie. I was only half surprised to realise that he'd been stealing from Rebecca and her parents for years. I'd hated him from the first moment I saw him. As Nathan Lynch's right-hand man, he must have had mandates that had allowed him, gradually over time, to syphon off millions.

I called home and Miguel picked up and confirmed that Miss Rebecca was working in her studio. An hour later I was having a beer with her on the terrace and spread out before us were the documents Mr Van der Guilt had entrusted to me. Incandescent with rage, Rebecca said that neither she nor her mother had ever authorised these transfers. She was as good as sure that her father knew nothing about them either. Rebecca didn't have a very high opinion of Ernie, but was terribly hurt by the discovery; first, because it highlighted her lack of vigilance and her naivety, but also because Ernie's betrayal dented her pride as a woman. Despite her strenuous denials, Rebecca knew perfectly well that Ernie was in love with her. My beauty had naively thought that these feelings made of him a devoted creature who would never dare turn against her, when that was in fact precisely what had driven him to this embezzlement.

'After everything my father's done for him! Did you know he paid for his law school? And helped him set up his first office? Can you believe it?'

I affected a look of sympathetic consternation.

'You're not saying anything!' Rebecca exclaimed. 'Doesn't this make you angry?'

'Of course it does, my darling, but we're going to settle this whole situation.'

For the second time that day, Rebecca came down into my office and, ignoring the chair opening its arms to her, sat on my desk – cross-legged this time – and called her father. For the second time that day, I positioned myself outside the door in order to follow Lauren's advice: to savour the present moment fully and intensely.

Arizona, 1974

'Have a good weekend, Professor!' the security officer called, raising the barrier.

Professor Zilch gave a half-hearted wave through the window of his bronze Chevrolet and left the Sanomoth site. As he did every Friday evening, he would be going to the Paradise, but he wanted to stop by the gunsmith first. If his new rifle hadn't arrived, he would buy a second revolver. He wasn't short of weapons at home, but the sheer number of them reassured him. As did handling them: he did firing practice twice a week using targets he'd set up in his cellar.

For several days now he'd felt he was being watched. It was a distant feeling, but he'd immediately implemented his security procedure: he changed his route to work and was careful not to stick to a regular timetable. Professor Zilch had learned to listen to his instincts, he had too much to lose. He'd been leading a discreet life for years, and had become as invisible as his stature and physique would allow. His work at Sanomoth had meant he was transferred on average every eighteen months, which suited him. He had no friends and didn't want any. He was polite to his neighbours, but always cut conversations short. He did not have lunch with his work colleagues and claimed he had an urgent file to deal with if they ever suggested having a drink together at the end of the day. He woke early each morning to go to the pool before work. In the evenings he watched television, listened to music or played number games in magazines. He had grown used to this disciplined life.

The bonnet of a Pontiac Executive appeared in his rear-view

mirror for the third time and his muscles grew taut. Five minutes later it was still following him. Even though the traffic light was turning to red, he accelerated and turned left past a no-entry sign. The Pontiac stopped: false alarm. Still cautious, Professor Zilch made a detour several miles long before parking outside Dury's gun shop. He waited in his car for a couple of minutes and didn't see the car that had attracted his attention go by. His automatic rifle hadn't arrived. The gunsmith apologised and gave him a substantial discount on a revolver. Professor Zilch paid in cash and asked to go out through the back. Before getting into his car again, he checked no one was posted outside.

Back home, he parked in the street: if there was a problem, he would need to make a fast getaway. He hesitated briefly; caution would dictate that he shouldn't go out this evening, but how many times had he hidden away anxiously at home when there was probably no need to? There wasn't much left in his fridge – he shopped on Saturdays – but he found some pâté, cut some slices of bread and poured himself a whisky. He turned on the television, watched the news, then settled in for the Friday evening film. It was a boring, mawkish comedy but the lead actress, an appetising little brunette, reminded him of Barbra. Which made up his mind for him. He took a scalding-hot shower which left his skin glowing red, shaved, and then filed his nails with implements from a small leather case. He used two different mouthwashes, and sprinkled his hands with surgical spirit and his torso with eau de toilette. He rejected three shirts for tiny creases on the collar before finding one he was happy to wear.

The car park at the Paradise was full of cars. Only men emerged from them. Above the sign was a neon outline of a naked woman with her arms raised and breasts thrust forward. Music with a heavy beat poured from an outdoor speaker. Professor Zilch joined the queue for club members and the doorman let him through straight away. Inside, Mrs Binson came to greet him.

'The usual table, Mr Zilch?'

The professor nodded and she opened the inner door. A blast of moist heat smelling of sweat and tobacco enveloped him. On small stages, girls danced around brass poles. They wore swimming costumes and high heels, and their bodies gleamed. The red lighting lent them a halo of surreal perfection. Professor Zilch spotted Sandy: with her ankles firmly crossed around the pole, she was twirling, head down, with her blonde hair skimming the floor. He was just admiring her arched torso when she whipped back up, gripped the pole above her feet and set off spinning around the pole again, gripping it with her knees. He scanned the room for Barbra but couldn't see her. She must have been preparing for her performance. He ordered a whisky and lit a cigar. His table was slightly isolated, which meant he could watch without being seen. He noticed a new girl, but she didn't appeal to him: she was executing her moves mechanically, with no grace.

After he'd eaten and watched the girls for a long time, he drained his glass and stood up. Mrs Binson came over to him.

'Who would you like this evening? Sandy or Barbra?'

'I'll take Barbra.'

Sandy gave Mrs Binson an enquiring look and when the manageress shook her head, Sandy looked relieved. Instead, a pretty brunette followed the professor into one of the lounges. Although Zilch was a very good customer, Mrs Binson was firm with him.

'I won't remind you of the rules, Mr Zilch,' she said. 'We had that conversation last time.'

The professor pushed the girl into the room and closed the door without replying.

It was two in the morning when Professor Zilch left the Paradise. He'd had a lot to drink. In his Chevrolet he took a bottle of ninety-proof spirit from the glove compartment and cleaned his hands and face. He started up the car and drove quickly through the moonless night. After turning a tight corner he became aware of a strange noise and thought the exhaust pipe must have come loose, but it was worse than that: the engine spluttered several times and stopped. When he opened the bonnet, there was smoke coming from the engine. He lit the flame of a lighter to see more clearly but quickly snapped it off when he noticed a significant fuel leak. He closed the bonnet angrily and thumped it with his fist. He was about twenty-five miles from home and there wasn't a light to be seen anywhere.

He took his coat, locked up the Chevrolet and started walking back to the Paradise. He changed his mind when he saw head-lights up ahead. What a stroke of luck! There was only one road so this vehicle was bound to pass him. It was travelling very fast, just as he had been only minutes earlier. It dropped in and out of his field of vision through the undulating landscape. He stood squarely in the middle of the road where he would be seen, but the car didn't slow when its headlights locked onto him. He waved his arms. The car flashed its lights. Professor Zilch thought at first this was a friendly sign, but when he recognised the Pontiac Executive his heart pounded. In a fraction of a second he understood the situation and started to run like a madman with the thundering sound of the still-accelerating car in his ears.

Sandmanor, 1974

It was a crisp sunny day. We let Shakespeare out of the Bentley and he immediately went to explore the gardens. I playfully lifted Rebecca into my arms to cross the threshold to our new home, but unfortunately knocked her shin on the door.

'That's a good start,' she said with a grimace but then smiled and kissed me.

In the hall, a bouquet of flowers the size of a chair was waiting for us with a note: 'Welcome to your new home. Marcus and Lauren.' Rebecca made a quick call to her father about Ernie, whose trial had just started. Nathan Lynch's former right-hand man had been fired and sued. Banned from every respectable home in New York, he'd been forced to close down his lawyer's office and sell his house. He now spent most of his time arranging his own defence. I didn't shed any tears for the guy . . . In the upheavals of these events, the tax inspection at Z & H had miraculously come to an end. I took this good news as a sort of apology on Nathan's part, but we hadn't seen each other since our altercation at the Phoenix. Rebecca firmly compartmentalised these two aspects of her life, and seemed in no hurry to bring us together. Neither was I. I knew how Judith and Nathan felt about me and it upset me, but it seemed impossible to change their views. Rebecca and I no longer talked of marriage, or children. That was the condition on which we stayed together. This saddened me, but I didn't want to stir up our quarrels again.

We stayed at Sandmanor completely alone for a week; I'd given the staff several days off so we could get to know the house. Mr Van der Guilt had taken his personal belongings and a very few objects he wanted to keep with him. He left the bulk of the furniture and works of art that his wife had so artfully chosen. We went on long walks with Shakespeare, and took siestas in the sun on those early spring days. My beauty moved into her studio in the bungalow that we used when we first stayed here. She was busy working towards her first exhibition in London, and it was that week that we received some good news: one of her pieces, a sculpture called *The City* comprising hundreds of figurines in hundreds of bronze compartments, had just been bought by a Frenchman. He was responsible for acquiring the collection for a future contemporary arts centre which was to be built in the heart of Paris – the Beaubourg project.

Miguel was the first to join us at Sandmanor and he was bowled over by the place. He was so taken with this house that would now be his responsibility that his eyes shone with tears the whole time we were showing him around. He was quick to tidy up the mess that we'd made as a way of taking possession of the house. Over the next few weeks, he drew up a meticulous inventory of the contents of Sandmanor: pictures, furniture, carpets, ornaments and books, but also linen, chinaware, glassware and silver. Once every last coffee spoon had been catalogued, he spent the first year researching the provenance of the major pieces in what he pompously called 'the collection'. He devoted the next year to writing a short biography of Kate Van der Guilt who had made the place what it was and whose portrait still presided over the main staircase. He paired this text with advice about the proper upkeep of a home. I sent a copy to Mr Van der Guilt who replied with a very kind note, emphasising how accurate its observations were and how delighted he was to know we were happy at Sandmanor. Miguel's book was so well put together that I recommended it to my editor friend, Vanessa Javel.

'Your friend? You mean your ex . . .' Rebecca muttered when I announced that the review panel were interested in Miguel's manuscript.

I was happy my beauty was jealous. Her absence and indifference had caused me too much suffering in the past so I liked it when she rebuked me and got her claws out.

Meanwhile, Lauren was making a big splash. Marcus's love had given her wings, and her well-being centre had become the place to be since a famous television producer had gone there. He had almost died of a heart attack a few weeks earlier, and wanted to get back into physical exercise. Lauren, who loved saving people from themselves, took his life in hand. Acupuncture, hypnosis, yoga, nutrition . . . she put together a bespoke programme for him and it transformed this stressed, aggressive and overweight smoker into a borderline thin man who walked around with an almost idiotic smile on his face and exuded kindness. Convinced that if he succeeded in sharing this revelation with millions of viewers, his karma could only improve (in spite of everything, he had a fiscal vision of his cosmic debt), he sold a programme pitch to ABC. The chain had recently switched entirely to colour and the set of *The Lauren Show* looked like a box of candy. On the show my sister trotted out all her hobbyhorses which, proving her visionary powers, had become very fashionable. Public enthusiasm was so fervent that she was contacted by an agri-food company. Working in partnership with them, she developed the first brand of diet products in the United States, spurred on by the thought of broadcasting the good news all the way to the supermarket shelves. This launch was followed by the advent of her range of sports clothes, then of plant-based cosmetics. Naturally, I still teased my sister: this girl who'd always criticised our materialism and the world of money was now heading up a constantly expanding business thanks to financial support from Z & H and Marcus's shrewd stewardship. This filled Lauren with shame, which I found as funny as it was endearing, and I threatened to take my retirement so she could now support me.

*

Marcus and I were indeed going through a difficult time. The real-estate market had been slowed by a series of restrictive laws that reduced the potential for loans and profits. This stagnation encouraged us to turn our attention to Europe, which meant we could stay afloat while diversifying our investments into vital commodities: powdered milk, biscuits, babies' diapers . . . We also took a number of very risky gambles, particularly in an emerging field: information technology. I'd set up a fund that gave some fifty newly established companies a chance. The young entrepreneurs were ten years our juniors and promised us the moon, swearing that soon every American would have his or her own computer, or a personal telephone no larger than a house brick that could make calls with no wires attached to it. Wireless phones? The guys were half crazy, but I was enthused by their vision and they didn't ask for much. I reached for my chequebook so frequently that I became one of the go-to investors in this area.

Rebecca and I were happy, but knew we were fragile, and Judith's health kept reminding us of that. Despite the resources that Nathan, Rebecca and I put into finding Kasper Zilch, the enquiry was going nowhere. Dane was doing everything he could, and his efforts had gone some way towards dulling my dislike of him. We had invited Marthe and Abigail to New York several times, and they had met Judith. Now completely free of Dr Nars's clutches, Judith started in-depth therapy with Abigail, calling her three times a week. These conversations did her good, but her anxiety attacks were still far too frequent, and her immoderate consumption of psychotropic drugs was seriously affecting her health. She alternated between periods of apathy when she hardly spoke at all and alarming hyperactive phases. She tried to take her own life twice, and if ever the telephone rang at an unusual time of day, Rebecca held her breath. Judith was suffering, and her daughter and her husband both felt powerless to help her. We were convinced that only solving the mystery of Kasper Zilch would deliver her from this torment.

United States, secret location, November 1978

A morning mist enveloped the buildings on the abandoned industrial site. The icy wind was not enough to disperse it. We could only just make out the dark dirty river beyond the wharf. With one hand I pulled my scarf higher, with the other I held Rebecca's hand. She glanced at me anxiously. Her mother had insisted on coming with us, and so had Marthe. Vengeance was finally within their reach and I could sense a disturbing febrile energy in them, a shared bloodlust. These two women couldn't have been more different: Marthe had short hair and not an ounce of make-up, while Judith, who was smothered with jewellery and whose hair escaped in wayward locks from her chignon, was almost theatrical in her fur coat over a long green skirt and a scarlet blouse. She was terrifyingly pale. Rebecca was as pallid as her mother and I probably had no more colour in my cheeks than the two of them combined. Despite his reservations about this – or perhaps because of them – Marcus was there too. I had insisted Lauren didn't come, not wanting her to be mired in this whole business.

We went into the disused factory where Dane had arranged to meet us. One of his partners, a hefty red-haired man of about fifty, was waiting to show us the way. Following him, we skirted around a puddle of foul-smelling liquid, stepped over metal pipes and lifted aside plastic sheeting that separated a succession of deserted hangars. Our footsteps rang out on the concrete floor, and the whole place had a musty smell of rust laced with putrefaction. The man led us down a metal staircase and brought us to the sort of round cast-iron door that leads to a strongbox.

'They're in there,' Dane's friend said, gesturing for us to enter. 'I'm going back outside.'

As he walked away, we opened the door to a cement-lined room with a single light bulb dangling at the far end, and seeping water dripping from the ceiling. Dane was waiting for us with the prisoner, who was tied to a metal chair and had his back to us. He was wearing a dark-red sweater and torn grey pants – he must have put up a fight when Dane and his team intercepted him. His eyes were bound and his mouth gagged.

Marthe and Judith looked at each other, and I watched Judith fall apart: she crumpled to her knees and then crossed her arms, gripped her shoulders with her hands, hunched her head towards her chest and curled up tightly. Rebecca rushed to her side where she sat rocking back and forth, and repeating the same unintelligible words. Rebecca seemed frantic and with Dane's help, she forced her mother back to her feet.

'Come on, Mom,' she coaxed. 'You don't have to do this, we'll do it for you. You mustn't see this man.'

She took her mother out of the room, almost carrying her. Dane wanted to go with them, but Rebecca stopped him with a sharp flick of her hand. I didn't dare offer to help, I knew the sight of me was offensive to Judith. Instead, aware of my thudding heart and clammy hands, I turned my attention to our hostage. I was hypnotised by his outline, and the size of him. His thick hair was very like mine, except that the years had turned it grey. He was thin and slightly stooped. I wanted to see his face, a face I'd been told was so like mine and my real father's. I wanted to look him in the eye and hear his voice, hear him talk about my parents, and the little stranger I once was. But I mustn't: if he became human, I wouldn't have the courage to see this through. I didn't have it in me. In a fit of anger, I could have gone too far, but to participate in the execution of a vulnerable, bound man, in cold blood . . . I wasn't sure I could. I knew all about this criminal's misdeeds, about his cruelty, but we were of the same flesh and he was the only link to my bloodline.

The man was tense, aware he was being watched. We'd decided to act as one, except for Marcus who did not want to participate in what he called an assassination and who stood a little way behind us. A couple of rickety tables were the only other furniture in the room and Dane had lined up five revolvers on one of them. We would share this act, in order to bear the weight of it together. No one person would be entirely responsible. Or innocent. No one would know which bullet finally brought an end to this infernal cycle.

Dane saw me look at the revolvers.

'They're loaded,' he said.

The prisoner heard these words. He struggled on his chair, screaming through his gag with furious energy. Dane yelled at him to calm down, his voice distorted with hatred. His barely contained violence chilled us, and the prisoner sat still. He was shaking. The sight of him was too much for Marcus.

'You have no right to do this,' he said. 'Who do you think you are?'

'He gave us this right, he gave it to Judith and me from the very first time he raped us,' Marthe snarled, bristling with anger.

Our hostage froze when he heard this; he had most likely recognised Marthe's voice. But Marcus wouldn't back down: his face flushed, he stepped in front of me and positioned himself between us and the prisoner.

'Marthe, you may be sure of yourself, but you have no proof. He has the right to plead his defence. He has the right to look his judges in the eye. To know why he's dying.'

'What do you want? A trial?' Marthe asked sardonically.

'Exactly, a trial. I want to hear his confessions. I won't let you execute this man without proof.'

Marthe moved towards him.

'I have proof from his voice, his skin, his smell. I have proof in my own memories and my scars. I have proof because he's frightened, now, he's shaking with fear because he knows it's the end. The truth will drive right into his skull. He knows that here in this place today, none of his lies will protect him.'

'But don't you have any doubt?' Marcus asked. 'Not one ounce of grey in this black-and-white world, a tiny corner of grey which might harbour this man's innocence? How can you be sure? It was more than thirty years ago, Marthe . . . You mentioned his voice, but you haven't even heard him speak. And his smell, but you haven't come near him yet . . .'

'Just seeing the size of him and his hair was enough. I know it's him.'

'Well, I'm a lawyer, and as you want to deny this man justice and a fair—'

'Justice! Fair!' Dane exploded. 'Do you think it's fair that our government took in these pigs who should have been hanged in Nuremberg, and even lined their pockets? If there were any justice in our country, if justice weren't a bitch who hid behind the veil of national interest and bowed down to power, then we wouldn't be here, because this man would have been dead years ago.'

'Don't you realise you're behaving just like them?' Marcus retorted. 'Worse than them, even. The Nazis followed their own state laws, however repulsive they may have been. You're undertaking this vigilante mission with no respect for any codes or laws.'

'Oh, so now he's defending the sick bastards!' Dane snapped, turning to Marthe and me to call us to witness. 'You're crazy, Marcus! Your principles have boiled your brains. You bleat away with your well-meaning ideas like all the others who've never suffered at all, but can't you see the world we're living in? Do you have any idea of the scale of the atrocities human beings are capable of? And this one is capable of more than most!' he added, giving the hostage's chair a kick while, restrained by his ties, the man was still trying to struggle free.

Dane stepped closer to Marcus, his fists clenched and his eyes glowering with threat.

'Either you're with us or you're against us,' he said.

'I'm with you, Dane. I'm with Wern, Rebecca, Judith and Marthe, but I want to hear what this man has to say.'

The prisoner stiffened when he heard our names. I watched him and was struck again by our physical similarities. I felt as if there were two of me. However hard I tried to remind myself that this man must be executed straight away before my courage failed me, my own curiosity and Marcus's arguments were making inroads into my resolve.

'I want to hear him too,' I announced.

Dane recoiled as if I'd struck him.

'Are you losing it? Oh, Rebecca's really gonna like that . . .'

I didn't back down.

'I want to be sure.'

Dane raised his arms and eyes to the heavens as if calling on the Lord, then stalked a few paces away with ill-disguised rage. I went over to the prisoner and lifted the back of the chair to which he was tied. With a grim scraping sound, I swivelled the chair around to face us. I removed his gag and then the rag around his eyes. I was looking at my own face after it had suffered the passage of time. For a few seconds he blinked, blinded by the light from the bulb, then he looked at me and was clearly as unsettled as I was.

'My son, you're my son,' he said. He had a deep voice and a strong German accent.

'I'm not your son,' I replied aggressively. 'I'm the son of Armande and Andrew Goodman, the most generous people and the best parents who have ever walked the earth.'

'You're Werner, I know you are. You have her eyes. You're exactly like her,' he insisted. 'It's as if she were here . . .'

'Don't try to soften him up, asshole,' Dane yelled, punching his shoulder. 'We all know who you are, Kasper Zilch, you tortured this woman,' he pointed towards Marthe, 'and you tortured Judith Sokolovsky and countless other women in the camps.'

The prisoner tore his eyes away from mine to respond to Dane.

'You're mistaken. I'm not the man you're looking for. Marthe, you know that. It's me, Johann. You of all people must recognise me . . .'

'Johann is no longer with us. We know what you did to him.'

The prisoner's forehead was beaded with sweat.

'It took me years to get here,' he said, desperate to defend himself, 'but I'm very much alive. Look at me, Marthe. Listen to me. Listen to my voice. You can't get us confused! Not you! I'm telling the truth. I'm Johann. I'm Luisa's husband, dear Luisa whom you so loved. I'm Werner's father. This madness will never end.'

'Don't you worry, it'll soon be over,' Dane said.

'Marthe, I took you in when you needed somewhere to go. I defended you when Kasper threatened you. I can tell you things about Luisa that my brother wouldn't have known. Ask me . . .'

I saw Marthe's conviction waver. Her eyes clouded. Marcus also noticed this glimmer of doubt and he stepped into the breach.

'Ask him, Marthe. I can see you're not so sure now . . . Prove to us that he's lying or, otherwise, that he's not.'

Marthe looked at the prisoner as if she wished she could probe the very depths of his soul. Her eyes scanned his ageing body for the evidence of a once-familiar young man. She moved closer cautiously, silently studied his earlobes and the symmetry of his eyes. He'd changed too much. She couldn't tell. As for his voice . . . How could she be sure? Kasper could mimic his brother perfectly, a talent he first developed to tease Johann and then to shoulder onto him the blame for his teenage misdemeanours . . . The voice was definitely Johann's, but that couldn't be taken into account. Marthe inspected the scars on the prisoner's scalp, but how could she know if they were the same as Kasper's scars? His hair obscured the shape of them. She gingerly felt his head.

Two voices warred inside her head. The first urged her to be decisive: 'Enough! You're being fooled! He's right here. You have him at your mercy! Don't hesitate for a moment. Not one. I recognise his features and his craftiness. Just look how he's manipulating your thoughts right now . . . Only Kasper could manage a *tour de force* like that. Stop thinking. It's him, for God's sake . . .' The other voice was less forceful and kept whispering that something wasn't right. Kasper, eloquent though he may have been, wouldn't have used those words. Yes, he was a good actor, but he wouldn't have had that aura of innocence and rectitude.

'I can't be sure,' Marthe admitted, defeated.

At that point the heavy iron door creaked, and Rebecca and Judith appeared. The fear on Judith's face had been replaced by an anger that lit up every inch of her.

'Isn't he dead yet?' she asked. 'You were right to wait for me. We must learn to savour good things . . . That's what you used to tell me, Kasper, do you remember? You and I are going to have some fun.'

She moved swiftly over to the table and picked up one of the pistols.

'Wait, Judith!' Marcus said, blocking her way. 'We're not sure this *is* Kasper. Even Marthe—'

'It's him!' Judith interrupted, shaking with indignation. 'Kasper, Johann, Arnold, I don't care. Whatever name he's using or you give him, this is the man who did this to me,' she screamed, tearing open the buttons of her blouse. The scars she'd shown me before were there for all to see. 'Who do you think you are, Marcus? A knight in shining armour defending the oppressed?'

Rebecca went over to her mother to cover her chest with her

scarf. She scowled angrily at Marcus but he didn't let this impress him.

'I'm very open to believing you, Judith, but right now what I see is five people standing free, confronting one man sitting tied to a chair. If you don't prove that this man is guilty, I won't let you execute him.'

'No one asked your opinion, my friend,' Dane thundered. 'You can't stop us doing anything.'

Sensing that the situation was not shifting in his favour, the prisoner looked Judith squarely in the eyes.

'It's not me you want. You're confusing me with my brother. People have confused me with him my whole life. And I'm deeply, deeply sorry for whatever he did to you.'

Judith's face flushed feverishly.

'You remember perfectly well what you did to me,' she said in a soft voice. 'Why are you trying to defend yourself, Kasper? It's pointless. You know I can prove your identity. I've been waiting thirty-three years for you, another hour or two won't hurt me. You want to know the charges, Marcus? Very well. I accuse Kasper Zilch here present of actively participating in the systematic extermination of thousands of people in Auschwitz where he was a *Schutzhaftlagerführer*. I accuse this man of directly or indirectly killing my father, Mendel Sokolovsky. I accuse this man of beating me, burning me with cigarettes and raping me over many months in Block 24 of Auschwitz Camp, the very aptly named Joy Division.' She took a step towards him before adding, 'I accuse this man of forcing me to behave in ways you wouldn't ask of an animal. I accuse this man of subjecting me to every horrific fantasy dreamed up in the perverted minds of his inferiors as his reward to them for their good and faithful service. I accuse this man . . .' her voice failed.

'Stop, Mom, this is so bad for you . . .' Rebecca interrupted, devastated.

'Oh no it's not, this is good for me. It's unhoped for. I never thought I'd see him again. You're right, Marcus, I don't just want him to pay, I want him to speak, I want him to acknowledge what he did to me, and Marthe and all those other girls, and those people who died. Do you hear me, Kasper? I want you to admit it,' she announced, aiming at the prisoner's forehead.

'Judith, he's tied up. Put down the weapon, you'll hurt yourself,' Marcus insisted, reaching his hand out to her.

'Step back, Marcus . . . Step back right now!' she threatened, pointing the gun at my friend. 'I'm not joking.'

'Mom, stop that!' Rebecca exclaimed.

'Don't get involved, Rebecca. You shouldn't be here . . . you should go.'

Rebecca didn't move.

'This is between you and me, Kasper. As Marthe can't be sure and Werner had no idea about anything, it's up to the two of us to settle the score. So look at me,' she said imperiously, moving even closer. 'I know the years haven't been kind to me but you can't have forgotten me.'

She came right up to the prisoner and straddled his lap, holding the revolver to his chin.

'So, Kasper, would you like me to remind you what you used to do to me? You'll see how nice it is,' she said, ramming the revolver against the prisoner's lower lip to open his mouth.

She slipped the barrel into his mouth. He tried to turn his head to one side to avoid it.

'No sudden moves! Accidents can happen so quickly. Those were your words, do you remember? "Accidents can happen so quickly," when I tried to get away, when you did this to me,' Judith said, pointing to the white line along the bottom of her neck . . . '"Don't move, little bitch," you used to say, "or you'll hurt yourself all on your own."'

We were paralysed. Only Dane, who was close to the table, remained very calm. He kept one hand on a pistol, ready to intervene. Judith seemed to have forgotten us. We were stunned by this scene that brought the bestial horrors she had endured back to life. Even Marcus had stopped protesting. When Marthe spoke, her voice startled us like a gunshot.

'Judith, I don't believe this is Kasper. I'm so sorry, but I don't think it's him.'

'You don't *believe*, you don't *think* . . . What sort of game are you playing, Marthe!' Judith erupted, taking the gun from the prisoner's mouth.

'Marthe is right, ma'am,' the man said quietly, breathlessly. 'The man you're looking for is already dead.'

'Don't you call me ma'am!' Judith roared, thumping him across the cheekbone with the butt of the pistol. 'Ma'am! As if you respect me . . . As if we've never met!'

'It's true, Kasper's dead,' he said clearly. A trickle of blood came from his mouth. He swallowed the rest of it with a grimace before adding: 'I know, because I killed him.'

This admission was greeted with silence.

'And think before making me suffer the same fate. Even though my brother was the worst of bastards, even though he took everything from me, the people who meant the most to me and the years I should have spent with them, I still don't know whether I was right to kill him. If you execute me, it won't set you free. The relief you're hoping for will be all the more elusive because I've done nothing to you . . .'

'Done nothing to me?' Judith howled.

She grabbed the prisoner's lined face, digging her blood-red fingernails into his cheek.

'Did you really do nothing to me?'

'Nothing!' the hostage said heatedly. 'Not only have I never touched you, but I've never even met you. So go ahead and shoot me in the head, hang me, cut me into little pieces if it will make you feel better, but don't pretend you're dispensing justice . . . and please get off my lap.'

336

He yanked his face free by tipping his head back sharply, almost toppling the chair and forcing Judith to stand up. For the first time she had her doubts. She took a step back and studied our hostage like a scientist poring over a new strain of bacterium. Then she was frustrated with herself for hesitating and this fanned the flames of her anger.

'Enough! This trial of yours is pointless,' she spat, turning to Marcus. She spun round to Dane and gave the order: 'Stand him up.'

Dane untied the ropes holding the prisoner to the chair and stood him up. Judith seemed cowed by the hostage's height which must have reminded her of her own comparative weakness in the past. She soon mastered herself and turned to me.

'Help us, Werner,' she said.

I gave Dane a helping hand and took hold of the prisoner by the biceps. He looked at me with a tenderness and reproach that disconcerted me. As did the contact of his shoulder against mine and his arm over mine. We were almost the same height. Judith took from the pocket of her fur coat a large purse in very worn red leather. She opened the zipper slowly to reveal a surgical tool kit.

'Do you recognise the sound, Kasper? That little tinkle you liked me to hear, when I was tied up . . . These are your tools, do you remember?' she asked, showing him the contents of the red pouch.

'That never belonged to me,' our hostage replied.

'Oh, come on . . . I stole it from you the day I escaped. I didn't have enough time, you see, and I thought I'd need it, when I found you again . . . I kept it with this very moment in mind. For a long time I thought it would never happen, but here we are now . . .'

'I'm not the man you're looking for,' the prisoner said again with suppressed anger.

Judith ignored him, turned to us and asked us to restrain him.

She took out one of the scalpels and brandished it in front of him.

'This is the moment of truth, Kasper.'

She came right up to him. With one hand she awkwardly loosened his belt, undid the top button of his grey pants and unzipped his flies. He struggled.

'What are you doing, Judith?' I asked, catching hold of her wrist.

She freed herself with a strength that surprised me, flailing her arm so the scalpel came just inches from my eyes.

'I have a very simple way of knowing . . .' she replied. 'I'm going to finish what I started the day I escaped.'

'Put the scalpel down. I want you to see justice done, but I won't let you emasculate this man in front of me,' I protested.

'I have every right over this man,' Judith rebelled.

Marcus had his head in his hands.

'This is madness,' he kept saying, 'pure madness.'

Rebecca, who had been frozen to the spot up to this point, came over to her mother. Very gently, she took her in her arms.

'Give me the scalpel, Mom, and check what you have to check. We need to know now.'

Judith looked intently at her daughter, hesitated for a moment, and then threw the metal blade to the far side of the room. With the same fury, she tore down the prisoner's grey pants and his underpants. Bracing himself for pain, he clenched his teeth and hunched his shoulders. She grasped his penis with brutal force and immediately let it go as if she'd picked up a hot coal. She seemed so demented that we didn't know how to interpret what she might have seen. Without warning and apparently reeling with shock, she turned on her heel and, with the sides of her coat flapping behind her, she left the room. Rebecca and Marthe ran after her while Marcus, Dane and I stayed by the prisoner in silence. I dressed him hastily before sitting him back down. Dane paced up and down the room and lit a cigarette. I took one from him, then another, my nerves shredded.

Thirty minutes went by and I was about to go looking for the three women when Marthe came back down the outside stairs. She was very emotional, and hurried over to the prisoner to free him.

'It's Johann. It really is Johann. My God, it's a miracle!'

Incredulity and relief flooded the man's face. He suddenly relaxed and succumbed to a tide of tears. Dane wasn't the type to give up so easily and he stopped Marthe who was trying to untie the prisoner.

'How can you prove it?'

'Ask Judith . . . the day she escaped from Auschwitz, she had enough time to . . . I'm not sure how to say this . . .' Marthe floundered for the right words.

'Tell us, Marthe,' I insisted.

'Kasper had been knocked out by the guard when he was on top of Judith. They tied him up. He was naked and she . . . well, she tried to . . .'

'Spit it out,' Dane yelled.

'She circumcised him. With this,' Marthe added, picking up the scalpel Judith had thrown to the floor. 'But this man isn't circumcised, so he must be Johann.'

I felt numb all over. Marthe's words flitted around inside my head. The prisoner looked up, first at her then at me. He wanted to say something but was too emotional to speak. Dane wanted to check: he took down the prisoner's pants and underpants again to inspect him. The man was indeed uncircumcised. Dane's disappointment was clear to see; years of searching had just gone up in smoke. This failure affected him deeply, it represented thousands more victims denied justice. I felt for him, and for the first time I grasped the full extent of his own suffering and the titanic efforts he made to avenge those he loved. Wracked with impotent rage, Dane gave a resounding kick to the wooden table on which four revolvers were still lined up. Then in a flash he turned around, came to stand in front of Johann and eyed him malevolently.

'And so where were you during the war?'

'I was at the military base in Peenemünde, then I was arrested by the Gestapo and sent to Sachsenhausen-Oranienburg.'

Dane appeared shocked to hear this name which meant nothing to me.

'Did you walk?' he asked.

'Yes,' Johann said in a muted voice.

Dane fell silent, and I didn't understand what they were talking about.

'And then?' Dane asked.

'Then I was taken on by the Russians, I was abducted and put under house arrest in Moscow and forced to work with Sergei Korolev.'

'Sergei Korolev?' Dane asked, for once apparently just as much in the dark as I was.

'The Sputnik satellite, Yuri Gagarin, the first man in space, that was all the work of Korolev and his team, and I was a member of that team,' Johann explained with a hint of pride in his eye.

He turned to me to see whether I was impressed by this revelation. Which I was.

'And so,' Dane said, abruptly changing the subject, 'you went ahead and killed your brother?'

'Yes, and I regret it.'

'How can you regret cleansing the world of filth like that?' Dane growled through clenched teeth.

'Because it wasn't for me to do and because, without realising it, I spared him retribution at Marthe's hands and the hands of the woman called Judith. I thought I was his only victim, and now I can see he had thousands. His death wasn't mine to take.'

'How did you find him?'

'I thought I'd never see him again. I'd heard that my wife had died and I didn't know what had happened to you,' Johann said, turning to me again. 'I was in Moscow, under constant surveillance, then twelve years ago Korolev died. I'd grown close to him and the things we'd done together. With him dead, I felt I had the right to claim my freedom. The British helped me and I told them I was happy to come over to the West on condition that they found my son and my brother. They succeeded with my brother.'

'How did you kill him? How do we know you're not trying to protect him?' Dane asked.

'I watched him for weeks. I'd studied his routines. He went to Sanomoth, where he worked, every day and then back home. He stayed in in the evenings. I think he was frightened of being recognised. The only time he went out was on Fridays, to go to a striptease club in the middle of nowhere. I tampered with his gas tank so he broke down in exactly the right place – five miles from the club and twenty-five miles from home. There was just one farm and a lot of fields. He tried to start the car up again, but couldn't so he opened the hood and saw the pool of gas spreading over the road. He punched the hood of the pick-up then locked it and started walking. I waited till he'd walked about 200 yards and come to a blind corner I'd spotted. We couldn't be seen from the farm there. I picked up speed and drove right at him.'

'And how can you be sure you didn't miss him?'

'Because I got out of the car. Because I checked he was dead. Because I put him in my trunk and because I buried him.'

'Where?'

'In the desert.'

'The desert's a big place . . .' Dane said sarcastically. 'What if I want to check?'

Johann shot him an icy stare.

'Then you would go to San Luis Potosí in Mexico, you'd drive nineteen miles west into the Chihuahua Desert and at precisely 22 degrees 8 minutes latitude north and 100 degrees 59 minutes longitude west, you'd dig.'

'I'll do just that, you know. And for your sake he'd better be there . . .'

'He'll be there. Which means I won't ever have to see you again. In the meantime, I'm tired of having my pants down,' Johann announced.

With an imperious flick of his hand, Dane gestured for Marthe to dress him. She did this and then took him in her arms. After a long hug, he released Marthe and turned to me. My mouth was dry and my mind blank. What are you supposed to say to your father when you meet him for the first time at the age of thirty-three? He took out a blue handkerchief and wiped it clumsily over his face to clear away the sweat and blood. Then he turned to Marcus with an outstretched hand.

'Thank you, sir,' he said. 'If it weren't for your sense of justice and your eloquence, I would no longer be here.'

Equally ceremonious, my partner shook Johann's hand and, his eyes full of kindly intent, he said, 'It's an honour to meet you, sir.'

I heard Dane sniff contemptuously, and Johann ignored him. I was about to say something but Johann stopped me and looked me right in the eye.

'Don't say anything, Werner. Let's get out of this grisly place first.'

I nodded and Marthe headed out first. We climbed back up the metal stairs, lifted aside the plastic sheeting, stepped over the metal pipes, avoiding the stinking puddles, and walked out of the factory. The morning mist had dispersed, and we were greeted by a pale winter sun. Two magpies were squabbling over a flashing piece of aluminium among the weeds. Cloud shadows scudded over the grey-green mass of the river that lapped gently at the abandoned wharf. Judith and Rebecca were sitting waiting for us on concrete blocks. The love of my life got to her feet, came over, huddled close to me and we hugged each other tightly for a long time. Judith, exhausted and drawn, gave me a small wave of her hand.

'I'm so sorry, Judith,' I said.

She gave me a look of heartbreaking despair.

'I'm so sorry for everything you've suffered,' I said.

'Thank you,' she replied.

I wished I could comfort her, find the right words, but was afraid that my presence was more unpleasant for her than beneficial. I nodded and moved some way away, holding Rebecca close.

'None of it was your fault, Werner,' Judith called after me.

I spun around to look at her and she spoke to Rebecca now: 'None of it was Werner's fault.'

I could tell what it cost her to say these words, and I felt all the good they did me, and Rebecca. My beauty went back over to her mother and kissed her tenderly. I thanked Judith, and I also thanked Dane who had come up to join us. I shook his hand. Marcus climbed into the driver's seat of the car. Judith said she'd rather travel back with Dane and, not wanting to leave her on her own, Marthe joined them. A great feeling of joy flooded through me when Rebecca stayed with me. Tactfully, she took the front passenger seat, while I sat in the back with Johann.

The limousine set off and we travelled in silence for a while, letting the wharf and the river dwindle out of sight behind us. When we reached the small country road that had brought us there, I needed a pick-me-up. I lifted the top of the armrest which concealed a minibar, and took out six miniatures of vodka. I poured a glass for Johann and handed it to him. Rebecca said she couldn't drink right now, and Marcus declined too. I downed my glass in one, and filled it again. I didn't know how to start the conversation, but Johann did it for me.

'I'm happy to meet you, Werner. It's a wonderful gift from a world which hasn't given me anything for nearly three decades. I know I can never be your father now. I know that at your age you don't need a guide or a protector, but I'd like to be at least a friend. A friend you can see whenever you want. A friend who can tell you where you came from, who we are and who we once were. I'll tell you about your mother who I loved more than anyone and who didn't see you grow up. I'll tell you about your grandparents who would have adored you. I'll tell you about the place that was your country, about our house which should have seen so much happiness, and I'll tell you about myself if you'd like. I'll tell you what I did and didn't do, what you can be proud of and what you don't need to feel responsible for. If you find some healing and joy in our conversations, if I have qualities you admire, I'd like to meet your parents. I know from what you said earlier that they were good to you. If they'd be happy to meet me, I'd like to thank them. Thank them for raising you. Thank them for protecting you. Thank them for loving you. Thank them for turning the baby I never met, and the boy I didn't see grow up, into the strong upright young man I see now.'

My eyes felt hot and there was a momentary silence.

In a voice that didn't feel like mine I managed to say, 'Yes, let's do that, and perhaps more.'

I reached out my hand to him. He took it and squeezed it. With one look we told each other almost everything there was to say about ourselves. It's impossible to articulate what was forged that day. It was a powerful connection that took nothing away from the people I loved but would in fact help me love them even more. Without a word, this man and I formed a binding, indestructible pact, a pact that would bring me, at last, a form of peace.

Acknowledgements

To Gilone, Renaud and Hadrien de Clermont-Tonnerre, Laure Boulay de la Meurthe, Zachary Parsa, Adrien Goetz, Susanna Lea, Christophe Bataille, Olivier Nora, Ulysse Korolitski, Marieke Liebaert, Malene Rydahl.

To the readers whose paths I was lucky to cross and who encouraged me.

To the booksellers who made the *Fourrure* adventure possible.

To Alfred Boulay de la Meurthe and Claude Delpech who accompanied me in thought as I wrote this book. I so wish you were still here to read it.

To Andrew Parsa, a luminous being, who left us too soon.

To Jean-Marc Roberts who gave me my chance like nobody had before him.

Do you wish this wasn't the end?

Join us at www.hodder.co.uk, or follow us on
Twitter @hodderbooks to be a part of our community
of people who love the very best in books and reading.

Whether you want to discover more about a book
or an author, watch trailers and interviews, have the
chance to win early limited editions, or simply browse
our expert readers' selection of the very best books,
we think you'll find what you're looking for.

And if you don't,
that's the place to tell us what's missing.

We love what we do, and we'd love you to be part of it.

www.hodder.co.uk